ONCE AND FOR ALL

WINDS OF FIRE
BOOK TWO

ANJU GATTANI

ANJU GATTANI

ONCE AND FOR ALL

WINDS OF FIRE BOOK TWO

ANJU GATTANI

ISBN: 979-8-9866524-5-0 (ebook)

ISBN: 979-8-9866524-4-3 (trade paperback)

ISBN: 979-8-9866524-3-6 (hardback)

PRAISE FOR ONCE AND FOR ALL

"Anju's phenomenal Winds of Fire Series returns with *Once And For All*, and this time, it's Downton Abbey meets Sleeping with the Enemy but set in India! I tore through the pages. Anju's sublime prose creates a truly visceral reading experience, making India come alive with all its sights, smells, and sounds. And the story itself...you better strap in and prepare because you're in for an unforgettable ride!"—Barbara Bos, Managing Editor, BooksByWomen.org

"Anju Gattani's second book in her Winds of Fire series is going to be a sensational blockbuster. I was shocked, surprised, and so engaged I was on the edge of my seat. Five Diamonds in the Pulpwood Queen tiara, has always been my highest mark but this read, the blaze of diamonds sparkling will have you searching for your sunglasses! — Kathy L. Murphy, The International Pulpwood Queens and Timber Guys Book Club Reading Nation

"How much can one woman endure before her world breaks into pieces forever? This is the question Anju Gattani asks of her marvelous protagonist in *Once and For All*, the gripping follow-up to *Dynasties*. Modern India provides a vivid and fascinating backdrop to the drama—all told with an unflinching eye toward emotional truth and psychological depth. Highly recommended!"—David Corbett, award-winning author of *The Truth Against the World*

"A page turner full of iron-wrought power, captivating characters and immersive storytelling... Anju Gattani's second novel in her Winds of Fire series keeps us on edge to a cliffhanger ending."—Kathryn Brown Ramsperger, Award-winning Novelist and Humanitarian Journalist

"A beautifully written tale of sacrifice and longing that will captivate readers until the very end. Gattani writes with her whole heart."—Rochelle B. Weinstein, Bestselling author of This Is Not How It Ends

"*Once And For All* by Anju Gattani is a visceral and compelling tale of privilege and pretense, where the glittering surface conceals the searing truth beneath. As secrets unravel, Sheetal's journey becomes the ultimate quest for liberation in the face of overwhelming odds. With a plot that amps up the tension as it weaves intrigue, *Once And For All* is a page-turner that draws readers into its world."—Veena Rao, Award-winning author

"A story rich in cultural detail and complete with the lush language and intense chemistry between characters that readers have come to expect from Anju Gattani. *Once And For All* spirals an emotionally abusive relationship to a level of self-destruction that you will never forget."—Barbara Conrey, USA Today bestselling author of Nowhere Near Goodbye

"The author deftly reveals the opulent lifestyle of the upper echelon of Indian society, but it is tempered with an undercurrent of painful secrets. What a page-turning read!"—Bobbi Kornblit, author of Red Carpet Rivals and Shelter from the Texas Heat

"With a richly evoked sense of place and culture, the series is a deeply engrossing depiction of one woman's struggle for love and independence. It will keep you turning pages until the end." – Ausma Zehanat Khan, author of A Deadly Divide

"*Once And For All* is a stunning and brilliant sequel in Gattani's Winds of Fire series. Powerful, emotional, it challenges the traditions that keep women in their secondary place and gives a voice to women seeking freedom." - USA Today Bestseller Lauren Smith

"Loved it! A delightful Indian saga giving us a vivid insight into the life of the wealthy, with deftly drawn characters, infused with human empathy and understanding. A very compelling read. Did not want it to end."—Qaisra Shahraz MBE, Peace Activist, Author of The Holy Woman

To Shruti Daga aka Little Sis...if only everyone could have a sister like you.
I am so very lucky to have you in my life.
Today, Always & Forever...

If the world doesn't seem to fit your mold
Look at all your accomplishments,
Successes, victories and goals.
Little slips, downfalls and losses.
Then put all those hallmarks on hold. Aside.
They were experiences. Merely rides.
*The Real **You** doesn't need to be defined.*

Look at yourself in the mirror
Then take a step forward and share your story
With someone who will listen.
Define Your place in Your world
Make Your story heard.

Remember...
You don't have to follow what you're told
Just listen to your heart
And create your own world.

—Anju Gattani

PROLOGUE

Her husband was often away on business and Sheetal thought that was a good thing until she found out why.

1

TRAPPED

A black Mercedes pulled up to the curb, and a security guard standing beside Sheetal opened the passenger door. The boot of the car lifted, and the guard gestured for Sheetal's shopping bag. "May I, Madame?" he asked. "I can store your bags in the boot, so you are more comfortable."

She tightened her grip on the bag's handle and the sari tucked inside. She didn't need more room and comfort in the passenger seat. He would never understand how precious the contents of this bag were. It wasn't just any sari, but a designer sari with elaborate red and gold trimmings, the *Karva Chauth* gift destined for Megha, to confirm her sister-in-law's marital bliss.

If only she could hold the silk between her fingers and squeeze its promise of love and happiness into her married life so she could reunite with her son. Her heart welled in her throat. Like every other married Hindu woman, she was to fast from dawn until moonrise and pray for her husband's welfare, longevity, and prosperity. Karva Chauth was intended to bring every couple together and strengthen the foundation of a marriage. It was the tradition of her ancestors.

Sheetal paused on the sidewalk and looked at the traffic flowing toward northern Raigun, the poorer part of town, where she had once lived with Mama and Papa. But that was in the past, before Papa's business succeeded and he was able to give her away in marriage to a prestigious family.

Sheetal's husband, the CEO of Dhanraj & Son, was away on business, as he was most of the time. The extra work hours, late nights and excessive travel were part of his efforts to recoup the three-hundred-and-fifty-million-rupee debt incurred by her other sister-in-law's wedding.

He was working hard. Too hard, perhaps? Like she was on her oil paintings and her ten-year marriage. The marriage ensured their son had a family to return to from boarding school. It gave Mama, who was battling cancer, a reason to endure the chemotherapy and live for another day. It validated that she had done the right thing in marrying the man Mama and Papa had chosen for her.

Did that mean it was her fault for failing her husband when it came to his health and well-being?

Sheetal ducked and slid into the car. The door slammed shut behind. She handed the guard a hundred-rupee note through the open window.

"*Dhaniyavad*, Madame," he thanked her and pressed both palms together in *namaste*, bowing his head several times.

"*Theek hai.*" She told him it was fine.

Was it? Her husband was the one suffering from weight loss and fatigue while she was fine. At least, that's what the public thought.

"*Aage kahan?*" The chauffeur, in his crisp, white uniform, asked where she wanted to go next.

"*Hira Moti.*" Diamond Pearl, the jewelry store where the Dhanrajs had their jewelry custom-made.

The car snaked through trucks, black and yellow taxis, private cars and auto-rickshaws. Pedestrians rushed along the pavements as diesel from the trucks' tailpipes clouded their bodies, causing them to cough and sneeze. Perhaps if they worked as hard as Papa, they too could rise from the middle class. But what if they weren't blessed for success or had erred in some way, causing the gods to withdraw fate and good luck?

Several pedestrians crossing the road paused between the bumpers of honking traffic, momentarily trapped.

Sheetal sank into the Mercedes' seat, took a deep breath and exhaled. If she'd married the man she once loved, she could have been trapped like one of those pedestrians. She bit her lower lip. She had been twenty-two at the time. Any sensible Indian girl would also have chosen wealth and prestige over love.

She ran her right palm over the glossy cover of the October issue of Vogue, India, that she'd been reading on the ride to the sari boutique.

The cover article entitled 'Jump-Start His Engine' was a Top Ten list of guaranteed ways to rake the honeymoon effect back into stale marriages. Suggestions like keeping open channels of communication, talking, being upfront that you want him, telling him you love him, demanding your man's time and attention, splurging on new lingerie and transforming dinners into dining with a candle-lit ambience "with you as dessert" had caused Sheetal to cringe. Her husband wined and dined clients after work. Where was the how-to for transforming dinners into a dining experience when they hardly ever ate together? On the few occasions when they did, mealtimes included the whole family, and he perpetually turned a deaf ear.

The family. Sheetal sighed. *They were always there. Everywhere.* Indian couples rarely expressed affection for one another in public. In private? Sheetal released her lower lip from her teeth. She had spent thousands of rupees on imported lingerie that stuck to her like a second skin by morning.

The next suggestion? If you were daring enough to not wait, the article suggested an alternative. Grab him in the nude and tell him you have to have him. Now.

Sheetal closed the magazine and left it face-down on the seat. Those suggestions worked for western women who were known to be forthright and demanding. Not Indian women who accepted their fate.

There must be another way. Sheetal straightened her posture. *A better way.*

"*Aa gaye,* Madame." The chauffeur eased the Mercedes to a halt in front of the shop with golden pillars and gold and silver letters.

Sheetal entered through the glass doors and was immediately greeted by the store manager dressed in a suit and tie. Waist-high glass cabinets displaying ready-made jewelry ran the shop's perimeter. Salesmen in lime green shirts and gray trousers, and saleswomen in lime green *saris* with a gray temple-border, were busy attending to several customers. Sheetal followed the manager to the private showroom sealed behind a wooden door on the right. Several customers, probably friends shopping together, turned to look, pointed in her direction, and whispered to one another.

Sheetal cringed and looked ahead, avoiding their gazes. Her left shoulder, covered by the heavily embroidered sari *pallu,* slumped beneath the burden of elite status. Out of habit, she raised a hand to her left earlobe and touch the two-carat diamond solitaire earring. Diamond bangles tinkled along her wrist. More people turned to look in her direction, and Sheetal wished she had kept her hand by her side. It wasn't the expensive pink georgette sari, the diamond earrings, the bangles on her wrist or the ten-carat diamond solitaire on the third finger of her left hand that drew everyone's attention. She was a renowned oil painter, but that wasn't responsible for disturbing the harmony of the shop's rhythm, either. The cause of the disturbance was simple. She was married to a Dhanraj, and the Dhanrajs had a way of making heads turn.

How she longed to be one of the women who stared and talked in hushed whispers. If only she had friends to confide in so she wouldn't have to bear the loneliness of living in a mansion of secrets. She could have lived her dream if she'd married the other man. But she didn't. That decision was in the past. Over.

Sheetal seated herself on a plush swivel chair at a round glass table in the center of the brightly lit private showroom and turned to the manager. "Please show me the latest full-set in precious stones and diamonds."

Several salesmen and women rushed back and forth at the manager's call to pull from the vault the latest in designer collections. Rings, bracelets, necklaces and earrings in diamond and gold cascaded along a cloth of black velvet on the glass countertop. Fiery rubies, blue sapphires and green emeralds spilled across the plush bed, reminding Sheetal of oceans and lands her husband flew across countless times in search of the next business opportunity.

The manager unfolded a dark blue velvet cloth. A necklace with pink diamonds, tiny rubies and white gold trim glittered in the yellow lights. "This one arrived yesterday."

Sheetal's breath caught. "How much is it?"

"Two *crores* for the necklace."

Twenty million rupees? The price of her husband's Lamborghini? Sheetal gulped. It matched perfectly with the Karva Chauth gift for her sister-in-law, but she couldn't spend that much.

"The earrings and bracelet are—"

"Just as beautiful, I'm sure," Sheetal cut him short. "But it's for a friend," she lied. "Do you have anything less formal?" He was bound to understand that she meant something less expensive. What he probably wouldn't understand was why a Dhanraj asked for something less expensive. He didn't need to understand. The debt was her business.

A good wife hid the family secrets and lived within her husband's means—the husband didn't mean to put the family in debt. Like every good Indian woman from a good Indian family, Sheetal's status at her in-laws', her position in society, and her sense of self-worth were measured by the strength of her marriage. Sheetal did everything possible to make her marriage appear intact.

The manager showed her a pendant of mini pearls, rubies and diamonds, and Sheetal laced her fingers through each string of pearls that supported the pendant. The pearls were white like the marble interior of the Dhanraj mansion. The mini-palace offered seventy-thousand square feet of living space, but lately, Sheetal had been suffocating beneath its sixty-foot-tall ceiling.

She ran her thumb over a pearl. Cold. Like the heart of her marriage. "How much is it?"

"Four *lakhs* for the pendant."

Four hundred thousand... Sheetal sat up. *The price of the Mercedes. Better.*

"The pearls are..."

Didn't oysters die when a pearl was extracted from its womb? What if she, like the oyster, had died eight years ago when her sari caught on fire? A shudder rippled up her spine. Like her husband, her son would have also grown up trapped under the cruel dictatorship of her stepmother-in-law.

She was lucky to be alive. Her marriage? Not so. She released the pendant and it fell onto the bed of plush black. She couldn't let her marriage collapse and risk her son's future.

A good Indian wife didn't give up. She forgave all sins, including those of her husband. *Especially* those of her husband because that's what kept the marriage intact. A good Indian wife was loving and caring. If she had needs and desires her husband couldn't fulfill, she forgave him and filled her life with all that he could give. Even if he wanted little to do with her.

"This," the manager held up a necklace, "is the latest in Jaipur *Kundan* work. Complete with earrings, rings, bangles..."

Sheetal took the inch-wide necklace constructed in segments and connected by tiny clasps. It, too, would match the sari chosen for her sister-in-law. She pulled the band of gold from both sides and tested the minute joints to see if they'd come apart. They didn't. The necklace was sturdy. It would endure and stand the test of time. Rubies. Sapphires. Emeralds. Didn't they weather the wrath of wind, water, earth, and fire to sparkle and shine? Her marriage would too. It had to.

Sheetal ran the index finger of her right hand over a single diamond dangling from the necklace's center. It slept in a bezel setting surrounded by an ocean of twenty-two-carat gold and held in position by four sharp prongs.

It was trapped.

She was trapped.

And there was no way out.

2

SAYONARA

Why was it that the people you trusted most betrayed you first? Rakesh leaned against the edge of the twenty-seater conference room table and tapped his fingers on the wooden surface while waiting for more Japanese board members of Tashukomo Electronics to take their seats. He strode to the pull-down screen in the Grand Hyatt's Platinum Meeting Room and looked at the men.

Identical mops of black hair capped their heads except for one bald, overweight man. *Five*, he counted. *Not good. Ten should be here.*

"Gentlemen." Rakesh addressed them but scoffed at the word. They looked anything but gentle. "Thank you for flying all the way from Osaka to meet here in Hong Kong."

The Japanese had a meeting scheduled tomorrow afternoon with the directors of Hutchison Whampoa, Hong Kong's leading investor in real estate, retail sales, and telecommunications. Hutchison was also the dragon Tashukomo Electronics had been trying to partner with for the last three years. Unsuccessfully. Rakesh had learned of the meeting and seized the opportunity to take Indo-Japanese trade relations to a new level.

"Should we wait for the others?" Rakesh pointed to the empty chairs.

"That won't be necessary." The bald man rose to his feet. "Others cannot come. I am Daichi Tanaka, CEO." He stretched the 'o' sound, bowed from the waist and righted himself. "We are pleased to meet you."

"Likewise. Thank you." Rakesh narrowed his attention on the man's navy-blue suit. Louis Vuitton. He nodded and smiled. You could tell a Vuitton a mile away from the signature cut. He reciprocated with a bow. Japanese customs were all the rage back home thanks to an influx of multinational corporate tie-ups. Rakesh had never bowed to anyone except Papa—not for long.

"We can begin when you are ready," Vuitton suit said. "But first, we would like to introduce ourselves."

Rakesh's shoulders relaxed. The six-hour flight, delayed because of Typhoon Susan, hadn't left enough time to check in and freshen up before the meeting. However, the temp Chinese employee had efficiently managed all those trivialities including setting up the meeting room prior to his arrival. The Japanese mattered most. If the deal went through, he wouldn't have to worry about the bank's threat to take over, and Yash wouldn't have to struggle in the future.

As the others introduced themselves, a pinprick of pain pinched his chest and rippled around his abdomen. Rakesh took a step back and held his breath. He'd never experienced anything like this before. Jitters? Butterflies? Impossible. He straightened his posture, pulled the edges of his jacket closed, glided the heel of a palm over a brown basket-weave silk tie and buttoned the jacket.

No mistakes. Not now. He took a deep breath. Not when thirty thousand employees and their families depended on him to seal this deal. He gestured for the temp Chinese assistant to close the door, dim the lights and await further instruction.

Rakesh tapped several laptop keys and began his presentation about the new era in India's growth. He ran slide shows and videos that had taken top executives of Dhanraj & Son a month to compile. He focused on today's tech-savvy, money-loaded, globalized generation, eager to buy the latest car, designer brands, clothes, and electronic gizmos. He shared a map of India that pinpointed the locations of hundreds of new malls built across the country in the last two years and described fortunes waiting to be reaped. More bar graphs, pie charts and statistics followed.

He finished with a focus on how Dhanraj & Son, importers and warehousers of major home appliances and luxury clothing brands, was positioned to help Tashukomo profit from India's booming economy.

The men's eyes widened, and Rakesh sensed their growing interest. "It's a shame your colleagues couldn't be here." He gestured to the empty seats. "I would have had the pleasure of meeting them in person."

"We didn't think it necessary for everyone to attend just yet." The Vuitton sat back. "But tell me, Mr. Dhanraj, how can you guarantee that you will fulfill all your tall promises? I don't see anyone else from your company." He looked around the room as if in search of someone. "Only you."

I alone am enough to take on all of you. Rakesh feigned checking his cell phone before returning his attention to Vuitton. "You'll meet them shortly on video conference. Isn't technology wonderful? Anyway, I just sealed a five-million-dollar deal with Hutchison Whampoa."

Vuitton raised his eyebrows.

"I understand your interest in Whampoa and can pull a few strings for you. So perhaps it's in your best interest to work with us." He toggled a few laptop buttons. The white projector screen fuzzed and then sharpened a livestream feed of Indian men and women dressed in dark business suits and seated around a rectangular conference table.

"I'd like to introduce you to the executive board members of

Dhanraj & Son. Live from Raigun, India. I hope they can address all your questions and concerns."

Two hours later, Rakesh shook hands with the board members of Tashukomo Electronics as they filed out of the room. Papa would have been proud. No, not proud. Surprised at how stellar the meeting had gone. Too bad Papa had died of a heart attack.

Rakesh experienced another pinprick. *Is this how Papa felt when the attack came on?*

The Vuitton broke away from the group and approached Rakesh. "Well, I must say, Mr. Dhanraj, I am very impressed. I think all our doubts have been cleared. I will discuss this with our colleagues in Osaka and contact you after two weeks."

Rakesh smiled. There was nothing more to discuss. He'd won them over.

RAKESH SCOWLED PAST A SHOULDER IN A NAVY BLAZER TO ANOTHER TWO MEN in the Grand Hyatt's reception queue and gritted his teeth. If not for the delayed landing, he'd have checked in hours ago and wouldn't be standing in line. Back home in India, employees jumped hoops to do his bidding. But on foreign shores, the value of the rupee lagged compared to all the major currencies and VIP treatment barely existed on a shoestring budget. Exhausted, Rakesh wanted to force the men out of his way, get his keycard and go up to his room.

Groups of noisy Japanese tourists littered the lobby in clusters, each one led by a tour guide armed with a clipboard and wearing a cap. On the other side of the hotel's glass wall that overlooked the entrance, a bus pulled up and one of the groups raced to board the vehicle. *Ridiculous!* Rakesh turned away, unaccustomed to such unrefined behavior.

A cramp tightened around his chest for a split second and Rakesh grit his teeth. Molar pushed against molar and pain seared along his jaw. He fished in his breast pocket, pulled out a thick, brown cigar and rolled it between his fingers. It felt good. He lit the tip in violation of the "No Smoking" signs. The aroma of roasted tobacco filled his nostrils, spiraled down his lungs and every tight-wired chord in his body sagged with relief.

A cough caused Rakesh to turn around. He fixed his attention on a man standing behind and his Adam's apple bobbing futilely beneath the brown flesh. Rakesh looked up at the blond-and-brown highlights tinting the man's wavy black hair, the coarse features and light stubble crusting the surface of his chin. A wave of excitement rushed through.

"Excuse me," the receptionist called out. "Next?"

His gaze drifted down past the wrinkled hem of the man's blue Nike T-shirt, which fluttered about his waist, past the frayed hem of the brown Bermuda shorts that encircled the man's shins and down the thick, black hairs curling on his legs' surface. But the tattered threads running the perimeter of the man's moccasins held his attention. *Nice.*

The man cleared his throat again, his expression blank, and then he pointed to the receptionist's desk.

Rakesh turned around, picked up his black-leather Versace briefcase and marched forward, leaving a cloud of smoke behind.

"Good evening. Welcome to the Grand Hyatt." The receptionist's high-pitched nasal, Cantonese accent jarred his hearing while the odor of fish thickened the air.

Rakesh chewed on the cigar held in the right corner of his mouth and blew away the salty sea odor with a fog of tobacco. Her face wrinkled in irritation. A strip of black plastic pinned to her maroon blazer pocket sparkled with 'L. Leung' in gold letters.

"Your name, sir?"

"Rakesh Dhanraj." The cigar vibrated with each consonant. He inhaled a mouthful of warm air and blew it to the right.

She coughed and then paused to look at him. "No smoking, sir. Is not allowed."

"What a shame."

She waved the air like his wife often did, scattering the smoke. "Hotel policy."

In India, in an unbalanced economy where wealth determined more than net worth and having too much money extended all privileges, he defied just about every policy. "Here." He shoved a hundred Hong Kong dollar note across the counter. "It's on me."

"Payment accepted at check-out." She slid the red note back across the counter. "No smoking in public places. Government policy."

He drummed his fingernails on the marble counter. Leung gave him *the glare*, the kind of glare his wife frequently did, and Rakesh's blood boiled.

"Please, sir, put it out. This hotel is smoke-free."

Not if I put your ass on fire. Rakesh grit his teeth harder. He turned to his left and right, then shrugged. "No ashtray. Government policy. Is not allowed." He drilled the burning end of the Robusto on the sparkling granite countertop and watched her lips freeze in an O. Surrounding people stopped to stare at the glowing red-hot tip of the cigar and then at him.

Leung immediately looked down, her shocked expression disappearing behind a curtain of falling black hair.

"Room four-three-three-four." She slid a plastic card at him and lowered her hands to the keyboard. "Enjoy your stay with us."

"How can I?" Rakesh asked. "This hotel is smoke-free." He was about to head straight for the corridor of elevators when he paused, turned to look at the receptionist one more time, and added as an afterthought, "Please send my suitcase up in two hours. Until then do not disturb."

Rakesh stepped into an empty elevator and a group of Asian tourists rushed in. They pressed him against the wall and out of reach of the control panel. Rakesh clamped his jaw as an ache welled up along his gums. Because people knew who he was back home, his stare would have been enough to cordon off the elevator for himself. Here, he was left to balance himself in the throes of the crowd. The odor of stale fish and sweat overwhelmed his lungs. Rakesh pressed his back to the wall tightening his grip on the briefcase's leather handle. Just as the doors started to glide shut, the front curve of a moccasin shoe plugged the closing door. *Oh fuck!* "Take the next one."

"I'm sorry," the man in the blue Nike T-shirt replied, the sound of crisp r's thickening his Indian accent. He stood two inches taller than Rakesh's six-foot-two. "I'm in a rush." He squeezed in and the doors closed, sealing in the fragrance of the man's Gillette aftershave.

One of the tourists, a frail-looking man, turned to Rakesh. "Ah... which floor?"

"Forty-three, please. Penthouse suite." The elevator made its way up.

"Ah, you speak good English. Like an American." The Japanese man, apparently the leader of the group, wearing a red baseball cap to signify his position as translator, touched the number crowning the metallic panel to his immediate right and turned to Rakesh again. Luminous red rings haloed the numbers forty-three and twenty-six.

"Urrr...which floor?" The Japanese tourist in the red cap, turned-button-pusher, asked the other Indian man.

"Same." He balled his fingers as thick as Rakesh's Robusto into fists and crossed his arms, double the size of Rakesh's biceps, across his chest while staring at the blinking panel above the elevator's door.

Rakesh's nerves tingled from head to toe, and warmth spread across his body. The zipper of his trousers strained against a swelling.

The button-pusher turned to Rakesh. "Where you study?"

"Harvard." After securing his US MBA, he returned to India to manage Papa's business empire. An empire he'd been promised upon return.

"You here on business?"

"Yes."

The button-pusher nodded to the others in his group and a chorus of "*Hai*" followed.

"We also here for travel. And business."

Rakesh smiled. Other business was always easier abroad where anonymity became a luxury.

"I here to meet new company." The spokesman spread his fingers, drew his hands apart, and then pushed them toward each other interlocking his fingers into one fist. "Partnership. Become strong." He smiled, revealing four golden molars. "Unite. One. *Hai!*"

"I too." Rakesh lowered his leather bag to the floor and straightened. He, too, had wanted to unite with Papa and run the family business as equals. As promised. Never happened. "Here on business. Come to meet new company." Rakesh made a fist, rammed it against his open left palm and curled all five fingers of the left hand around the closed knuckles' edge. "Become stronger. Unite." *Takeover.* "Hai." The elevator paused on the twenty-sixth floor, jolted as if the doors were meant to open and then rushed up against the force of gravity.

The tourists frowned and mumbled.

When the elevator stopped and the doors glided open on the forty-third floor, Rakesh picked up his briefcase and stepped forward. He elbowed the button-pusher out of the way, leaned his arm across the metallic panel as if to regain balance after a stumble and dragged his arm down pushing all forty-two buttons. The Indian man hopped out, and Rakesh turned back to face the audience. "*Sayonara.*" Manners were important. "Last floor, guys. You won't miss your stop this time. Promise. Only way is down." Then Rakesh stepped out and turned around to watch the tourists' appalled expressions before the elevator door closed.

Rakesh headed right and dug into his jacket pocket for the plastic card. He slipped it into a paper-thin slit below the doorknob. The door buzzed and a light flashed from red to green. Rakesh pushed open the door to his suite.

Golden knobs, hand-pleated upholstery, roses in a crystal vase and chandeliers greeted him. A welcome basket of fruit rested on a glass coffee table. *Perfect.* Rakesh put his briefcase down and took a deep breath. The scent of tea roses cleared his lungs of the fish smell that had nearly suffocated him during the elevator ride.

Then came a knock.

He spun round and yanked the door open.

The Nike T-shirt man entered.

Rakesh slammed the door shut and locked it. The fragrance of lemony Gillette filled his nostrils. Every molecule in Rakesh's body throbbed with excitement. Ions of electricity tingled his skin. His heart beat harder, quicker. He ran his fingers along the soft Bermuda shorts. The flesh beneath the fabric yielded under the pressure of his fingers igniting a thrill that rushed through his veins. *Fucking sweet.* Heat threatened to consume him alive. Rakesh touched the hairs running the length of Kartik's arms and each strand curled, pricking him with needle-like static. "I missed you."

"Same here, man."

Kartik yanked his shirt buttons open, and Rakesh inhaled long, deep breaths as the zipper mounting his growing bulge tightened. Every inch of exposed skin shivered under the silent breeze of air-conditioning and his body yearned toward Kartik's hungry pull.

When they were done, Rakesh sat up. Their clothing lay in a mismatched heap on the floor mirroring the tangle of their dark and pale limbs on the bed. Rakesh freed himself from the man's giant arm and lit a Robusto.

Hard to believe five months had passed after their first meeting at a business convention in Raigun. They'd been together since. He chewed on the tip of the cigar and exhaled. It felt good. So good, these moments. Moments that evaporated like the smoke from the cigar, all too quickly. Moments to be hushed behind hotel doors away from public view because their love was an act of sin. He regarded Kartik. How would Papa react if he could see him now? *Surprised? Shocked? No.* Rakesh blew a halo of smoke. *Mortified.*

He tapped his cigar against the edge of a Swarovski ashtray. Four days, three nights summed up their time together before he had to return home to his wife.

A pain-in-the-ass wife.

Sheetal.

3

DIRTY LAUNDRY

W hen one of the servants informed Sheetal of Rakesh's return from his Hong Kong trip, Sheetal rushed to their bedroom thrilled that Rakesh was home again.

Rakesh had placed the sixteen-inch soft-top suitcase horizontally on their bed and didn't turn when Sheetal entered. He dragged clothes out of the suitcase, dropped them on the floor and a heaviness appeared to weigh the lethargic motion of his hands.

"How was your trip?"

"Good." He dropped a white shirt on the papaya-colored carpet, rust-colored and stained from alcohol that had spilled five days ago and been left to dry. Sheetal hadn't bothered to inform the servants to clean up the mess because alcohol stains were such trivial matters.

"Dr. Kishore called while you were away." Sheetal paused. One more step within Rakesh's radius would be equivalent to invading his privacy. "He wants to see you and we should schedule an appointment."

"Look, I just got back from a six-hour flight. I'm fizzed." He let the suitcase lid flop down apparently oblivious to a white shirt dangling on the edge of the bed. "Let's talk later."

Rakesh had been suffering from bouts of fatigue for several months, so before Rakesh left for Hong Kong, Sheetal suggested that he visit the family doctor. Rakesh said he didn't have the time to schedule an appointment, so Sheetal took the liberty of doing so herself.

Sheetal narrowed the distance between them, pressed her palm on Rakesh's left shoulder and firmed her grip. "I scheduled an appointment for Wednesday next week at five-thirty."

He flicked the white shirt on the floor, and the fabric crumpled.

"I think it will help in case you need to go through any testing or just have a check-up."

He said nothing.

Was he afraid? No. Rakesh didn't fear anything. He just didn't like being told what to do. "Who knows? I could be wrong." She faked a laugh to ease the tension and shifted closer. "And this could be one big mistake—"

He brushed her fingers off his shoulder.

"Be reasonable, Rakesh."

"I am." He turned around and narrowed his gaze on her. "He'll say the usual. Stop drinking. Stop smoking. Kick the habit. I'm not going to. So, there's no point. Ditto?" Ditto meant a forced agreement.

The weight of his stare pressed down on her. "What about us?"

"Us?" He unbuttoned his shirt.

"Yash is only eight." Sheetal placed a hand on her hip and leaned against the edge of the bed for support.

"He's away at boarding school."

"For a reason. We put him there to—"

"Not we. You."

Sheetal had never wanted their only child, Yash, to live away from them but she couldn't keep him here, either. With a tyrannical step-mother-in-law, Pushpa, whom she referred to as Mummyji, and a thirty-year-old clinically depressed, divorced sister-in-law, Naina, all living under the same roof, Sheetal didn't want Yash growing up in a dysfunctional family the way Rakesh had. So, when Yash turned five, Sheetal convinced Rakesh the best alternative was to enroll Yash at a boys' convent boarding school in the northern foothills of the Himalayas. "I enrolled Yash at St. Paul's for his own good."

"He needs you. Me. A family for his own good."

She stepped away from the bed. Their mansion with a sixty-foot tall ceiling, separate living quarters for the help, an infinity pool that overlooked a lake and extended to a grand view of a mountain range offered luxury that fell short. "He needs stability and that's something we can't give him here. You know that." Sheetal slid her hand down her thigh and the bangles on her wrist clinked. "What if your aches and fatigue are serious?"

"Aren't you overreacting? It's not like I'm dying. Why do you always get Yash involved? And why are you always so highly strung? Have some wine. Champagne. Something to lighten up." His strong American accent rounded off vowels and swallowed consonants. His pronunciation presented a stark contrast to Sheetal's crisp, Queen's English with a light Indian accent. "Everyone drinks nowadays. Except you, of course."

Sheetal didn't drink alcohol because good Indian women from good Indian families didn't. Rakesh had forced Sheetal to indulge in his whims during the initial years of marriage, but when Sheetal declared it went against her norms and values he surrendered. "You know I don't agree with—"

"Anything I want." He narrowed his eyes.

Their arranged marriage had forced them together under one roof and into one bed but Yash, the only proof of love between them, was all they shared. Sheetal fidgeted with the decade-old ten-carat diamond engagement ring on her finger.

The debt had to be eating at him, and she needed to think of something quick. "What if we sell my ring? I'm sure it would fetch a decent amount and the bank—"

"Are you out of your mind?"

Sheetal cringed. So, what if love didn't exist between them? The ring must mean something to him. How could she be so stupid?

"I don't need your ring to bail me out. I can handle this on my own."

"I meant that we—"

"This isn't a family event, God dammit, where everyone has a say. No one else needs to know. My problem. I fix it."

Everything was still 'I,' not 'we.' Their relationship could be so much better if he agreed to professional help.

Eight years ago, Rakesh had come up with the solution to seek counseling and therapy, and Sheetal elicited a promise from him to work on their marriage. However, the decline in business and mounting tension of the debt had only increased the friction between them. "I have so much jewelry from our marriage that I hardly wear, and it's all just sitting in the bank locker. I can take it to *Hira Moti* and find out its current worth." She followed him to the fading peach-colored sofa arrangement on the right, its back to a mirrored wall. "You are not alone. We're in this together. You are in our lives as we are a part of yours."

"Yes, apart." He turned away from her. "I don't have time to waste with all this *drama—baazi*."

Rakesh didn't waste a minute. Thirteen years ago, shortly after Rakesh turned twenty-seven, his father, Ashok Dhanraj, died of a heart attack and in less than twenty-four hours Rakesh took over Dhanraj and Son. Rakesh, meaning 'Lord Of The Night' in Hindi, proved he was just as bold and powerful in every waking hour and didn't need anyone in his life. Others needed and wanted to be with him.

"My problem, I deal with it."

He flicked the white shirt off his shoulders revealing smooth titanium contours. Tufts of black hair sparsely scattered over his body and graying at the roots were the only signs of Rakesh maturing into his forties.

Her attention wandered to the *Vogue* magazine lying face-up on a sofa cushion as Rakesh paced the room. Yesterday's cover article "Jump Start His Engine," glared from the upper right corner in bold red letters.

Could she really seduce Rakesh in the open when couples in her generation didn't even hold hands in public?

According to culture, marriage was a means to procreate, to carry on the man's family name and to establish the woman's duty to her husband and his family.

The words circled her head. *Don't wait. Grab him in the nude and tell him. You have to have him. Now.* Sheetal gulped and headed toward him.

Rakesh raised a hand to his forehead, stretched the palm across his eyes and rubbed his temples. His fingers and thumb moved toward and then away from each other, repeating the motion he so often did when he had a headache.

Sheetal was about to sit down when Rakesh headed for the bathroom door. She followed his magnetic force, the pull of his minty fragrance but stopped short at the huge pile of filthy laundry. She bent to gather the clothes, trapped the cuffs and collars of Rakesh's shirts and the hem and waistbands of his trousers between her chest and arms, struggling to hold the soiled socks and handkerchiefs in her grip. She almost lost balance and tripped but quickly regained composure. However, tiny articles of alcohol-cigar-and-sweat-stained clothing slipped and Sheetal raised the index finger of her right hand to snag an item. Another scent, a lemony disinfectant-type that Rakesh didn't wear. She turned and regarded the bedroom behind her. Her attention paused on the chipped wood and paint of the closet door to her left. No...not from there. The fragrance hung like a cloud, so heavy and thick she could hardly breathe. She lowered her head to the clothes pressed against her chest and sniffed. She'd found the source. She loosened her grip and followed, determined to ask Rakesh if he'd picked up a new fragrance in Hong Kong.

Sheetal peered right and down at the bathroom floor. She walked in measured steps ever so carefully between the clearly defined outlines of each tile ensuring each movement fell within the limits of Rakesh's boundaries. Then she dropped the clothes into a hamper and parted her lips but stopped. Rakesh hated being questioned and might lose his temper.

Rakesh stood next to the glass shower box, his back turned to her. He loosened the pair of black trousers hugging his waist and let go of the waistband. The fabric slid down his legs, folded and pooled into two conjoined hoops around his feet.

A decade ago, Sheetal, like many Indian women, would have blushed and turned away in embarrassment at the sight of her husband's nudity. But now she watched mesmerized.

Light blue veins branched wild and unrestricted up Rakesh's pale calves and thighs to a pair of kidney-shaped mounds tucked tight behind a pair of black G-string Jockeys. He slipped both thumbs between the strips of fabric clinging to his hips and rolled off the underwear causing the fabric to tumble down to his feet.

A sigh escaped her lips. *May, June, July, August, September, October...six months since they had made love.*

Rakesh pulled open the glass shower box, stepped into the five-by-seven-foot enclosure and turned a knob to the right. Streams of water thundered down Rakesh's chest, waist and hips and snaked down the fine black line running between a pair of his pebble-smooth mounds.

A rise-sink feeling clenched her stomach. Oh, how she ached to press her body to his.

Rakesh flexed his arms, and muscles across his shoulder blades rippled and tightened.

Sheetal's breathing quickened and she bit her lip unsure where to look and what to do. She tapped her fingers along her thighs to refrain from wanting to touch him. Her attention darted to the hamper's lid tilting to one side and the urge to straighten the square rattan tingled her fingers. She made for the hamper watching Rakesh from the corner of her eye.

Rakesh turned the knob further to the right, stepped aside, grabbed a blue bottle from a niche and shampooed his hair. Then he pumped soap from a dispenser, lathered himself and resumed his position under the spray. Suds melted down his frame, pooled near his feet and clouds of vapor rose with another yearning to press her body to his, but Sheetal aligned the rattan on the hamper's rim and sealed the lid tight.

Rakesh abruptly turned off the water, stepped aside, and water sloshed. Wetness distilled between her thighs as the mist between them evaporated. What if women abroad found him attractive? Was he drawn to them in the same way? Her throat ached. *Be forthright. Demanding*, the article had said. *He wants to know you want him.* The tip-tip of the leaking showerhead pattered to the rhythm of her heart.

Rakesh pushed open the door, grabbed a towel from a rod on the wall and wrapped the fabric around his slim waist as the fragrance of mint, soap and whiffs of herbal shampoo lifted with the lacy curtain of steam making her dizzy. He ran his fingers through strands of pepper-gray hair, and she inched toward his towering frame a swelling, pulsating sensation throbbing within.

"You're hurting me, Sheetal. Let go." He grabbed her wrist and flicked open her fingers that were curved around the pendulum of his organ.

"Please." She pressed her mouth against his nape and nuzzled, oblivious to what she'd just done.

He pulled away her hand, let go and rungs of bangles collided and clumped along Sheetal's wrist. "I'm tired." Rakesh marched up the three marble steps, swung open the bathroom door and left her standing alone.

4
LOST & FOUND

The next morning, Sheetal stood before a white canvas in her studio determined to complete the assignment at hand. With nine years' experience under her sari pallu and the 'S.Dhanraj' signature on every work, Sheetal kept up with orders for her paintings from hotels, restaurants, posh clubs, the occasional art exhibition and balanced her finances with ease. However, she wanted to be better and reach the heights of Indian artists who had claimed international fame like Husain and Tagore. She had a long way to go and to attain that caliber meant commitment, dedication and focus.

Painting offered more than just a career. Painting meant diving into a world of colors, shades, hues and then bleeding her heart out on canvas. Several careful strokes of the brush and she could erupt mountains, wash lakes, or field forests to life. The right combination of light and dark and she could preserve objects in still-lifes.

Two weeks ago, Sheetal had delivered a series of orchids to Mr. Bhattacharya, the PR manager for Sheraton Hotel, New Delhi. The rush order was then delayed by two days because Mummyji had taken off a week to go on a cruise and left Naina in Sheetal's care.

Last week Sheetal called to follow up on the delivery of her paintings and payment worth three hundred and fifty thousand rupees, but Mr. Bhattacharya assured her corporate would not hold the delay against her. Since Mr. Bhattacharya had not called, Sheetal assumed the remaining ninety percent balance payment would reach her soon.

A series of ten oil paintings of the Himalayan Mountain range on four-by-five-foot canvases destined for the Renaissance Hotel's newly renovated west wing was also due by December fifteenth. Two months was ample time.

Sheetal's cell phone rang, and she took the call. "Hello?"

"Hanh! Helloji! Bhattacharya calling from Delhi."

"Hello, Bhattacharyaji." *He's probably calling to confirm the balance payment due.* "I trust all is good?"

"That's...uh...why I'm calling. We...uh...the paintings, you know. They arrived two days late. So, I...uh...am having them delivered back to you."

Sheetal tightened. "Surely, Bhattacharyaji, we spoke about this and—"

"I know uh...how disappointing all this is. But please be assured it was not...uh my decision. Corporate didn't get your paintings on time and purchased another artist's collection. They only told me—"

"Didn't you explain the situation? We talked last week, and you said—"

"Big people, Madame. Inauguration of new hotel. Corporate wanting everything in order."

"You can't just send them back. Surely, you'll pay—"

"No, no, Madame. We will not take back the ten-percent deposit. It will be an insult if we ask money back from a Dhanraj. But we cannot pay you more."

Seven huge orchid paintings. Four by five feet tall. What was she going to do with them? Barricade the windows of the studio?

He ended the phone call, and Sheetal tucked the mobile into a velvet cell phone pouch that hung off the waist of her sari by a metal hook. This was all Mummyji's fault!

At forty-eight, Mummyji believed that any activity on the Dhanraj premises was her business. It didn't matter whether Sheetal and Rakesh argued, Sheetal received a phone call concerning her paintings, or Naina grew upset with Sheetal over some trivial matter, Mummyji had to know everything. Thirteen years ago, shortly after Rakesh's father, Ashok Dhanraj, died from a heart attack, Mummyji inherited the mansion and estate. According to Ashok's will, Rakesh inherited the business, and Naina and Megha received a fixed percentage from their ten-percent shares of Dhanraj & Son. As if Mummyji's intrusion wasn't enough interference, Mummyji and her biological daughter, Naina, had to be priority on everyone's list, which is precisely why Sheetal had lost the Sheraton Hotel account and now her earnings from the sale of the orchids.

Money had never been an issue for the Dhanrajs because Rakesh earned enough to cover the running expenses of their home, local charities they supported, social events they hosted and he secured enough in savings. However, with the mounting pressure of the debt, Sheetal wondered how much longer this could continue. At least she had not been a burden for Rakesh and had managed overheads like the cost of brushes, canvas, paints, other supplies and saved some money to tuck into her personal bank account as profit.

Not that it mattered much because Rakesh labeled Sheetal's revenue pocket money. According to him, her income would never amount to anything substantial. No matter how well Sheetal painted or how many pieces she sold in a quarter, her earnings equated to loose change in his pocket. Rakesh claimed painting was a useful hobby to keep her busy and her revenue would buy her a few designer saris. And when he wanted to be particularly vindictive, he claimed the only reason her paintings sold was because of the Dhanraj label.

Sheetal cringed. Oh, how she hated the reminder that the Dhanraj label allowed her to bypass the hassle of selling artwork through dealers and being subjected to the standard fifty-fifty share of the revenue or sixty percent share on the sale of her paintings to art galleries. Hotels, clubs and restaurant owners came to Sheetal for business because owning a work of art by a Dhanraj meant status and pride. For Sheetal, painting also represented her independent working-woman status and that she was not just another pretty face as were so many other wives who shared her elite lifestyle.

Sheetal's cell phone chimed again. She withdrew it from the pouch and pressed it to her ear. "Hello?"

"Hey, Kavita here."

Kavita's sing-song voice warmed Sheetal's heart. "How are you? It's been so long since we caught up."

"Oh, I know. I've been tied up. The whole flat is full of boxes. There's barely any space for me and the girls to move around."

The girls were Kavita and Gaurav's three and five-year-old daughters.

Kavita, Gaurav, Sheetal and Arvind used to be a four-some in college and hung out together all the time. Shortly after graduation, and against the wishes of both families, Kavita, a career woman from the northwestern region of Punjab, had eloped with Gaurav, a *Gujarati* from the west. Ostracized by their families with no financial support, Kavita and Gaurav's meager combined incomes forced them to live in a run-down locale in northern Raigun.

"What's going on?"

"We're moving."

Sheetal's heart sank. Had their struggles to make ends meet forced them to move to a smaller city? "Outside Raigun?"

"No way. Just to a better locale where we'll have electricity, running water, and decent amenities compared to this dump."

A weight lifted off her chest and Sheetal ran her thumb down the edge of the white canvas. "I'm sure you must be excited. Are you buying?"

"Are you kidding? Rent is all people like us can afford."

Sheetal bit her lip. She hadn't meant to offend her one true loyal friend since high school. "I didn't mean it that way. I was just—"

"Hey, no offense taken. I'm cool. But I wanted to meet you."

Sheetal longed to see Kavita, too. They'd last met three years ago at a mall but didn't have time to do more than exchange a quick hug before Kavita and her family rushed to make it to the opening of the evening show. What could be so important that Kavita was willing to endure an exhausting, sweaty ride on an overcrowded bus just to meet her? "Is it important?"

"I need to return something."

She couldn't invite Kavita to the Prasad's because Mama still used Kavita as an example of disgrace and waved Kavita's banner of dishonor as a warning to Sheetal to stay with Rakesh and avoid bad influences. For years, Sheetal had wanted to invite Kavita over for the Karva Chauth puja where women honored their husbands with a day of fasting and evening prayers at the Dhanraj's, but Mummyji would equate Kavita with the servant rank and openly insult her before their snobby, wealthy friends. "Can you tell me on the phone?"

"It's personal."

"Like you and Gaurav, personal?" Were they breaking up? What about their daughters? Her heart fisted in a knot at the thought of children who suffered because of their parents' broken marriages.

"Why would I ask to meet if we could discuss this on the phone?"

Because she perpetually cut short their phone conversations? Guilt weighed on her chest. Sheetal preferred not to burden Kavita with the weight of her worries because Kavita had enough to deal with. Friends helped each other, they didn't burden each other, and she needed to find neutral territory. "I'll be meeting Mama at the Raigun Cancer Center this Thursday afternoon. I can meet you there at around 4 p.m."

"Sounds good. I'll give you a buzz when I leave."

· · ·

SHEETAL DRAGGED A PAINT-FILLED BRUSH DOWN THE OUTLINE OF A mountain range she had just sketched. Trees rustling in the breeze outside reminded her of Yash's laughter. The morning sun filtering through the open window flooded Sheetal's paint-zone—marble floor cordoned off from the surrounding beige carpet—with yellow light like the warmth of Yash's smile.

She closed her eyes and imagined the tip-tap of Yash's shoes making their way in from the corridor outside, across the carpeted entrance to the room's center. How she longed to put her arms around Yash, hold him tight and press his body to hers. She opened her eyes, and her heart sank at the surrounding emptiness.

She dipped a two-inch thick brush in some pthalo-blue, then some cadmium-white paint on her palette, and swept the brush in horizontal strokes along the bottom third of the canvas. Another pretty picture to hang for public satisfaction and alleviate the starkness of some wall.

Fifteen minutes later, Sheetal lifted the brush off the canvas and exchanged it for a palette knife. The thud of footsteps on the carpet closed the distance between her and the intruder behind. The scent of mint thickened like a cloud. *Rakesh.* She pressed the ball of her left index finger on the point of the knife's blunt tip.

His breathing filled her ears. The fabric of his shirt crinkled against her spine, and the beating of her heart fell in sync with his rhythm.

"What's this?" he asked.

Sheetal picked up another brush, dabbed the paint on her palette, and began whipping a series of clouds in the upper third of the canvas circling the sky with gray paint. *A storm.* She stepped forward, away from the lure of his masculine pull because custom ordained it wrong for them to be in such proximity with the studio door wide open. If anyone saw them, she would be labeled 'shameless,' 'too broad-minded and outgoing' and 'too western' in behavior. Perhaps she'd lose her position as an example for others to follow. Besides, why give in after yesterday's rejection?

The warmth of his tobacco breath burned the hairs on her nape, and when he snaked a blue shirt sleeve around her bare mid-riff, Sheetal reeled in tight against his body. The silky-smooth Geoffrey Beene shirt crinkled under her weight and the light woolen fabric of his trousers entangled her silk sari causing a tingling sensation to run through her nerves *He wants me after all.*

"I have something for you."

That deep, throaty 'you' clenched a knot within as he came around and handed her an envelope.

"What is it?" She looked up.

"Two-way train tickets to Mansali to bring Yash back for the holidays."

A holiday would give them quality time away from Mummyji, Naina, and the business and put their marriage back on track. For the last three years, Sheetal and Rakesh took week-long vacations around late October near the foothills of the Himalayas in Mansali close to Yash's campus, and then returned with Yash for the holidays, the Hindu Festival of Lights.

Road and rail offered the only modes of transport to and from Mansali. However, the rural areas of India presented considerable risk for a lone woman traveler. Sheetal pulled three tickets out of the envelope and read the names on each. A return ticket for her. A one-way ticket for Yash. A return ticket for Janvi, the maidservant. The maidservant? Why was Janvi going? She checked the envelope again, but it was empty. "Where's yours?"

"I'm not going. I told you."

"I'm not going alone either. You said tickets for two."

"I said two-way tickets. Janvi and you. Janvi will accompany—"

"But I thought—"

"Think less and listen more."

Sheetal dropped the brush on the palette. Didn't he understand that a vacation meant their alone time?

"You'll get the usual ten days in Mansali before you return." He spun on his heels and left.

"Rakesh!" She followed him down the south wing past richly carved marble balustrades on the right and a wall of closed doors on the left. He turned right and lengthened his stride. He was probably heading to their bedroom. Sheetal hurried to catch up, but Rakesh took another right, marched past their bedroom and took the stairs that sliced through the middle of the south wing and flared on the ground floor like an A-line skirt onto a tessellation of black and white marble squares.

"Rakesh?" She leaned over the balcony running the mansion's inner perimeter.

Two monstrous chandeliers, suspended equidistant on either side of the stairs, dangled from the ceiling like earrings. The left chandelier on the east wing looked over a nine-seater Bradford Brown sofa and the one on the right hovered above a sixteen-seater Fulton White seating arrangement.

"Rakesh, what about you?"

He paused and turned to look at her. "What now?"

"Aren't you coming? You promised you would."

"No."

Sheetal hoisted the front pleats of her sari and made her way down, but her flat sandals slipped on the silky fabric. She lunged forward and slammed against Rakesh's chest, but he caught her in time.

"Careful."

He cares. She pulled away from him and straightened, crushing the envelope in the process. "I don't want to go alone."

The sharp upward slant of his jaw and cheekbone tightened. "Sheetal," he whispered, "the loan. I have to focus on that right now. I might have to travel again. On business."

Always traveling. Always business. "But—"

"Be by yourself for a while." He ran his palm along the length of her arm. "Learn to be a little independent." He let go.

"What exactly will I do?"

"Paint...stuff? Walk? Take tours. See the mountains." He said the words soft and slow.

"But—"

"Look, I can't be around all the time. Learn to be alone."

How much more was she supposed to do alone when they spent most of their time away from each other anyway? She tightened her grip on the crushed envelope.

"I'll use the time to finish up with my meetings and work before Yash's home. Promise." The pale skin tightened around the corners of his face which meant he wanted her to leave. "Anything else?"

The unsaid words lodged in her throat and melted on her tongue.

"Ah, there you are! I was looking for you, I tell you." Mummyji appeared at the foot of the stairs, no doubt with some personal favor that demanded attention as a way of reminding Sheetal who was in charge. "I'm on my way to the club, I tell you. I have lunch and a game of cards today." Mummyji always ate lunch at the Royal Society Ladies' Club and spent her afternoon playing cards.

"Now run up and bring down my purse, I tell you because Janvi's gone out. The white one with flower beads." Janvi and Roshni were the only servants allowed in the bedrooms and whenever Janvi was out on an errand, Mummyji cast Sheetal next in line.

With over twenty servants in the house surely one could fetch the purse. Sheetal marched down past Rakesh and turned to Mummyji. "What about Roshni?"

"*Hai Ishwar*! Not Roshni." Mummyji pumped both hands on her hips and her Amul chocolate lips curved in a sneer.

"But—"

"No buts in this house, I tell you. I would get it myself, but the trip upstairs will ruin my sari pleats. You go." She flicked an index finger.

The order bore no connection with sari pleats but tied in with cellulite pleating every fold of Mummyji's skin. Over the last eight years, Mummyji had doubled in dimension and struggled to balance without toppling over. She also owned a closet full of white purses to match every white sari she owned. White, the color Hindu widows wore, reflected the subdued lifestyle a woman should lead after her husband's death. Widows didn't dot *bindis* on their foreheads, adorn their wrists with colorful bangles or participate in religious festivals like Karva Chauth meant for married women.

After Ashok Dhanraj died, Mummyji, only thirty-five at the time, suffered a forced sedentary lifestyle. Over time she compensated for the loss by substituting all her rubies, emeralds and sapphires for diamonds and pearls. She sacrificed all her gold *zari*-bordered saris for silver ones and replaced multi-colored bracelets with diamond bangles.

"I said, I need my purse." Mummyji waved a thick, brown finger in the air.

"I'll bring it down in five minutes. First, I need to talk to my husband." Sheetal was about to pivot on the step and face Rakesh when Mummyji frowned and a spider web of wrinkles raked from the circumference of her round face to the one-carat nose pin. "Now. Naina is on bed rest. Spend some time with her, I tell you."

Sheetal would much rather spend time with her Mama, Indu, who had been diagnosed with ovarian cancer six months ago. Sheetal accompanied Mama for the monthly chemotherapy treatments and couldn't wait for the day Mama would be diagnosed cancer free.

"I expect you to have all of Naina's meals wheeled up to her room while I'm away and check-in on her, I tell you."

Naina married Ajay Malhotra nine years ago with all the pomp and glory of a nine-hundred-million-rupee wedding. However, Ajay and the Malhotra in-laws soon discovered Naina's clinical depression and accused the Dhanrajs of duping them. The illness Mummyji had tried so hard to hide inevitably led to Naina's divorce and sunk Naina deeper into depression.

"Now then." Mummyji waddled over to the Fulton White sofas, the barrel of her white sari swinging with each step. She almost tripped over the front sari pleats, circled her arms wildly in the air, and collapsed on an ottoman. The flab around her midriff compressed and protruded like two tires, one atop the other. "Hai Ishwar! What else can go wrong? Servants keep mopping floors all day. No wonder I keep slipping. They have nothing else better to do, I tell you."

"Perhaps the servants shouldn't mop the floors so frequently then?" Sheetal suggested.

"Yes, my fault—no? Is that what you're trying to tell me? You, young women nowadays. No sense of respect. No consideration for..."

During the initial years of her marriage, Sheetal tried to strike a cordial balance with Mummyji. However, Mummyji made it clear from day one that she held the matriarchal position in the Dhanraj household, and in accordance with customs and the extended family system, Sheetal would do better to follow her lead. If Sheetal chose to break away, the family would label her a rebel and treat her like an outcast.

"...I don't need your sympathy or advice, I tell you. God knows what I did to deserve this."

Sheetal's throat tightened. 'This' referred to her presence in the Dhanraj's lives, not the incident just now. Sheetal turned around, but Rakesh had gone. She trudged upstairs to Mummyji's room, grabbed a white purse from her closet, and soon handed it over. Then she returned to her studio. *A storm.* Wasn't that where she'd left off? She dipped the brush's tip in dark blue and pressed it against the canvas, but as usual, the magic of that moment was gone.

5
TRUTH OR DARE

In the Japanese garden behind the mansion, Sheetal and Rakesh shared a ritual on this rare occasion when Rakesh returned home early from work. A decade-old Paris Evening tea set from Sheetal's dowry graced with black and gold décor held Sheetal's coffee in one pot and Rakesh's chai spiced with cardamom, cloves and saffron in the other. Sheetal swirled her coffee with a silver spoon that had bronzed and tarnished. Rakesh raised a cup to his crisp, thin lips for the fifth time in the last three minutes, took a sip, and then sailed it back down to the saucer clinking porcelain against porcelain. Rakesh didn't gulp quick mouthfuls like other men and from the lethargic motion of his hands, he didn't appear to care if brown skin crusted the liquid's surface, steam clouded his eyes when he blew across the cup, or if brown rings from his cup stamped the saucer beneath. Rakesh didn't care for life's trivialities and carried on with whatever fell next on his agenda. He withdrew his hand and placed it on his lap.

Time for a smoke? A thought had been weighing on Sheetal's mind for several weeks and she parted her lips to speak. However, Rakesh reached over to the tea trolley, opened the cigar box, pulled out a thick, brown cigar and lit it with precision. Sheetal took a quick sip of her coffee and watched from the corner of her eye as Rakesh chewed on the end, gulped, and exhaled.

Now that he'd released the day's stress he might just listen. "Megha arrived this morning."

"Oh."

Megha, twenty-seven, and the youngest of three Dhanraj children had married Raj Saxena for love at the age of nineteen. The couple eloped and tied the knot with a quick wedding ceremony at the local temple because Rakesh would have otherwise forced Megha to marry a man of his choosing.

In her second trimester, Megha had called that morning to remind Sheetal about her duty. In accordance with Indian tradition, first-time mothers were supposed to have the baby at their parents' home.

Rashmi Dhanraj, Rakesh and Megha's biological mother, had died twenty-seven years ago and Mummyji wanted nothing to do with Megha or the Saxenas because Megha was another woman's daughter and therefore not Mummyji's responsibility. So, responsibility for the baby's birth fell on Sheetal.

"Megha's due in May and that's six months from now, so I figured we should speak to the Saxenas ahead of time so she can have the baby here."

Rakesh looked up.

"I think *you* should talk to the Saxenas."

"I think *you* should figure this out."

He obviously wasn't in the mood to discuss the birth of Megha's baby, so Sheetal changed the topic. "There's an appointment with Dr. Kishore this week. Wednesday, at five-thirty. I can meet you at—"

"What appointment?"

"He asked to see you. Remember?"

"I said no. Remember?"

"It's important."

"Nothing is unless I say so." The evening sun cast a light against Rakesh's left cheek, slicing the distance between them at a diagonal.

"He wants to talk—"

Rakesh stood, headed back to the Marquette Dining Room, and slid closed the glass door.

THE NEXT DAY SHEETAL WOUND UP WORKING AHEAD OF TIME TO ACCOMPANY Mama for the chemotherapy session later that afternoon. She headed downstairs and was about to step onto the ground floor landing, paused, and turned left. Naina lay sprawled out on the Bradford Brown sofas, her favorite spot.

The informal seating arrangement located adjacent to the mansion's main entrance served as a vantage point because it offered visibility and access to all those who came and went, and this entrance connected the palace to the outside world. The dark brown fabric and E-shape arrangement of cushions camouflaged Naina's raggedy, sun-roasted, five-foot-tall weedy frame. Raisin-like buttons dotted each cushion's center point like Naina's pupils and raked in the fabric from all four corners of the cushion's edge like the perpetual scowl she wore. The Russet Legacy coffee table stretched from one end of the sofa to the other like her flat and broad nose.

A short stumpy vase of artificial white buds gracing the table's center and a stack of *New Woman, Vogue,* and *Elle* magazines haphazardly stacked on a corner table presented two bright spots in the drab seating area. Naina trailed a stubby brown finger along the hump of a black telephone beside the magazines as Sheetal stepped on the landing.

Nine years ago, when Ajay Malhotra had divorced Naina, the catastrophe occurred in this enormous living room. Since then, Naina spent the majority of her time flipping through magazines and answering the telephone even though servants had been designated to do the chore. From the manner by which she trailed her finger over the receiver and glared at Sheetal, she appeared eager for Sheetal's marriage to unravel like hers.

"So, are you feeling better?" Sheetal held her breath at the odor of stale chutney.

"Eh, na? What makes you think I'm sick?"

"I didn't say you were. It's just that I haven't seen you in a while."

A while usually meant several weeks with Naina locked in her room all day, neither asleep nor awake, but in a catatonic state of depression. During this phase, she mulled over the dark color of her skin, uneven teeth and features set too close, to lips that ran like two brown Camel crayons. She blamed her looks, failed marriage, and stuck being single on Mummyji while her ex-husband, Ajay Malhotra, had re-married shortly after the divorce and successfully fathered two children.

"I just thought you might be on bed rest." Sheetal headed for the door.

"I've been busy, na."

'Busy' meant Naina had been going through her wedding albums or trying to figure out some cosmetic remedy to enhance the scant beauty she had been born with.

"So, *Bhabhi*,"— Naina addressed Sheetal with the term of respect reserved for an older brother's wife—"Where are you going?"

"To my parents' place. But I'm meeting Mama at the hospital for chemo first."

"Will it take long?"

"The rest of today." Sheetal quickened her steps, thereby minimizing the opportunity for Naina to interrogate further.

At that moment, Megha, dressed in a creamy-brown *salwar kameez* suit trimmed with white leaves and vines rose from the Fulton White sofas and headed toward her. The detergent-strong fragrance of Mountain Blue Rexona deodorant refreshed Naina's odor. Because of Karva Chauth tomorrow, which entailed a day of fasting followed by evening prayers with a group of women, Megha would stay over for the next two days.

A tiny mound of Megha's tummy showed from behind the knee-length *kurti* that hung over a pair of baggy white trousers, cuffed at the ankles. A chiffon stole in brown and white tye-dye colors hung in a 'U' from shoulder to shoulder and the remaining fabric drifted behind like two pigtails. "Bhabhi? You're leaving?" Megha's voice was as delicate as wind chimes.

"The chemo is at three and I'll go home with Mama and stay there overnight," Sheetal replied. "But I'll be back tomorrow morning."

"Eh, na, did you check with Mummy?" Naina intervened.

"For what? Permission to take my mother for chemo?" Ten years ago, Sheetal had needed Mummyji's permission to go anywhere, but she proved herself by taking control of her life, her marriage and her career.

"I expect to see you back home tonight, I tell you!" Mummyji's voice floated from above.

Sheetal craned her neck to find Mummyji staring down. "I'll return tomorrow morning, Rakesh knows." As long as Rakesh knew, no one else's opinion mattered.

"Bhabhi?" The tone of Megha's voice shifted, and Sheetal's gaze lowered in concern.

Megha's hazel eyes darted to the left and right as if in search of something and then she blinked. "I..." she pushed a falling lock of hair around the curve of her right ear. "You will come back tomorrow morning, right?"

"Of course." Sheetal nodded. "It's Karva Chauth. I have to."

Megha leaned toward Sheetal. "I'm not used to... you know... being here without you." Ten years ago, Megha's incoherent speech gushed without a pause or break, and she stammered. Shortly after marriage, Sheetal assumed the role of Megha's mother figure and instilled enough confidence and femininity in the girl to help her emerge from her shell and blossom into a woman. Now, Megha prepared to be a mother.

Unlike Sheetal who stayed back while Rakesh travelled abroad, Megha accompanied her husband, Raj Saxena, a cardiologist in private practice, to several medical conferences. A month ago, the couple had returned from a New York trip—their first abroad—and Megha dropped in to visit the family. She fawned over how American women had blonde hair that sparkled like gold in the sun. She praised their blue and green eyes, compared them to the colors of the ocean, and went on and on about several women blessed with breathtaking beauty and model-like figures. She highlighted their career-oriented, determined personalities and marveled at their ability to balance work and family without the help of servants.

A bitterness crept on Sheetal's tongue as Megha droned on. Did Rakesh spend the majority of his trips abroad with these blue-and-green-eyed beauties and return to find she didn't measure up? "There are some interesting articles I bookmarked in those magazines." Sheetal pointed to the stack on the corner table. "While you're here you might want to read up on silly things like how to put love and romance back in a marriage."

"Why silly?" Megha asked.

"Because it's... Isn't it obvious? These reprints from American magazines are great fillers but western ideas simply don't work here. Don't tell me a bag of tricks can put your marriage back on track especially when we have to work harder on relationships because we don't have their easy-going culture."

"Things are changing here too." Naina snorted. "Only, now it's coming out in the open—na? Half the marriages here. They're lies. Ask me. I know, na. Because—"

"Every marriage goes stale after a while. You know, after the honeymoon phase is over," Megha cut her short. "But you don't give up. You keep trying. Besides," she shrugged, "love is the same in any culture. It speaks a language of—"

"Language?" Naina smirked. "I needed the truth. What did

Mummy tell Ajay's family about me? What did she hide? So many lies, na. If I had known, my life wouldn't be a mess."

Sheetal's chest tightened and her sides hurt. So many secrets in her own marriage.

"Anything built on lies," Naina yelled, "crumbles and dies."

Sheetal turned and left.

THE CHAUFFEUR PULLED THE BLACK MERCEDES OUT OF THE DHANRAJ mansion, drove around the semi-circular driveway, and braked before a security guard's cubicle on the left. The uniformed guard pushed on a button and a pair of black, wrought iron gates topped with gold knobs parted to the sides. The chauffeur eased the vehicle through the widening gap and careened down a gently sloping road toward Raigun city. Sunlight dappled between overhanging leaves and cast playful shadows along the length of Sheetal's left arm. Sheetal glanced behind and the white mansion grew smaller until it sparkled on the hilltop like the diamond crowning her ring. She flexed the fingers of her left hand and her skin crinkled around the ring's band. Desperate for some fresh air, Sheetal rolled down the window and the scent of eucalyptus rushed in. She ran four fingers through her tangled hair causing the shoulder-length strands to fly wild, free, and caress her cheeks with the gentleness of Arvind's touch.

Arvind. She rolled her tongue and pressed it against the roof of her mouth to soften the 'd'. She played the name on her lips, twirled a lock of loose hair, and curved it around her ear. However, the ringlet broke free, leapt back to the corner of her mouth, and Sheetal played the name on her lips again. Wasn't it only yesterday that she'd been madly in love with Arvind, and they'd planned to spend their lives together?

Powerless against Mama and Papa's wishes that she marry Rakesh, she'd managed to meet Arvind one last time and kiss him goodbye. That kiss. She ran her tongue over her lower lip. Ten years later and the flavor of his mocha breath still aroused a tingling within.

The car turned left at a four-way intersection and snaked between trucks, black and yellow beetle-shaped taxis, private cars, and autorickshaws. Pedestrians rushed on sidewalks coughing and sneezing as diesel from the trucks' tailpipes clouded their bodies.

The odor of gasoline, sweat, and the day's heat flooded the Mercedes. Sheetal took a packet of wet tissues out her purse, pulled one out of the sleeve and the fragrance of sweet vanilla permeated the air. She wiped her hand and arms clean, rolled up the glass window and sank back against the smooth leather seat. Sheetal's phone chimed. She fished it from her handbag, flipped it open, and pressed the device to her ear.

"Hey, it's Kavita. How far away are you? I got here just now."

"On my way. I'm meeting Mama in the lobby." She glanced at her watch. She'd escort Mama to the chemo room, get her settled, and then find a way to slip out and meet Kavita.

"I can meet you there too and say hi to Aunty."

"You know what happens whenever Mama sees you. She picks at you and says things I'll regret. How about I meet you in the parking lot at the back entrance? I'll get Mama settled first and meet you at around four?" The vehicle picked up speed and glided through the traffic. "You really can't tell me on the phone?"

"We'll talk when we meet." Kavita hung up.

The Mercedes broke through the traffic, turned off the main road, and cruised along a roundabout near Raigun Public Gardens.

Better. Sheetal rolled down the window again and the scent of hundreds of floral fragrances reminded her of better times with Rakesh. Days when he came home on time from work and took her and Yash out to the Raigun Cricket Club, the zoo, or brought them here. Yash was two at the time and occasionally napped in his pram while Rakesh pushed the stroller and Sheetal walked alongside, her fingers curled around his arm.

The vehicle braked before a red traffic light at a four-way intersection, and a wave of human traffic on the left sidewalk rushed across. A woman in her mid-thirties, dressed in a faded red and white salwar kameez and squatting beside several canvases displayed on paint-splattered wooden easels called out to pedestrians. Several oil paintings on two-by-three-foot canvases had been pushed to the pavement's edge and angled for drivers to see: flowers in a vase, a bowl of fruit, a horse on a farm, villagers working in fields, and a scenic mountain range.

Sheetal pressed her face to the window. The paintings presented such a stark contrast to imported bronze, metal-leaf, and sparkling gold frames crusting the edge of her works on display at the Raigun Sports Club. Her throat tightened. The woman's work was full of depth. Passion. Not just good. But excellent. Sheetal caught her lower lip between her teeth. *Almost*—she gulped—*as good as mine?*

The woman waved for pedestrians to look at the works and name their price, but no one glanced at the display.

Sheetal raised a hand to her earlobe out of habit and touched the diamond solitaire earring. A man on a scooter turned to look through the window and Sheetal dragged her hand down wishing she had kept still and not drawn attention again. The woman made eye contact, angled one of the paintings toward Sheetal, and gestured for her to buy one, but Sheetal shuddered and turned away.

Five minutes later, she arrived at the Raigun Cancer Centre.

A NURSE IN A WHITE UNIFORM HUNG A BAG OF CLEAR LIQUID ON AN IV POLE, connected it to a tube that fed into Mama's elbow, then tapped the drip chamber to adjust the flow of the liquid dripping from the bag into the IV tube. She looked at her watch. "You are feeling fine, Ma'am?"

Mama nodded. The movement appeared to exert a toll and Mama nestled back into the padded concave curve of the cushioned hospital bed. Dressed in a pink silk sari, Mama covered her head with her sari pallu, and the fabric outlined her face like a halo. Most women from previous generations covered their heads as a sign of respect to their elders. Despite Dadi's death last year—Papa's mother—and Mama's elevated status to the oldest Prasad woman alive, Mama continued to maintain the practice of covering her head to hide the loss of hair from chemotherapy.

"Ten minutes and I will come to check again," the nurse said. "If you need anything, just push the red button." She pointed to a red 'panic' button located on a wall behind Mama and left.

Mama closed her eyes and her chest heaved gently. Thin lines etched across her forehead and the corner of her lips quivered.

Sheetal planted a hand on Mama's shoulder. "What happened?"

Mama opened her eyes and kohl, running along the cradle, moistened. "Feeling sick. Very sick. Like I need to vomit," she croaked. Almost every chemotherapy session nauseated Mama and lately, she started feeling sick even before the hour.

"Why do you need to cover your head?" Sheetal slid the pallu off Mama's head but stopped at the sight of more milky white patches of skin. Mama had lost more hair over the last two weeks.

"The more I hide the better, Beti." Mama used the term of affection parents lavished on daughters. "You must be so tired, braving all that traffic for me."

"Really, Mama. I just sit in the car and here I am." With several cars parked in the Dhanraj's garage, Sheetal couldn't drive a single vehicle and didn't need to learn thanks to her chauffeur-driven lifestyle.

"You make it sound easy, but it's been hard ever since *Maji*, your grandmother, died." Mama referred to Papa's mother, Asha, and fell silent. For thirty-four years, Mama had lived the married years of her life under the woman's iron-fist reign. Now she appeared lost without the woman and confused about everything, including herself.

It's the cancer, Sheetal reasoned. The doctor had warned the family to keep an eye out for signs of anxiety and depression, common side effects patients experienced over the course of treatment. The doctor also suggested to keep Mama's morale high, but from Mama's haggard expression and raspy voice, the success of accomplishing that feat seemed highly unlikely.

"Your father is so confused all the time. He doesn't remember anything nowadays, and I think Maji's death has affected his memory."

Was Mama losing her mind too? Papa had a penchant for precision and never missed the fine details of any event. But she didn't want Mama to burden herself with more worries. "You need to get on with your life."

"Promise me you'll take care of your father after I'm gone."

"Mama—"

"Promise me."

Sheetal nodded. *So many people survived cancer. Mama would too. She had to.* "Why do you start with all these depressing—"

"It's the truth. I'm not strong like you."

Strong? If only Mama knew. Sheetal looked past Mama to the wall behind and a vase of flowers on a corner table. "You think too much of me."

"I'm your mother. I know everything about you. Where do you think all my strength—"

The nurse entered, and Mama stopped. The nurse checked the liquid in the bag and the drip chamber again. "Are you feeling all right, Ma'am?"

"Tired. Weak. I'll feel much better when all this is over."

At that moment, Mama's cell phone rang, and the nurse took leave. Sheetal reached for Mama's velvet green sari pouch on the corner table, pulled the phone out of the holder, and looked at the caller ID. "Anjali."

"Tell her I'll call back later."

Anjali, Vikram Choudhary's wife, was the daughter-in-law of Hemlata Choudhary, Papa's younger sister from the village of Vilaspur. Eight years ago, Vikram and Anjali had been forced to move from Vilaspur to Raigun because Vikram couldn't secure a job. A strong believer in the policy of 'family must help family' Papa employed Vikram in his telecommunications company, Induslink Corporation, and arranged for the couple to live with them at Prasad Bhavan. Vikram and Anjali had two children, took over three bedrooms at the Prasad's residence, and Vikram now helped support operations in India while Papa's younger brother, Uncle Ashwin, ran operations from New Jersey, USA.

The ringing stopped. Sheetal slipped the phone back into the pouch.

Mama extended an arm back and pinched closed the open mouth of the phone pouch. "You still don't like them."

"Who?"

"Anjali and Vikram."

"I didn't say that."

"Then why didn't you take the call?"

"I don't trust them." Sheetal didn't agree with how quickly Papa had put his faith in Vikram and shared business matters with him. However, what really hurt was the manner in which the Choudharys dominated the Prasads and treated Mama and Papa like caretakers for their children.

The creases at the corners of Mama's eyes tightened. "You think I give in to them every time but there's no choice, Beti. If I don't, they'll spread rumors."

What rumors could Vikram and Anjali possibly spread when Mama and Papa never said anything to hurt them, and the Choudharys clearly didn't have the means to afford such luxuries in the first place?

"Being comfortable—" Mama was too modest to use the word wealthy "—and coming from a good family is your good fortune. But not everyone is lucky to be blessed with such comforts. And to think at one point you were ready to throw it all away. I don't know what you were thinking at the time."

Sheetal winced. What was there to think about when she had loved Arvind? So what if she was twenty-two at the time, a final year student at Raigun University's Master's program, and Arvind, twenty-four, was studying for his Ph.D. in Biochemistry? They had been going steady for eight months.

"I knew when we first met Rakeshji, at the party,"—Mama added the suffix ji after the son-in-law's name as a sign of respect— "he was the right choice for you. So well mannered, well spoken, refined..."

The feel of Arvind's palm and the first time they'd locked eyes flooded her memory. So outgoing and caring, friendly, and warm-hearted...

Arvind had sprinted out of the library to give her a textbook she'd left at the check-out counter. She thanked him and when she took the book their hands touched, and a warm tingle surged through. Sheetal didn't want to let go. She offered to buy Arvind coffee at the 'Barista' on campus after the day's lectures to thank him and the friendship budded into romance.

"I'm sure you now look back and see how irresponsible you were." Mama sighed. "And how you left us no choice in the end."

"If you'd listened—"

"To what? Living a poor life full of struggle and hardships?" She shook her head.

"Anyway, you're a grown, mature woman now and responsible..."

Sheetal crossed her arms. First honor, then duty, prestige and now, responsibility. "Really, Mama."

"All a part of life. So easy to hold on to what you have but the difficulty is in letting go. When you give, you rise in the other's eyes and that's when reputation builds."

"Just let go of everything you work so hard for makes no sense." She'd let go of Arvind, and what did she end up with? Rakesh?

"The more you let go the more you grow. Trust and respect are two things you earn not with hands and mind but by winning the hearts of others. Start by giving your heart without expecting anything in return."

She'd given her heart to Arvind and then had the heart of her marriage ripped out by Rakesh. "You can't just—"

"If I say anything to Vikram or Anjali they will create a fuss, speak ill of us, and spread gossip."

A throbbing pulsed at the front of Sheetal's head. Unhealthy gossip and rumors spread with the speed of Raigun's breeze and when fortunes and business empires grew to accommodate fifteen and twenty-two-bedroom mansions, word of mouth ruined reputations.

Anger welled up her throat and Sheetal rose to leave.

"Where are you going?" Mama asked.

"Out for some fresh air." She headed for the door. "I'll be back in a few minutes."

"Something I say hurt you?"

When she'd wanted to marry Arvind, Mama and Papa put family on the line and held her accountable for any calamity that would befall them. But when Megha married for love to a man outside their caste, Mama refused to discuss the affair, claimed the Dhanrajs could do as they pleased, and what they did was their business. Sheetal turned the doorknob and firmed her grip on the handle. What more could Mama say to deepen the pain when she was already a victim of double standards and had learned the art of selective listening from Mama?

"You take rest, Mama." She swung open the door, stepped outside, closed it softly behind, and headed for the lift.

The lift doors rattled open on the ground floor, Sheetal stepped out, wove through several corridors, and headed for the hospital's back entrance. A pair of glass doors emblazoned with a red cross glided open, and Sheetal raised her palm above her eyes for a visor as she entered a chunk of sunlight that bathed the parking lot in hot white. Scorching air blasted. It was like walking into a furnace. She looked past the hoods of cars and minivans parked in neat rows but saw no sign of Kavita. Did Kavita tire after waiting and leave? Possibly. Guilt roiled at her heart. She couldn't blame her.

"Hey!" A woman called from behind. "You walked right past."

Sheetal turned and hugged Kavita. The odor of sweat, stale perfume and diesel filled the embrace. "It's been so long. How are you holding up?"

"Busy moving house. The girls and I have been packing box after box for a whole week now. Amazing how much rubbish you can collect in ten years."

Sheetal grinned. "How can anything be rubbish when you're living with the people you love? All treasures, yes?"

"Love or no love, *yaar*." Kavita used the slang for 'friend. "Life comes with baggage. It doesn't hit until you move, how much you've been holding on to. All week, I've been feeling like the biggest fool on earth because I didn't get rid of so much stuff before. Baby toys, infant clothes, and hand-me-downs. So, I cleaned out all the crap and packed whatever was left, which boiled down to half. Moving guys should be here in three days' time."

Kavita's hair sparkled in the harsh daylight. Had her strands turned white or were they reflecting the sun's rays? Kavita's leathery skin was a shade of burnt latte and when she smiled wrinkles formed along her jawline. Well, at least one person still smiled. Kavita pressed a hand against Sheetal's back and urged her through the sliding doors. "It's cooler inside. We can grab those." She gestured to a row of padded black chairs that lined the left wall.

Sheetal wanted to invite Kavita for the Karva Chauth puja tomorrow but knew better. Mummyji didn't want Megha over for the festival because the Saxenas fell rungs below the Dhanrajs in rank. Where was the question of inviting Kavita who by comparison wouldn't even qualify to live on the same planet? Mummyji would throw a fit.

"So, what's the latest with you?" Kavita asked.

"The same as always." Sheetal took a seat. "Rakesh is forever tied up with business and travel. Yash settled and happy in boarding school, and here I am with Mama for chemo."

"What's the doc say?"

"He insists on chemo even though it wears her down. It's her best option."

"Can I pop in and say hi to Aunty?"

Sheetal sank against the backrest. "Mama doesn't know I'm meeting you and I'd... I don't want Mama saying anything. Besides, what's so important that you couldn't tell me over the phone?"

Kavita reached into her handbag, withdrew an envelope, and handed it to Sheetal. The edges were a dark shade of turmeric as if marinated by time.

Sheetal flipped the envelope back to front. "What is this?"

"A letter."

Sheetal opened the flap, pulled out sheets of yellowed paper, and unfolded the pages. Her handwriting in faded blue ink danced across the sheets...the letter she'd asked Kavita to give to Arvind before her marriage to Rakesh. Which could only mean one thing. "Arvind's here?"

"I have no idea where he is."

"Then where'd this come from?" She folded the letter and tucked it back in the envelope.

"I-I never gave it to Arvind."

The air thickened. "What do you mean?"

"I read the letter when I got home and thought long and hard about what to do."

Anger revved her heart. "Why did you read the letter? It was for Arvind, not you." If Arvind had received the letter in time, he would have stayed in Raigun as she'd asked him to. "You had to do nothing more but give him this letter."

"Which is precisely why I read it, so you don't end up making the same mistake I did. After the shit-hole life I've been living, you really think I'd let you do this to yourself? Do you know what Gaurav and I have gone through? I didn't want that for you. I figured it best if I—"

"Who gave you the right to decide what's best for me?"

"You think you could sustain the life I lead?"

"That's not for you to decide."

"If I didn't care, perhaps. But I do. Arvind could never have given you a fraction of what you're used to. Just look at me." She held out her wrists scarred by burn marks. "My gold medal for cooking *chapati* after chapati for the last ten years and slaving over a hot stove every night where we lose electricity most times and running water is still rationed. Thank God, we're finally moving to a better place now. After ten shitty years."

Sheetal swallowed a lump in her throat and slipped the envelope into her handbag. "It could have been different for us."

"Different? How?" Kavita's tone iced. "Maybe Arvind could have earned fifty thousand rupees more than Gaurav after his Ph.D., but that buys peanuts in today's world. And why the regrets when you're at peace and life is rolling perfectly for you?"

"Who says I'm at peace?"

"Whenever we talk, you assure me you're happy and thrilled that things are running the way they should."

She'd said that because Kavita had always wanted the best for her as sisters do, and the last thing she wanted was to burden Kavita with the guilt of a supposedly privileged life she'd never have. "So why now after all these years?"

"I found it when cleaning out my desk and figured I owed you the truth."

Regret welled up her chest and she ached. Is this what real friends did? Stab you in the back when you trusted them most?

"What are you going to do with it?"

"It doesn't matter." Sheetal slid the zipper of the handbag. "Chapter closed."

SHEETAL RETURNED TO THE CHEMO ROOM AND HEADED TOWARD MAMA.

"Tell me, how is Rakeshji?" Mama really meant to ask how things were between her and Rakesh.

Sheetal fidgeted with the princess-cut diamond ring. During the last chemotherapy session Sheetal had confided how she felt like something between her and Rakesh wasn't quite right and a distance had crept between them. Mama had been quick to shoulder the blame and suggest Sheetal dedicate more time to her husband and family and let Anjali take over her treatment. However, Sheetal didn't trust anyone else with Mama's care, least of all Vikram and Anjali. There were times when Papa accompanied Mama for treatment, but Sheetal still made it a point to attend.

"Focus more on your family and husband. Take off some time together like a holiday away from all the pressures here and myself."

"You're not a pressure, Mama. Besides, I tried." Sheetal leaned against the chair's backrest. "I planned for us to spend a week in Mansali before we bring Yash home for Diwali break, but Rakesh has work."

"He's a hardworking man and he suffered a rough childhood. Losing his mother so young when he was only thirteen. And Meghaji was just a newborn then. Imagine how they would have grown up without a mother if it wasn't for Pushpaji?"

Sheetal raised her eyebrows. *They would have been better off, for sure!*

From what Rakesh had told her, Mummyji stormed into their home with three-year-old Naina shortly after Rashmi's death. Mummyji and Ashok had a quick wedding at a nearby temple with no more than a few witnesses, and Mummyji took over as mother to Megha and Rakesh.

"Growing up in boarding school," Mama continued, "is so difficult for a little boy." She stopped and pursed her lips as if she'd realized she'd said something she shouldn't have.

The Prasads had never agreed with Sheetal's decision to send Yash to boarding school, and they tried to rationalize that despite Mummyji's dictator-like temperament Mummyji would mellow with age and Naina would eventually get better one day. But after ten years with the Dhanrajs—Sheetal knew better.

"Financial pressures, problems at the office and at home can easily affect the relationship between a husband and wife."

Along with the debt. No point in sharing details because if Mama were to accidentally share the information with anyone, gossip would follow and mar the Dhanrajs' reputation. "You just get better, Mama. We'll fight this together." Some medical breakthrough would cure Mama for good and a clear course of treatment would follow.

"You're not listening, Sheetal. I have perhaps a few months left. But you have your whole life ahead and Yash's future."

With just a few patches of hair left on her head and merely an ounce of energy in her body, Mama still expressed concern for Sheetal's welfare and her future after she would be gone. Sheetal's concern, however, lay in Mama's happiness and the time she had left. The invisible and endless bond stretched well beyond the length of both women's sari pallus, tying daughter to mother and mothers to daughters.

"You don't feel respected by your family? Is that it?"

Over the years Sheetal had given Mama the impression she was running the Dhanraj household so Mama wouldn't think Sheetal was living under Mummyji's authority the way Mama had under Dadi's. "It's not that."

"Just having money means nothing without respect. Money is what everyone naturally yearns for. But true wealth comes from giving and sharing what you have. Let go of other people's negative traits and narrow-mindedness and move forward."

Sheetal ran the fingers of both hands through her hair and pressed the palms on her eyes. Her head pounded.

"Perhaps all this talk is too much for you to handle right now, but you will understand in your own time."

Her and Rakesh's bedroom alone equated to double the size of the dingy flat they had lived in *Nariyal Ka Rasta*, the poorer northern side of Raigun.

"With God's blessing, we have more now than ever before. And because we have more, we have more to lose. Always."

GARDEN LIGHTS FANNED LONG NETS OF YELLOW UP A STONE WALL THAT RAN the length of Rosewood Street and marked the boundary between Raigun city and the Prasad's home. The Prasad's blue *Maruti Zen* cut through the main gates and pulled into the quiet darkness of Prasad *Bhavan* under a thicket of night sky. The vehicle headed toward a double-story mansion and the calming fragrance of jasmine rushed in the open window. Two double-story, rectangular wings branched left and right off a central tower in a V that reached toward Rosewood Street like a pair of open arms. A light on the tower's ground floor directly below Sheetal's room, Papa's office, called her to safety like a lighthouse and she relaxed in the comfort of being at home.

A HALF-HOUR LATER, SHEETAL OPENED A GLASS BALCONY DOOR IN HER ROOM and stepped out. Garden lights glittered like jewels in the back lawns and the stone mosaic floor cooled her feet.

Arvind had climbed this balcony on the day of her wedding and begged her to elope. She wrapped her fingers around her right wrist exactly where he had tightened his grip and proposed to her on one knee. If Arvind had read the letter, he would have stayed in Raigun, not left abruptly and they could have married. She leaned against the wall for support and sighed. Then she would be fasting for Arvind tomorrow and praying to the moon for his long life and their happy marriage on Karva Chauth instead of Rakesh.

The fatigue of living with past regrets tightened a lump in her chest and she headed for her handbag lying on the queen-size comforter and removed Arvind's letter. She was about to rip the sheets to shreds but stopped. The letter was all she had left of him. Was it so wrong to keep one last memory?

Sheetal reached to the back of her cupboard drawer and tucked the envelope between her clothes. Then she turned the key in the lock and shut the cupboard.

That night after dinner, Papa entered the living room dressed in his pajamas. The vertical blue stripes firmed against the brown fabric as he took his place on a corner sofa seat and straightened his posture. He ran his fingers along the finely trimmed edge of his graying moustache, coughed gently, and aligned an arm along the armrest as the sound of children's laughter permeated the air.

Anjali's children were next door, and her heart ached with yearning. Oh, how she missed Yash. Two more weeks, she reminded herself.

Papa removed his glasses, left them on the right corner table—sunken behind the armrests of two sofas at right angles to one another—and drummed the fabric. "Just think, if Yash were here, you'd be with him right now."

At fifty-six, with numerous accomplishments and a successful business to his credit Papa's posture and harsh tone reflected an affirmation that he was always right about every decision, from having forced Sheetal to marry Rakesh, and inviting the Choudharys to live with them, to sharing confidential business matters with Vikram. Not only had Papa grown overbearing, highly opinionated and stubborn with age, but whenever Sheetal sat down to talk their discussions inevitably ended up in arguments.

No more disagreements. With two more months of chemo ahead for Mama, she would focus tonight's discussion on the doctor's recommendations for Mama's treatment.

"So how are you?" Papa asked.

"Fine." She leaned toward the coffee table, picked up the remote, and switched on the T.V. to fill bouts of anticipated silence in their conversation.

"Meghaji?"

"She's at the mansion and will be celebrating Karva Chauth with us tomorrow."

"Nainaji?"

Sheetal sighed at Papa's bullet-style questions and imagined him mentally ticking off a pre-meditated list with some invisible pen. "Naina's fine," she lied. *Thank God no one discussed Naina's health issues anymore!*

Naina's divorce had front-lined The Raigun Herald nine years ago, depicting the extent that a family lied to secure a girl's future. But Mama refused to discuss the topic because she didn't want to comment on other people's business.

"Rakeshji?"

Sheetal glanced at her watch. It was nine-thirty, and she should call Rakesh to check how his doctor's appointment went. "At work, as usual."

"Your work?" He referred to her paintings.

"I have a series of the Himalayan mountains and waterfalls due for—"

"And how much will they pay you this time?"

"Whatever they are worth." Best to leave the answer open-ended, avoid another comparison to the Dhanraj's net worth, and more on how instead of painting art to grace the wall of some club she should better utilize her time in raising Yash who was destined to earn millions in the future like Rakesh. Sheetal didn't blame Papa for his money-mindedness because he had worked very hard to break out of the lower-middle class. Perseverance and determination coupled with good luck and good business timing had freed him from the lower rank and elevated him to the elite class of society, but why did he always have to be so hard on her?

"Yash?"

"I'm picking him up next week from Mansali for the Diwali holidays."

"What is it with you younger women nowadays? Sending your children away and abandoning family for career? What will you do with a career when your son needs you more? Isn't working for the lower and middle class who can't make ends meet?"

Like Kavita and Gaurav who struggled and somehow managed to make ends meet, while Vikram and Anjali conveniently took shelter under Papa? Sheetal sank against the backrest. Papa was so glued to his conventional ideas of women and their place in society that any attempt to explain happiness couldn't be measured by currency or corporate success was useless.

"People who struggle..."

They were struggling.

"...work to put food on the table..."

Food perpetually graced the Marquette Dining table, but Rakesh was never around to eat anything.

"You have everything!" He threw his hands up in the air. "Why work when you have a comfortable, happy home?"

Comfortable? Happy? Home? Sheetal lowered her hand and let the remote rest on her lap. Would the 'off' button work on Papa and others who believed such nonsense?

"Why not keep Yash with you?"

"It's the trend with so many families, nowadays," Sheetal lied because the ways of the wealthy worked in favor with Mama and Papa. "Everyone wants the best for their children. Besides, Yash will have to take over the business someday and he should get the best education."

"Fine! Fine! Doesn't just mean you pack up and ship off your child like one of your paintings. New generation. New ideals. What economics is this, of running life in some new balance?" He crossed one leg over the other. "You will achieve nothing by keeping your child away from you except breaking up what you have."

Sheetal tightened. "I wanted to talk to you about Mama's treatment. There are two more months of chemo left and—"

Just then Vikram sauntered in with several sheets of paper. "Uncle— Oh." He looked at Sheetal. "I didn't know you were here. I presume you've come to spend the weekend with us?" He was confirming the duration of her stay.

"I leave tomorrow morning."

"Good that you're here." Vikram handed the papers to Papa, took an adjacent seat across Sheetal, and leaned forward. "Please sign these, Uncle."

Papa patted Vikram on the arm and held up the papers. "You work too hard. Now then, what do we have?"

"Papers from Brown and Polson."

"I...I thought I signed those yesterday. All of them. Didn't I? I'm sure—"

"No, Uncle. You didn't." Vikram laced his fingers together and rested both elbows on his knees.

"I remember you brought them over to my office yesterday afternoon," Papa said. "I know, I—"

"You're confusing this document with something else again." Vikram leaned back against the cushions. "You did see the doctor, didn't you?"

"But I remember—"

"Did you remember to take an appointment, Uncle? You promised me last week you would."

"Too busy. Too much work." Papa waved a hand in the air and placed the papers on the table.

Vikram pulled out a pen from the front pocket of his shirt and handed it to Papa. He leaned forward and waited. "Well, if you can't, then I'll have to take the appointment for you."

"What appointment?" Sheetal intervened. "What's wrong with Papa?"

"Nothing." Vikram's attention fixed on Papa's pen still poised in the air.

"He thinks I'm losing my mind," Papa said. "What if I forget a few things here and there? I'm not in my twenties or thirties anymore. Little slips are allowed with age."

Didn't Mama mention the same thing this afternoon?

"Not losing your mind, Uncle, it's your memory."

"Mind. Memory. All the same things." Papa waved a hand. "Finally, it's all in your head. Now," he turned to the left, then right. "My glasses. Where did I put them?"

"What glasses?" Vikram frowned.

Papa reached for the corner table and tapped the surface. "I put them here just now when I sat down to, to "

Vikram leaned toward the corner table. "There's nothing."

"I saw Papa put them there."

Vikram brushed a hand across the surface and turned to look at her. "Nothing here. See for yourself if you don't believe me."

Sheetal stood and tightened the fingers of her right hand into a fist. How dare Vikram speak to her in such a harsh tone. "I'm not saying I don't believe you. But I saw Papa put his glasses there."

"Never mind, Uncle. We'll do it next time." Vikram grabbed the documents, but Papa gestured for him to sit down.

"It's fine. Just tell me where to sign."

Vikram pointed to a line running beneath layers of fine print. "There."

Papa signed.

"And there"—Vikram pointed to another line—"and—"

"Shouldn't you read the document first?" Sheetal interrupted.

Vikram glared at her again.

"It doesn't matter," Papa said. "What's to doubt?"

All his life, Papa read and checked everything he signed, not once but twice. How could he have such blind trust in Vikram?

Sheetal lunged forward and was about to grab the sheets when Vikram snatched the lot from Papa.

"Sheetal!" Papa grabbed her by the wrist and forced her to sit down as Vikram headed for the door. "I don't know what you're all upset about. They're just a bunch of office papers that are not your business."

"Then why did he grab them so quickly? What is Vikram trying to hide?"

Papa turned from Sheetal to Vikram and back. "You didn't need to—"

"Checking, Papa." Sheetal raised her voice to make sure Vikram heard as he left. "Just checking,"

"Oh, come now. I can still..."

Sheetal turned and her heart skipped a beat. The glasses lay on the corner table, exactly where Papa had left them, but Papa didn't appear to notice a thing.

6

GOD AND DEBT

Rakesh swiveled in his chair on the forty-fifth floor of Dhanraj & Son Towers as cream-colored walls and a series of abstract geometric paintings careened in and out of view. He paused and reached for a rectangular envelope beside a glass of scotch and a half-full bottle of Blue Label on the teak table as sweat beaded down the side of his face.

After the bank had refused to lower its interest rate, Rakesh wined and dined seven CEOs in Raigun's finest restaurants, unfolded his request for an unsecured loan over dinner, and ensured the meals ended with dessert, sweet talk, and a promise to pay back the full amount after ten years. Back-ups were mandatory in case negotiations with the Japanese didn't go as planned.

He grabbed a letter opener from a pen stand, filled with four black and one silver cross pens, slit the envelope along the topmost edge, and pulled out the folded letter. What if this financial institution, his last hope, said no? His heart raced and he thumbed open the sheet.

He skimmed the customary salutation below the letterhead and narrowed his attention to the second paragraph.

"We regret to inform you that your request for a loan in the amount of three hundred and fifty million rupees has been declined."

Fuck! Rakesh took a swig of the scotch and gulped it neat. All Pushpa's fault. If Papa hadn't given in to Naina's whims and fancies and allowed Pushpa to spoil Naina, he wouldn't be in this mess. A mess because of a fucking wedding he had to throw Naina. If only Mumma hadn't died.

He remembered it like yesterday. He returned home after playing a game of cricket with friends and was heading up to his room when the doorbell rang. A servant opened the double doors, and the odor of rotting potatoes and raw onions flooded the large hall. A fat, dark-skinned woman with a pock-marked face barged in with a suitcase and a three-year-old girl clutching onto her sari pallu.

Must be the bai, Rakesh assumed she was the nanny Papa had hired after Mumma died last month to take care of his new baby sister, Megha.

"She's your new mother," Papa told him shortly after.

Rakesh's biological mother, Rashmi, a gorgeous woman with fine features and a silky fair complexion had given birth to Megha one month before. Rakesh remembered visiting Mumma at the hospital, hugging her tight, and Mumma wrapping him in her arms and raining his face with kisses. Then he never saw Mumma again.

She died from complications, problems the doctors couldn't fix, Papa explained, but Rakesh refused to believe Papa. So many of his friends had younger siblings, but their Mumma hadn't died. *Why me?* he asked the Hindu gods and goddesses decorated in all their finery in the temple at home, but they watched in silence. The funeral rites and prayers for Mumma went on for thirteen days, in accordance with Hindu customs. But Rakesh didn't pray. *You took Mumma away from me,* he accused the idols, his heart turning to stone. *Why pray for her journey to heaven when she should be here with Megha and me?*

Desperate to find a little of Mumma's love and caring qualities in Pushpa for Megha's benefit, Rakesh tried to please Pushpa, but quickly learned this buffalo of a woman could never be satisfied. Pushpa fussed over her biological daughter, Naina, and left Megha to the servants. If Rakesh jumped out of his seat on the dinner table to attend to Megha crying upstairs in the nursery, Pushpa would grab him by the arm and sit him down with a stern warning she'd have a bai attend to Megha later.

However, when Pushpa ordered the servants to remove every photo and trace of Mumma's existence, Rakesh's heart boiled with anger, and he couldn't bear Pushpa's presence in their home any longer. "I hate her," he told Papa two weeks later.

"You will love and respect your new mother," Papa commanded. "And Naina is now your sister. My blood," he added matter-of-factly. "So, learn to love her too and adjust."

Your blood? How? Rakesh wanted to ask but the discussion ended. Rakesh was labeled a rebel and whisked off to boarding school with a warning that he would learn the true value of family in its absence.

He ended up learning who he really was instead.

Rakesh picked up the glass, swirled the contents, and ice clinked against the glass side. He carried the drink to the floor-to-ceiling window overlooking the city of Raigun, broadened his shoulders, and flattened one palm against the sheet of glass. *Cold.* Just the way he liked it. He exhaled and his breath misted the city. He narrowed his attention on people crawling like ants between the looping traffic. So tiny. So helpless. Like he and Megha had been under Pushpa's authority. Rakesh leaned forward and touched his forehead to the glass. He pointed the toe of his leather shoe above their minute heads and pushed down hard as gray smoke puffed from factory chimneys in the distance. He breathed the same air, lived on the same land, but towered above them all like God. He curled the fingers of his free hand into a fist. *God!* He almost laughed out loud.

God dammit! Where were all the gods when Mumma was dying? When Pushpa stormed into their lives and wreaked havoc? Weren't the gods supposed to block obstacles in his and Megha's lives? Why did Papa make him "work his way up in the company" but give

Pushpa all the controls? He pressed a palm against his forehead and tried to suppress the throbbing pain. Would the injustice ever end?

Tomorrow thousands of married Hindu women worldwide would fast all day long to appease the gods, then wait for moonrise and drink seven sips of water from their husband's hands to break the fast. And Sheetal? She would dress up like a bride again, then fast all day and pray. *For what?* Bile burned his throat and he almost gagged. *Me! Even though this isn't the real me!*

A good Indian man was supposed to study hard, marry in accordance with the family's wishes, have children and provide for the family. Society condemned anyone who deviated from the norm. Trapped, Rakesh had married Sheetal and proved to investors, the board members and other CEOs that he could lead a normal-happy-married life. However, several months into the marriage, despite Sheetal's stunning looks and curvaceous figure, he felt no excitement when he touched her, no rush of adrenaline in their lovemaking, and no feeling of coming alive after they were spent. Some damages couldn't be repaired. But when Sheetal became pregnant, there was no turning back and he was stuck in the moving vehicle of a stagnant marriage. No one ever asked what he wanted; they all just took from him in the name of love.

Fuck love! He took a swig of the drink and the cool liquid glided down his throat. His muscles relaxed and he looked at the glass. Half-empty again. He had promised Sheetal to sober up and become a better father for Yash's sake, but nothing he did was good enough by her standards. She demanded he first find a permanent solution for Naina so that they could keep Yash at home. Rakesh tightened his grip on the glass. Boarding school! What kind of place was boarding school for a child and how much did Sheetal know about what really went on there? Saliva lodged in his throat, and he swallowed. He knew because he'd been cursed to grow up in one!

The fair complexion, fine features, paper-thin flaky skin, lanky frame, and hands that were naturally over-expressive when he had something to say worked against him. He hated everything about himself! At Harvard in the US, he blended with white foreigners, and no one cared. But in India, he was scrutinized, surveilled by the media, and picked on to no end. Pick. Pick. Pick! How could he forget the times at school when other boys picked on him for looking like a girl and he ended up a sexual target of bullies? Oh, the shame. The alienation. The loneliness.

The magnetic pull toward bigger boys with ripped muscles, towering frames, and tanned skin were clear signs that something was wrong. But it felt right. So right. And he had been living in silent shame since because if Papa ever found out, he would detest Rakesh even more, disown him, and cut him out of the inheritance.

Rakesh headed for the desk when footsteps in the corridor outside his door grew louder. He resumed his position in the chair, tucked the letter back in the envelope, took a deep breath and slowly exhaled. He had to do everything in his power to keep the Japanese happy and make sure they didn't back out.

He was trapped.

And there was no way out.

7
KARVA CHAUTH

Every year on Karva Chauth, Sheetal and thousands of married Hindu women across the world fasted all day and prayed to Goddess *Parvati* before sunset to seek her blessings for the longevity of their husbands' lives and their marriages. Sheetal didn't plan to just fast and pray. She was going to beg for a miracle cure.

Most Indian women assumed they would be happily married with children and a bustling household by the age of thirty. However, at thirty-one, divorced and alone, Naina didn't qualify to merit any position in society, so she spent Karva Chauth isolated in her room. Sheetal didn't need the shadow of a divorcee's marriage to fall on hers and she didn't wish Naina any ill, but logic ordained she take precaution. So, while heading upstairs to dress for the evening puja, she opened Naina's bedroom door a crack, saw her asleep on the bed and content, headed down the north wing toward her bedroom.

With Naina out the way she had to make sure Mummyji kept her distance from today's celebration because if the shadow of a widow

fell on any married woman during such an auspicious occasion, bad
luck would follow.

As the wealthiest among her group of friends, Mummyji maintained her dignity by hosting the members of the Royal Society
Ladies' Club and their daughters-in-law for the annual evening
prayers at the Dhanraj mansion. However, she maintained physical
distance from the religious celebrations during prayer time by
waiting behind the curtained sliding patio doors in the dining room.
Mummyji joined the group after the prayers ended to socialize and
bid the women goodbye before they returned home to their
husbands. Because Megha was going to celebrate this year's Karva
Chauth at the Dhanraj's, her husband, Raj, would be dropping in
later that evening to celebrate the festival with the family.

"Were you spying on me?" Naina called from behind.

Sheetal lengthened her stride, rushed to her bedroom and closed
the door. She pulled a heavy embroidered magenta and silver sari off
a hanger, an extravagant sari she'd asked Mama to have custom-
made for her in accordance with tradition where the woman's family
paid for the clothes and jewels she was to wear on Karva Chauth.
Though Sheetal monitored her personal expenses and the costs
Mama and Papa had incurred for her attire this year, she consoled
herself with the logic that tonight's puja would change her life for
the better.

Sheetal filled the crescent of her lips with magenta, applied glittery pink blush and slid rungs of matching pink and diamond
bangles along her wrists. She pressed a mango-shaped bindi, half
the size of her index nail, between her eyebrows and frowned at her
reflection in the mirror. *Too small.* She peeled off the glittery sticker
that represented a woman's married status and replaced it with
another, double the size, with elaborate diamond work skirting the
edge. *Better. And makeup?* She sighed at her complexion, applied
another coat of lipstick and darkened the blush to give the impression her marriage held strong. She sprayed the bun behind her head
and the bangs down her forehead when a knock came.

"Bhabhi?" Megha called.

"Yes?"

"I'm ready. Do you want to go down?"

Sheetal opened the door and took a step back. Megha looked stunning!

Megha had lightly dusted her whole-wheat complexion in a shade of natural taupe and applied a neutral eye shadow and dark red lipstick. Rubies, emeralds and diamonds glittered along the Jaipur Kundan necklace Sheetal had purchased from Hira Moti. Red and green pools of enamel embedded in the chunky, gold necklace swirled into one another as precious stones dotted their banks. Chandelier earrings dangled above the gold temple border that ran along the edge of Megha's sari.

Sheetal had tried to talk Megha out of fasting several times because of the pregnancy. However, Megha insisted that the ritual validated her happy marriage to Raj but made an exception this year by having a light lunch of fruits and milk.

Jealousy roiled Sheetal's heart. She had married a year and a half before Megha and owned one extra Karva Chauth to her credit. How could Megha be happier? Maybe she could share or rub off some of Megha's marital bliss for herself? "I need some more time. Why don't you come in?" She swung the door wide open with the hope Megha would enter and erase the sterility of her bedroom.

"Thanks." Megha raised her eyebrows. "But I'll wait outside."

Fifteen minutes later, the two women made their way down to the Japanese garden, and Sheetal couldn't believe the cobweb of miniature lights crowding the trees. In her apparent quest to outdo last year's décor, Mummyji had imported fluorescent, waterproof lights from Japan and ordered they be placed along the bottom of the Koi Pond. However, when Mali Kaka, the gardener, heard of the news he retaliated and declared the fish would boil before moonrise. Last year five servants had decorated the garden. How many servants were involved this year considering Mummyji had outnumbered the leaves with light bulbs? Eight? Ten? Would Mummyji ever give up all these show-and-tell expenses which only reversed Sheetal's attempts to save money?

The ground lay covered in a mosaic of multi-colored *dhurries* with an open square in the center for Goddess Parvati to be seated on a decorated *chowki*, footstool. Colorful *rangoli* powders sprinkled in intricate henna-like designs covered the open area.

Mummyji rushed out of the dining room and hurried toward them. "Hai Ishwar!" Her white sari billowed and the pleats near her toes swished. "So much time you take, I tell you. How will I get any work done at this rate? No value for—"

"No one's even here yet," Megha cut in.

"Well obviously not." Mummyji frowned and the brown freckles on her cheeks darkened. "I just wanted all of us ready ahead of time since we're hosting the event. Now stay here, I tell you." She nodded and marched off.

"We always host the event." Sheetal leaned against a tree for support.

"Nothing's changed, huh?" Megha muttered under her breath. "She just gets worse every year."

Speaking ill of any family member, especially the in-laws, could turn against her so Sheetal kept quiet.

"You've changed, Bhabhi."

So much about Megha had changed, too.

Megha tapped her shoulder. "Are you ignoring me?"

Sheetal diverted Megha's attention to two plates adorned with pools of rice, grains and colorful powders on a table. "Our *puja* thalis are ready." An earthenware crucible, *diya*, filled with oil and a cotton wick graced each thali. A small metal *karva*, an urn of water, with a fresh flower, one coin, one cardamom pod, one clove and one string bean had been sealed at the mouth with a red cloth tied at the neck by a *moli*, religious yellow-and-red thread. Each thali also held a *baya*, the sari each married woman would offer her mother-in-law after the prayers concluded. Tiny gold *ghunghroos*, bells, dangled from the edge of Sheetal's thali in five-millimeter intervals whereas Megha's thali bore silver ones.

Fifteen minutes later twenty-two women in glamorous pink, orange and maroon saris entered the garden with their thalis. Their pallus sashayed to their swinging gait and red *sindoor* powder marked the *maang* running down each woman's middle parting to symbolize their married status. The women laid their thalis to rest beside Megha's and Sheetal's and rungs of colorful bangles tinkled up and down their wrists. Intricate mehndi designs exploded in a firework of leaves, tendrils and petals, and Sheetal sighed. She'd forgotten to call the henna girl this year to decorate her and Megha's hands. With Mama's chemo, her commissioned paintings and planning for Megha's baby she'd been absorbed with so much else. Well, she'd have to do a better job next year and remember ahead of time.

Some of the married women her age, plump and out of shape, tried to hide the width of their bodies with sari pleats fanned across their chests. Because Sheetal had maintained her physique by following a strict regime of cardio-fitness, Pilates and a healthy diet, she didn't have to worry about those issues. However, even though she was blessed with curves in the right places, she no longer had the model figure from her twenties and tucked dollops of post-pregnancy flab and stretch marks behind her petticoat.

"You know, little Sasha took her first step yesterday." A high-pitched voice broke from the midst of surrounding chatter.

"Why, how lovely!" Prerna squealed. "You guys should come over for dinner sometime so we can meet up."

"Oh, and you won't believe this," someone said. "But ever since that awful stock market crash, Dinesh refuses to go anywhere. He just comes home from work, eats, sleeps and acts as if sticking to a routine will reclaim the loss. You think that'll really do the trick, Sheetal?"

Rakesh had been living in debt for eight years but appeared to show no desire to mend his habits. Sheetal smiled. She didn't dare complain out loud because any sign of trouble with the in-laws or problems in her marriage provided fuel for gossip and held the potential to make tomorrow's headlines. Sheetal wove between groups scattered around the garden, her heart heavy with regret. Maybe she should have invited Kavita. At least she would have had a friend—a friend who had betrayed her too. A hand rest on her shoulder and dragged her aside.

"Surely, you'll understand my dilemma," Vinita pouted. "I just don't know how to keep Ronit away from video games; he's going to fall behind in class. You have an eight-year-old too. How do you handle the technology craze?"

A knot fisted her heart. "Yash is usually on holidays when he's here and St. Paul's has strict rules against video games."

"Oh yes, I forgot." Vinita slapped her thigh. "Yash is at boarding school! Must be so lonely without him, no?"

Sheetal swallowed.

"Will you see him soon?"

"I'm going to Mansali next week to bring him home for Diwali."

"Alone?" Vinita raised her eyebrows and four other women ahead turned to look.

"Rakesh doesn't have time."

"Well, make time." Another woman joined in. "You certainly can't travel alone."

"One of the servants will accompany me."

"Tch, tch, tch." Vinita shook her head. "You're asking for trouble traveling to Mansali without a man. The number of thefts, I hear. And so much instability in Dholakpur. Anything can happen." She leaned in close and whispered, "So much violence. So many cases of rape."

Sheetal turned away and her attention drifted to the clearing at the far back where she'd almost burned alive when her sari caught fire.

"Now then, I tell you." Mummyji pulled Sheetal away from the group and turned to Prerna. "Your mother-in-law's not here?"

"She's at home sick with a cold," Prerna said.

"Why, that's terrible, I tell you," Mummyji frowned. "She's the only other person who knows the prayer by heart. How on earth are you all going to do the puja now?"

"Who else knows the prayer and stories?" Vinita asked.

"Why, me, of course." Mummyji smiled.

A debate ensued and the women agreed that Mummyji should recite the prayers as long as she stood well out of sight behind the curtained patio door. Mummyji agreed and headed over to the dining room as Janvi brought out an idol of Goddess Parvati seated on a gold, red and green chowki.

The women sat in a lotus-position in a circle around the goddess with their puja thalis and Mummyji narrated the centuries-old tale of Karva Chauth. The women passed their thalis sparkling with lit diyas to the right in a clockwise motion like a game of pass-the-parcel. The story told how seven brothers created an illusionary moon on Karva Chauth to trick their queen-sister, Veeravati, into praying and breaking her fast. As a result, Veeravati's husband, the king, died. To win back her husband, a devastated Veeravati had to appease the goddess. So, the young widow fasted and prayed to the moon every month on *Chauth*, the fourth day after the full moon. Pleased with the queen's devotion, Goddess Parvati restored the dead king to life.

Story after story unfolded over the next forty-five minutes, highlighting the significance of Karva Chauth and Lord Ganesh, the remover of obstacles. Hope and warmth flickered with the swaying motions of the thalis perambulating from one woman to another. Sheetal took care to face the burning diyas away lest the flames come too close. She held a breath, closed her eyes and prayed for the success and blessings of the thali in her hands. Then she passed it right. She held up the queue of perambulating thalis, but desperation clawed her heart for a little honesty from one and acceptance from another. After a whole day of swallowing saliva to keep her throat moist, she yearned for water. *A promise of my husband's food and protection.* She passed a thali right. *A promise my husband will be faithful.* She shuddered, took another breath and the stagnant lake of her marriage throttled her. *Let the light of this person's happiness shine into my life.* She gulped and passed a thali right.

One wish. Surely, she was allowed one last desperate wish. On the seventh perambulation, she closed her eyes and tightened her grip on the thali in her hands. *Let all the love from this woman's marriage pour into my life. Give me her happiness. I want her marital bliss. Once. Just once. I want it all.* A chilly breeze brushed the hairs on her arms. She raised the thali to her forehead as a sign of respect, lowered it and opened her eyes. Silver ghunghroos skirted the perimeter. Megha's thali! Dread filled her heart. No. This was wrong. All wrong! She quickly passed the thali and took her own to the left as the sun set behind the trees and raked in the last of the day's light. She had to take back the wish before the sun disappeared. The sky turned a shade of gray. The sun dipped behind a tree and disappeared. It was too late.

"Let the offerings of this Karva bring long life to my husband." Mummyji's voice wafted with the cold breeze. "And may my *bhagya,* my joyful state of married bliss, be everlasting."

Sheetal raised her gold thali to her forehead like the others. The plate's edge touched the sindoor in her maang and she gulped.

"May my death precede that of my husband," Mummyji continued, "so that I can enter the *chitta,* the funeral pyre, as a bride."

She was dressed in bridal attire in the nightmare before her wedding, perambulated the sacred fire behind her husband, and just before completing the seventh *phera,* jumped in the fire and burned alive.

A hot wetness rolled down her cheek. The thali tilted to the left. The contents slid. Her back grew hot. Very hot. Where was the heat coming from? Sheetal turned. The baya, karva and thali hit the ground.

"Arrey *dekho!*" one of the women screamed.

Sheetal jumped to her feet.

The women called for water and help.

"Arrey, *bachao!*"

"Her pallu. Hai Ishwar!" Mummyji screamed. "Her sari pallu is on fire!"

A storm of dhurries beat down on her. Her lungs clouded with dust, and she fell to the ground. Everything in sight spun from gray skies to sparkling lights to a tessellation of dhurries and the hoops of sari hems.

"She's in shock," someone declared. "The diya fell on her sari pallu."

"Oh! What bad luck!" Mummyji exclaimed.

The odor of burned fabric roasted the air.

"No damage to her, thank God." A deep female voice rose in sympathy. "But how unfortunate something like this should happen on such an auspicious day."

"Oh my!" Vinita gasped. "Bad luck. Truly bad luck."

Sheetal's head spun. The pallus of the women's saris filled her horizon. *All Mummyji's fault for conducting the prayers and casting her widow's shadow.* Mummyji's bad luck.

"*Choti Memsahib.*" Janvi unraveled her from the dhurry's cocoon and pat her mid-riff with cold, wet towels. "You're so lucky to be alive."

Sheetal coughed. Not luck. An omen from the gods. Bad luck.

THAT NIGHT AT TEN-THIRTY, SHEETAL LOOKED OUT FROM BEHIND A STAINED window in the dining room as a gibbous moon peeked from behind thick gray clouds. She had called Rakesh several times all afternoon, but he didn't pick up the phone. He should be home anytime now, she reasoned making her way to the Marquette Dining Room.

Raj and Megha stood in a halo of the moon's light in the garden, and Sheetal watched from behind the folds of curtain panels.

Dressed in a sparkling cream and burgundy *kurta* pajama, Raj watched Megha perform the final puja to mark the end of Karva Chauth.

Holding the puja thali in her left hand and a steel sieve in the right, Megha raised the sieve and looked at the moon through the silver mesh. Then she laid the sieve on a nearby bench, dipped the third finger of her right hand in some red *kum kum* powder, dry grains of dry rice and flicked them gently toward the moon. She offered the moon a libation of the karva water, picked the sieve and looked at Raj through the silver net.

Sheetal's chest thickened with the abyss of Rakesh's absence. He must be on his way home. Perhaps stuck in traffic, she reasoned, because most husbands returned home on time to celebrate Karva Chauth with their wives.

Then Raj held the karva, and Megha cupped her lower lips with her right palm. He tipped the karva toward her open palm, and water flowed into the hand trough and trickled down Megha's chin. She drank seven sips. Then Raj slipped a piece of sweet meat between Megha's lips.

Sheetal's stomach growled as a hot wetness rolled down her cheek.

Then Raj encircled Megha and they locked in an embrace.

Sheetal clenched her sides tight at the salt of her own tears.

8

LIVING CANVAS

The train pulled out Raigun Station as Sheetal rested her left elbow on the train's narrow windowsill and cupped her chin in her palm. The concrete remnants of the city were left swirling in the afternoon dust and a ribbon of platform flaked off with the day's heat. Metal awnings, roofs of shanty huts, and makeshift homes supported on bamboo poles in the distance surrendered to a mosaic of lush green fields and blue sky peppered with fluffy white clouds.

Sheetal pressed herself to the wall and tucked her feet under her hips on the berth, despite ample space in the luxury coupe. The train's rickety motion swayed her from side to side in rhythm to the *thaka-thaka-thunk* grate of metal against track. Janvi had fallen ill that morning, so Sheetal was on her own. She hoped for no delays on this journey because she couldn't wait to hug Yash, smother his cheeks with kisses and run her palm down the sides of his face.

An overhead light bulb flickered, and the force of the air conditioner's breeze and a mini whirring fan on the ceiling puckered goosebumps along her arms, so she pulled the pashmina shawl over her shoulders.

The train rolled west, and bushes and wild grass swayed in the train's direction. Huts with thatched roofs, acres of farmland, ponds and mudholes brimming with silt-brown water careened into view. Lush green mountains, padded with a thicket of clouds, and trees and sliced in thirds and quarters by waterfalls, dominated the horizon. A group of ragged shepherd boys on a pond's edge swung wooden sticks and yelled at a herd of black buffalo that were submerged in dirty gray waters. The beasts rose on all fours, dragged themselves out onto fields of yellow grass and the disturbed waters lapped the banks. An uneven tessellation of rice paddies now matted the rustic landscape, and Sheetal placed a palm against the glass for some warmth from the world outside. However, the cold made her tuck her hand back in her shawl and tighten the soft fabric around her chest. What if the train got delayed and the taxi *wallah* hired to drive her to Upper Mansali abandoned her? What if she got caught midst a robbery or riots or the train derailed? Who would she turn to for help? The train chugged on with a never-ending cascade of calamities whirring in her mind.

Someone knocked on the coupe door. Startled, Sheetal looked up at the orange and pink sky seizing the last of the day's light as the sun dipped behind a horizon of mountains. When did she doze off?

"Kholiye." The knocking resumed louder, and a deep male voice demanded she open the door that was rattling with the train's motion. "Ticket checking. Conductor," he said in broken English.

Sheetal pulled a sheet of paper the size of her palm out of her handbag, rose to her feet and headed for the door. She snapped open the door's lock and slid the gate several inches to the right, wide enough to slip the ticket across. The conductor plugged the front curve of his shoe between the doorway and wall and yanked the ticket out of Sheetal's grip.

Her gaze was travelling up his beige trousers that filled the narrow opening to watch for any sign of a forced entry when the train curved around a bend and screeched, throwing Sheetal against the door. Sheetal grabbed the handle in time and prevented the door from sliding open any further.

The conductor wrapped his fingers around the door's edge and his knuckles turned a lighter shade of brown. *"Aap akele?"* He asked if she was alone in Hindi. "Such a long journey, thirteen hours, for a woman to be alone."

"There are two of us." She handed him Janvi's ticket and the confirmation slip with both their names. He tried to peek in, but she barricaded the narrow gap with her body and slanted her foot against the door in case the conductor tried to take advantage. If he so much as made an attempt, she would kick his foot out the way, slide the door back against the wall and lock it shut. Never mind if his finger got in the way!

"Next stop, Dholakpur. Must keeping door locked, Madame. Don't open even anyone begging. You understanding, Madame? Problem area. Hooligans. Always catching free rides and looting passengers. All this religion and politics doing no one good."

The residents of Dholakpur, totaling about twenty thousand, were destined to a lifetime of farming and other menial jobs. The impoverished town had been suffering religious unrest over several months and the curfew lifted last week.

"We are locking doors from inside of all carriages. Still, I am warning you and other passengers not coming out. Not open doors if anyone knocking. About fifteen minutes train stopping. Stay inside for some more time even after train moving." The conductor handed the tickets back, then placed a blue cap on his head and left.

Sheetal locked the door and returned to her berth as the train slowly screeched to a halt. A network of low voltage bulbs, suspended from thick black cables running below a station's roof, highlighted Dholakpur in the curled Hindi alphabet where characters huddled under one horizontal line. Hawker-boys, about Yash's age, wheeled food carts under the luminous glare of flickering fluorescent tube lights that now lit the platform. Woks of hot oil and sizzling griddles serviced by portable gas cylinders steamed above the fiery jets as cries of *"khana garam"*, *"pakoras"*, *"garam nescoffee"* and *"garam chai"* muffled through the thick glass.

Sheetal sniffed to inhale the aroma of hot dinners, vegetable fritters, steaming coffee and hot tea but ended up breathing more rusted metal odor and recycled air. Her dinner, perfectly packed in aluminum foil and portable mini hot cases from the Dhanraj kitchen by Laal Bahadur's skilled hands, lay tucked in a black carry-on below her seat. Cramped from being rocked side to side over the last six hours, Sheetal stretched her muscles and pressed her left cheek to the sheet of glass craving a hot drink.

A hawker boy busy serving passengers cups of chai and packets of food bundled in paper through the open windows of second-class compartments grabbed several rupee notes handed to him, dug in his pocket and returned the passengers' change. With no calculator or cash register to aid monetary transactions, dressed in ragged clothes and barefoot he clearly possessed the gift of a strong mind, a will to endure and could survive any obstacles life threw in his path. Sheetal knocked on the glass. However, he didn't pay her any attention. Is this what it meant to be invisible or perhaps a still-life on canvas? She felt around the window's edge for an opening. However, the glass was sealed to the wall, and she remembered the conductor's warning to stay put.

Wasn't Dholakpur a fifteen-minute stop? She glanced at her watch. *The train should be moving anytime soon.* A thump from the other side of the coupe door rattled the metal hook in the notch and the hairs on her neck stood on end. *Hooligans. Bandits?* Sheetal lowered the shutters on the window and squeezed back in her corner. The train jerked, whistled, inched forward and the thumps stopped. Another knock. Another thump. Sheetal waited as the train pulled out of Dholakpur, expecting the door to forcedly slide open. She struggled to focus on the lock as she rocked gently from side to side. Then a blackness took over.

"Arrey, *jaldi karo, Bhaiya! Saman ootaro!*" Someone called on the other side of the door for help to unload their luggage as footsteps thundered back and forth, and doors slid open and shut in frenzy to the tune of people's hollers in Hindi.

Sheetal jumped to her feet, rolled up the window shutter and harsh daylight flooded the coupe. She'd slept a long while. Passengers had already spilled out of the coach with their luggage and clumped in groups as a train on the opposite side of the platform prepared for departure. Coolies, porters, dressed in red shirts with bronze tags bracing one arm, unloaded beddings, suitcases, and metal trunks on the concrete platform.

"Kholo bhai kholo." Thump-thump-thump. A male voice commanded she open the door as an open-air kiosk outside with 'Mansali Chai Walla' in Hindi caught her attention.

Confusion whirled with the crowd spilling on the platform. The train jerked, whistled and Sheetal stumbled. She grabbed the upper berth for support, lunged toward the door, slid it open and peered to the left and right. The carriage was empty. *"Arrey koi hai? Sunno."* She called for assistance begging to be heard.

From an adjacent cabin, an elderly coolie in a red shirt and tattered white pajamas with an orange towel on his shoulder popped his head out

"Mera saman!" She pointed to her suitcase and hand-carry tucked below the berth. The train jerked, and she grabbed her handbag and hitched it to her shoulder.

The coolie darted in, looped the orange cloth into a knot, and dragged out the suitcase as the train eased out of the station. He positioned the cloth on his head for a makeshift turban, swung the suitcase on top and hurried Sheetal down the corridor toward an open door on the left.

Sheetal grabbed hold of the vertical metal bars on both sides of the door, angled herself right so her feet aligned parallel to three steps and dangled a foot over the steps' edge. The platform trailed like a thick gray sliding ribbon as hordes of passengers made their way up a staircase to a footbridge. The train rolled forward at a lazy momentum, and Sheetal rocked to a steadying rhythm as wind rushed past.

"Jump, *Behnji*." The coolie referred to her as Sister out of respect.

She looked over her shoulder as the coolie balanced her luggage on the coiled turban. "How can I when the train's moving?"

"If train catching more speed, then you really can't jump," he continued in Hindi.

Sheetal let go of the right handlebar as the gray platform thinned, abruptly cut off and a tessellation of rice paddies filled the horizon.

"*Arrey, Behnji, jaldi karo.*" The coolie urged she hurry against the gentle *thaka-thaka-thunk* of train against track. "Just step down and jump."

The wind pricked Sheetal's eyes, rushed in her ears and pressed the blue salwar suit to her chest. She tightened her grip on the pole, inched her left foot over the edge and rammed her elbow against her chest trapping the handbag in place. She glanced left as several carriages ahead curved around a bend. She lowered herself. *One... two...* She let go, jumped and slammed against the earth as the train whizzed past. Her head spun, and she struggled to sit up, her body burning on impact.

"*Theek ho, Behnji?*" the coolie asked if she was all right from behind.

She had grazed her palms and elbows and reached for her handbag. "I think so. And you?"

"I do all the time. My everyday job." He dusted himself, got on his feet, recoiled the loose turban and adjusted it back on his head. Then he hoisted the luggage on the turban, walked over and held out a hand plastered with lines and cracks. The thick sweet-sour stench of cheap cigarettes caused her to hold a breath, and Sheetal declined the offer, dusted the grit off her hands and rose to her feet. The coolie shrugged, marched past, headed for the ramp, and Sheetal followed.

"So many tourists coming to Mansali, Behnji. But government not allowing trains to stop more than five minutes. Everyone always rushing in, out, in, out, train. One day someone will fall and die on tracks." He paused and turned round to look at her. "Hurry up, Behnji!"

Sheetal struggled against a tide of incoming human traffic, but the red of his shirt blurred with other coolies' uniforms. *Where'd he go?*

"But it will be too late by then." The coolie turned and waved climbing up the steps. "No compensation for small people like us. If someone big"—meaning wealthy— "dies, that is cutting the government's nose and forcing them to do something."

Sheetal quickened her gait to keep up.

"Last year, Madame, one coolie, a union member, losing leg when unloading luggage. Foot get stuck between steps of the train. Can't pull out. Train start. No time to pull chain and stop train. He is dragged for so long with a dangling foot."

Sheetal shuddered. Had she invited trouble by dangling her foot and jumping off the train?

"And what is Railway Minister doing? Sending letter of regret with barely enough to cover his medical expenses. Finished." He took a left on the footbridge and charged past the crowd.

The stench of onion-and-garlic sweat forced Sheetal to cover her nose as she struggled past the thronging crowd. She tightened her shoulders petrified of being touched by several leering men who 'accidentally' brushed past and groped her breasts.

"Now Behnji, he is selling tea on same platform with one leg and making living somehow. God only knowing how. Half of what he is making before, which not enough to feed his wife and seven children..."

"Can you slow down, please?" Sheetal yelled above the din. The coolie stopped, and Sheetal caught up.

"If I getting hurt today—nothing. No difference to anyone. But a big person like you?" He surveyed her from head to toe, and Sheetal instinctively crossed her arms. "Uproar. Headlines in tomorrow's paper. Government is coming down to railway track, making fuss, and cutting Railway Minister's nose." He pivoted and marched ahead. "Our lives, Sister, having no value because we are poor."

Free, Sheetal wanted to correct him.

"You having someone? A taxi? Waiting?"

She nodded and followed him across the bridge above rows of trains as one took leave. Thick, gray sheets of smog puffed from below and drifted across several platforms to vehicles parked outside the station.

Cycle rickshaws and autorickshaws *tr-r-r-inged* and buzzed outside the station's entrance zigzagging through a claustrophobic maze of traffic queued up. *Tanga* drivers held up placards with the awaiting passengers' names in Hindi as their horses clip-clopped and swung their tails at swarms of flies. The odor of diesel, urine, fodder, and manure billowed as she followed the coolie down the stairs and to the left where sturdy beetle-shaped Ambassadors and Fiat cars littered the station's parking lot.

A dark, short, stout man in a green turban ran up to her bearing a placard with 'Dhanraj'. He slid a pair of thick, black glasses up the bridge of his nose. "You are Madame, Dhanraj?"

"Yes."

"Namaste." He pressed his palms together and nodded. "I am coming from Holiday Inn. Upper Mansali." He referred to another part of Mansali up in the mountains that constituted half of Mansali's geography and population. "Car is there, Madame. Fourth from left side." He led her toward a queue of Ambassadors, signaled for the coolie to follow and helped unload the luggage into the trunk.

"How much?" Sheetal turned to the coolie.

"My apologies, Behnji, for speaking more than I should." The coolie smiled, revealing several missing teeth she hadn't noticed till now. "We small people sometimes getting carried away with our stories. You give a poor, old man whatever you feel."

"Here." Sheetal fished in her purse and pulled out a five hundred-rupee note. He could use the extra money. *"Paanch-so."*

"No, Sister." The coolie shook his head. "Too much. Two hundred is good."

"Go on, take it. The extra will help you." She raised her voice above the din.

"Five hundred for one suitcase?" The taxi driver turned to look from the coolie to Sheetal and back. "So, now your coolie union is starting some money-ripping scheme? Two hundred rupees, Brother. All you deserve." Then he turned to Sheetal. "Two hundred is what you should pay him, Madame."

Sheetal firmed her jaw in irritation. What right did this cab driver have to dictate what she should do? She turned to the coolie. "Take the five hundred, please. If it weren't for you, I would have missed my stop."

The coolie grinned. "Three hundred is enough, Behnji."

"The money will help your family. You were so courageous to jump off that train with such a heavy suitcase."

"Only doing my duty, Behnji."

What duty called someone to put their life at risk for another?

Then the coolie pointed to a shabbily dressed boy, about ten years old, who led a blind woman in a tattered sari away from the sweltering crowd toward a broken strip of pavement on an empty corner. Flies swarmed around their heads and arms as the boy helped the woman sit down. The old woman scoured the fume-filled air with her hands, as if in search of something, and then lowered them to her lap.

How did people survive on chips of broken pavement? Sheetal turned to the coolie. "Do you know them?"

"That one-leg coolie I am telling you? She is the wife. And that boy, one of his children. This mother and son beg here every day like some miracle will change their fortune. That, Behnji, is courage. Hope."

"Look," she deepened her tone, "don't argue. Just take the five hundred, please."

The coolie took the note, folded his hands together in namaste and headed toward a ticket counter. He handed over the crisp five-hundred-rupee bill to a cashier, took several notes in exchange, separated a few from the bunch and tucked them in his front shirt pocket. He pressed the remaining notes into the beggar boy's hands before disappearing into the crowd.

The boy opened the crinkled note, whispered something in his mother's ear, and the old woman hugged him tight.

ONE OF INDIA'S FAVORITE HOLIDAY SPOTS, THE TOWN OF MANSALI, THREE thousand feet above sea level peaked with tourists during the summer months from April to June. So, Sheetal figured the uphill mountain ride would be free of traffic.

An hour later the blue Ambassador droned up the steep incline, its wheels crunching stones and boulder droppings littering the mountain road. Broken white lines separated the two-lane road with oncoming traffic passing on the right. Sometimes cars whizzed a fraction too close around sharp bends, but the driver maneuvered crisp turns with skill and control as the Ambassador held ground.

Rakesh's Lamborghini, a high-tech piece of stunning Italian machinery needed minimum wind resistance and perfect road conditions to function best. Unlike the Ambassador, an ancient model that was rough-and-tough and solid-to-the-core like the sturdy locals, the vehicle needed no frills to survive the mammoth mountains carved by Indian gods.

An oncoming lorry headed right for them as it careened around a bend. The lorry driver blared his horn, and Sheetal stiffened. They were going to crash. The lorry swerved back on its side of the road, spluttering black clouds from its tailpipe as it whizzed past.

"You coming before, Madame?" The driver looked up in the rear-view mirror.

"Yes, my son studies here." Sheetal sank into the seat and closed her eyes to recover from the near-death impact just now. The ripped faux leather nipped her finger, and she pulled her hand away.

"Ah, *acchha!*" He nodded, and threads from his frayed turban jiggled. "He is at boarding school?"

"At St. Paul's."

"Very good school." He rolled and crisped the 'r'. "Very good boys from very good families studying there. Now Diwali holidays is coming." He persisted in broken English, probably so she wouldn't think he was illiterate.

"*Hanh.*" Sheetal switched to Hindi for his benefit. "I'm here to take my son back home." She looked at the time on her watch. Three more hours until she would see Yash.

"Very good. If you are needing taxi, go down again tomorrow—"

"I'm here for a few days."

"I am good tour guide. I take you see *Shivaji, Parvatiji's* famous temple, Echo Point, Hot Spring Point where hot water coming naturally from ground and..."

"I really don't need a tour, but thank you." Sheetal cut short the string of promotional offers taxi drivers frequently advertised to secure their next pay. She preferred to spend time up in the mountains and go sightseeing on her own free will. Dealing with Mummyji and Naina's incessant complaints presented more than enough challenge and she didn't need to deal with a chatterbox on holiday. A wall of lush greenery surrendered to a majestic view of valleys sweeping up toward snow-capped mountains, and Sheetal realized she'd never noticed the shifting landscape on previous rides because Rakesh's presence perpetually distracted her from the beauty of the mountains.

Rakesh always spent the duration of the journey on his laptop tracking the stock market, calling his broker to do this and that. When he lost internet connection, he switched over to proposals that needed attention or documents that needed approval. Now, if he had worked in a calm and patient manner that would have been fine. Just fine. However, Rakesh's idea of a good conversation centered around Sheetal's paintings, her income from some recent sale, or family matters. If Sheetal didn't say what he wanted to hear, he lost his temper, and she spent the duration of the ride defending what she'd said.

Rakesh would complain incessantly about mountain weather like it was too hot, too cold, or too windy. He advised the taxi wallah to slow down and complained he drove too fast, too carelessly, or with too much caution. The end result—they never reached Upper Mansali on time because the driver's nerves were on edge. And when Rakesh couldn't take the boredom of the ride anymore, he'd scream at the driver to go back to driving school. By the journey's end, Sheetal would be on edge and the driver a nervous wreck.

For the first time, Sheetal's lungs didn't constrict. She could breathe. A cascade of trees gave way to clear terrain, and she hooked her fingers along the edge of the half-open window. The rustling breeze caressed her skin. She was alive.

"All reservations confirmed, Madame?"

"Thanks for reminding me." Sheetal grabbed the phone from her handbag and called the hotel.

"Thank you for calling the Holiday Inn, Mansali," a male voice greeted her. "How can I help you?"

"I'm calling to confirm my reservation."

"Please hold while I transfer you to reservations." A click filled the receiver and instrumental music played.

"Hello." Static interrupted the call. "Thank you for calling the Holiday Inn, Mansali. This is reservations—"

"I want to confirm my booking. Sheetal Dhanraj." Sheetal cut short his greeting convinced a row of trees ahead would interrupt the connection.

"Please hold while I check." Silence followed with instrumental music. "I'm sorry, Madame. Can you repeat the name, please?"

"Sheetal Dhanraj. D-h-a-n-r-a-j."

"Dhanraj..." He paused. "I'm sorry, Madame. But I don't see any reservation in this name."

"That's impossible. My husband made it over a month ago and—"

"Madame," the taxi driver interrupted. "I am having guest house. Jatinder Singh my good name. I am taking you there?"

"Please." She covered the mouthpiece with her free hand and glared at the driver in the rear-view mirror. "I'm on the phone." She removed her hand again and trees curtained a view of the valley on the left. "Can you please check the reservations and call for the manager? It's for a suite. Booked in—" The line went dead.

"Very good one, Madame. My guest house. Spiceality. Offering all kind spicy vegetarian, non-vegetarian food, with single-double rooms. Also..."

She didn't need a double room at a guest house. She needed him to park at a location with fewer trees, get some clear cell reception and confirm the booking. She looked out of the open window for a possible parking space ahead and her heart skipped a beat at the hundred-foot drop skirting the road's edge. No fence. No railing. Nothing to divide them from certain death in the abyss except the driver's control of the steering coupled with good timing and good luck. Better to stay quiet she decided as Jatinder Singh prattled on. His jovial chatter wafted with the rush of cool mountain air as the trees gave way to shrubs and flora. "How much longer?" She glanced at her watch.

He accelerated, and the car groaned. Then he jerked his wrist as if to glance at his watch but much to Sheetal's relief he didn't take his hands off the steering. "Two hours more, Madame. Now we are two thousand feet above sea level."

"How do you know these mountains so well?"

"My home. I am growing up here and know every turn, every inch of this place. I am going up and down all my life. I am even driving with my eyes closed. Like this, Madame."

"No. Just keep your eyes on the road." Sheetal grabbed the backrest as branches of deodar cedars lining the cliff drummed the car's chassis, threatening to send them crashing down. "Please, hands on the steering wheel. I hope your car is sturdy?"

"*Hindustani* car, Madame," he pressed on in English. "Long lasting. My Chamkeeli is strong."

"Chamkeeli?"

"Name of car, Madame. She is shining, always, like a star. *Dal and roti* for my family." He referred to the vehicle as his bread and soup and sturdy source of income.

The ascent grew steeper, and Sheetal's nerves tightened, but she calmed herself with the rationale she couldn't have been in better hands considering this was a first solo travel. She'd made it so far on her own and in a short while she'd have Yash all to herself.

9
DOUBLE SHOT

hit! Four-fifteen already. Rakesh threw aside the quilt, bolted upright in bed, and looked over his shoulder at the rumpled sheets and Kartik's sleeping frame. He should have been in the office over an hour ago. Not only had he missed the three o'clock teleconference, he was late for the four o'clock board meeting. He sifted through the pile of mixed clothing and dressed quickly, tightening the tie around his neck. How much longer could he sustain this double life and living in two places at once?

Rakesh slipped on a gray blazer and straightened the collar. If he hurried, he could make it to the office in fifteen minutes and say a stubborn client held him up after the extra-long lunch meeting or—his mobile rang. He grabbed the beeping instrument and glanced at Kartik, still asleep, and pinned the phone to his ear. "Hello?"

"Dr. Kishore, here. Good to know you're back, my son."

Son?

"I left several messages for you over the last few weeks. Did you get them?"

"No," he lied, lowering his tone so as not to wake up Kartik. "I've been traveling, working and—"

"You missed your appointment last week, and it's important." Dr. Kishore's voice strained. "Can you be here in an hour?"

Rakesh glanced at the time on his watch again. 4:20 p.m. He had to get to the meeting now. He slid his foot in the leather black Ballys when the room tilted right. He pressed a hand to the wall for support.

"Hello? Are you there?" Dr. Kishore asked. "Are you all right?

"I'm—" He closed his eyes and gulped. "I'll be there."

IN HIS LATE FIFTIES, DR. KISHORE ROSE FROM BEHIND A BROWN DESK, reached out to shake Rakesh's hand and then gestured for him to sit in a chair in front. A neat stack of folders and loose sheets of paper had been piled on the left. Photographs of a woman in a blue sari and a teenage boy were sealed behind silver photo frames that graced a long, wooden cabinet behind. Medical books filled open bookshelves above and detailed charts of the human body, certificates and plaques honoring the doctor's achievements, adorned the wall.

"I should have returned your call much earlier." Rakesh pulled back a chair for himself and sat down.

"It's fine, Dhanrajji." Dr. Kishore flipped open a folder, attaching 'ji' to Rakesh's name as a form of respect.

"Call me Rakesh, please." Manners were important.

"How are you feeling now, Rakesh?"

"Tired. Fed up." He left out the dizziness and recent pain in his chest.

"Are you eating well?"

He looked past the doctor to the teenage boy's photo.

"Have you cut down on drinking alcohol like we discussed last time?"

"Yes," Rakesh lied.

Dr. Kishore raised his left eyebrow without a change in expression. "And the fatigue is still there?"

"All this pressure at work."

"I'm very sorry to hear this. But based on results from recent bloodwork you had, your liver tests are high. You must take care of your health first." Dr. Kishore picked the topmost sheet from the pile with a list of about thirty items boxed in a table, and Rakesh leaned forward as Dr. Kishore circled 'Ultrasound'. "I'd like you to get this test done as soon as you can." He slid the paper to Rakesh. "Once I get the results, I'll have my office call you and schedule an appointment."

"Doctor, I don't have time for all this. I'll be fine. I'll just take a vacation or—"

"The kind of pressure you're dealing with can damage your health in the long run. You have to understand..." Dr. Kishore continued without a pause like Papa when he had gone back on his promise for Rakesh to take over Dhanraj & Son after Rakesh graduated from Harvard.

Rakesh's head throbbed.

"I don't want you to wait until it's too late..."

After Rakesh had kept his end of the promise, Papa decided to go public with Dhanraj & Son, and Rakesh lost all scope of keeping full control of the company. However, life continued to roll. Three years later Rakesh married Sheetal. A year later he paid for Naina's over-the-top wedding and the never-ending tirade of bills drowned him in debt like the walls closing in on him. Rakesh pressed a palm against his forehead and spread all four fingers away from his thumb to erase Papa's droning voice.

"You must take this seriously."

Papa had been serious when he insisted Rakesh work his way up while he planned for the company's public future. Bile rose up his chest. Why work his way up when Papa had promised Dhanraj and Son would be his as long as he kept his end of the deal?

"I'm afraid if you don't stop drinking..."

Afraid... Fear chilled like an ice-cold glass of scotch at the memory of stumbling out from behind the curtains for a clearer view. Papa had thumped a hand on his chest and was gasping for air as Naina, seventeen at the time, staggered back and screamed.

"Rakesh? Are you listening?"

"Yes."

"I've been talking to you. Where are you? What's wrong with you?"

"Just distracted, lately. That's all. Work pressure."

"The results from all the prescribed tests will help determine next steps. I'm sure you'll have to make a few lifestyle changes, but I want to emphasize you must stop drinking immediately or..."

"It's hard, doctor. I'll try. But—"

"This is serious! Rakesh..." Dr. Kishore's voice grew louder. Too loud. He went on and on, but Rakesh ignored him like he did with Papa. Papa couldn't just go back on his word and make him work his way up from the bottom. Rakesh pushed his chair back. An acute pain sizzled to the back of his head and he clenched his jaw.

"... all right? Rakesh? What's wrong? Come. Sit down. Nurse!" Dr. Kishore called out. "Come quickly..."

Rakesh rose to his feet, pushed away the doctor's hand and left.

RAKESH CROSSED THE STREET TOWARD THE PARKING DECK WHERE HE'D parked his black Lamborghini when a boy about Yash's age walked past with a man. What a spitting image. Dressed in a pair of navy trousers, a white shirt, a tie and a gray school bag humped on his back, the boy chatted to the gentleman and looked like his son.

Probably a father picking up his son from school. Rakesh's heart knotted with regret.

Four men in business suits marched past the two, and the

gentleman put an arm around the boy's shoulder and pulled him close.

Rakesh ached to pick up Yash from school and have him spend an afternoon at the office like other dads. But how could he when Sheetal had banished Yash to the mountains so Yash would be away from the family? *So, fucking overprotective!* He crossed the road and relaxed his clenched jaw thereby releasing the pressure of molar pushing down on molar.

No matter how hard he tried to give Yash the best of everything, from imported toys, clothes and customized furniture, Sheetal complained.

The buildings on his left blurred in a cloud of gray like the finely printed rejection letter from last week that he'd read countless times until his eyes grew dry. At first, the board members expressed shock when he informed them about the denial of the loan and showed empathy at his dilemma, but Rakesh knew they were secretly mocking his failure and waiting for the Japanese to bail out on him. The board had organized today's meeting to resolve the financial crisis before Rakesh scheduled another discussion with Tanaka. *Fuck!* He smacked his heel against concrete. With only six months to repay the loan, he'd have to do everything in his power to coax the Japanese to buy into his scheme—even if that meant kissing their ass.

10

YASH

Sheetal stood outside the principal's office at St. Paul's School, an all-boys school, knocked on the door, straightened the collar of her jacket and ran a palm down her jeans. No response came so she knocked again.

The door opened, and the smell of worn leather and eucalyptus oil wafted from the room.

"Come in." Dr. Pramod Chaturvedi, in his sixties with a hunched back and white strands of oil-slicked hair, opened the door. Using the support of a wooden cane, Dr. Chaturvedi stepped back as Sheetal entered.

A thick panel of maroon curtains covered the wall in front, and a sliver of light sliced through an opening between the folds of fabric.

Sheetal would have preferred to deal with the general office, but the staff was only authorized to grant permission for students to go off campus during one school term for a total of three days. If a parent or guardian wanted permission to take a student off campus for longer, Dr. Chaturvedi's permission was required.

Leather-spine books filled a bookcase on the far right. School trophies and plaques that should have graced the empty hallway outside were stacked behind a wooden cabinet with glass doors. A yellow shade hooded a lit table lamp casting a golden halo on the four-foot-long cherry wood desk illuminating a pen stand, paper-clip holder, stacks of paper, folders, a glass of water covered with a porcelain saucer and specks of dust.

"So good to see you again, Mrs. Dhanraj." Dr. Chaturvedi closed the door and shuffled to his chair on the other side of the desk. He propped the hook of the cane against the table's edge, pulled his chair and sat down. "Please, have a seat." He emphasized every consonant, motioning for Sheetal to sit in one of two chairs on the other side. "Mr. Dhanraj didn't come?"

Sheetal curved a lock of hair behind her left ear. Diamond bangles tinkled down her wrist, and Dr. Chaturvedi's attention shifted. She lowered her hand out of view. "Rakesh is tied up with work."

"Yes. Yes. Big people with big responsibilities are always busy."

"I've come to request permission to take Yash off campus for the week and then home for the Diwali holidays right after."

"Yes. Yes. Of course. We have six more days of school and curfew is still six thirty each evening." He sang the words with apparent pleasure.

"I'd like to spend afternoons with my son off campus." Even if curfew was at 6:30 p.m., surely Dr. Chaturvedi would allow a half-hour leeway. "I'll have him back by seven."

"Yes. Yes. Of course, that's what you'd *like* to do. But you know rules are not made to be broken, Mrs. Dhanraj. Six thirty is the limit."

Sheetal glanced at her watch. "I guess I can sign the forms then? We have five minutes until the bell rings." She was thrilled to have made it to St. Paul's on time despite the confusion that followed after her arrival at the Holiday Inn. Rakesh hadn't made a reservation for her at all. However, she'd managed to get a room pretty quickly since it was non-tourist season and plenty of rooms were available.

Dr. Chaturvedi put one hand over his mouth, turned away, and

...eak free, but she held on with fierce determination to never let go. ...ash was her world. Her reason for living.

"Agh! I can't breathe!" He laughed, and Sheetal let go.

She rolled to the side, sat up, cupped his cheeks in the palms of ...oth hands and ran her thumbs below the lower cradle of his eyes. ...ash was and always would be the one true perfection in life and no ...ainting would ever come close. She tousled his hair, freed her ...ngers from the loops and ran her hands over a little bulge of his ...oulders. "You've grown, Yash." An urge to joke and fool with him ...ked. "You look so...beautiful. Totally beautiful!"

"Beautiful!" He pouted and his rosy cheeks puffed. "Yuck! It's a ...irly word."

"Well, what do I use then?"

"Handsome."

"How about toothless? For two molars. One on the right and ...nother on the left." Her heart sank. She gestured for him to open his ...outh and pinpointed the exact location of two missing teeth. He'd ...rown up some in her absence. "I missed you."

"I missed you, too. Where's Dad?" He looked over her shoulder.

Dad? Didn't Yash call Rakesh, Daddy? "He couldn't come because ...f work."

"Always work, Mum! Why does he always have work? Can't he ...ake a holiday?"

"He wanted to, *Beta*, but there were so many important meet-...ngs." Including repayment of the bank loan in six months.

"More important than me?"

"Nothing can ever be more important than you. I promise he'll ...ome next time, and you can spend as much time with him as you ...ant."

"I don't want to come next time, Mum. I want to stay at home ...ith you and Dad. Can I?"

The dreaded question. She looked into Yash's eyes and her heart ...ched. "We'll see."

"You always say that."

coughed. He paused to breathe, but phlegm rattled his throat and he coughed again.

"Are you all right?"

"Yes. Yes. I'm fine." He uncovered the glass of water, took a sip, and then handed her six forms requesting permission to take a student off campus, one for each day.

Sheetal skimmed the fine print and signed each, the nib of the pen grating the wooden table beneath the paper and marking the silence impregnated by Dr. Chaturvedi's heavy breathing. "How are things at school? Have you had a chance to meet Yash?" Sheetal didn't expect Dr. Chaturvedi to personally know Yash; after all, the man ran a school with over eight hundred students, but polite conversation always helped break the ice.

"Yash? Yes. Yes. A good student. An all-round, well-mannered, attentive boy, interested in learning. A very confident boy. No complaints. Second standard, yes?"

"No. He's eight, in the fourth standard."

"My mistake. I forget, sometimes." He coughed. "However, I can make an exception for you. I will grant you an extra half-hour with Yash in return for a small donation?" His attention diverted to the bangles on Sheetal's wrist, and Sheetal flinched. "A series of paint-ings, perhaps?"

Newspaper and magazines occasionally featured Sheetal's works, so she wasn't surprised that Dr. Chaturvedi had heard about her accomplishments.

"Or one for my office or the library, perhaps? Your work is so renowned. What a privilege for our school..."

The series of orchids lying stacked in a corner of the studio would brighten this room ten times. However, Yash was not a commodity to barter. "Six thirty is fine." Sheetal smiled. "You know the rules, Mr. Chaturvedi, not made to be broken." Then she handed all six sheets back and left.

Sheetal left the building housing the school library and Dr. Chaturvedi's office, slipped on her leather gloves and stepped on a thick sheet of snow padding the ground. With her back to the building, she marveled at the full view of St. Paul's campus.

A stone wall bordering the campus' perimeter and crowned with shards of glass to bar intruders ran the campus' vast perimeter. Mall Road, a nearby town's arterial road, several kilometers away, cut through the mountainous terrain then branched out and crept into St. Paul's campus from behind, cutting past the school's main security gates and running alongside Dr. Chaturvedi's building. The snow-covered road continued to cruise past a large area of open land also covered in a carpet of snow that separated the school from the boarders' lodging far ahead.

Sheetal headed toward the open ground so she was in clear sight of Yash irrespective of which direction he came from. She pulled back the cuff of her jacket and looked at her watch, her heart pattering in excitement. Would he descend from the monstrous flight of stairs on the right that leveled before a portico and grand doors to the auditorium? Or did he have class in one of the many buildings behind the auditorium which meant an additional five or ten-minute wait? St. Paul's School was renowned for its four-hundred-meter running track, indoor gym, swimming pool and equestrian center nestled behind the auditorium and the enormity of the campus grounds.

The tips of white mountain tops along the left and the blue sky sprinkled with clouds were like one huge wall painting. Rows of conifer trees ahead hid a tall iron fence separating the boarders' lodging from St. Paul's campus. A service gate in a far corner on the right allowed boarders to come and go from their lodging to the campus and back and was manned by a security guard. Perhaps Yash would come out from the service gate in which case he'd be here even sooner. Excitement revved her heart. Any minute now.

The school bell clanged and several boys in gray trousers, white shirts, navy blue ties and matching blazers emerged at the auditorium's portico, sauntered down the stairs and dotted the snow-covered ground in rows of twos and threes like sapphires. A boy separated from the group and headed in her direction.

Yash? Sheetal inched toward him, her heartbeat q[...] each step. *Was that him? No. Can't be.* The boy looked [...] appeared too broad at the shoulders. She blinked for [...] but couldn't make out the details from the distance. [...] her strides mentally molding the boy's features to the [...] memory of Yash six months ago when she'd helped [...] then said goodbye outside the cottage. Accustomed t[...] absence with her imagination, every trip to Mansali [...] guessing game of how tall Yash might have grown. H[...] he matured? How much more did he look like Rakes[...] her? Then they'd meet and she adjusted to a new v[...] knowing he would change the next time around.

The boy, about five-and-half feet tall, a few meters[...] armed with a thick book walked with a confident b[...] step, a thick Oxford Dictionary in his gloved hands. "G[...] Ma'am." He walked past and smiled.

"Good morning!" *What a fine young man! Would Y[...] confident teenager like him?*

"Mum!"

Yash? Her heart leaped. Couldn't be. Yash called her[...] "Mum!"

A boy waved from the bottom of the staircase a[...] direction. She hurried toward him, desperate to run he[...] the curve of his eyes, cheeks and chin.

He smiled from ear to ear and pounded one foot [...] other. "Hey, Mum!"

Sheetal leaned forward, stretched her arms out [...] coat sleeves pushed against her as Yash filled her [...] keeled back on the edge of her heel and landed on her b[...] on top. Something tickled her ear and laughter bu[...] throat. She ran her palm over his head, and black lo[...] sprung back. She couldn't believe it. Yash. Her son. [...] arms once again. She tightened her embrace and raine[...] kisses as flurries of snow drifted. Yash squirmed an[...]

coughed. He paused to breathe, but phlegm rattled his throat and he coughed again.

"Are you all right?"

"Yes. Yes. I'm fine." He uncovered the glass of water, took a sip, and then handed her six forms requesting permission to take a student off campus, one for each day.

Sheetal skimmed the fine print and signed each, the nib of the pen grating the wooden table beneath the paper and marking the silence impregnated by Dr. Chaturvedi's heavy breathing. "How are things at school? Have you had a chance to meet Yash?" Sheetal didn't expect Dr. Chaturvedi to personally know Yash; after all, the man ran a school with over eight hundred students, but polite conversation always helped break the ice.

"Yash? Yes. Yes. A good student. An all-round, well-mannered, attentive boy, interested in learning. A very confident boy. No complaints. Second standard, yes?"

"No. He's eight, in the fourth standard."

"My mistake. I forget, sometimes." He coughed. "However, I can make an exception for you. I will grant you an extra half-hour with Yash in return for a small donation?" His attention diverted to the bangles on Sheetal's wrist, and Sheetal flinched. "A series of paint-ings, perhaps?"

Newspaper and magazines occasionally featured Sheetal's works, so she wasn't surprised that Dr. Chaturvedi had heard about her accomplishments.

"Or one for my office or the library, perhaps? Your work is so renowned. What a privilege for our school..."

The series of orchids lying stacked in a corner of the studio would brighten this room ten times. However, Yash was not a commodity to barter. "Six thirty is fine." Sheetal smiled. "You know the rules, Mr. Chaturvedi, not made to be broken." Then she handed all six sheets back and left.

Sheetal left the building housing the school library and Dr. Chaturvedi's office, slipped on her leather gloves and stepped on a thick sheet of snow padding the ground. With her back to the building, she marveled at the full view of St. Paul's campus.

A stone wall bordering the campus' perimeter and crowned with shards of glass to bar intruders ran the campus' vast perimeter. Mall Road, a nearby town's arterial road, several kilometers away, cut through the mountainous terrain then branched out and crept into St. Paul's campus from behind, cutting past the school's main security gates and running alongside Dr. Chaturvedi's building. The snow-covered road continued to cruise past a large area of open land also covered in a carpet of snow that separated the school from the boarders' lodging far ahead.

Sheetal headed toward the open ground so she was in clear sight of Yash irrespective of which direction he came from. She pulled back the cuff of her jacket and looked at her watch, her heart pattering in excitement. Would he descend from the monstrous flight of stairs on the right that leveled before a portico and grand doors to the auditorium? Or did he have class in one of the many buildings behind the auditorium which meant an additional five or ten-minute wait? St. Paul's School was renowned for its four-hundred-meter running track, indoor gym, swimming pool and equestrian center nestled behind the auditorium and the enormity of the campus grounds.

The tips of white mountain tops along the left and the blue sky sprinkled with clouds were like one huge wall painting. Rows of conifer trees ahead hid a tall iron fence separating the boarders' lodging from St. Paul's campus. A service gate in a far corner on the right allowed boarders to come and go from their lodging to the campus and back and was manned by a security guard. Perhaps Yash would come out from the service gate in which case he'd be here even sooner. Excitement revved her heart. Any minute now.

The school bell clanged and several boys in gray trousers, white shirts, navy blue ties and matching blazers emerged at the auditorium's portico, sauntered down the stairs and dotted the snow-covered ground in rows of twos and threes like sapphires. A boy separated from the group and headed in her direction.

Yash? Sheetal inched toward him, her heartbeat quickening with each step. *Was that him? No. Can't be.* The boy looked much taller and appeared too broad at the shoulders. She blinked for a clearer view but couldn't make out the details from the distance. She lengthened her strides mentally molding the boy's features to the last snap-shot memory of Yash six months ago when she'd helped him move in, then said goodbye outside the cottage. Accustomed to filling Yash's absence with her imagination, every trip to Mansali turned into a guessing game of how tall Yash might have grown. How much had he matured? How much more did he look like Rakesh and less like her? Then they'd meet and she adjusted to a new version of Yash knowing he would change the next time around.

The boy, about five-and-half feet tall, a few meters' distance, and armed with a thick book walked with a confident bounce in each step, a thick Oxford Dictionary in his gloved hands. "Good morning, Ma'am." He walked past and smiled.

"Good morning!" *What a fine young man! Would Yash grow up a confident teenager like him?*

"Mum!"

Yash? Her heart leaped. Couldn't be. Yash called her Mamma.

"Mum!"

A boy waved from the bottom of the staircase and ran in her direction. She hurried toward him, desperate to run her fingers over the curve of his eyes, cheeks and chin.

He smiled from ear to ear and pounded one foot ahead of the other. "Hey, Mum!"

Sheetal leaned forward, stretched her arms out wide, and the coat sleeves pushed against her as Yash filled her embrace. She keeled back on the edge of her heel and landed on her back with Yash on top. Something tickled her ear and laughter bubbled up her throat. She ran her palm over his head, and black locks of his hair sprung back. She couldn't believe it. Yash. Her son. He was in her arms once again. She tightened her embrace and rained his face with kisses as flurries of snow drifted. Yash squirmed and wriggled to break free, but she held on with fierce determination to never let go. Yash was her world. Her reason for living.

"Agh! I can't breathe!" He laughed, and Sheetal let go.

She rolled to the side, sat up, cupped his cheeks in the palms of both hands and ran her thumbs below the lower cradle of his eyes. Yash was and always would be the one true perfection in life and no painting would ever come close. She tousled his hair, freed her fingers from the loops and ran her hands over a little bulge of his shoulders. "You've grown, Yash." An urge to joke and fool with him irked. "You look so...beautiful. Totally beautiful!"

"Beautiful!" He pouted and his rosy cheeks puffed. "Yuck! It's a girly word."

"Well, what do I use then?"

"Handsome."

"How about toothless? For two molars. One on the right and another on the left." Her heart sank. She gestured for him to open his mouth and pinpointed the exact location of two missing teeth. He'd grown up some in her absence. "I missed you."

"I missed you, too. Where's Dad?" He looked over her shoulder.

Dad? Didn't Yash call Rakesh, Daddy? "He couldn't come because of work."

"Always work, Mum! Why does he always have work? Can't he take a holiday?"

"He wanted to, *Beta*, but there were so many important meetings." Including repayment of the bank loan in six months.

"More important than me?"

"Nothing can ever be more important than you. I promise he'll come next time, and you can spend as much time with him as you want."

"I don't want to come next time, Mum. I want to stay at home with you and Dad. Can I?"

The dreaded question. She looked into Yash's eyes and her heart ached. "We'll see."

"You always say that."

"I know, Yash."

"You say we'll see every time."

Sheetal took his gloved fingers in her hand and pulled him close.

"I don't like living here alone."

"You said you had so many good friends."

"I do. But it's not the same without you or Dad. I really miss you."

Yash loved Rakesh, and Rakesh would give up the world for his son, but with Naina and Mummyji around she simply couldn't make false promises even though she desperately yearned for them to be a normal family.

"So, what's with all this Mum and Dad business?"

"It's what all the big boys say when they talk."

Sheetal smiled, relieved she'd diverted the conversation. "So, you're a big boy now?"

"That's what Chopra Sir says."

"Ah, your new House Master, right?"

At the start of the school year, only male members of the teaching faculty were assigned charge of residential cottages that accommodated up to sixteen boys. They acted as guardians for the students under their care and were known as House Masters. Other faculty members led extracurricular activities after school hours. However, shortly after the first term began, the House Master designated for Yash's cottage had to leave because of a family emergency and a substitute replaced him.

"So, how's this new House Master?"

"Oh, Chopra Sir. He's a little strict and teaches me science."

"I bet you're one of his favorites."

"He doesn't have favorites. There are so many in the class and he says he has to be fair to everyone, but you know what? He watched me audition and said I did great."

"What audition?"

"Announcer. Compere for the spring concert next year."

"Oh, yes. I remember." Sheetal and Rakesh talked to Yash every weekend and about two weeks ago Yash mentioned something about auditioning for a school concert. But they hadn't talked about it, since.

St. Paul's held an annual spring concert in April, two weeks prior to the students' final exams. Parents were invited to watch the school's theatrical production which took months of preparation and rehearsals and reeled in the best talent. Competition to secure a leading role was fierce because boys who came from families with strong business backgrounds competed with children of politicians and Bollywood celebrities who were naturally gifted.

"How many others auditioned?"

"Seventy-five. And guess what?"

"What?"

"I was chosen!"

"You what?"

"I was selected to be a compere for the concert."

"Oh, Yash!" Sheetal's heart soared with pride, and she hugged him again. The achievement proved Yash's talent and confidence and validated her rationale to have enrolled him at St. Paul's. He would have never thrived at the Dhanraj's. "I'm so proud of you and so happy!" She rained his face with kisses. "Why didn't you tell us on the phone?"

"Because..." He giggled through the shower of kisses. "I wanted to surprise you and Dad!" He turned left and then right. "Stop, Mum! They'll tease me."

"Who?"

"My friends." He wormed out of her grip and jumped to his feet. "Snow fight, Mum."

"Next time. Let's go out somewhere so we can talk. Anywhere you want. We have so much to catch up on."

"Home?"

Sheetal rose to her feet and dusted snow off her jacket and jeans. "Not so soon. You still have another week to go—" Something smacked Sheetal in the face and she numbed. She raised a hand to her nose and snow crumbled to the ground.

"Sorry." Yash took a step back.

Sheetal bent down, picked up a handful of snow, and threw it at him.

Snow cupped his blazer pocket and crumbled. "You got me!" He squatted on his haunches, scooped another ball and threw it at her.

Sheetal retaliated and received another blow in return. "Come back, here." She chased Yash, zigzagging back and forth, hitting, missing and tumbling to the ground. Oh, how she wanted to freeze the moment and remain giddy in a world that spun only with Yash's laughter.

11

FROZEN

Sheetal walked down a concrete slope leading away from the Holiday Inn as a chilly breeze rippled the lower seam of the red kurta around her knees. Gravel crunched under the soles of her Nike shoes and Sheetal kicked pebbles in her path, sending them reeling down to nestle in pockets of melting snow and chips of broken asphalt. A few leaves still clinging to overhanging branches rustled, and the sun cast nets of yellow on the flora-filled landscape tinting everything in in a golden hue before hiding behind a thick gray padding of clouds. She tightened her jacket's hood.

A light blue Fiat cruised past, and the driver poked his head out the window as he slowed down. *Kahaan jaana hai, Madame? Mein aapko chodh deta hoon."* Prepared to drop her at any destination the taxi driver waited, but Sheetal wanted to walk by herself for a while and be alone with her thoughts. The freedom of anonymity, of living carefree and not being boxed behind four walls was a treasure to savor. "You carry on, and I'll figure out my destination." She replied in Hindi.

"I can drop you off at Mall Road," he insisted, but Sheetal shook her head and waved her hand. An easy downhill walk Mall Road stretched for two kilometers and cut through the quaint town of Mansali. Shops, hotels, open-air food stalls, street vendors and family-owned restaurants lined both sides of Mall Road while bungalows and private schools were scattered all over the hillside.

"Where are you going, Madame, in such cold weather?"

Sheetal tightened her grip on the strap of her handbag dangling off her shoulder and crossed her arms. "I'll figure it out."

The town of Lower Mansali peeked from a cut in the mountain's edge. The valley nestled like a patchwork quilt of green, yellow and brown squares. Ponds the size of her nail glistened like mirrorwork stitched on the lush thicket of fabric. A bed of clouds shielded the sun's rays, smothered the land in shades of dark green and stole the sateen from the water's surface. The air rustled the leaves with force, the temperature plunged, and Sheetal rammed her fists in the side pockets of her jacket as tendrils of hair flew about her face. Then the clouds drifted away, the sun burst forth, and Lower Mansali took on its previous sparkle of a living and breathing canvas.

What beauty! What brilliance! Warmth spread across the land, and she descended toward an overhanging cliff looking out on the valley bordered by metal railings.

This vacation would have done Rakesh so much good—maybe not, considering he harbored no patience when it came to appreciating natural beauty. She imagined Rakesh standing next to her lighting a cigar to keep warm and complaining about the wind chill. Rakesh would have had the taxi driver follow close on their heels, checked his cell phone for email updates at least five times by now. He would have lost connection a few times, cursed the town, the mountains, and when done, he'd have jumped in the vehicle and ordered the driver to take him to a five-star hotel for a drink.

Her muscles tensed, and Sheetal exhaled the breath she hadn't realized she'd been holding until now. Maybe Rakesh's absence would do some good. Her shoulders sagged from the relief of lifting weight. No expectations. No responsibilities, for now. Oh, to be free and soar like a bird every day without a care. What must it be like to live up in these mountains? What if she could make this life permanent?

Impossible, she reasoned. After marriage, her status had transferred from Papa's responsibility to Rakesh's, and she would always be Rakesh's property, even if Rakesh proved unfaithful to their relationship. Where was the chance of a second marriage? Because after the first she was now damaged goods and would likely be fit to marry a widower who needed a mother substitute for his children. *Shouldn't think such thoughts.* Sheetal bit her lower lip in guilt. How could she be so selfish and desire what was clearly out of reach? She shouldn't desire anything in any way or form. Even if it was an escape from Rakesh.

AS SHEETAL WALKED ALONG MALL ROAD, RESTAURANT OWNERS CALLED passers-by to come in for a meal or some hot masala chai. The fragrance of spicy dals, bubbling tomato gravies, steamed Basmati rice, deep-fried fritters and oven-baked *naans*—white-flour flat bread—peppered the air. The restaurants gave way to an open-air market on both sides of the road where stalls jostled for space and were separated from each other by colorful tarpaulin sheets tethered to wooden poles and manned by vendors. The make-shift stores sold colored glassware, crochet table mats, runners, potholders, fridge magnets and a variety of trinkets.

"Arrey, *gori gori Memsahib!*" A vendor waved and referred to Sheetal as Beautiful Madam. "Three for the price of two. Buy as many as you like for yourself and your friends."

Sheetal walked toward the vendor, picked up a multi-colored glass jewelry case and held it against the sun. Light flounced off the slanting orange, green and pink triangular facades, and she turned the case so that each side faced the light. She thumbed open the lid and all three colors flooded the four-by-four-inch hollow cavity.

"Buy it, *Memsahib*." An elderly lady in a faded salwar suit and stringy-knit jumper smiled to reveal four missing teeth. "I give you special. Only three hundred and seventy-five rupees."

Sheetal closed the lid and returned the box to the stall. "I was only looking."

"What's there to look when you can buy?"

"*Arrey, Memsahib*." A neighboring vendor in a multi-colored sari and black shawl called. "Come take a look at my collection."

The Dhanrajs gave gifts of gold and silver to friends and families, not jewelry boxes purchased from open stalls run by a toothless old woman out in the middle of nowhere. Even if she were to buy the box for herself, could she find a place on the dressing table crowded with crystal bottles of imported perfumes? Maybe she could get rid of extra magazines on her bedside table and position the box beside the lamp under a halo of yellow light.

"*Khareed lo, Memsahib!*" The old lady beckoned her to buy the jewelry box.

"Thank you, but maybe next time." Sheetal walked on and ignored the lady's request to buy the case.

A gust of icy wind slithered down the collar of her jacket and freed a lock of hair that brushed a corner of her lip. Sheetal tugged the wisp behind the curve of her ear, but the strands leaped right back. Her legs ached from the three-hour walk, and she longed to sit down and rest. She pulled the sleeve of her jacket to look at the time on her watch. It was 2:30 p.m. and she had another hour and a half until Yash's classes would be over.

The door to a restaurant on her right swung open and a man in a turban carried a thick tube of carpet on his shoulders. Sheetal thought she recognized him but couldn't be sure because of the bundle obscuring his face. The carpet slipped from his grip and the man lowered the tube and slanted it diagonally across his chest. The taxi driver. Sheetal looked the other way to avoid risking more chatter.

"Ah! Hello Madame!" he called out. "So nice to meeting you!"

Sheetal nodded. *His name? What was his name?* "Hello. *Kaise ho?*" She asked how he was doing.

"Always good, Madame. Jatinder Singh always good."

That's it! Jatinder Singh.

"My restaurant here, Madame. Spiceality." He pointed to a sign above the door he had just exited. "Please come in. Most welcome. Always welcoming new customers." He turned around, walked back to the door and pushed it open with his back as Sheetal followed.

Overhead windchimes tinkled as the door gave way and warmth flooded. "Really, it's all right," Sheetal pressed on in Hindi. "You don't have to—"

"No problem, Madame." He persisted in English. "I am coming back in little minutes, please. You sit anywhere you are liking and my staff taking your care." Then he hollered a few instructions to a skinny teenage boy in a faded white, full-sleeve shirt and tattered brown trousers, a gray towel draped over his shoulder. "I go now, Madame. You treat like your home."

The door closed and wind chimes tinkled furiously as the aroma of thick onion gravy and damp wood spiced the air. Several customers seated at wooden tables for four, draped in solid blue, red and green tablecloths, looked up. A gentleman apparently unperturbed by her entry rustled the pages of a newspaper before him and then flipped a page.

A waist-high wooden counter equipped with a cashier's register paralleled the back wall and separated the kitchen from the dining. Sheetal looked for an empty table unsure about sitting too close to the cream-colored walls peeling with paint. An elderly woman in a purple salwar suit manned a mini kiosk that displayed comics, books, trinkets and souvenirs. A haphazard arrangement of light bulbs suspended from overhead beams on thick black cables convinced her this place would fall apart any minute. Maybe she should leave.

The gentle rustle of paper caught her attention. The gentleman behind the newspaper, dressed in a pair of black trousers and matching shoes appeared to be decent. Perhaps this restaurant would suffice for a short rest and a cup of coffee before she headed over to St. Paul's. The teenager approached, gestured to an empty table on the gentleman's left and Sheetal followed. A whiff of musk caught her off-guard. Perhaps the scent was coming from behind the newspaper?

"*Yeh table theek hai, Madame?*" The teenager asked if the table to the man's left would do.

Crumbs and oil stains littered the surface. "Can you wipe the table, please?"

The boy yanked the towel off his shoulder, swiped it on the table's surface and gestured for her to take a seat.

Sheetal took out a wet tissue from her handbag, flattened it on the chair's headrest and pulled out the chair. Then she wiped clean the table's surface closest to her. The boy snorted, but she didn't care. She was about to sit down when the gentleman lowered the paper.

"Sheetal? Sheetal Dhanraj?"

Her heart welled up in her throat and she swallowed. "Arvind?"

"How are you?" He smiled. "You're looking great."

"I'm fine. *Tum bhi.*" She paused to weigh her comment in Hindi. "*Acchhe lag rahe ho.*" He looked good like he always did. A French beard and a rounded, softened jawline added to the elegance of his thirties and a thick layer of flesh padded his frame. His copper-bronze complexion had lightened, but jet-black hair still curved back in waves.

Arvind rose to his five-foot-eleven stature. A slight paunch protruded from behind the blue shirt and his body filled the cave of the garment stretching the fabric tight. "I can't believe it's you."

Warmth crept up her shoulders. Was it really Arvind?

"Like to join me?" Arvind set the newspaper aside.

Was it him in flesh and blood after all these years? She slid her hands into the jacket pockets. "So, what are you doing here?"

Arvind cocked his head back and laughed. "Nice intro!"

Sheetal sucked her lips in tight. "I meant, do you live here? You know, suddenly meeting you after all these years up in the mountains."

"I teach at St. Paul's."

Sheetal sat down. "Oh, what do you teach?"

"Science. Yash is in my class." Arvind sat down. "And, I'm also his House Master."

Chopra Sir.

"He's an intelligent and bright boy, always ready with the right answer. A lot like you."

Warmth crept up the nape of Sheetal's neck as he folded both hands in a fist on the table. The memory of running her fingers over those very hands while he caressed her cheek and promised to love her forever made her heart tingle. "So, you knew all along, Yash is my son?"

"Who doesn't know the Dhanrajs?" He emphasized the last word like a contagion. "Hard not to notice."

And yet he'd never made any attempt to contact?

"I'm guessing you're here to pick him up for Diwali break."

"Rakesh and I usually take our vacation around this time."

Arvind's fist paled just a little at the mention of Rakesh's name and he motioned to leave. "I have extra-curriculars in about an hour. This place is like home where I come for some peace and quiet. It's like my corner away from all the hustle and bustle of campus life, plus great food and great company with Jatinder *Bhai*." He rose to leave. "Maybe we'll meet again?"

Sheetal jumped to her feet.

"You only just got here. Do stay. The food is excellent, but if you're not hungry a hot coffee will do wonders against that cold out there."

"I'm meeting Yash at four on campus."

"Oh good! So, you have time to kill." He headed for the exit, and Sheetal followed. "You'll find deals in the local bazaar. Remember to bargain." He turned the knob, opened the door, and wind chimes tinkled as he stepped out.

Sheetal followed, her heart in her throat as several auto-rickshaws passed by. How could he leave so soon?

"Memsahib! Gori gori memsahib!" The toothless old woman called out, referring to Sheetal by her fair complexion. Sheetal turned and the old woman beckoned her to return. "Arrey! Give me three hundred then!"

"Looks like she's trying to sell you something," Arvind said.

"I was just looking around. I picked up something to look at and she's been after me, since."

Arvind hailed for an auto-rickshaw, and one veering close to the sidewalk pulled up. Arvind ducked his head so he wouldn't hit the roof and slid across to the other side. "I can drop you off if you want." He patted the empty seat.

Sheetal hesitated.

"I forgot. You probably have a car waiting. Anyway, this auto would be a bumpy ride." He patted the driver on the shoulder "St. Paul's School." He waved Sheetal goodbye and left.

THAT AFTERNOON SHEETAL AND YASH VISITED SOME OF THE FAMOUS TOURIST spots including Echo Point, an overhanging cliff surrounded by mountains. Yash cupped his mouth and screamed "Mum." The word echoed and faded.

Sheetal grabbed the metal railing, leaned forward, and screamed, "Y-a-a-sh!" Her voice echoed louder.

Yash cupped both palms around his mouth and yelled, "D-a-a-d!" The word echoed louder than Sheetal's. "If I say it louder maybe Dad will hear me and yell back from Raigun."

"Go on then, try." Sheetal feigned a smile for Yash's benefit. "Maybe when your daddy's here next time you can both yell each other's names out loud."

"He's always busy on the phone with office work."

"Should I call him and ask if he can hear you?"

"Okay."

Sheetal checked her watch. It was five, which meant Rakesh must be in the office. She'd ask Rakesh to pretend he could hear Yash's echoes all the way in Raigun. Sheetal called and pressed the phone to Yash's ear.

"He's not picking up." Yash frowned. "I told you, he's always busy."

"Maybe he left the phone somewhere and didn't hear it ring? How about we try again later? I have to get you back on campus before six-thirty."

"Okay."

Sheetal reached for Yash's hand and tightened her grip around his fingers. Since she'd arrived, she'd tried calling Rakesh several times, but no answer. He could at least have called once to speak to Yash. Didn't he notice her missed calls? What held him back from answering just now? First, he messed up on the hotel reservation. Before that, he didn't come home before moon rise on Karva Chauth and when he did finally walk in, he was stone drunk and went straight to bed. And now he had the audacity to ignore them?

The taxi pulled up outside the boarders' lodging at 6 p.m., and Sheetal spent the next half-hour with Yash walking past rows of cottages. Strings of lamp posts cast wide nets of yellow on the snow-crusted ground as Yash prattled away about homework, friends and roommates.

"And my friends, Mum, they said I should..."

She paused at the front door of Yash's cottage. What if Arvind was inside? What if he decided to step out for some fresh air? Her heart raced. She stepped in a circumference of yellow light and turned to face Yash's cottage so Arvind wouldn't miss her.

"Mum?"

Sheetal looked down at Yash and smiled. Maybe Arvind would have an errand and a reason to come out.

"Are you listening?"

She should apologize for the way their relationship had ended and how she turned her back on him. "What a coincidence that Arvind is your House Master."

"Arvind?" Yash asked.

"I mean, Chopra Sir."

"Why?"

"Isn't anyone else in charge around here?"

"The twelfth standard captains are on duty until the House Master returns."

"Oh." Her heart sank. "So, when does he return?"

"Who?"

"Your House Master."

"I don't know."

"Do you think he'll be back soon?"

"Who?"

"Your House Master." Her voice rose sharply without meaning to, and Yash stepped away. Sheetal squatted on her haunches, met Yash's gaze and gulped. "I'm sorry, I didn't mean to sound angry."

"Chopra Sir might be in. Should I check? Do you want to meet him?"

"No."

THAT NIGHT SHEETAL CALLED RAKESH ON HIS CELL PHONE FOR THE fifteenth time. The ringing continued. Sheetal looked at her watch. It was only ten. Was he with clients at dinner or in the office? Exhausted from chasing Rakesh, she switched off her phone and dumped it in her handbag.

12

FOREST RAIN

The next afternoon Sheetal drove up to St. Paul's where a crowd had gathered at the main entrance and along the raised portico. Overnight, more parents and families had arrived to take students back home and were waiting for the afternoon bell to ring. However, Sheetal made her way across campus to the boarders' lodging and hooked her fingers in the metal loops. She pressed her forehead to the gate and waited.

"Hey, Mum!" Yash called from behind, and Sheetal looked over her shoulder. "What are you doing?"

"Waiting for you."

"But the classrooms are back there."

"I forgot. Silly me." Sheetal turned and walked toward him. "Where would you like to go today?"

"Mall Road."

An hour later, Sheetal and Yash walked hand-in-hand along Mall Road's snow-covered path as vendors yelled their wares and asked tourists to name a price. A gust of wind tore across the mountains, ripped the tarpaulin sheets off wooden poles and shook the scaffolding.

"Hurry!" a vendor yelled. "Storm!"

"Pack up, quickly!" A woman pooled her items in metal trunks and boxes as others hurried. "Put all the show pieces here."

"Arrey, not there, boy!" a man bellowed. "Here. In this box." The bang, clatter and snap of locks smacked the air as gray clouds thickened and another gust of icy wind whipped from behind. Snowflakes spun as Sheetal pulled Yash to her side.

"It's freezing, Mum. We need to find shelter."

Vendors systematically rolled the sheets, dumped them in boxes, dismantled the pillars and bundled them on the edge of sidewalks. Cries of *"Jaldi Karo"*, *"Phatafhat'* and *"Havaa! Tez havaa!"* urged people to hurry and escape the oncoming storm. Surprise storms, a commonality here, had clearly trained the locals to survive in the mountains controlled by mammoth gods.

Sheetal tightened her grip on Yash's hand and ran toward numerous brick shops ahead. Another gust of wind whirled a wall of snow obstructing her view, and Sheetal bent her head to keep the flakes from pricking her eyes. She veered right hoping to run into a coffee shop or restaurant where they could take cover and tried the first door within reach. However, the door was locked. They trudged ahead, shielding their faces from the wind and Sheetal tried another door. This one gave way. Sheetal pushed Yash in, followed and slammed the door behind. Wind chimes tinkled furiously, and several people seated at tables looked up.

"Arrey, *Bhai!*" A thick heavy voice rang, and Jatinder Bhai emerged from the kitchen. "Welcome! Welcoming again to my humble Spiceality."

The air tingled with the aromas of cumin, hot oil and burnt garlic.

The taxi driver wiped his hands on a green towel draping the left shoulder and rushed toward them. "Oh, ho ho! Who is coming today? Welcome, welcome!" He ruffled Yash's hair "Chotta Baba—" he referred to Yash as 'Little Boy' "—is in good mood, I am seeing."

Why couldn't he just speak in Hindi like he did with everyone else? Sheetal dusted the snow off her jacket and gloves and helped Yash do the same.

"And you, Madame. Last time coming and then going so quickly-quickly. No time for eating anything."

"I wasn't hungry."

"No problem, Madame. No problem. Please sit on any seat you are liking." He led them to an empty table and pulled out two chairs. *"Aloo matar, chole garam, rajma rasiya, paneer do pyaza, chicken tikka..."* he recited a roster of vegetables, meats and lentil soups on the menu. "We are also having *naans, rotis, chapatis...*" he continued the list of Indian breads, savory rice and dishes from the southern region of India. *"Dosa, idli, uttapam..."*

The pungent smell of turmeric and burnt spices wafted and Sheetal held her breath struggling to focus on the items. "Do you have a menu?" she asked in Hindi.

"Sorry, Madame," he pressed on in English. "I am reciting menu every day to all customers. Cannot fixing here because items changing depending on what vegetable and meats is being available in market."

"We're really not that hungry. We just came in to get away from the storm."

"No worrying, Madame. Most welcome to staying long as you like." He wiped his masala-stained fingers on the green hand towel again and then scratched his beard. "My home, your home! One and same thing."

Sheetal looked past his shoulder to a row of windows, the storm intensifying outside, and sat at a table. "I'll just have a coffee. And Yash—" The wind chimes tinkled and Sheetal looked up.

The blustery wind raged in through the opening door and a gentleman dressed in black from head to toe slammed the door behind. He dusted himself, pulled off a woolen hat and shook it free of white flakes.

Arvind! Her heart skipped a beat.

"Chopra Sir!"

"Hey, Yash! Sheetal." Arvind nodded. "Good to meet again. So, what brings you here?"

"The storm," Sheetal replied. "I didn't expect the weather to change without warning—"

"It's normal. We just run, take cover and make new friends along the way. *Aur Jattu Bhai?*" Arvind shook Jatinder's hand and sat at the next table. "How about your soup of the day?"

"*Tomato shorba!* And you, Chotta Baba?" Jatinder turned to Yash. "What you having?"

"A *masala dosa.*" Yash asked for a crispy, white rice-and-lentil crepe with a spicy filling of potatoes and onions.

"Yes, yes! Good choice. My wife making fresh dosas, hot and crisp with her own hands." He held out his palms. Cracks ran along the surface and yellow-and-red stains of Indian masalas dotted his fingers.

Sheetal pulled out a packet of wet tissues and leaned close to Yash's ear. "How about you have a dosa later and take a hot chocolate instead?" she whispered. "I'll take you someplace better, more hygienic, for dinner."

"I want a dosa now." Yash frowned.

"Aah! Chotta Baba knowing what is good here." Jatinder nodded as two waiters carried tray loads of dirty dishes back to the kitchen. A customer signaled, and Jatinder acknowledged the call with a wave of his hand. "Please, Madame. Other customer needing me. I am coming, one minute." Then he wove through a maze of tables.

"You shouldn't eat in such places," Sheetal whispered to Yash.

"Why?"

"You could end up with a stomach infection and then—"

"Why don't you two join me here?" Arvind peeled off the leather jacket and rolled up the blue-and-white-checkered sleeves of his shirt.

Sheetal peered above the rim of Yash's head. "Like I said, we're not really here to eat, just to get away from the storm outside."

"That storm isn't going away anytime soon, and you're stuck for a long while. Where are you staying?"

"The Holiday Inn."

Aur dost?" Arvind referred to Yash as 'friend'. "What did you order?"

Yash walked over and cupped Arvind's ear. "A masala dosa."

Sheetal rolled her eyes and pulled a chair beside an electric heater perched on a low-rising stool. Anyone within a meter's radius could hear.

"Why are you whispering?" Arvind asked.

"Because Mom says not to eat in such places."

"That's not what I meant." Her attention flew to the window behind Arvind and the curtain of white outside.

"Really, yaar?" Arvind grinned.

Sheetal's heart melted. She hadn't heard a casual, easy-going, arguably affectionate tone like that in years. Arvind used to debate for hours over sweet nothings and she hung on his every word.

"Mum said it's not clean and I could get a stomachache and fall sick and—"

"That's enough, Yash." Sheetal planted her hands on the table's edge and firmed her grip.

"But that's what you said," he argued.

"And you don't have to tell everyone."

"Chopra Sir is not everyone."

"Whoa!" Arvind intervened. "I think I'm in the middle of a mother-son debate."

"I'm going to the comics." Yash rose to his feet and ran to the kiosk.

"Yash!" Sheetal called after him.

"Just one look, Mum."

"Come back, Yash."

"Aww!" he whined. "Once."

"Let him be," Arvind suggested.

"I know when to let him be." Sheetal firmed her voice. "I'm his mother."

Arvind raised both hands in surrender. "My mistake. Happens when you spend months with other people's children and forget you're just a custodian."

Sheetal wiped her hands clean with the tissue and dusted a few crumbs off the table.

"Beautiful ring by the way. Expensive?" He gestured to the princess-cut diamond.

Dhanraj blood rushed to Sheetal's head, and she straightened her posture. "Ten carats."

"I'm not surprised. A beautiful woman like you deserves beautiful things."

Sheetal sucked in her lip regretting her tone. Did it really matter if the ring was ten, twelve or fifteen carats? Arvind had simply shown appreciation, and in typical Dhanraj manner, she patronized him. "I'm sorry. I didn't—I shouldn't have said that. How's your family?"

"My parents died a few years after I left Raigun. They were driving from Lower Mansali to meet me up here, but their bus swerved to avoid colliding with an oncoming lorry, over-turned and fell down a cliff. Everyone died."

Her throat tightened. "I'm so sorry. How did you cope?"

"The same way everyone else does with loss and grief."

Sheetal swallowed the lump. "Mama told me you had visited my family after I married."

"I did. To let her know she need not worry. That I was out of your life forever and leaving Raigun. What was I thinking when I came for you that day?" He shook his head. "How on earth did I think I could barge in and whisk you off? Such a fool!"

"You're not."

"So, you're saying you would have come with me?"

"You know, I—"

"Of course not. I understand now but I didn't then."

"I had asked Kavita to give you a letter some time before I married but found out recently, she didn't."

"A letter for what? Another goodbye?" His tone mocked.

"A letter asking you to wait for me. I needed time to prove my marriage to Rakesh wasn't working. I planned to divorce Rakesh and then I'd be free to marry you. But you'd already left."

"What else did you expect? I risked my life climbing your balcony, but you were hell-bent on marrying Mr. Millionaire."

Why couldn't he leave Rakesh alone? "So...what about your Ph.D?" She broached the topic.

"What about it?"

"I'm assuming you must have taken a transfer and completed your degree."

"Delhi University."

"And your family? How many children do you have?" A knot clenched her stomach.

"Sixteen."

Sheetal reached for the *mangalsutra* around her neck and rolled the sacred gold and black beads validating her married status.

"Boys. All sixteen of them by the way."

He hadn't lost his sense of humor.

"Oh, come on, Sheetal. It's a joke, for God's sake. Every single boy under my care is like my own. Lighten up."

"What about your wife?"

"What about her?"

"Where is she? Here?"

He raised his eyebrows and grinned.

Her forehead throbbed. "So where is she?"

"Who?"

"Your wife."

"Why?"

"Why, what?"

"Why do you want to know about my wife? What difference does it make where she lives, how she lives and what she does?"

"What difference does the size or cost of this ring make? You asked. I answered. Now it's your turn."

"In ten years did you think of me?"

Why was he using that rigid tone of voice? "I'm married, Arvind. I have a child and family."

"And I was nothing but a joke in your life."

"I didn't have a choice."

"You didn't have the guts."

Anger seethed. "I was going to end my marriage to be with you. I just told you but the letter—"

He jumped out his chair, pulled the seat in front, grating metal against floor and sat across the table. "Did you?"

"How could I when you left? What was I supposed to do?"

"Did you have the guts to end your marriage first and *then* come find me?"

"How do you expect—"

"Did you ask around for me? I had told a bunch of our friends where I was heading—Kavita and Gaurav included."

"Kavita never told me." It wasn't just Kavita's fault. Sheetal had also not reached out to Kavita because the distinction in her status as a Dhanraj elevated her to a level where Mummyji would have only belittled her friends who didn't measure up. Still, Kavita could have at least called to share the information. "If Kavita had called me—"

"Forget it, Sheetal. Some things are not meant to be. Besides, I'm over it."

Guilt clawed at her heart. "Well, I guess that makes two of us then."

"Where's your sense of humor?"

"I don't see anything funny in what we've discussed, and I don't see either of us laughing."

"You used to. Seems like you don't anymore."

She looked past him to several waiters serving customers as the storm raged outside. She used to be so much more.

"Do you know I was supposed to pick up my parents from Lower

Mansali, but they said not to bother and they'd manage on their own because it was just a three-hour uphill ride. They died, but I'm still here. How do you think that makes me feel?"

What if he had died? The breath caught in her throat. How would she have ever known?

Just then a beeping disturbed the silence between them, and Arvind flicked open his mobile. "Hello? Arvind speaking. Yes. I know. I'm stuck at Jatinder Bhai's because of the storm."

The wind howled, and Sheetal reached out to warm her hands near the heater.

He switched off the phone and placed it on the table. "I was naïve and foolish to choose you above everything. But that's how much I loved you. Gave up everything for you, and you left me for everything."

The blood rushed to her head. What was there for him to give up when he had nothing to lose? How could she have left everything for Arvind when Mama and Papa never meant for her to go with him in the first place? He just turned up on the balcony on her wedding day expecting her to elope.

"So how is that husband of yours?"

"His name is Rakesh."

"All these high-flying marriages make headlines, you know. Sometimes ordinary people like us happen to read. Rakesh has been in the papers quite a bit. Just wondering, that's all."

The company, no doubt. "We're happily married."

"Acchha hai." He nodded. "Even though I didn't ask. Still, good to know you're both still together."

"Why wouldn't we be?"

"You read about so many break-ups and divorces nowadays."

"We're very happy."

"Good. At least one of us is."

"What do you mean?"

"One tomato shorba. Very, very hot. And one hot coffee." Jatinder bellowed rushing over with two trays. "I bringing myself." He planted one tray with the bowl of soup and another with a cup of black coffee, a small steel pot of milk and cubes of sugar in a steel bowl on the table. Then he wiped his hands on the green towel and placed two metal spoons, one on each tray. "Chotta Baba, dosa. I know. I remember and come back again. Bringing, Madame."

"Arrey, *yaar. Jattu Bhai!*" Arvind's eyes sparkled with mischief as he addressed Jatinder with the camaraderie reserved for close friends. "Be cool. What's with all the formality? Join us and have some..."

"Many customers waiting. I must attending first." Jatinder Bhai left.

Arvind poured milk into the coffee. "Sugar?" he asked.

In ten years, Rakesh had never asked how much sugar she wanted.

"Three, please."

He added three cubes of sugar in her cup and swirled the liquid with a spoon. "That's a lot. Not good for you." He tapped the spoon gently against the cup's edge and laid it to rest on the saucer. "Be careful. It's hot." He slid the cup and saucer toward her with both hands.

"Still giving free advice?"

"It's for your own good. Besides, bad habits are hard to break."

Sheetal wrapped her fingers around the cup, her attention on the wall of snow outside. Would they be stuck here all night? Soft warmth seeped and she pressed her fingers down on the cup absorbed in the warm towel-like comfort. She ran her thumb along the porcelain's rim and closed her palms tight around the cup to soak in the moment. A fire ignited her soul.

"Sheetal?" Arvind said.

Was the heater on too high?

"Sheetal, my hands."

She looked down. Her fingers were wrapped around Arvind's. She pulled away. "I'm sorry. I didn't—"

"It's okay. Bad habits are hard to break." He pinched the cup by the handle, centered it in the palm of a free hand and offered her the drink. "Just the way you like it. Hot and sweet."

Sheetal opened her palm, but he didn't hand over the cup. Clearly, he wanted her to make the first move. She pinched the cup by the handle, laid an open palm below the raised cup, and the coffee slush-sloshed gently lapping the past and present against the porcelain's edge. One cup. One moment to keep. She lowered the cup in her open palm trapped between the warmth of Arvind's hand and the coffee's heat. "Your soup is cooling."

He curled his fingers around her palm and said nothing.

"Arvind, let go."

"I did, ten years ago."

"The cup. The coffee. My hand."

He slid his fingers away out the hammock of her palm, and Sheetal curled her fingers around his.

"Sheetal, let go."

"I didn't mean to."

He pulled away and drops of coffee spilled over the cup's edge and dribbled down Sheetal's fingers.

"Hot, hot dosa coming!" Jatinder returned with a tray of food.

Sheetal put the cup to rest on the saucer's center.

The paper-thin white and golden rice crepe, about one-foot wide and rolled into a tube, oozed with a spicy yellow potato filling. The top fold hung over the crepe like a tongue and pointed at two bowls, one filled with *sambhar*, a spicy brown lentil soup, and the other a light green coconut chutney.

"Hot off *tava*!" Jatinder referred to the large iron griddle the white liquid dosa batter cooked on. "Arvind, yaar..."

Sheetal looked up and gestured for Yash to come back. However, Yash shook his head and held up a comic. "Your dosa is here," Sheetal mouthed. "It will get cold."

"Not now," he mouthed back. "I'm reading."

"So, you two knowing each other?" Jatinder asked.

"From college," Arvind replied.

"Good. Very good."

"We're just old acquaintances," Arvind added.

"You tell me acquaintancing?" Jatinder teased Arvind in Hindi. "But I am seeing more in your eyes."

Heat steamed from the dosa, rose up Sheetal's neck, spread along her shoulders, and she turned away in embarrassment.

"Don't mind him," Arvind interrupted. "Jatinder's like an older brother, always watching out for me and saying more than he should."

"An old friend, Madame. Who is knowing more, but not understanding why Arvind Bhai still not marrying. For whom he is waiting? When some woman he loving many years ago is long time married."

"Jattu Bhai." Arvind's tone tensed. "I'll have a coffee as well."

"First you say soup, then coffee." Jatinder shook his head. "Drinking two-two at same time not good for digestion. It not taking troubles away. Chotta Baba looking like he is reading so I am changing this dosa and getting another hot, crispy one." Then he left with the dish.

"So, who are you waiting for?" Sheetal asked.

"No one." Arvind looked away.

"Jatinder said you never married."

"So?"

"You're alone." She was married and still so alone.

"It means nothing."

"But you're not sharing your life with anyone."

"You share a life when you have someone to live for. To live with."

"Then find that someone."

"I did. She left me."

"I'm here," Sheetal whispered.

"You're not the Sheetal I know. What does all this mean anyway? You, here, in front of me one minute and gone the next."

"You can marry and start a new life."

"I'm not like you. There's a difference."

"What's happened, happened. We should forget it and move on." By not marrying and settling down Arvind only worsened the pain. She sipped the hot coffee and almost burned her tongue.

Arvind stirred the shorba and raised the spoon to his lips.

She remembered sitting across from him at the Barista on campus and listening to him talk about playing cricket in scruffs and ripped jeans with friends on *maidans*, deserted barren grounds. Whenever the ball went off-field, Arvind volunteered to sidle between ripped wire fences and slide through the gaps between broken walls despite scratches and bruises from previous games, and she would listen about his brave feats. "I'm sorry."

"For what?"

Sheetal took a sip, lowered the cup on the saucer, swiveled the cup's handle and hunched over her drink.

Arvind leaned forward and their foreheads almost met.

"Turning you down that day. I didn't mean to hurt you." She ran a thumb over the cup's rim.

"Like you said, what happened, happened. We should forget it and move on with our lives. I want you to know I haven't forgotten our time together. I've never forgiven myself since." The warmth of his mocha breath washed over each exhale.

"Neither have I."

"For turning you away the way I did."

"For loving you the way I did."

"It's different."

"What's different?" She dipped the spoon in her coffee and swirled the milky brown liquid. "Look, what I did to you was wrong and I live with the guilt every day."

"Every day?" He stirred the soup.

"Every day."

"Every hour?"

"Every hour."

"Every minute?"

"Every minute."

"Every—"

"Second." She stole the word right out of his mouth.

"Then it was worth it because at least you thought of me and didn't forget."

The air thickened. This conversation was only going to stir up the past and fill her cup with more regrets, but she couldn't help it. "I don't think I ever stopped loving you."

"Then tell me, if things had been different, would you have chosen me instead?" He stirred the soup again.

She leaned against the chair's backrest and looked at the wall of snow outside the window. "Does it matter? It's over. We can't change—"

"Anything. I know. But for my peace of mind so that I can believe you really did love me."

"I gave Kavita a letter. Isn't that proof? I can't help or change the fact that she didn't give it to you and didn't tell me of your where-abouts. I wish I had an answer, but this is all I can offer for now."

He laid his spoon to rest. "I still wish you'd run away with me that day."

Her attention flickered from his soup to the coffee and back. Two different liquids in two different worlds and ten years later here they were stirring up the past on one table.

"*Dost?*" He held out a hand in an offer of truce.

She stretched out her hand. "Friends." She slid her fingers between his warm brown skin. His grip tightened, and her breath stilled. Then he coughed, she withdrew and fished her wallet out of the handbag and placed it on the table. "I'm paying."

"No arguments. I've been paying all my life." He winked. "Now, no more of the past. How about a new beginning and a new intro-duction? Hi. I'm Arvind Chopra."

"Sheetal Dhanraj."

"*Arrey! Garam garam dosa!*" Jatinder Bhai meandered toward

them, armed with another tray. "Crisp. Crunchy! Hot. Very hot." He set the tray on the table, excused himself, and left.

Sheetal glanced at Arvind, the steaming dosa, and then back at him again. Desire rose whirling up her soul in a vortex of hunger.

Yes. This one was hot.

Oh, so very very hot.

THE TAXI PULLED UP OUTSIDE THE HOLIDAY INN, AND SHEETAL FISHED IN HER handbag for her wallet. However, her fingers scraped the interior of a pocket lining, and she bit her lower lip in despair. She zipped open another section and then another but in vain.

The valet opened the passenger door, but Sheetal didn't step out. "I seem to have misplaced my wallet." She looked at the driver in the rear-view mirror.

The driver raised his eyebrows. "Waah, Madame! You are forgetting your wallet somewhere, but I still having to feed my family tonight."

"Oh no. I'll make sure you get paid. Please, wait here." She exited the *Fiat*, walked up the granite steps, through the sliding double-glass doors and headed for the reception counter.

"Good evening, Mrs. Dhanraj." A young man in a suit and tie looked up from behind his monitor. "How can I help you?"

"I think I left my wallet somewhere and I need to pay the taxi driver outside."

"Not a problem, Ma'am. We can pay him for you, in cash?"

"Yes, please. And charge the amount on my card."

"Will do. Please enjoy the rest of your evening."

THAT EVENING, SHEETAL FLIPPED OPEN THE LID OF HER SUITCASE, RAN HER fingers along the inner pockets and corners of salwar suits, trousers and jumpers—but in vain. She searched under the duvet, the floral bed skirt, and ran her hand between the narrow slits of the sofa cushions. Nothing. She pulled open two drawers in the bureau and sifted through an array of lipsticks, cases of compact powder, blush and lip pencils then slammed the drawers shut. How could she be so absent-minded? She'd planned to have an early dinner, pack the remainder of her luggage for tomorrow's journey back home, and give herself what was left of the evening to watch a little TV and settle her edgy nerves. She had to start forgetting Arvind and return to life as a Dhanraj.

She mentally retraced her steps, recalling that she'd paid for the meal at Jatinder's cafe, dropped Yash off at St. Paul's after the storm passed, then rode the same taxi back to the Holiday Inn. Which meant only one thing. The wallet was at Jatinder's café.

A ringing pierced the silence. She glanced at the phone docked beside a digital clock and lamp on the bedside table. It was 8 p.m. Whom could it be at this hour? Laundry? Room service? She hadn't ordered anything. She grabbed the receiver and pressed it to her ear. "Hello?"

"Hello, Mrs. Dhanraj?" a male voice asked on the other end.

"Yes?"

"There's a gentleman here to see you."

"Who?"

"He says he has your wallet."

Jatinder Singh! Sheetal exhaled in relief. "I'm coming." She returned the phone to the cradle, took the elevator down to the lobby and rushed over to the young man behind the reception desk.

"Excuse me. I got a call just now about someone here to return my wallet?"

The receptionist pointed behind her shoulder.

Sheetal turned and the breath caught in her throat. "Arvind. What are you doing here?"

"You left this." He handed the wallet over. "I figured you couldn't leave without it."

Sheetal reached for the leather wallet and pressed it between her palms as two bellboys helped guests check in with their luggage. "Thank you. I turned my suitcase, clothes and the whole room upside down looking for it."

"I'm not surprised. And since I was on my way here, I thought I'd give you something I picked up the other day." He gave her a cardboard box that fit in the palms of both hands.

Sheetal pulled open the upper flap and gasped at the glass jewelry box the toothless old woman had been trying to sell her. "It's beautiful!"

"The lady told me you liked it. Nothing much but something perhaps to remember your trip here?"

Feeling the press of the receptionist's and bell boys' stares, Sheetal led Arvind to a corner sofa on the far left, held up the jewelry box against the crystal chandelier and marveled at pink, green and orange blocks of light on the walls behind.

"Arrey, can you believe she charged me four hundred and fifty? I told her I was buying it for you, the gori gori memsahib she had quoted three hundred the other day. But the old croon refused to back down. Anyway, it's worth every rupee as long as you like it."

"I love it."

"Well...I guess I should get going. You leave tomorrow, right?"

"Yes."

"Have a safe trip and take care." He turned and headed for the glass doors.

"Wait."

He stopped and turned.

She melted in the liquid brown of his eyes, desperate for him to stay. "Yash!"

"What about Yash?"

"Tell him I'll be there after school to pick him up tomorrow."

"Fine." He nodded. "Any other message for a messenger at your service?"

"No." She pressed the wallet close to her chest, ran her thumb over the leathery texture and clung to the fragrance of musk as Arvind walked out the door.

Sheetal returned to her room, changed into a lace-frilled white satin nighty, switched off the lights and pressed the wallet between both palms, lying awake in bed. She tried to sleep, but sleep wouldn't come. She tossed and turned thinking about how the strands of Arvind's hair cascaded in black waves. And what about the warm glow of his coppery skin in the lobby's light? And the feel of his palm against her hand. She closed her eyes.

A knock sounded, and Sheetal sat up. Another knock came. "Who is it?" she called out.

"Arvind."

She glanced at the clock. 10 p.m. What could Arvind possibly want to discuss at this hour? Her heart raced. "What are you doing here?"

"We need to talk."

"I—" Sheetal swung her feet over the mattress and switched on the table lamp. Then she walked down the narrow passageway and pressed her palm on the door. "Arvind?"

"I understand it's late but—"

"How did you know my room number?"

"Yash told me."

"I can't let you in."

"We need to talk, Sheetal."

She slid the chain latch in place, cracked open the door and peered through the inch-wide slit. Their eyes locked and she ran a hand down her hip. Seven thin diamond bangles tinkled along her wrist. "Just give me a minute." She closed the door, donned a matching silk gown and tied the ribbon around her waist. They would talk in the corridor outside, certainly not in the privacy of the room. She unlocked the door, swung it open and stepped out on the velvety maroon carpet when a lift door on the far right glided open.

Sheetal grabbed Arvind by the sleeve of his jacket, pulled him in and locked the door.

The scent of musk filled every corner of the room, and she let go.

"This isn't a good idea. I shouldn't be here." He turned round to leave, and Sheetal grabbed him by the arm.

"You're obviously here for something important."

"I...I had to see you one last time."

She closed her eyes and took a deep breath. Musk. Musk. Everywhere. "And here you are, with me."

He leaned toward her, and the soft hairs of his French beard grazed her cheek. "And you with me."

She raised her head, glided her lips across his jaw and the fuzz of his beard pricked ever so gently. She took a deep breath, dragged herself away and looked into his eyes, her reflection a watery imprint. He slid an arm around her waist, and she pulled herself to him running her fingers up the blue-and-white-checkered shirt. She peeled the jacket off his shoulders. The garment hit the floor with a thud as bangles tinkled down her wrist.

"Sheetal—"

"Shhh." She slid seven white buttons running down his chest out the checkered holes, parted the ocean of cotton fabric and rolled the shirt off his shoulders. His taut copper contours gleamed in the soft yellow light and he tilted his head down. Sheetal joined both hands behind his neck, pulled him to her, and the scent of mocha revved through her veins as his lips pressed on hers.

"We shouldn't." His manhood pulsed through the thin film of her nighty and a wetness surged between the 'V' of her legs. She ran her fingers along the gentle swell of his chest, so soft and comforting like a Geoffrey Beene. The fabric of a true man.

"Sheetal."

"Shhh." She raised a finger to his lips. *Hot.* She shivered. *Cold.* She tightened her lips. *Dry.* She rubbed her legs together. *Moist.* She brushed her lips across his, but he stiffened and pinned his hands by his side. "What's wrong? Aren't you... don't you?" She let a finger trail down his chest.

"I can't."

"I belong to you. I always did." She kissed him long and hard and swallowed. Sadness whirlpooled into the empty karva of her soul.

He swelled. He throbbed. He pulsed. He hardened against her with a mountain lion's force as desire burned. His lips coaxed hers apart in warm undulating waves. He teased her lower lip with gentle licks, then ever so slowly trailed a finger down to her waist and the satin belt came undone. "We don't have to do this." He pulled away and curled his fingers into a fist as the gown slid down her arms.

She coaxed his fingers out from hiding and pulled them to her waist.

He wrapped her in a pashmina embrace and ran his fingers through her silky hair gently brushing the spaghetti straps aside. The nighty peeled off her shoulders and the satin hooped around her feet. He trailed his finger along the curve of her breast, and her nipples hardened. A cool blast of air caused her to stagger and lose balance. Then he removed his belt and trousers, scooped her into his arms and laid her on the bed.

He eased on top and rained kisses on her eyes, cheeks and lips with the gentleness of snow flurries. She rubbed against him, and a vortex of heat spiraled. She loved him. Oh, how she loved the feel of him and yearned to be loved by a man. She pulled him closer, tighter, harder, and melted in the sweat oozing between their bodies as the air-conditioner hummed in the background.

An eerie chime pealed, and Sheetal waited for the ring to die.

Arvind pulled away, his attention fixed on a center point between her eyebrows.

She touched her forehead. The bindi. She peeled it off.

"You're married, Sheetal. This is so wrong."

This was wrong. But it felt so right. Sheetal flicked the bindi and the earthy scent of his forest rain filled her with a euphoria she had never known. She rained kisses on his chest, and he ran his fingers down her thighs, tugging off one last fabric between them. She felt so loved. So warm. So free. "Take me."

He peeled the bangles down her hand and coined them on the bedside table.

Inhibition. Clink.

Restraint. Clink.

Honor. Clink.

Prestige. Clink.

Integrity. Clink.

Unacceptable. Clink.

Forbidden. Clink.

He kissed her long and hard and tides of pleasure welled up her being. He entered and filled her with forest rain quenching hidden desires.

Sheetal dug her fingers into his arms with a promise to never let go.

SHEETAL RAN A HAND ALONG THE MATTRESS, HER EYES HEAVY WITH SLEEP. She willed them open, and in the soft yellow light discerned an empty pillow crowned with the jewelry box. She rolled to the side, and something wedged between her and the mattress. She scooped it out, curled her fingers around the wallet, pressed it to her cheek and inhaled the scent of musk.

Here one minute and gone the next, like a dream.

13
RETURN

The next morning, Rakesh pressed the phone to his ear and a trail of rings thrummed away. He ended the call and glanced at his watch. Nine thirty. He had called Sheetal last night—not once, but twice—to let her know he had taken her advice and would take care of his health from now on. He paced the office and called again.

"Hello?" It was Sheetal. "Rakesh? Is that you? I was going to call this morning, but I overslept."

He pressed the phone against his ear. The sound of her voice didn't feel right. She sounded too casual. Too carefree. "I called last night. Where were the hell were you?"

"Here. In the room. Where else would I be?"

Attitude? "So why didn't you pick up the phone?"

"I was asleep."

At ten? "You never sleep early."

"I... I was tired from all the packing. You won't believe what happened yesterday. Yash and I—we..."

She ranted on about some snowstorm they got caught up in yesterday afternoon and how they took cover in a dingy restaurant.

Then some bullshit about the freezing weather and the greedy school principal. Going on and on. "How is Yash?"

"Fine. He's grown. A little taller. Smarter. Chatty. I didn't realize how much I miss him."

"We wouldn't be missing Yash if he was with us." First Pushpa. Now Sheetal. Both out to keep him away from his son. "I saw Dr. Kishore yesterday."

"What did he say?"

"If you were here and not in Mansali, you would know."

"I told you to see him last week when I was there, but you didn't listen. And now when I'm away you go on your own and conveniently blame me?"

"If you were here, I wouldn't be alone."

"Rakesh, you knew I was going away for the week. You gave me the tickets yourself and you didn't even book a room for me. I tried calling you several times, but you don't pick up the phone or bother to call back."

"I told Reshma."

"You leave my hotel reservations for a member of staff? Couldn't you do this one thing yourself?"

"Reshma handles all travel arrangements. Besides, I was tied up with work."

"I'm your wife, not a client. I go out of my way to do everything for you, and you don't even have time to…"

She was not going to let this go.

"Do you know how much trouble I had at check-in? They—"

"I'm getting a series of tests done this morning. More blood work and CT scans."

"Is it serious?"

"We'll talk later. You leave today."

"I know."

"You sound—never mind."

"I missed you."

His attention meandered to the Raigun skyline and buildings jostling for space.

"Oh, and I forgot to tell you. Yash got a lead role in this year's spring concert. He's presenting and—"

"Give me a call when you're thirty minutes from the station. I'll pick you up."

14
SNAKEBITE

Sheetal, Rakesh and Yash were playing a game of Snakes and Ladders on the carpet in Yash's room. Sheetal rolled a die, moved her counter two spaces, and waited for Yash to play his turn.

Rakesh lay on his right propped on an elbow, parallel to the board's black and white tiles across from Sheetal. He cupped the right cheek in his palm while the other hand rest gently along his thigh. He cracked jokes and laughed every time he moved his counter down one of the colorful snakes, carefree and at ease in a way Sheetal hadn't seen in a long time.

Yash sat cross-legged between the two, his back to the bed. He scooped the die and rolled it on the board. "Six!" he squealed. "Extra turn for me!"

According to the rules, a six did not give the player an extra turn. However, Sheetal and Rakesh allowed Yash the bonus with the hope he'd win.

Yash moved his yellow counter and Sheetal's attention wandered to clusters of miniature 'Thomas the Trains' printed on the light blue duvet behind him. His bed, in the shape of a sports car, had been custom designed and imported from the U.S. six years ago. Since Yash had grown taller, the bed now fell short and would need replacement. The panel of curtains stamped with matching smiley-faced trains reminded her as if it had only been yesterday when she'd chosen the theme and coordinated the accessories well before Yash had transitioned from the nursery where she spent the last few months of her pregnancy into a room of his own.

Yash rolled the die, and the red cube bounced and glided across the board and stopped at the tip of Rakesh's finger. "Six again!" Yash slid his counter forward by six. "May I have the die please, Dad?" He straightened his back against the bed and waited.

"Of course, you may." Rakesh handed over the die.

May? Please? Sheetal remembered when Yash was six and how he grabbed the die on every turn. Last summer, however, he tucked a napkin in his shirt collar and waited until he finished chewing before popping in the next mouthful. Six months later, here he was, waiting politely for his turn and using a grown-up voice. However, this morning when she caught Yash in Rakesh's closet secretly trying on Rakesh's leather Bally shoes, her heart knotted. She asked what he was doing.

Yash raised his foot with the shoe dangling on the tips of his toes and despite the six-inch gap between the heel and the back curve, he squealed, "Look, Mom! I'm almost like Dad!"

Her chest tightened. Yash didn't need to fill Rakesh's shoes.

Yash rolled the die, moved his counter by four spaces, and handed the die to Rakesh.

Rakesh blew some air into the crevice between his thumb and index finger, made a wish and let go. "Five? Come on, five!"

The die knocked against Yash's toe and stopped. "No, two!" Yash moved Rakesh's counter to ninety-seven, then all the way down the snake's body to thirty-five. "Now, you're last. I'm first."

"Oh no." Rakesh feigned disappointment.

"My turn." Yash waited for Rakesh to hand over the die and then rolled it on the board.

"Ah-ha!" Rakesh sat up. "Three, and down you go."

Yash slid the yellow counter down a green snake, then drilled both elbows into his knees and cupped his chin in the palms of his hands. "Not fair. Now I'm last."

"That's life. You can't always be number one. Sometimes life is fair, sometimes it isn't."

"But I want to win," Yash whined, like his former five-year-old self.

"Don't we all? Anyway, it's just a game. One minute you're up a ladder, next minute down a snake. You'll be up again, soon. Your turn." He rolled the die toward Sheetal.

Sheetal scooped the die and tossed it on the board. The diamond bangles tinkled down her wrist, and she saw the jacket peeling off Arvind's shoulders. "Seven." She moved the counter seven spaces.

"Sheetal—"

"Shhh." She wove the counter in and out of the tiles' borders, remembering the feel of seven buttons sliding out of Arvind's checkered shirt. "We shouldn't."

"Shouldn't what, Sheetal?" He sounded annoyed.

"Oh, it's nothing."

"Seven, Sheetal?"

She blinked, and the board crystallized into view. She'd crossed seven tiles with the roll of a die. "Oh, I didn't realize." She pulled the counter back one space.

"You rolled a five. Look." He pointed to the '5' on the die. "How can you miss that?"

"Like how you forgot my hotel reservation? Besides, didn't you say it's just a game."

"Little slips happen. It's not like you were out on the streets because you didn't get a room. Anyway, in case you didn't notice you missed two turns before. If you're not interested, you don't have to play." Rakesh played his turn and the die accidentally whacked Sheetal's counter and threw her off several squares down to one.

Yash followed Rakesh's lead, not bothering to give Sheetal a turn and leaving her at the bottom, alone.

A STRING OF ADVERTISEMENTS BLARED ON THE TV AS YASH SLEPT ON THE sofa with his head on Sheetal's lap and his feet pointed three cushions away toward Rakesh. Sheetal ran her fingers through Yash's hair as the TV cast shadows on the half-empty bottle of Blue Label to Rakesh's left and a cigar burning on an ashtray.

"How did the appointment go with Dr. Kishore?"

Rakesh raised the glass of scotch to his lips and drained the liquid. "*My* problem. *I* deal with it."

"It's not just your problem."

"It is."

"I can help."

"How?"

"Tell me what the doctor said."

"Fuck off alcohol. Can you help? No. Happy?"

Sheetal winced. "At least mind your language when Yash is here. When will we know the results of recent blood work and scan?" She looked across at the burning cigar. "Can you put that out? The smoke is harmful."

"I was minding my own business and you two decided to join me. I didn't ask you to. Besides, Yash's sleeping, and he doesn't know."

"He's breathing the same air."

"He can't see."

Sheetal turned to the TV screen. "He doesn't need to know. The secondary smoke will affect him."

"Don't know what your problem is. Every time..."

Sheetal closed her eyes, placed her palm on Yash's ear and

pressed her head into the sofa's backrest. The cushion absorbed her in the warmth and comfort of Arvind's embrace.

"What the hell am I supposed to do? Just give it up? Who do you think you are? And what fucking…"

You share a life when you have someone to live for. Arvind's voice melted her heart. *To live with.* She cracked her eyelids open and shadows flickering on the ceiling reminded her of that night. *I did. She left me.* She tightened the pallu around her shoulders. So warm. So silky. Like Arvind's pashmina embrace.

"Sheetal!"

She swallowed and semi-sweet mocha glided down her throat.

"Are you fucking listening to…"

She gently woke up Yash, helped him to his feet and from the corner of her eye noticed the stub of the cigar at the end of its life.

"That's it? Walk off? Are you…?"

Sheetal left Rakesh with his alcohol, cigar and advertisements blaring in the background. The way he deserved to be left. Alone.

THE ENTIRE DHANRAJ MANSION HAD BEEN THOROUGHLY CLEANED AND strewn with strings of colorful light bulbs and tinsel for Diwali, the Hindu Festival of Lights. Sheetal, Rakesh and Yash were dressed in their finest to join the family for prayers and were ready to go downstairs when Rakesh ducked into his closet, pulled out a shiny blue package and gave it to Yash.

"A surprise? For me?" Yash's eyes twinkled in excitement.

"That's right. For you." Rakesh sat on the carpeted floor beside Yash, tucked the cream-colored knee-length kurta trimmed with brown and gold embroidery under the seat of his baggy silk trousers that were tapered at the ankles and crossed his legs. Sheetal had never seen Rakesh sit on the floor and give anyone so much time and attention which could only mean the gift had to be something special.

"Is it my Diwali gift?" Yash peeled off the shiny blue wrapper.

"It's more than that."

Yash tossed the wrapping, cracked open the box's lid and unraveled the neatly folded clothes. "It's a kurta pajama." He frowned.

"Like the one I'm wearing. I had one made for you so we can look the same."

Yash dropped the kurta and the creamy brown shirt littered Rakesh's radius.

"Wear it. We'll look the same. Like father and son."

Sheetal turned to Yash. "You'll look just like your dad. Isn't that what you've wanted for so long?"

"I don't want to look like him," Yash replied.

Sheetal placed a hand on Yash's shoulder. "Why do you say that?"

"Because all he does is drink that stuff and stink of smoke. And if I'm like him, I'll have to do the same."

"That's not how it—it's not all your dad does." From the corner of her eye, she saw Rakesh's expression fall. She had to act quick before Rakesh lost his temper.

Yash leaned toward Rakesh, took a deep breath, and wrinkled his nose. "He smells. See! You can smell him. My teacher says smoking is bad."

Rakesh's expression tightened and he looked away.

"Yash, I understand. There are some not-so-good things in life. How about if Daddy promises not to do it again?"

"I heard you both talk last night. All he ever does is shout at you. I don't want to shout at you." Yash marched toward the door, stamped the clothes on his way out, then slammed the door behind him.

Rakesh rose to his feet. "Who asked you to bring him into the TV lounge last night? I was sitting by myself, minding my own business but you just had to ruin it. See what you did? And now you make promises on my behalf?"

"He didn't mean it that way," Sheetal protested in Yash's defense. "He's only eight. He probably just—"

"Knows what he wants. It's not me. And it's all because of you."

That evening Sheetal convinced Yash to wear Rakesh's gift for the Diwali Lakshmi puja. The Dhanrajs congregated in the home temple at 6:30 p.m. and Sheetal stood between Rakesh and Yash as Mummyji conducted the prayers.

Both Rakesh and Yash stood palms pressed together in prayer, postures erect, heels of both feet touching and toes fanned slightly apart. Even the way their heads bowed ever so slightly in prayer to show reverence but not submission, was identical. Rakesh's once titanium-and-steel complexion tarnished over time, however, contrasted with Yash's milky-white skin that glowed with highlights of pink around the ears, cheeks and lips. The left side of Rakesh's temple pulsed in sporadic intervals. Cracks ran along the contours of his face as his nostrils flared intermittently while Yash barely flinched.

Carved from death, Rakesh reflected ice.

Carved from blood, Yash reflected life.

That night as firecrackers whistled in the night sky Sheetal rolled on the bed to face Rakesh, unable to sleep from the noise and fatigue of the day's celebrations.

Rakesh's bare skin and blue veins branching across his body glowed under the light of the moonbeam spilling in through the window and a net of yellow cast by her bedside lamp.

Sheetal rolled to the other side and chunks of pink, green and orange light from the jewelry box stamped the walls. Sheetal ran a thumb around the glass case's edge and dangled a finger in the hollow cavity flooded with colors. Rakesh hadn't commented about the case. Perhaps he didn't notice it, or like most things, he didn't care to. Perhaps now that Yash had spoken the truth and pointed out Rakesh's deficiencies Rakesh would change for the better.

Something cold touched Sheetal's arm, and she edged away, toward the lamp. Rakesh locked her wrist and yanked her to him, but she peeled off his fingers. He grabbed her by the thigh and drilled the pointed tips of his chapped, rough fingers causing pain to sear up her leg. She was not giving in. She dug her toes into the mattress and pushed away. However, he pulled her with force. She kicked, but he locked her legs with his. She opened her mouth to breathe, but he clamped against her lips, and his breath filled her with the stench of stale alcohol and cigar fumes.

Sheetal flattened a palm on his chest, spikes of cactus-coarse hair pricked, and she pushed him away. "What's wrong with you?"

"You turned Yash against me." He grabbed her by the wrist. "You brought him in the lounge on purpose last night so he'd hate me."

"What are you talking about?"

"You want Yash all to yourself. Admit it."

She struggled against his grip, but he held on.

"You're so fucking overprotective; I wouldn't be surprised if he turned out to be the biggest coward on earth like you."

Bile raced up her throat. "You don't know what you're saying. I only wanted to talk to you about Dr. Kishore. But you're so obsessed with yourself—"

"Fuck Dr. Kishore! You don't care about anyone but you." His acrid breath washed over.

"Rakesh. Let go."

"Why? Don't you want me now?"

"That was then, Rakesh. Before...before—"

He stamped her with saliva-coated kisses reeking of vomit and pummeled her inside until he was done. Then like shreds of shiny, blue wrapping, he left her bruised, in pain, turned his back to her and slept.

15
KALEIDOSCOPE

With Diwali out the way, Sheetal found relief in the series of Himalayan Mountain ranges due on December fifteenth. With a two-week deadline and one completed painting in the series of ten, determination crept in not to compromise the caliber of work and earnings for anyone this time. With a fifty-thousand-rupee advance in her bank account, Sheetal was not going to lose out on the remaining portion.

She was heading for her studio, mentally mapping out the position of lake, mountains, and the angle at which sunlight should crack through the clouds to cast a net on the valley for the next painting when Mummyji's voice and Yash's giggles caught her attention. Sheetal peered over the balcony railing to the ground floor.

Mummyji and Yash sat on the Fulton White sofas and Mummyji squeezed fingernail-sized discs of Gems—chocolate discs coated in colorful, glossy enamel—in Yash's palm. Since Yash's return, Mummyji had been pampering Yash with Cadbury chocolates and trips to the toy store like every grandmother was entitled to. However, it was really a strategy to barter private information about her and Rakesh for chocolates which meant Mummyji was up to no good.

In the past, Sheetal had managed to coax Yash to refrain from divulging details, but with a stockpile of chocolates and toys pooled in plastic bags above the pewter elephants' heads, these grand-motherly sessions would lead to more than tooth decay.

Sheetal rushed downstairs. "Oh my. All that will upset Yash's tummy." She feigned surprise at the Gems overflowing Yash's palm.

"Now, now, I tell you." Mummyji looked up and scrunched her nose. "No need to get fussy over a few small treats. Not like he'll eat it all at once. All you young mothers nowadays, Hai Ishwar! Always complaining. Too much sugar, too much fat, too much—"

Yash tilted his palm a little too far, and Gems scattered on the floor.

"He can barely manage what you've given. Besides, too much of anything is bad for him." Sheetal refrained from picking up the fallen Gems and leading Yash away because she'd trigger a chain reaction. Mummyji would rave about the incident for weeks until gossip fueled their household and the households of her friends at the club. No doubt everyone would blame Sheetal for instigating a verbal battle and asserting authority over an elderly widow. As long as Mummyji reigned supreme, Sheetal would always be the outsider and a shoulder to carry blame. "Yash, why don't you come with me? I could use some help with my painting." The perfect pretext to lure Yash away considering he loved to watch her paint. Sheetal's cell phone rang, and she pulled the phone out her sari pouch, took the call and turned her back to Mummyji. "Hello?"

"It's me." *Rakesh.*

So, an apology for what he did four nights ago? "What's wrong, now?"

"I was just thinking it would be good for you and Yash to come down to the office today and I could show you both around."

"No."

"I want to spend some quality time with Yash, here."

"I can send Yash over." That would prove she wasn't being over-protective.

"No." He paused. "You, too."

A sudden bout of care and affection? She looked over her shoulder as Mummyji watched her intently.

"I thought time together would do us some good."

"I don't need to be there." She firmed the tone in her voice, moving away from Mummyji's range of hearing.

"As a family, Sheetal. For Yash."

A sudden concern about being a family? Where was this coming from? She pivoted and watched Mummyji pop a Gem in Yash's mouth.

"Hello? You there?"

"Yes." She sighed. Always here and always falling behind on work because of everyone else.

Mummyji pulled out a toy construction set from one of the bags and held it out of Yash's reach. Yash jumped to his feet and grabbed the box from Mummyji.

"We'll be there."

Sheetal and Yash had been waiting for over twenty minutes on leather sofas tucked in a corner in Rakesh's office, but from the pile of papers stacked on his desk, Rakesh didn't look as if he'd be free anytime soon. Yash played on his electronic hand-held PSP while Sheetal flipped through a business magazine. She yawned and breathed in the thick scent of stationery, paper and men's cologne.

"A few more minutes." Rakesh looked up from a document. "I'm almost done."

The wait would extend beyond a few more minutes as always. Experienced in waiting for Rakesh whenever she stopped by the office to go out with him for dinner in the city or shopping after work, Sheetal predicted an hour more of waiting ahead.

A knock sounded.

"Come in," Rakesh said.

The door opened, and Vipul Swampat, one of the company's oldest employees, walked in. Vipul Sahib—a suffix added as a term of respect to Vipul's name because he had worked for Rakesh's father for twelve years and then became Rakesh's right-hand man shortly after Rakesh took over as CEO, was the CFO of Dhanraj & Son. With a career spanning two decades of service to Dhanraj & Son, Vipul Sahib witnessed the company's boom ten years ago when Dhanraj & Son grew into one of India's industrial giants under Rakesh's reign. Vipul Sahib also witnessed the company's recent decline into debt.

Rakesh rose to his feet, marched across the room and greeted the elderly gentleman with a handshake. "Ah, I haven't seen you all morning, Uncle." Renowned as the most trusted employee, Rakesh treated Vipul Sahib with the respect reserved for older members of the family and referred to him as Uncle out of respect.

"I've been busy with that proposal and hope this partnership works out." Vipul Sahib glanced right and opened his arms wide as a huge smile lit up his face. "Well, well!" He crossed the office and his gray eyebrows arched. "Look here! Yash, my boy. How are you?" He hugged Yash.

"Good, *Dada.*" Yash referred to Vipul Sahib as grandfather, out of respect.

"And Sheetal, Beti. How are you?"

"Fine, Uncle," Sheetal replied further respecting the man by calling him Uncle.

"Good, good." Vipul Sahib ran his hands down Yash's shoulders. "With this young man here I'm sure both of you must be fine. It's amazing what children can do in your life—eh? They bring out the best in people. Now, I'll have to catch up with you later, young man." He headed to Rakesh's desk. "We need to schedule more meetings and talks with the Japanese. Open lines of communication. What do you think?"

Sheetal turned a page to a black bottle of Givenchy's men's cologne centering the advertisement.

"I'm thinking partnership. A joint venture," Rakesh said. "We form a third company with them. They give us cash, the brand, and the technology of all their gizmos like washing machines, microwave ovens, refrigerators and stereos. The whole lot. We throw in a few factories, start local manufacturing, handle marketing and distribution and sell their toys. The whole network. 'Toys', according to Rakesh, meant home appliances. "We know the Indian market. They don't."

Tashukomo Electronics wanted an elephant's share of the prospering Indian economy. However, according to India's government policy, the only way any foreign brand could enter the Indian market was through a local partner.

"Tashukomo Electronics agreed to chip in fifty percent." Rakesh handed Vipul Sahib several documents.

"Yes...and two...perhaps three years down the line as we progress...they get to buy us out at a fifty percent premium. That should give them enough incentive to sign the contract and give us the cash we desperately need."

"Check out page six," Rakesh said.

Vipul Sahib ruffled several sheets of paper.

"We'll add a clause that if their products fail, we buy them out at half the value of their stake."

"That's useless," Vipul Sahib shook his head. "Their products will never fail."

"What if we make them fail? It's a question of timing. We keep them buoyant for the initial two years and when their products fail —which we make sure from the get-go—we let go. Meanwhile, we build ties with Borgon. Those multi-national German giants are just waiting to enter the market."

"And what about the Japanese?"

"Use their cash. Improve our balance sheet for now. Repay the bank. Later, they walk out with a loss."

"It's wrong."

Sheetal's throat tightened, and she looked up.

Rakesh glanced in her direction almost as if he'd forgotten she was in the room and sighed. "You're only looking at short-term gain. I'm in for the long haul. Don't you see? Once the Japanese fail, they lose their rep in the market and never sell here again. No one will partner with them in the future."

"It's not right." Vipul Sahib laid the papers on the table. "We're setting a trap for them to walk into. They trust us, and we cheat to win?"

"Whoever wins with the truth anyway?" Rakesh loosened the navy-blue tie around his neck. "It's our only way of bailing out this debt alive and a chance to stand on our feet again with dignity—or be screwed for life."

If anyone found out what he was up to, he'd be in so much trouble. Sheetal pursed her lips. Ten years ago, Mummyji had suggested Sheetal work with Rakesh in the company. However, Rakesh threatened that if she tried, he would never step foot in the house again. Sheetal didn't interfere with company matters and she wasn't about to start now.

"I want to pin them down."

Bubbles of anxiety rippled up her throat. "I don't think it's a good idea, Rakesh." The words slipped, and Sheetal bit her lower lip.

"Really?" Rakesh turned to look at her. "And how does this involve you?"

"You're putting yourself and all of us at risk."

"I think I know how to run this company, thank you." He turned his attention to Vipul Sahib.

"Sheetal is right. There has to be another way." Vipul Sahib ran his fingers through his gray hair. "We'll ruin our reputation forever. Twenty years ago, your father had visions of Dhanraj & Son becoming a household name and a publicly listed company."

"We are." Rakesh paced the room, his forehead creasing with wrinkles. "But we are staying private. This way we have control. We do what we want."

"I agree and we have a responsibility to carry forward that reputation of strength, trust, reliability and—"

"Papa died," Rakesh cut him short, "and his visions for the company are gone. I had never planned to use the company's money for Naina's wedding. But what choice did I have? You know it all, Uncle. You've been with me from the beginning." He stopped pacing and stood behind the black leather chair. "If there's one thing I'll do, it's repay that three hundred and fifty million. I'm a man of my word and I will not shut down the company. I will recover that money however I have to, even if it means squeezing the Japs dry."

"You need to think this through." Vipul Sahib took a seat. "Take a break, son. A vacation. Something. I..."

Rakesh arrested and imprisoned behind bars? Sheetal swallowed. Surely Vipul Sahib would ensure Rakesh changed his mind and did the right thing. However, from the way creases marked Vipul Sahib's forehead and how his shoulders were beginning to droop, she wasn't so sure.

"There's also something I've been meaning to ask you." Vipul Sahib rubbed his chin.

"What?"

"One of our employees, Girish Sharma, he's been with us for five years and came to me last week. His younger sister, twenty-five or twenty-six was in a car accident two weeks ago and has been in the ICU since."

"Shit. How is she now?"

"Not good from what I hear. Everyone's been talking about it. Girish came to me last week asking if we could lend him some money to tide over the medical expenses. They're looking at surgery. Girish's sister—her husband's company, doesn't provide medical insurance like we do."

"How has Girish's performance been?"

"Made quite a name for himself and always on top of things."

"What does the Distribution Department think of him?"

"Their go-to person for any problems. Loyal as hell."

"How much is he asking for?"

"Around three lakhs."

Rakesh paced the room.

"Perhaps you two should meet him first, hear him out and give it some thought," Vipul Sahib suggested.

"Give him the money."

"We don't have to make a decision right now. It can wait."

"I don't think his sister can."

"Are you sure?"

Rakesh nodded.

Was this the same brute in bed four days ago?

"Give money to one and we'll have a line of people outside asking for this, for that. We don't want to start a trend of money lending."

"Ask him for medical papers as proof and see if you can send someone over to verify."

"Think it through, son."

"I'm still taking care of Naina's medical expenses. And if something happened to Megha, I'd do whatever I could to help."

"There's no guarantee he'll pay back the sum."

"He will." Rakesh was firm. "We'll earn his loyalty for life and make sure we charge him a nominal interest fee, lower than the banks do, so he doesn't turn to anyone else."

"He's just an employee, not your family, Rakesh."

"All the better." Rakesh paused at the table's edge. "No strings attached."

"You're a good man at heart, son." Vipul Sahib nodded.

Rakesh's attention flickered to Sheetal and back to Vipul Sahib. "If only others could see that."

Sheetal winced.

"I'm doing all this for him." Rakesh gestured to Yash. "The last thing I want is to leave a debt for him to carry on."

"Is there anything we wouldn't do for our children? Lay down our lives if we had to."

"Then you agree with my plans for Tashukomo, and this stays between us."

"It's not right. Perhaps Ishwar"—he called upon God—"will somehow help us through. But Yash will have to live with the burden of your deeds forever. Think again." He rose to his feet, turned and headed for the exit. "What example are you setting for your son? Is this the legacy you want to leave behind? Because everything you do could become his undoing someday." Then he left and closed the door.

An hour later, much to Sheetal's surprise, Rakesh introduced Yash to important members of his staff and explained their roles. He flipped open folders of all the foreign brands Dhanraj & Son sold, pointed out their warehouses and agencies and used Lego vehicles to explain the distribution processes. Then he showed them several meeting rooms and explained how the department heads came together and monitored the progress of each division.

Rakesh's efforts, no matter how small, gained recognition here. Every rupee earned went toward an employee's paycheck, to the bank or was pumped back in as capital. Zeroes held a value and emphasized Rakesh's significance on the country's balance sheet. People looked up to him for guidance and direction whereas in the mansion he lived like a misfit. No wonder Rakesh preferred not to live at home. Mummyji's incessant tooting her own horn and fawning all over Naina must make him feel so out of place. Perhaps that explained his bouts of intense anger.

Rakesh made Yash sit at the head of every boardroom table and watched Yash from a far corner.

In one room, Yash pretended to conduct a meeting. He called out for a glass of water with the excuse his throat was dry from too much talking. In another boardroom, Yash drew a stick figure of a man holding a cricket bat upside down and explained to invisible board members why Dhanraj & Son had just lost a deal. He used four-and-five-syllable words in his speech like 'photosynthesis', 'respiration', 'monopoly', 'opportunity', 'opponent' and 'challenge' and waited for Rakesh's reaction. He was trying so hard to live up to Rakesh's expectations. Every time Rakesh nodded, Yash's face lit up.

Then Rakesh called for a member of staff. He ordered Pepsi, pizzas and French fries from a coffee shop across the street and had a picnic spread out on a conference table. He pulled a chair, sat across from Sheetal and patted a swivel chair next to him. "Come here, *Beta.*"

Yash sat down, grabbed the table's edge and swiveled from side to side.

Rakesh propped an elbow on the table, cupped a cheek in his palm and leaned against the edge. "Enjoyed your day so far?"

"So much, Dad!"

"I want you to know how proud I am of you. Your Mummy told me—"

"Not Mummy. Mum."

"Yes, Mum. She told me about your excellent marks and that you were chosen to compere for this year's spring concert."

"Out of so many boys, they picked me, Dad!"

"You must be really good." Rakesh cupped Yash's face in his palm and ran a thumb over the swell of his cheek.

"The judges told me it was a hard decision, but I won because of my fluency and confidence."

"That's a big word," Sheetal commented. "Do you know what it means?"

"Hmm..." Yash nodded. "Like I am sure of myself, and I know I'll do my best no matter what happens."

"Very close." Rakesh leaned away from the table.

"You'll come and watch me perform?" Yash asked.

Sheetal nodded, but Yash's attention fixed on Rakesh.

"Promise." Rakesh ruffled Yash's hair. "And I'm going to whistle and clap the loudest and tell everyone how proud I am of you."

Yash hopped off the chair, hugged Rakesh, and Rakesh folded

Yash in his arms. "When you're old enough, I'm going to make sure all of this—this building, company—is yours. All yours. It's what your grandfather and I built, and as long as you study hard and get good marks..."

Sheetal bit her lip. Wasn't Yash too young to know all this information? Not only would the inheritance go to his head, he might become proud and conceited. "The future's far away. Let's not think about it right now."

"I guess your Mum's right." Rakesh ordered for digital equipment to be wheeled in on a trolley. An attendant pulled down an enormous white screen, no doubt used for presentations, and darkened the room. The equipment beeped, the screen fuzzed with a thousand black and white dots, and Rakesh had three cushioned chairs aligned in a row. He sat between Sheetal and Yash as colors filled the screen and sharpened to a Walt Disney cartoon movie.

Sheetal's attention meandered to the luminous needles ticking away on a wall clock. They'd been here for two and a half hours. Didn't Rakesh have more important things to do?

"What do you think of me now?" Rakesh cradled Yash who'd taken comfort in his lap.

"Like you Dad." Yash yawned, rubbing his sleepy eyes. "I want to be just like you."

16

GAME OF LIFE

A white T-shirt, a pair of matching trousers and a sleeveless white sweater with thin, navy bands running around the perimeter of the 'V' neckline and sleeveless shoulders had been laid out on the bed.

Rakesh ran his fingers across the white fabric and gulped. The last time he'd played cricket, his childhood favorite and the country's national sport, was twenty-seven years ago. Papa used to say that he was gifted and a natural, but like everything else he'd ever loved, the sport was jinxed. He couldn't jinx life again. He had to find an excuse to avoid playing. He'd tell Yash that he was feeling sick, or something came up at work. No. No. Not on a Saturday.

"Look, Dad!" Yash ran in the open bedroom door dressed in the matching attire. "I look like you!"

Rakesh sank to his knees, ran his hands down Yash's back and tightened his grip around the boy's shoulders as he looked into the brown pools of Yash's eyes. He used to look like Yash when he was a boy. He pulled Yash to his chest, hugged him tight and held on, wishing Papa had hugged him so. "How did you put this whole uniform together?"

"It was a secret, and I told Mum not to tell you."

"Well, she sure didn't."

"You will play, won't you? You promised."

Rakesh tightened. No chance of running away from one of the hundred promises he made and assumed Yash would naturally forget. "How about tomorrow? We can go bowling today and to the video arcade instead?"

"Today." Yash frowned.

"But, Yash. It's been ages and I don't remember the rules."

"I'll help you. We play cricket at school all the time."

"But I—"

"For me, Dad," Yash pleaded. "Do it for me."

YASH HAMMERED THREE TWENTY-EIGHT-INCH-TALL WOODEN STUMPS NINE inches apart into the front lawn for a batting wicket. A semi-circular driveway bordered with red, pink and yellow carnations arched around him and ended at a pair of wrought iron gates manned by security posts. Yash edged back closer to the flower bed, scratched his chin, cupped the edge of his mouth and turned to Rakesh. "I'm not losing to you, Dad."

Rakesh surveyed the lawn's expanse from centerfield. Professional cricket consisted of two teams of eleven players each; both teams took turns bowling and batting. However, with just the two of them, could Yash strike the ball past the mansion's lower step without the ball hitting the ground? That feat would equate to scoring the maximum in one strike according to their kiddy made-up rules, professionally known as a sixer. Rakesh cupped a palm on his forehead for a visor. Probably not, because it was out of Yash's reach, even though he was bending the rules for Yash's benefit. He couldn't let Yash lose heart. A score of four runs on the other hand where the ball hit the ground and made it to the perimeter looked to be an easier task. But he could easily bring in the boundary line a little for Yash to score a sixer.

Yash shook each of the stumps and aligned two white pegs along their flat tops until the pegs balanced—the pegs indicated the stumps had been hit and the batsman was out. Then he walked over to another set of wooden stumps then drilled and hacked away at the grass with the pointed end of one.

"Ai-ee!" Pushpa rushed out of the mansion. "My lawn! Hai Ishwar! You are ruining my front lawn. *Mali! Chowkidar!*" She called for the gardener and security guard. "Stop them."

Jinxed. "He's setting up the pitch." Clearly, Pushpa wouldn't let them dishevel a blade of grass. So, they'd have to manage with the lawn as is.

"Don't you hear me? Have you all gone deaf, I tell you?"

"We're not ruining anything," Rakesh shouted. "We're just setting up the other batting wicket. We'll be careful."

"Careful to knock my flowers down, you will." Pushpa pumped her hands on her hips.

"If you insist." Rakesh grabbed the cricket ball near his feet and pretended to aim at a bush of roses in bloom when Pushpa screamed. He rolled the ball and relayed hand signals to Yash. "Ready?"

Yash marched to the opposite wicket, picked up the two-and-a-half-foot-long cricket bat by its thin round handle, pointed the tapered end to the ground parallel to his body and nodded.

A security guard watching from the guard post's cubicle rushed out as several gardeners tending shrubs and plants along the mansion's periphery dropped their tools and hurried to watch.

"Ready." Yash signaled.

Pushpa waved her arms, her bangles jingling in fury. "Play some-where else, I tell you! In the back garden."

"And knock down the bushes and fish?" Rakesh got in his about-to-bowl position. "Look, I'm going to play with my son whether you like it or not. If you don't want to get hurt, I suggest you back off."

"Go play in the back then, I tell you," Pushpa suggested. "Far back in the clearing where Mali burns wood."

Rakesh shook his head. "No good. We need grass on our turf and a barren strip only between the two wickets."

"Yash." Pushpa folded her arms across her chest. "No playing here, I tell you. You know the rules."

The rules dictated by Papa's will left the mansion and estate to Pushpa which was why her sole mission lay in maintenance of the property. Pushpa frowned and clusters of brown freckles tightened on her face.

Rakesh ran toward Yash swinging the ball in a clockwise motion. The moment his toe landed on the bowler's crease-line—a makeshift stick—he let go. The ball bounced, missed Yash's swinging bat by an inch, knocked two stumps before ramming into the hedge of carnations and knocked out several flowers.

"Out!" Rakesh yelled. "One ball down, five to go." Six balls equaled one over. After which another batsman took over.

"Out!" Pushpa wagged a finger in the air.

"Practice ball," Yash rebelled. "That doesn't count." He drilled two stumps back in the ground and the game continued. Yash missed almost every ball and hacked away at the ground until the lawn turned into a patchwork of upturned grass and soil.

Pushpa cupped a hand on her mouth and shook her head.

"How about you field and I bowl now?" Rakesh changed positions with Yash.

"*Kaka!*" Yash waved to the security guard and gardeners, and they all came running to his aid. "All of you can help me field. I can't handle Dad alone." He appointed one staff member to stand behind the bowler's wicket. "And you must go stand all the way there." He appointed another to the mansion's front entrance. In less than two minutes Yash secured nine fielders, delegated Laal Bahadur, the chef, to be umpire and collated the first Dhanraj cricket team. Then he resumed play. Cheers and laughter lifted with the Raigun breeze as the servants cheered for Yash while darting left and right, palms cupped above their heads to catch the flying ball.

"What's wrong with you all, I tell you?" Pushpa screamed again. "Back to work! Enough nonsense."

"Not until game over." Rakesh prepared to bat again. He looked up just as Sheetal peered from behind the edge of her studio window. He winked, but she slipped out of view. Rakesh narrowed his attention on the fielders closing in.

Yash bowled. Rakesh swung his bat and a 'puck' sound carried on the breeze. The ball sailed over Yash, over Pushpa, over the four Venetian pillars holding up the portico. The sound of broken glass shattered the silence. The servants numbed. Yash froze.

Pushpa marched across the lawn and jabbed a finger at the studio behind. "I hope you're happy now, I tell you. Look what you've done!"

"A sixer!" Rakesh threw his bat on the ground and ran to scoop Yash in his arms. He'd played cricket until his teenage years for recreation, but he'd never scored more than a four. "It's my first sixer."

"*Waah! Waah!* Rakesh *Babu!*" Applause filled the air as gardeners and servants left their positions to join in the excitement.

"Teach me, Dad!" Yash squealed in delight. "Can you? Will you? Huh?"

"Of course!" Rakesh spun Yash in circles. Sunlight pierced through the clouds and, in that moment, a heaviness lifted and filled him with light. The sky shimmered an ocean blue. The leaves sparkled an emerald green. The roses blazed ruby reds. And the air! Rakesh took a deep breath. So light. So breezy. So cool. For the first time, he felt weightless. Free.

RAKESH RAN UP TO SHEETAL'S STUDIO AND FOUND HER KNEELING ON THE floor picking up shards of glass. He helped her up by the arms and pulled her away from the mess. "Don't. You'll hurt yourself. I'll call the servants to clean up."

Sheetal handed Rakesh the cricket ball and turned away.

"Look, I know you're still angry about that night on Diwali. I'm sorry."

She picked up the brush and resumed working on her painting, her back to him.

"I didn't mean to break your window. The ball—"

The sound of her jingling bangles raking momentum cut him off.

"I shouldn't have behaved like—done that to you. I'm sorry. I was angry. I don't know what happened. What overcame me."

"*You* don't know what happened? Then who does?"

"It was a mistake, Sheetal. I admit it. I made a mistake. I'm human—"

"Oh? And I'm not?"

"Things are going to be different from now on. Promise. I—Dr. Kishore called yesterday."

Her brush paused mid-air.

He had her attention. "I...he told me I'm suffering from cirrhosis of the liver. You were right. But I'm only at the initial stages, so it's not that bad. I can fix this."

"This isn't about right or wrong." She turned to face him. "You're sick and need professional help, like rehab."

"I'm going to stop drinking. Make changes. Dr. Kishore said it's what I need to do. Get better. I'll do what it takes—"

She dipped her brush into the palette and continued without so much as a glance. "I've heard that before."

Words and talk wouldn't win her over. He'd have to earn her trust and prove himself. Rakesh left with the ball and took the stairs two at a time. He helped Yash pull all six stumps out of the ground then got down on his knees and began patting handfuls of loose soil back in place.

"Arrey, Sahib!" The gardeners rushed to his side. "We'll fix the lawn. Don't you worry. Don't get your clothes dirty, Sahib." The security guard rushed over and got down on his knees. "Sahib, we fix. You no worry."

"Nothing will happen if I pitch in." Rakesh wiped the sweat off his brows. He dug his fingers in the earth and moist soil filled the crevices of his fingers with warmth as servants straightened the shrubs and bushes. Instead of running away, the servants fussed over him expressing concern at the dirt covering his white clothes and creeping under his fingernails. They cared for him in the same way he needed to care for and hold on to his family.

TWO DAYS LATER RAKESH ENTERED SHEETAL'S STUDIO, AND THE SCENT OF paint, turpentine and oil thickened the air. The broken window caught his attention, and he made a mental note to call someone and have it fixed.

Sheetal was dotting crests of snow along a range of the Himalayas.

"Hey." He closed the door softly behind him. "Busy?"

"I have a series of ten paintings due in ten days." Diamond bangles clinked up and down her wrists with each stroke.

"I came to talk."

She paused, turned around and raised her eyebrows. There it was. The stare indicating he wasn't worth her time.

"About your window the other day. I'll have Janvi cover it up with something and call a repair guy to come and take a look. Next week, maybe."

She laid the brush to rest on a table, wiped her fingers on a paint-smeared rag and turned to face him.

"I played cricket with Yash again yesterday, and we had fun. I want things to stay like this between us. Not lose what we have." He gulped. "I... I want us to be a family."

"We are." She crossed her arms.

"I mean a real family. A normal family like everyone else."

"Oh, just like that?" Her tone sliced the air.

Why did she always have to be so judgmental? Why couldn't she just listen? "Our son needs to live with us. Here. There are things you don't know about boarding schools and what happens there. Older boys *do things* to the younger ones."

"What things?"

"It's an all-boys hostel, Sheetal. Do I have to spell it out for you?"

"What are you trying to say? And how do you know?"

"Look, you've lived a sheltered life. There are things you don't and will probably never know. I know because—I just do. I grew up in a boarding school and sometimes it's not just the older boys but the staff, the custodians, can be perverts."

Her jaw dropped.

"Why put Yash at risk? Think of the opportunity as a chance for us to come together as a family—only if we are together."

"We tried for a long time. But with your stepmother and Nainaji around—"

"It'll be different this time. I'll try harder to—"

"To what? How will this time be any different from before?"

The back of his head throbbed. "I don't know. I don't have all the answers but give me a chance. We need Yash here. I know it. I feel it. There's so much happiness with him around and we're laughing and doing things like a normal family. Like how you two spent the afternoon at my office the other day. We can do it right and make our family right. I want you to know I thought hard about what you said. I could tell from your expression you don't like my idea of using the Japanese and their money to fix our problems."

"You're not fixing anything, Rakesh. You're going against the law and—"

"I get it. I'm wrong. I'll talk to Vipul Sahib and find another way."

Sheetal leaned against the table and folded her arms across her chest.

Finally, she was listening. "See! I'm already changing. I can feel the change in me. I can do it. I'll stick to my promises. I've already given up smoking and I'm cutting down on drinking."

Wrinkles creased the corners of her eyes. "For a few days, Rakesh? And then you'll go back to what you were before."

"I even went to the doctor like you asked me to and I'm taking care of my health. I'll do everything Dr. Kishore says." The thoughts raced at lightning speed. "Look, I cut down to a few glasses of scotch over the last week. I almost stuck to my promise but then I got this letter from the bank—"

"The bank. The company. There's always going to be an excuse. I need you to be in your senses, to be a father, a sensible father, a responsible father if we're to keep Yash here. I can't handle Mummyji and Nainaji and raise a child—a sane child—by myself."

"You're—"

"I'm his mother. I feel the same way you do. Our son can never have a normal life with our million problems. He doesn't deserve any of it. He needs an environment that's predictable and safe."

"Safe?" He wanted to laugh but resisted the urge. "We have servants and guards all the time. What more security does he need?"

"Stability, Rakesh." Sheetal pressed a palm to her forehead. "A stable home so he's not living in fear of his own family. Can you change Naina and put some sanity in her? No. Because Mummyji won't allow her to go for therapy. Can you change Mummyji and make her less of a control freak? No. Because Mummyji owns the property. It's hers. All of this is hers!" She thrust a hand in the air.

"I lost out on a huge order for the Sheraton Hotel because of Mummyji. All the paintings were ready to go. Seven orchids on four-by-five feet canvases and each worth three hundred and fifty thousand. But Mummyji decided to go on a cruise on the spur of the moment and I'm stuck babysitting Nainaji, a fully grown adult, mind you. And because of that, my work was two days late. Two days late for delivery is no excuse! I lost the entire contract and now I have ten paintings due by the fifteenth worth five hundred thousand..."

"Your career is more important than Yash?" He glanced at the time on his watch. Almost 5 p.m. He should be at Kartik's place in half an hour.

"Our conversation has nothing to do with career or money. Not everything about my career is tied to family."

"No matter what I do, nothing is ever good enough."

"How is this about you? How can Yash's well-being have anything to do with you when you're hardly ever around? I put aside my work to make sure your mother and sister are not poisoning Yash's mind. Can you move us out if I asked you to? No. Because it'll affect the company and confidence of your board members and stakeholders. I want Yash here with us too but it's impossible."

He ran a palm along the back of his head and pressed hard, but his head pounded. He had to make changes. He couldn't be in two places at once anymore. He had to let one go.

At the apartment, Kartik drained scotch from a bottle into a tumbler, and cubes of ice rattled and clinked. "I don't get it. Why you doing this?"

Rakesh's attention traveled up several threads dangling from the seams of Kartik's blue shorts to the wrinkled and tattered gray T-shirt. From Kartik's casual dress style no one would ever expect a man like him to afford a plush condo in downtown Raigun and a life-style as carefree. Rakesh wiped the sweat from his brows and turned away from the glass Kartik offered.

"She found out—no?" Kartik's eyes hardened. "You scared? That it? A double scotch on the rocks is what you need." He poured himself a glass and lowered the tumbler on the table. "Bottom's up. Go on. Take it."

Rakesh slid the glass back to Kartik and left a trail of sweat on the wood. "She doesn't know. And I've given up drinking."

"You joking—no?" Kartik took a swig of the golden liquid and stared at him. "What? You serious?"

"About everything."

"You—"

"I can't do this anymore." He took a deep breath to hold his composure and slowly released. "They deserve better."

"And me?" Kartik's eyes narrowed on him. "What about me?"

His jaw tightened. Did anyone care about him? A gentle whirring erupted from nearby followed by clicks. "You know what we have is temporary and good for as long as it lasts, but we can't go on anymore."

Kartik snapped his fingers. "So, this is how it ends?"

Rakesh's head pricked with needles.

"Just like that? And now where do I go from here, man? You just kick me out and that's it?" His voice deepened with anger. "I gave up a high-paying PR job with perks for some small-time shit-hole stint at the local pharmacy. Be discreet and be invisible, you said. And this is what I get?"

"Shut up!" Rakesh thwacked the air with his hand.

"No. You fuck up..." Kartik thumped an empty glass on the table. "You fucking..." He roared like all twelve cylinders of the Lamborghini. "You can't just fucking walk out on me as if I'm nothing."

"My son is living away and my marriage is a shit-hole. I'm screwed." Arrows of pain jabbed his forehead. His hands were flying all over the place in a wild gesture and he couldn't hold them down. "I can't take it anymore. Just go fucking wherever you want."

Kartik paced the room fingering the light stubble on his chin. He poured a second drink for himself and edged Rakesh's glass back toward him. "All right, man. If this is it. One last scotch for old time's sake."

17

LETTING GO

T hat afternoon Sheetal and Yash were waiting on the Fulton Whites for the driver to return from an errand and drive them to Mama's while Naina and Mummyji argued on the Bradford Browns. Sheetal was reading an article in the November issue of *Vogue* but couldn't focus with Naina's yelling. She closed the magazine and her attention meandered to the thick anklets on the elephants' legs. Perverts in an all-boys hostel? Surely, the staff underwent a background check before they were employed. Rakesh was probably making things up so she'd cave in. Or maybe he was trying to—Mummyji and Naina's discussions deafened the great hall, and she could barely think.

"No husband. No one to answer to." Mummyji glowered at Naina. "Doesn't give you the right, I tell you, to do whatever you want. How long will this sitting by the phone all day go on for, as if Ajay will call? He divorced you, re-married and has two children now. He got on with life, but you still keep waiting for that Ajay to call like he will want you back."

"Maybe he will." Perched beside the black telephone, Naina rolled a plastic medicine bottle back and forth in her palm.

Yash looked up from the book he was reading.

"A lone woman gone wrong. That's what you are." Mummyji rose to her feet and towered over Naina's skinny frame. "Society has no place, I tell you, for a woman without a husband."

"Like you, na?"

"What do you mean?"

"You're alone. You answer to no one either, na. Keep dumping me on the servants and Bhabhi." She screwed off the cap and tilted the bottle so that the open mouth faced her palm.

"Cannot, I tell you, spend the rest of my life running after you. I gave you a chance to marry and settle down."

The Dhanrajs had gone beyond a chance. They bribed Ajay Malhotra with an ostentatious dowry into marrying Naina. Ajay divorced Naina nine months later and returned her with all the dowry. Though Sheetal had initially disagreed with the plan, the relief of Naina's absence felt like a blessing because shortly after Sheetal had married and moved in with the Dhanrajs, Naina ruined Sheetal's paintings and damaged her studio in a fit of rage.

"Janvi?" Naina yelled. "Water."

Janvi hurried in with a glass of water, placed it on the table and left.

Naina tossed one pill in the air, cocked her head back and opened her mouth swaying to the left and right. The pill landed on her tongue and Naina downed it with the water. "Look, Yash!" She repeated the feat several more times, missing several tablets and catching another and then another. Yash's jaw dropped.

"Look, Yash." Sheetal pointed to a photospread of a fluffy brown dog in a dog food advertisement, but Yash showed more interest in Naina's antics.

"No shame, playing with those medicines like they are some toy. No value for anything, I tell you because you've always had everything. Never had to work or live on that side of town surrounded by filth, dirt, heat and little to eat and wear. No, Sheetal?"

Why was Mummyji picking on her? "Not everyone is born a Dhanraj."

"Exactly what I say, I tell you. But not everyone understands. How can you appreciate what we have if you have never lived without our life of plenty? No, Sheetal? You would know."

Was Mummyji on a mission to openly insult just because Papa had worked his way up from the middle class? "How dare you speak about me like that in front of—"

"What to do now?" Mummyji cut her off. "No one of our rank will marry and take Naina as wife. Thirty-one is far too old and she's —well, touched." Mummyji meant damaged.

"I did live a life without plenty," Naina interrupted.

"And how long did you last, I tell you? Nine months? Now put those away!" Mummyji gestured to the bottle.

"I was like a servant there." Naina ignored Mummyji's order.

"More like my mark of shame."

Naina raised a palm to her face and rubbed her nose. "What's there to hide now when everyone knows?"

Naina had studied up to the twelfth standard and surrendered further education for a life of anticipated luxury. With no vocational training or work experience, she wasn't qualified to secure a job and work outside the house, and she didn't want to volunteer to help the needy either.

Mummyji pumped both arms on her hips. "Can't get rid of you and can't live with you, I tell you. You make my life impossible. What about the proposal that came in just the other day? What's wrong with that fellow, Praveen, I tell you? He's thirty-three and divorced with one child and he lives in a three-bedroom apartment."

"Ordinary, na?"

"What do you expect?" Mummyji paced the length of the Legacy table and the freckles on her face darkened. "No handsome, young prince is coming for you, I tell you."

"Ajay will come back." Naina crossed her arms. "Just you wait and see."

"That's what you think. I am fed up trying to put sense in your head. Never listen. Never think. But think the world of yourself, like some *maharani* in a palace, I tell you. Take whatever man you get and be happy."

"I don't take leftovers." Naina rose to her feet, thumped the bottle on the growing pile of magazines near an open candy dish of Gems and walked off.

"You." Mummyji turned to Sheetal. "Why don't you teach her something useful so she can figure out what to do with her life."

The car honked its arrival. Sheetal grabbed Yash by the hand and rushed out the door before Mummyji suggested she take Naina to Mama's. There was simply no helping a woman who couldn't help herself.

THE SITUATION AT MAMA'S WASN'T ANY BETTER.

Mama had grown weaker and now stooped. She could barely stand without support, struggled to breathe and her life revolved around Anjali's shopping trips, Anjali's children and keeping up with Anjali's social life. Papa had also grown dependent on Vikram for business matters.

That evening, when the day's activities subdued and Sheetal found some time alone with Mama, she went to Mama's bedroom, closed the door and sat beside Mama on the bed while Yash played on the front lawn with Anjali's children. "You need to rest, Mama, and stop running around after everyone. Look how tired and weak you've become."

Mama wrapped the pastel pink sari pallu around her head and tightened a gray shawl around her shoulders. "Never mind me. You should be proud of the smart young man Yash will grow up to be. Like Rakeshji someday."

The credit for Yash's confidence went to St. Paul's and Arvind's efforts, not Rakesh who only fathered Yash when he had the time. "I thought I should tell you, I...uh, I met Arvind when I was in Mansali."

"Why?"

Didn't Mama care to know where or how? "He's a teacher at Yash's school and also his House Master."

"Oh." Mama frowned. "He must be settled by now."

"He never married."

"Probably couldn't find a good enough girl to marry."

"He didn't want to, Mama."

"How do you know?"

"He told me."

"You talked to him?"

"What's wrong with talking?"

"Everything." Mama shook her head. "The more you talk, the more you know and talking leads to other things. You should have walked away."

Sheetal wrinkled her nose in irritation. Women from Mama's generation assumed talking to another man, who was not considered family, in private implied something more.

"Don't nose me. You are a married woman, and you have a son and a family, and I suppose he wants all that now. Don't even think of ruining it for him."

Sheetal turned away.

"That look on your face tells me you're still thinking of him."

"Mama—"

"Didn't you say you and Rakesh were having trouble?"

"Not trouble. But something feels wrong in our relationship."

"And now you meet and talk to that Arvind again. What else do you expect to happen?"

Shouldn't have told Mama anything! Sheetal fluffed two pillows and placed them between Mama and the headboard. "You're acting like I went out with him on a date or I—"

"Things go wrong when you wish for something and want it bad enough."

Had she somehow secretly invited Arvind back with that wish on Karva Chauth? "He was a friend and nothing more."

"Put your heart back in your marriage," Mama wheezed and sat up. "Or there will be nothing left." She shook her head. "There's something I want to talk about."

From Mama's tone, the talk didn't sound good.

"I've decided—and you can't change my mind about this—but I'm not going ahead with the chemo."

Sheetal's heart skipped a beat. *Was Mama cancer free?*

"I'm tired of all the medicines. doctors, hospitals and—" She coughed.

Sheetal rushed to support her. "It's my fault, isn't it? I forgot to take you to the doctor's last time. I'm so sorry, Mama."

"Silly girl. How could you when you were in Mansali? Your father and I went, and I just can't do this anymore." She took deep controlled breaths as Sheetal reached for a jug of water on the bedside table and poured Mama a glass. "I'm exhausted and I just want to go."

The air thickened. Did her absence cause Mama to feel neglected? She should have called from Mansali or after she returned, but she was so wrapped up with Rakesh's health issues, keeping Yash away from trouble and her own work. "It's my fault. I should have remembered to check on you."

"I made up my mind weeks ago. Your father argued so many times and tried to reason, but I don't have the strength to go on."

Mama was clearly falling into depression. "Let's talk about this later. We can ask Vikram and Anjali to go somewhere with their children for a while." Their presence exhausted Mama and she wasn't thinking right. "That way you won't have to deal with all their—"

"It's got nothing to do with the Choudharys. This is my decision."

"Then you and Papa take a holiday." Her mind raced. "Go somewhere for a while and get away from everything. Mansali's the best place for some fresh mountain air, relaxation, and you will feel better.

"You're not listening, Sheetal. I don't want to go to Mansali. I want to go in peace and not live with this incurable pain anymore."

"But Ma—" Her throat choked, and the walls blurred.

"I don't have the strength to fight a losing battle." Mama pressed a palm against Sheetal's chest. "I'm always here in your heart."

Sheetal squeezed her eyes tight to hold back the tears, but they rolled down her cheeks. "You don't have to do anything, Mama. The medicines and treatment will cure you." The chemo wasn't as effective as they'd hoped and Mama's tummy had bloated to twice its size, but she had to give Mama hope.

"Chemo will prolong my life by several weeks or months and then what? I live in fear of death?" She looked down and ran her hand over the bulge of her tummy. "This pain continues day after day and the cancer is growing out of control. I want you to promise when I am no more, Yash will light my pyre."

The Indian custom of cremating the dead originated with the belief that a person's soul was liberated from the corpse and attained *moksha* only when the deceased person's son or a male family member lit the pyre.

"Promise me you'll take care of your father when I'm gone."

Her heart fisted her throat and she nodded.

"And that you will put your heart back in your marriage."

Sheetal pressed her elbows on the studio's windowsill, cupped her cheeks in the palms of both hands and watched Yash and Rakesh play cricket on the front lawn. The servants had knocked out the remaining shards of glass, and the open window had to be temporarily shielded until fixed.

Rakesh mocked the servants with empty threats to halve their pay, have them clean the house from top to bottom and sparkle every leaf if they didn't ensure he won, but the staff no longer feared Rakesh and openly cheered for Yash. Rakesh mockingly deviated Yash's attention with a snarl, growl, or animal noises. One time Rakesh pointed to an invisible bird taking flight from a tree. Another time he yelled ice cream and pointed to a cloud in the shape of an ice cream. Then, when Yash screamed "Da-a-a-d!", threw his bat on the ground and stomped off, Rakesh would run after Yash to coax him back into playing.

"Time for a break. Mali Kaka, you all get some cool water for yourselves to drink and some juice for Yash." Rakesh headed for the mansion's entrance.

The gardener ran over to a cooler spot under the shade of a tree, flipped open the lid, took out a Tetra Pak of apple juice and gave it to Yash. Then he walked over to a huge earthenware pot near the security guard's post and doled out glasses of water to the staff.

Sheetal forced herself away from the windowsill and headed toward the half-completed canvas on an easel. The happy family distractions were causing her to fall behind again but in a good way.

"Hey." Rakesh appeared at the studio's doorway, his hair ruffled as sweat rolled down the side of his face. "Why don't you join us?"

"I don't know how to play, and I have to finish this."

"It'll be more fun with you. Besides, we only have a few more days with Yash."

"I know. I've been thinking..."

"What?" His expression blanked.

"What you said the other day about keeping Yash here with us. I know it's going to be hard, but if you're serious about going sober, changing and becoming more responsible, we can think this through."

"Oh, Sheetal!" He grabbed her hand. "We?"

Her heart thumped. Yash would help bring them together. Besides, what if Rakesh was right about things that went on in boarding schools? "Let's start looking for a school here and give it a try."

He wrapped his arms around her and kissed her full on the lips. Then he tightened and pulled away. "You mean it, right? You're not going to back out?"

"We won't know until we try. And as for that loan, I was thinking if we sell some of my jewelry—"

"No." He was firm. "I won't hear of it."

"Just listen to me. I was willing to listen to you. It's stuff I haven't worn in years that's gone out of fashion and just sitting in the bank locker. I'm sure the pieces will sell for a good price which will be enough to get the banks off your back for a while."

"I'll find another way, Sheetal. I promise. But the fact that you're willing to take the first step for me, for us—calls for a celebration!" He hugged her again. "And we won't tell Yash now. Only later once we're completely sure."

"READY, MUM?" YASH TWIRLED THE BALL BETWEEN HIS FINGERS.

Sheetal wrapped the pallu around her hips and tucked it at the waist. She stood before a wicket and positioned the bat parallel to her body, its flat tip touching the ground.

"You can do this." Rakesh nodded. "Keep your eyes on the ball."

Perhaps Rakesh really meant to keep his promise this time. The sun bore down. The tour of Rakesh's office last week, his coming home early from work every day, dinner and movie thrice this week, the bouquet of flowers three days ago, and just yesterday he'd bought her a book on the world's fifty-most famous oil painters. Life was too short to hold on to grudges and maybe this turnaround would help put the heart back in her marriage. "Ready!"

Yash scrambled to get in position, and her attention flew to a gardener-turned-fielder at the far back in tattered shorts, a faded blue shirt and open-toe sandals. Is this how Arvind used to play in scruffs, on maidans? She imagined a barren sand-crusted open ground in place of the lush lawn and a ripped wire fence running its perimeter. The ball torpedoed in her direction. Sheetal swung the bat, raising her hands higher and higher until her hands felt weightless and free. She was free. A whoosh followed by the clatter of wood on wood echoed with surrounding laughter.

Sheetal looked down at her feet and then over her shoulder.

The wickets and bat lay clattered on the ground.

SHEETAL TUCKED YASH IN BED THAT NIGHT WHEN HE HELD ONTO HER WRISTS and forced her to sit down on the mattress' edge. "I don't want to go back, Mum. I want to stay here with you and Dad."

She cupped his face in her palms and ran her thumb over his hairline. One more week before his return to Mansali. *Tell him.* Her heart skipped a beat. *What could possibly go wrong in letting Yash know?* "Your Dad and I have been thinking."

He tightened his grip.

"Perhaps you can stay with us and not go back this time. I'll start looking at schools here for you."

He sat up, swung his arms around Sheetal and hugged her tight. "Really, Mum? Really? I can stay?"

She pressed him tight to her chest. "It's a secret and nobody knows. I'm not even supposed to tell you."

"I won't tell anyone." He pulled away. "Promise."

"Not Aunty Naina. Megha. Or even Dadi. No one."

"But won't they find out?"

"When we tell them later, yes. You can't tell your dad you know either."

"Why?"

"Because he wants to tell you and surprise you later, once we're sure. Until then it's our little secret."

"You promise, Mum? Right? You won't let me go? You'll let me stay?"

"I promise, Yash. You are my light, and you will always shine bright. I will never let you go."

18

COFFEE KISSES

Rakesh and Yash marched back into the house, exhausted from having played two hours of cricket. Rakesh pressed all six stumps to his chest with thoughts of Kartik and the break-up several days ago.

Yash tugged the lower rim of his sweater. "You don't look happy, Dad."

Rakesh looked down distracted. "What makes you say so?"

"You're not smiling."

Rakesh swallowed. His throat was parched from not having had a drink in six days.

"Dad?"

"Here." He forced a smile. "Better?" Good fathers always smiled at their children and didn't plug their children into boarding schools. Such a relief to know Yash would be living with them soon and not holed up with boys who could easily make him their bitch, and scar him for life. He couldn't let Yash grow into the sissy-weakling Sheetal had turned him into. He would teach Yash to be rough and tough and to survive in the real world. He would teach Yash to be stronger than he'd ever been like all good fathers did.

"You're angry you lost again, aren't you?" Yash tapped his hand.

"Of course not, I'm proud of you. Every father wants his child to be better than himself."

"Like your father was of you?"

Funny, how Yash assumed all good things automatically trickled down through generations. He'd spent his entire childhood trying to please Papa, but Pushpa had planted so much doubt in Papa's mind that Papa lost all confidence in him before he even had a chance to prove himself. He returned with the promised MBA degree from Harvard and spent the next three years standing up for himself and dodging Pushpa's maneuvers. He would never let anyone do that to Yash.

"Dad? Say something."

"What, Beta?"

"Was your father proud of you?"

"Yes."

"Did you win him in every game?"

"Almost."

"And did he get upset or was he happy when he lost to you?"

Papa's expression before he died? "Very upset, especially the last game when I won the final round."

Yash patted him on the lower back. "Just so you know, I think you were an outstanding opponent."

"Why, thank you. That's a very grown-up thing to say." They passed several rooms on the north wing, took a left on the west and stopped at Yash's bedroom door. "Who taught you such good manners?"

"No one really." Yash shrugged. "I just hear Chopra Sir say it's good manners to let your opponent know you enjoyed the challenge. It shows sportsmanship."

Rakesh decreased his strides to match Yash's. "Who's this Chopra Sir? I've never heard of him before."

"My House Master. The new substitute. He teaches us science too. Don't you know him?"

"No."

"Mum does. He had lunch with us. But Mum had coffee."

The stumps started to slip, and Rakesh tightened his grip. "Lunch and coffee?"

"In the restaurant, Dad."

He sucked in his chest.

"Mum, me and Chopra Sir. You're not listening, Dad."

"So how does Mum know him? This Chopra Sir."

"She said they were friends from school. Old friends. Good friends."

Chopra. The word circled his head. Hadn't Sheetal been close friends with that guy by the last name Chopra, before they married? "Did she say anything else about this Chopra Sir?" He opened the door to Yash's room and dumped all the stumps in a box.

"No, but they talked a lot."

Jinxed!

"You don't look happy, Dad. You're not smiling."

Rakesh forced himself to smile again. "I'm smiling. Happy?"

"You're not angry, are you?"

"Of course, not." He wasn't angry. He was furious.

THAT EVENING NAINA GRABBED THE ALMOST-FULL BOTTLE OF ELAVILS FROM the Russet Legacy coffee table she'd left earlier during the day. She flicked off the cap and emptied several in her left palm. However, she tipped the bottle too far and a stream of shiny orange enamel-coated discs landed on the magazines, an open candy dish and scattered all over the table and floor. Naina picked a few off the table, popped four in her mouth, slipped the bottle into her pocket and sauntered up to her room.

RAKESH SAT IN BED WITH A STACK OF PAPERS ON HIS LAP AND TWIRLED A PEN as Sheetal slipped between the sheets. Exhausted, she snuggled her head into the pillow content she shared her bed with her husband like any normal couple. Proof, her heart was finally in her marriage.

The aroma of coffee and chocolate hung in the air. *Arvind?* No. She reasoned. Her mind was playing tricks. She had to get Arvind out of her head. "Rakesh?" Sheetal ruffled the covers this way and that, but Rakesh didn't appear the least interested in what she had to say. "Rakesh?"

"What?" He didn't move.

"Please turn off the lights."

"I'm working."

"Can't you do it tomorrow?"

"Why?"

"I want to sleep." The scent of Arvind grew almost as if he were here in the room and in their bed. She sniffed the sheets. "Do you smell something?"

Silence.

The aroma grew stronger. Who drank mocha at this hour of the night?

Rakesh reached over to his side table, and Sheetal waited for him to put away the papers and switch off the lamp. However, he lifted a brown mug, raised it to his lips as curls of steam piped and took a sip.

Was this some kind of a healthy substitute for scotch?

Wrinkles creased his expression on contact with the drink.

"What are you drinking?"

His lips curved into a crooked smile, and he raised the mug in a toast. "Hot brown coffee. Want some?"

THAT NIGHT, YASH WALKED ALONE NEAR THE BRADFORD BROWN SOFAS IN the dimly lit Dhanraj's great hall, sipping apple juice from a Tetra Pak. He stopped near the Russet Legacy table, scooped a handful of Gems and tossed one in the air. He cocked his head back, opened his mouth and staggered to the left and right. The first Gem hit his cheek and bounced on the floor. The second hit the corner of his mouth and rolled under the sofa. The third landed on his tongue. Yash sipped the juice, swallowed the candy, and picked up a handful of orange ones scattered all over the table and repeated the feat until they were all gone.

AN HOUR LATER PUSHPA FOUND YASH UNCONSCIOUS ON THE FLOOR AND screamed.

19
BROKEN GLASS

Rakesh and Sheetal spent the night at the hospital as machines monitoring Yash's heart rate and breathing beeped and whirred. In the time they'd been here, Rakesh had turned into a nervous wreck. If a machine clicked, Rakesh examined all the devices to make sure they all worked. If the ECG machine beeped too loud, he pushed a red panic button beside the hospital bed and called for a nurse. He looked out in the corridor every five minutes and demanded any doctor passing by attend to his son and the nurses keep continued surveillance on monitors in the room.

At five the next morning, Rakesh returned from his fifteenth trip to the nurse's station, closed the door and walked across to Yash's bed. "I just spoke with the doctor. Yash is going to be fine. Hopefully, they'll discharge him soon after he wakes up."

A wave of relief washed over her, and Sheetal nodded. The doctors had used twenty-eight grams of activated liquid charcoal and spent two hours clearing Yash's system of the Elavil overdose.

A nurse entered the room, drew a sample of Yash's blood and left.

Rakesh stepped away from the edge of Yash's bed, and the

vertical steel rail pushed aside the lower right flap of his blazer, revealing a hip flask.

"You're drinking alcohol again after everything that's happened? You promised to stop."

"I need to calm my nerves."

"Dr. Kishore said—"

"I know what Dr. Kishore said."

Sheetal brushed away a lock of hair from her forehead. "How can you go back on your promises? So easy for you. God knows what would have happened—"

"Nothing," Rakesh cut her short. "Nothing will happen to Yash. You have my word. I will never allow anything to happen. He's *my* son."

"Our son." She almost choked on the word. "Do you realize we almost lost him because of Nainaji? Because—what was I thinking? How did I let you talk me into believing we could keep Yash with us? I told you our home is not safe. He has to go back because whatever happened was not in your control and will never be in your control. There's nothing you or I can do to control anyone in this family."

"What happened was an accident."

"If Naina didn't live here, this accident wouldn't have happened."

"Look, I did everything—" He grazed his fingers through his hair. "I blew up all the money possible to give Naina a future and get her away from us. I put myself down by three hundred and fifty million. If nothing works out, it's not my fault she's still here."

"What if the next accident is fatal?"

"There won't be a next time."

"Of course, there won't be a next time because you'll just go right back to your alcohol and pretend everything is under control."

He sank into a chair, stretched his thumb and fingers across his head then covered his face with his palms.

Sheetal turned to Yash. If it weren't for the hip flask, she might have tried to comfort Rakesh.

Just then Yash's finger twitched.

Sheetal inched to Yash's side. "I think Yash is awake."

Rakesh rose to his feet, his forehead caked with wrinkles. "Yash," he called out gently, "Wake up."

Sheetal walked around the bed to stand beside Rakesh. Yash should see them together, so he'd believe everything was fine. The cold metal flask wedged between their bodies, and she winced.

Yash opened his eyes for a split second, and his lids closed.

"Yash?" Sheetal reached out and took his fingers in hers. "Wake up, Yash. It's me. Mum. Look, Dad's here too. You're fine now. Everything's going to be fine."

THE HOSPITAL DISCHARGED YASH LATER THAT AFTERNOON. SHEETAL TUCKED him in bed and sat with him. However, when Naina's and Mummyji's loud debates from the floor below reached her, she rushed out of Yash's room and peered over the balcony railing.

"You, I tell you!" Mummyji bellowed from the Fulton Whites. "How irresponsible and careless of you leaving medicines around. What were you thinking?"

Huddled in the left corner of the Bradford Browns, Naina hugged her knees close to her chest. "It's Janvi's fault. She should have cleaned up after, na."

"Clean up, my foot!" Mummyji marched toward Naina. "Your fault that my reputation falls in this family, and everything goes wrong."

"My fault?"

"Yes, and you should apologize to Sheetal."

"Never!"

Revolted at the spectacle, Sheetal turned her back to the railing. How would Yash ever recover with all this yelling? She needed an alternative. Have him stay with Kavita? No, Kavita had enough to manage with a job, two children and her own problems. Besides, sending Yash off to a friend's would create gossip. Yash would be safe with Mama and as soon as he was better, she'd whisk him back to St. Paul's whether Rakesh agreed or not. But how to tell Yash that he must return?

Sheetal called St. Paul's main office and informed a member of staff that Yash had been hospitalized and would return when he was better, in about a week. Then she called the Raigun Railway Office, canceled Yash's return ticket to Mansali tomorrow, and booked two flight tickets to New Delhi on November twenty-third and two train tickets from New Delhi to Mansali for Yash and Rakesh. She hadn't asked Rakesh if he'd take Yash back to school but he'd have to agree given the incident.

Sheetal called Mama. A servant took the call and asked her to wait. Seconds later Papa and Vikram's voices exploded through the receiver.

"Hello?" Sheetal whispered.

No response.

"I'll throw you out of the company," Papa said. "How dare you..."

"Hello?"

"I didn't force you to sign anything." Vikram's tone hardened.

"Hello, Sheetal?" Mama came on the line, rasping for air.

"Are you all right, Mama?"

"I'm—a—little—tired. That's all."

"Papa sounds angry. What did Vikram do?"

"Nothing. It's just office talk and the usual business matters."

"I heard Papa threaten to throw Vikram out. Last time I was there, Vikram got Papa to sign papers—"

"Sheetal, what happens here is not your problem."

The Prasads, like most Indian families, believed that once a girl married, her responsibility and duties lay with the family she married into and not the one she left behind.

"But Mama, I heard—"

"I have to go," Mama whispered, and then the line went dead.

LATER THAT EVENING SHEETAL LEFT THE HOUSE FOR SOME FRESH AIR TO think and sat near the pond of Koi in the Japanese garden. The pond's surface darkened with a black shadow, and the sound of gravel crunched.

Rakesh sat beside Sheetal and ruffled open pages of The Raigun Herald.

Rakesh had shown no remorse for going back on his promise or Yash's accident and behaved as if life had returned to normal and he was here for his evening chai. In no mood for casual conversation, Sheetal mentally listed the priorities requiring his immediate attention. "The Saxenas called earlier today to ask about Yash." She referred to Megha's in-laws. "I told them Yash is doing better and was wondering what to tell the Saxenas about Meghaji having the baby here?"

Rakesh clapped the pages of the paper together, turned a page, fanned the sheets apart and held it before his face like a barrier.

"Rakesh? Are you listening? When should we—"

"Isn't that your responsibility?"

"Isn't she your sister?"

He lowered the paper. "As you are my wife. Ditto? We have several invitations for New Year's Eve, and I said yes to the Singhals. Make sure you have something nice to wear."

"Of course." She softened her tone. "I just want to know what you think."

"Women matters are yours to sort out. Pushpa is no help. Do what you think is right. Besides, how does what I think matter?"

"I've never handled another woman's delivery before."

"There are many things you've never done before. But that

shouldn't be a problem considering you're doing lots on your own nowadays without permission."

Did he know about the change of plans to send Yash back to St. Paul's? "I don't know what you are talking about."

"You do."

"Yash will have to go back to St. Paul's. I've made my decision, and I was right all along. You can take him since I brought him home. But this isn't about Yash. I'm referring to—"

The sound of porcelain rattling on a trolley disturbed the moment.

Rakesh folded the paper in half and then in quarters. "No tea from now on. We should change because change is good."

"What change?"

The servant filled two cups with hot, brown liquid and the aroma of coffee hung in the air. She leaned closer for a better view and from the almost black color it looked like a dark roasted blend.

"I'm changing my habits to suit you." He took a cup, sniffed it and then he turned to the servant. "Lots of milk and sugar for me. This drink is far too cheap for my taste. Don't know what people see in it."

The servant followed Rakesh's instructions and left.

Rakesh raised the cup to his lips and took a sip. "Burnt. Brown. Pathetic." He tilted the cup over a bonsai plant and the coffee seeped into the soil, leaving a moist imprint on the surface.

SHEETAL OPENED THE DOOR TO YASH'S ROOM AND FOUND HIM FAST ASLEEP. She had secretly packed his suitcase that afternoon and planned to tell him first thing tomorrow morning. No, not *first* thing. She would wait until after breakfast. She caressed his left cheek and ran her fingers through his hair. Wasn't it only yesterday that she'd brought him home from Mansali and then recently promised he could stay? How quickly her world had turned from hope to loss. She looked at the time on her watch. Ten. Twelve hours until Yash would catch tomorrow's flight. She had informed Rakesh of the reservations that afternoon but didn't understand why he showed no reaction and said nothing about it.

She touched the corner of Yash's lips and traced a finger over his eyes, nose, cheeks and chin. Her heart tightened, wanting to hold on, but she pulled away.

Sheetal entered the darkness of her bedroom dimly haloed by Rakesh's beside lamp and the stench of scotch reeked.

Rakesh sat in bed, a quarter-full bottle of scotch and an empty glass near the bedside lamp.

She walked across the room and stopped at the footboard "You're back to drinking?"

"No," he slurred.

She marched toward the bedside table, grabbed the open scotch bottle and cap and noticed another empty bottle near her feet. "You had this too?"

"Looong time ago." He leaned over the bed's edge, groping for the tumbler. However, his fingers tapped the glass and moved it along the table's surface. The glass toppled and fell.

She screwed the cap back on. "How are you going to take Yash on the morning flight in this state? You need to leave by seven sharp."

He lunged for the bottle of scotch in Sheetal's hand and landed on all fours on the duvet, but she circled the drink behind and stepped back.

"Give it." Two words.

She firmed her grip, shocked at his pathetic animal-like state. She hadn't meant to keep Yash's return a secret from Rakesh but didn't expect Rakesh would be so devastated.

"Give!"

She took a step back. "I won't."

"Oh?" He curled his lips in a sneer. "You won't?"

"No."

"I will."

"Will what?"

"Take it from you."

"Why are you doing this? You promised to stop."

"Like you? Told you to stop fasting on Karva Chauth so many times. You starve for me. Worship the moon for me—eh? And look what happens when I'm not around?" He crawled on the bed.

"Rakesh. You've had too much."

"Too much of you. So now you give someone else a turn—eh?"

"What are you talking about?"

The light from the bulb flickered. "Give." He commanded.

She backed away. "You promised to stop."

He fanned open his fingers and lowered one foot on the carpet. "Now hand it over like a good girl. Promise. I won't bite." He grinned, and the bars of his teeth sparkled in the light.

Something pressed into her back and Sheetal stopped. She swung a hand behind and hit a cold glass surface.

Rakesh rose and swaggered toward her. "You did this, Sheetal."

She turned away from the thickening stench of his acid breath.

"Shame. Shame-on-you." He waved an index finger, singing the words in a haunting melody. "Married-and-with-another-man? You-shouldn't-have." He lunged for the bottle, lost balance and fell against the mirrored door. The door swung open, and Rakesh clung to the side struggling to balance. The faint glow of light from the artificial fireplace paneled against the left brick wall, casting orange shadows on a sofa in the room's center and Rakesh's desk. "Shouldn't with another man."

Her heart filled with dread. "What other man?"

"You-didn't-tell-me. You've-been-hiding." The mirror swayed back and forth as Rakesh struggled to stay upright. The reflection of the bedroom's interior swung with his momentum from the tossed duvet to the faded wallpaper and stained carpet. "I-know-everything."

Calm. Be calm. "What are you talking about?"

"You and your friend."

"What friend?"

He grabbed Sheetal's hand, swung her into the den and pushed the door closed with a heel, struggling to balance. The thick slab of wood almost touched the wall's edge, stopped and a photosphere of light from the bedroom illuminated his hand reaching out. "Give."

Sheetal swung the bottle behind again. "You've had enough."

He pounced, wrestled the bottle out of her grip, unscrewed the lid and gulped the liquid neat.

"Stop, Rakesh, you'll hurt yourself."

He paused, cupped his lips around the bottle's rim and resumed drinking.

"Talk to me, Rakesh. Let's talk this through."

He lowered his hand and let go of the empty bottle. "You want to talk?"

"Yes, Rakesh. Let's talk."

"About what?"

"Any—"

"Who is he?"

She numbed.

"You had lunch with him, right?"

"Who?"

"Some Chopra? Old friend? Old memories? Good memories?"

"He's Yash's House Master and Science teacher."

"Oh come, Sheetal. You know this man from before, don't you?"

He couldn't know it was Arvind. "We got caught in a storm and ducked into this restaurant for cover. He happened to be there."

"Oh, so you'll join any man sitting alone in a restaurant for lunch?"

"I just had a coffee, Rakesh. He knows Yash."

"He knows *you*, Sheetal. Tell me, does he still like you?"

The breaths drew in quickly and her heart pounded.

"Do you like him?"

She couldn't breathe. "He's Yash's teacher, Rakesh. How can you think—"

"My mistake." He staggered forward, slipped on the bottle and lunged, but Sheetal scrambled aside, and Rakesh fell face down.

"Look at how drunk you are." She grabbed him by the arm, forced him to his feet and swung an arm around her shoulders while supporting him by the waist. Her back hunched under the burden of his weight. The stench of vomit and urine made her gag. She helped him back to the room away from the darkness before she retched.

Rakesh wrenched himself free, turned around and staggered back to the den.

"Was he better than me? Did you enjoy each other's company? Must have." He sank onto the couch. "So different, so changed since you returned. You think I wouldn't know? How was he? Good?" He rose to his feet, staggered past to the desk on the right, yanked a drawer open and grabbed another bottle.

Fear clawed at her heart. Did he know the friend was Arvind? Her mind raced to change the topic and stop him from drinking himself to death. "Dr. Kishore said—"

"Fuck the doctor!" He smashed the bottle against the table's edge. Shards of glass and puddles of scotch littered the wooden surface and carpet. "What the fuck were you doing, bitch?"

"Listen to me, Rakesh." Her chest tightened. "You don't know what you're saying."

"Out to get me? Ruin me?" He pulled a belt out of his trousers and coiled it around his knuckle, leaving the end hanging free. He whipped the table with a crack.

"Listen, Rakesh," she pleaded.

"Fucking slut." His spittle sprayed her like bullets.

The belt came down.

She raised her arms in defense. "Stop, Rakesh!"

The belt came down again.

"You don't know what you're doing."

"That son-of-a-bitch?" The belt snaked up in the air and cracked down. Again and again.

Sheetal caught the strip of leather, held on with all her might and yanked it out of his grip, but he held on. And then he was tilting, falling on her and she tried to scramble out of the way. The force of his weight pounded her against the floor and venoms of pain seared along her mid-riff, legs and feet. She pushed him off, rolled away, and the hot needles pierced.

Tiny pools of blood dotted her body. Particles of glass crusted her arms and feet. She pulled out the shards and shrapnel, hot tears running down her cheeks.

Broken.

Shattered.

Glass.

20
GONE

E arly next morning before sunrise, Sheetal called Mama in desperation, shared Yash's travel details to Mansali and asked Papa to buy tickets to take Yash back.

Two hours later the Prasads arrived at the Dhanraj's.

With her feet, arms and upper torso covered in gauze and bandages, Sheetal hobbled toward Mama and Papa seated on the Fulton Whites.

Mama gasped and rose to her feet, and Papa rushed over to help. "What happened?"

"I had a slight accident." Sheetal sat down with Papa's support and perched her right heel on her left ankle to keep it elevated. She hid the left wrist below the shield of her sari. "I fell on some broken glass. But it's not as bad as it looks."

"Let me see." Mama bent at the waist and raised the skirt of Sheetal's sari up the length of her calves, but Sheetal gently pushed Mama's hand away and fanned the pleats around her feet.

Sheetal had spent the night pulling out splinters and shards of glass then disinfected the open wounds with Dettol antiseptic before patching them with gauze and thick, white bandages. She wrapped the pallu around her shoulder to hide the bruises on her collarbone, arms and mid-riff. Wearing a salwar suit would have been so much easier, but saris hid bruises and enveloped pain in their pleats and folds.

"Tell us, Beti." The skin on Mama's face hung in folds desperate for anchor. She had grown weaker and gray circles stamped her eyes. "What really happened?"

How could she tell Mama the truth when Mama was dealing with so much already?

Mama leaned in and whispered, "Did Rakeshji do this to you?"

Sheetal gulped.

"Did you tell Rakeshji about Arvind?"

Did Mama think she deserved to be beaten by Rakesh for having revealed Arvind's chance meeting? "Why would I?"

Mama gestured to the bruises. "I thought...maybe you had, and—"

The blood rushed to Sheetal's head. "He's just a *friend*." She emphasized the last word. "That's all."

"That's enough to make any husband suspicious. All these bruises can't be from a fall. I can tell."

"You need to see a doctor," Papa added.

Had Papa been eavesdropping? "Please take Yash away from here. I know it's wrong to ask Papa to travel at such short notice, but Yash is better off at St. Paul's."

"Don't worry about Yash. Your father will take care of him. But look at you. I'm so worried about you now." Mama dabbed a tear with the end of her pallu.

"I can handle myself."

"Is Yash well enough to travel? Has he fully recovered?" Papa asked.

"Much better, but I'm still worried about the psychological effects of the overdose."

"And you?" Mama touched her lightly on the right arm, and

Sheetal winced. "What are you hiding?" She applied a little pressure and the touch burned. "I want the truth."

Pain seared all over and she couldn't hold back. "Rakesh had a little too much to drink last night and—"

Mama leaned forward, the pallu slipped off revealing her bald head, but she quickly draped the sari in place.

Sheetal had woken Yash early that morning, broke the news that he was to return to Mansali with Papa instead of Rakesh and hugged him tight as he cried in her arms. Now her heart squeezed, and Sheetal held back the urge to cry. "I can handle it, Mama. Just take care of Yash. I'll manage the rest."

"Now, now. What's all this?" Mummyji marched into the grand hall. "Oh. I didn't realize you had come so quickly. So nice of you, I tell you, to take Yash back to Mansali. Would have done so myself, but you know how it all is. The accident with Naina's medication last week has the girl upset to no end. Poor girl, I tell you, is on bed rest again. Not eating. Not drinking...nothing. She just stares into space, regretting what happened to Yash. So sorry she is, poor girl, I tell you."

"I'm so sorry to hear about Nainaji," Papa said. "But looking at Sheetal and hearing about Rakeshji—"

"Yes. Very unfortunate, I tell you." Mummyji made herself comfortable on an ottoman. "If only Rakesh did all his drinking outside, I tell you. That is, outside the house." She scrunched her nose. "His bad habits stink the whole mansion! Hai Ishwar! Whole house smells of alcohol all the time."

"Isn't that something you should be taking care of?" Mama asked.

"Why me? First, I manage this house, and now manage their marriage? Only this morning five servants were on their hands and feet, cleaning their mess for six hours straight."

The servants brought Yash's suitcases downstairs.

Mama glanced at Sheetal, but Sheetal turned away and went upstairs.

Sheetal entered Yash's room to find him sitting on the bed pulling threads out of the duvet. She made her way across the room gritting her teeth as sharp spasms of pain rippled through every nerve. She sat on the mattress edge and ran her fingers through Yash's hair. "I know you don't want to go, and I broke my promise. But after what Aunty Naina has done, I have no choice, Beta."

Yash lowered his head.

"Look at me." She put her index finger under his chin and raised his head gently. "Yash, look at me. Just once."

He stiffened, refusing to look up.

"You know how much I love you and how much I'm going to miss you. It hurts me so much to let you go."

He said nothing.

Yash always grew upset when the time came to leave. First, he would argue to stay. Then plead. Sheetal remained adamant, and eventually he cried. After much cajoling and sweet-talking him into the next holiday, Sheetal earned a goodbye hug before he left. Then of course the never-ending wait to speak with him because Yash initially refused to take her calls for the first two to three weeks from Mansali, However, over time the pain of separation healed, and he gradually got back to normal and started speaking to her again.

"How about a new promise? I'll come to your school concert this year and stay on until your exams are over and bring you home." She waited, but he kept his head bowed. "Let's see... January, February, March and April." She counted the months on her fingers. "Four months. Just four until summer holidays."

Yash resumed pulling more threads and dropped them on a growing pile.

"Are you worried about me? Is that it?"

Silence.

"I had an accident last night. But I'll get better soon. You believe me, don't you?"

His attention flickered to the gauze padding her wrists then the skirt of her sari, and Sheetal pulled back her feet under the pleats.

"Oh, I know why you're angry. Your Dad isn't taking you back. Is that so? I promise, Yash. He meant to. He had tickets booked for the two of you, but he's fallen sick." Her throat ached and she gulped. "You've already missed a week of school and it's important you go back so you don't fall behind. We almost lost you, Yash, and I can't bear to lose you again. There's so much outside my control here. Please understand." Her heart fisted in her throat. She blinked to hold back tears, but they threatened to spill.

Silence.

"You're going to leave without goodbye?" She slid off the mattress, crouched slowly, gritting her teeth in pain, and looked up into his eyes. "Remember, you're my little light and you must shine bright. Before you count the months, I'll be there. We'll be together again." Then she pulled away.

SHEETAL YANKED ASIDE THE PEACH-COLORED CURTAINS, AND THE HARSH late-morning light drove away the night's broken shadows.

The contours of Rakesh's body glided under the cream blanket. He raised a hand to his head and slowly woke. "Ugh. My head." He mumbled. "What time is it?" He struggled to sit up but fell back against the pillows. "Shit! What the hell happened?"

"*You* don't remember?" Sheetal tightened her hold on the curtain.

Rakesh pointed at her wrist. "Why are you covered in bandages?"

"You really don't remember anything?"

"I need some chai."

"You of all people need chai to wake up after what you've done?" Anger raged through her gut. "Must be hard to remember with all that scotch in your head. Think." She pulled another curtain pleat aside, bathing him in light. "Who do you think did this?" She pulled the boat-shaped collar of her blouse off her shoulder revealing more bandages. "How's this for morning chai? Awake now? Want to see more?" She raised the skirt of the sari and pointed to her feet caked in crimson. "I was bleeding, but you didn't stop. You didn't listen. You kept whipping me with that." She pointed to the belt hanging across the footboard and let go of her sari. "I begged you to stop, but you didn't."

He shielded his eyes and rolled to the other side. "I don't...don't even remember. I...I must have had too much to drink."

Sheetal walked around the bed and towered two feet above Rakesh. "You're always drunk."

"It's not my fault."

"Are you ever at fault?"

Rakesh dug his right elbow into the mattress, pushed himself up and turned away. "I... didn't mean for anything to happen. It was a mistake."

"You mean I'm making all this up?"

"I don't know what—"

"How can you know anything when you're always drunk?"

"It's not—"

"Of course, it's not your fault." Sheetal raised the pitch of her voice. "The only reason you haven't drunk in the last nine hours is because you were asleep—thank goodness—or you would've surely beaten me to death."

"Sheetal, I—"

"Didn't do such a thing, right? Rakesh Dhanraj, at least wake up to what you've done for once in your life if nothing else."

He pressed his fingers down on his scalp.

"You accused me of cheating on you? I've been faithful to us for ten years. I've given this marriage all I have and look at what you do. What am I supposed to tell everyone?"

"It was an accident."

"Accident?" Sheetal ambled around to his side of the bed. "Your sister drugs my son, and it's an accident. You beat me to death, and it's an accident. What's real, Rakesh? Tell me, what part of my life is real and what is an accident?"

He slid his palm down his forehead, nose, mouth and cupped his lips.

"Go on Rakesh. Speak. You've never held back. Why now? I sent Yash to Mansali today because of you and Nainaji. Our son returned without either of us because of you and your family. What's there to stop you from doing the same to Yash? You let us down, Rakesh. All of us."

Rakesh leaned over the edge, let his hand go and retched. Vomit, the color of rotting mango chutney, splattered Sheetal's pleats.

Sheetal unclipped three safety pins from her sari, unraveled six yards of fabric, trashed the sari on the carpet and hobbled to her closet.

WITH HER DEADLINE FOR THE RENAISSANCE HOTEL'S ORDER JUST AROUND the corner, Sheetal had been working aggressively on the Himalayan Mountain series and had one more painting to complete the assignment.

She had also spent the last two days researching cirrhosis of the liver and learned that instead of efficiently eliminating toxins Rakesh's damaged liver was recycling waste. Rakesh may not want to consider his condition serious because he was in the initial stages, but he only stood a chance at recovery if he abstained from alcohol. Symptoms like jaundice, fatigue, confusion, disorientation and changes to his person-ality fell under 'common occurrences'. However, no sick person—no matter how sick—deserved to get away with beating another.

Sheetal hoisted an incomplete painting on the easel. Despite having worked on this painting thrice, the corrections demanded endless fixes in some tiny corner or the other. Despite all her efforts, she just couldn't do justice to the work. In a fit of anger last week, she finally put aside the project with the rationale she couldn't afford to waste any more time and energy pursuing something that demanded more than she could ever give.

Sheetal squeezed out some titanium white, midnight black, and several blue, yellow and red paints on a palette. She dipped a two-inch wide brush in the white, then dipped it in blue to form a bluish-gray color and spread a thin layer along the bottom edge of the canvas. She lifted the brush halfway up to the carved mountains and dabbed small strokes. Something didn't look right, and she sighed. She could easily put this aside and give up, but after having invested so much of herself she couldn't just let go. Dedication demanded persistence and if she wanted to reach the heights of Tagore and Husain's caliber she couldn't surrender.

A cold gust of air rushed in, and Sheetal's attention drifted to the broken window. So typical of Rakesh to leave a mess for others to clean up! Her best bet was to hang one of the rejected orchids on the window and get the point across, so he'd realize the next time he visited the studio.

She swept the brush in horizontal strokes on the lower third of the canvas creating shallow waters to hide defects in the mountains' base. Then she stepped aside to gain a different perspective. The error distorted the piece like yesterday's one-way conversations with Yash.

She'd called him twice since he returned to Mansali and listened to the slow and steady breathing in the silence of his answers. He needed time to adjust and now, possibly more time to overcome the added trauma of the overdose.

Sheetal added touches of greens, browns and white on snow-capped peaks to give the mountains height and dimension. She dabbed the tip of her brush in white and lifted some of the blue from the lake's surface, creating mist between the crevices. However, the intended effect wasn't coming across.

Mint scented the air. *Rakesh.* Sheetal tightened. They hadn't spoken in two weeks, and she certainly didn't intend to start now.

She picked up another brush, fanned open the bristles with the pad of her thumb, dipped it in some yellow, ochre and green and streaked a line of conifers along the bank. She dabbed away highlighting the left of the trees facing the sun with tinges of yellow. She filled the empty banks of the lake with bushes, wildflowers and pebbles all the while feeling the press of his stare on her back.

"Sheetal?"

Her bangles jilted back and forth with the brush's steady movement.

"We need to talk."

Talk? She pursed her lips and lifted the brush higher. The bandages were off, the scars healed and whips of his belt almost faded. Now he wanted to talk? "What more do you have to say?"

"Put down the brush, Sheetal. It's important."

Bile fire worked up her throat and she firmed her grip on the filbert. "Don't you order me to put the brush down after what you did. No apology since. Did you once stop to think about what I've been going through and how I feel?"

"Your father just called."

She threw the brush on the palette. "And you told him what you did to me? Right? And what a perfect son-in-law you turned out to be."

"Your mother..." He looked past her shoulder.

"What about Mama? She stopped the chemo a while back. I know that. We all know that. Except you, of course. Because you're so busy beating me up."

"She's—"

"She's what? What happened?" The blood rushed to her head. "Did you tell her what you really do with a belt? It would have killed her. She would have died right there and then."

"Gone, Sheetal. I'm so sorry. She's gone."

21
FREE

Sheetal entered Mama's bedroom at the Prasad's.

Mama lay on the bed, serene in a blue sari and in the same position and on the same side of the mattress as when they were last here together. Papa's face had caked dry with tears, and he sat slumped in one corner of the room, his arms hanging limp by his sides and both legs extending out like a marionette that had lost its strings.

Mama's sleeping or unconscious like Yash. The chemotherapy wore her out and we should schedule the next treatment. Sheetal leaned over Mama and shook her gently. "Mama. Wake up. It's me." She withdrew from the cold feel of Mama's arm.

Mama didn't move.

Sheetal waited for Mama's lips to quiver, for feather-like wrinkles to tighten at the corners of her eyes, or for a change in her blank expression, but Mama lay motionless. "I'm here, Mama." Sheetal kneeled beside the bed, cupped the side of Mama's face and numbed. So cold. So stiff. Mama couldn't leave. She was sleeping. She turned Mama's face in her direction, and Mama's head flopped to hit the pillow's edge. "Take her to the hospital." She turned to Papa, but his expression drew a blank. "She needs the chemo. Ma—" The word lodged in Sheetal's throat and tightened her chest. She ran a palm across Mama's forehead and brushed the blue halo-like mantle aside. "Mama. I'm here now." The sari blurred in her vision. She rubbed her eyes, and hot tears burned down her cheeks. Then a heaviness weighed on her left shoulder.

"She's gone," Rakesh said.

"She's sleeping." Sheetal ran her thumb along the contours of Mama's eyes, waiting for the upper curve of Mama's lips to release a tiny gush of air.

"Sheetal." Rakesh knelt beside her and tightened his hold on her shoulder. "She's gone."

Then a cry like the wail of an animal tore through her heart and ripped her soul to shreds.

INDU PRASAD WAS CREMATED LATER THAT EVENING, AND VIKRAM SET FIRE TO her pyre.

22

ILLUSIONS

Despite being in her second trimester, Megha visited Sheetal every day after the thirteen-day mourning period ended. Megha lent Sheetal her full support and attention, offered her a shoulder to cry on, and Sheetal was grateful to have a friend.

However, after six days of being shadowed, Sheetal paused mid-painting to gaze out the studio window and noticed Megha stood right behind. When Sheetal went downstairs, Megha followed. When Sheetal canceled a business lunch scheduled for that afternoon, Megha listened close by.

Despite being married and therefore an 'outsider', Megha assumed her position at the Dhanrajs as if she were still one of them. Sheetal couldn't have cared less except that she wanted her privacy back and found Megha's presence suffocating. Sheetal's phone chimed, and she took the call.

"Hello? Mrs. Dhanraj?"

"Speaking." From the corner of her eye, Sheetal glanced behind and Megha stood so close she was almost breathing down her back, so Sheetal spun on her heels and left the studio with the phone clutched to her ear.

"This is Nisha Trivedi, a member of the Board of Directors from Solange Art Gallery."

Sheetal's heart quickened. Renowned for exhibiting works by elite artists, Solange Art Gallery carried a notorious reputation for scrutinizing every artist's works before hosting them. The artists selected to showcase their masterpieces received ample media coverage, attention from the cream of Raigun's art community, and, as a consequence, received more offers to display their works from prestigious art galleries.

"What can I do for you?" Sheetal walked along the south wing, careful not to sound overanxious.

"We'd like to feature twenty of your paintings at our next exhibit on April thirteenth."

Sheetal paused at the railing. April thirteenth meant after her return from Mansali she'd have about a week to prepare for the event. "Twenty paintings?"

"That's right. We're exhibiting works from foreign artists and some of our own celebrities like Husain and Tagore Sahib. We thought something new to represent the modern generation would be a great addition."

Her heart soared and she swallowed, but couldn't feel a thing. "How did you hear about me?"

"Who doesn't know a Dhanraj?" Nisha's wind-chime voice played music to her ears. "Your name and the family's reputation speak for itself. But we have been hearing some great things about your work and saw several on display. You're incredibly talented."

Sheetal pressed a hand to her chest. Her latest series, "Basking at the Feet of Mountain Gods", shipped to the Renaissance Hotel on time and if accepted, would add to her credibility. "Thank you. I'm so flattered that I don't know what to say."

"Just say yes."

A weight shadowed from behind and Sheetal looked over her

shoulder. Megha again. "Please give me a minute so that I can take some notes."

"Of course."

Sheetal sped down the south wing, took a right on the west, another right and entered her room. She grabbed a pen and notepad from her bedstand and sat on the mattress' edge. Clearly, the invitation was a result of the Dhanraj label. Perhaps she could use the opportunity to break away from the family name and claim independence in her career with her ethics, professionalism and continued caliber of work. "Is there a specific theme or collection you'd like me to put together?"

"I was thinking..."

A shadow from behind closed in. Sheetal looked over her shoulder, and Megha had made herself comfortable on the sofa backed to the mirrored wall. Sheetal jotted notes and ignored Megha. When she was done, she exited her room, slammed the door and left Megha behind.

A WEEK LATER SHEETAL WAS IN THE STUDIO WHEN SHE RECEIVED A CALL from the Renaissance Hotel.

Megha lay sprawled on the studio sofa reading a book but every so often she lowered the book so that the rim rest below the lower cradle of her eyes.

"Hello? Mrs. Dhanraj. Kannada here."

"Hello, Mr. Kannada." *He was probably calling to confirm the remaining balance.* "Sheetal speaking. Just give me a minute, please." Sheetal covered the phone's mouthpiece with her free hand and turned to Megha. "Why don't you go and lie down in another room? That sofa doesn't look too comfortable."

Megha sat up and hoisted both feet on the coffee table. "Oh, don't worry about me. It's my duty to be with you at all times. I mean, it's only been a few weeks since your mother passed away."

Since when had she become Megha's duty? And why did Megha

assure Rakesh before he left for the office every morning that she would stay on for the day? Didn't she have a life to lead with a husband and in-laws? "Yes, hello, Mr. Kannada." Sheetal pressed the phone to her ear and turned her back to Megha. "I understand you received all ten paintings. I got the confirmation—"

"Yes, yes, we did," he said. "All in perfect order. But I'm afraid there's a slight problem."

Sheetal tightened. She'd fixed the problem with that one painting and ensured on-time delivery despite Mama's funeral and thirteen days of mourning that followed. "What's wrong, Kannadaji?"

"The paintings are good. Very good. Bright, happy, and full of life. But others...we cannot use them for the new wing in the hotel. They are too dark. Too depressing."

Sheetal bit her lower lip. How was that possible when she'd stuck to the theme? "I don't understand." She could feel the press of Megha's stare and moved toward the door's edge.

"I'm keeping ones that we are finding suitable, but I already return the rest."

"How many did you send back?"

"About six. By tomorrow you should get them."

She leaned against the wall for support. "I'll take a look and see if I can fix or—no. I can paint another six for you—No. Wait. I have a series of six orchids I can ship today."

"No time, Mrs. Dhanraj. The ribbon-cutting is three days away. Also must be scenery painting. Not flowers..." Kannadaji went on to describe four of the paintings that had been accepted. Sheetal concluded she'd completed those before Yash's accident. Thanks to Naina, she lost focus and now half the order! How would she ever establish herself as a professional if work kept getting returned?

"What's wrong, Bhabhi?" Megha asked.

"Nothing." Her attention wandered to five orchids lying against the wall and one against the broken window. Six rejected flowers and now another six mountains on their way back? What was she supposed to do? Pile them like a stack of magazines on the coffee table downstairs? She walked across to an open window for some fresh air.

The flower-bordered driveway resembled a garland of flowers—hung on a deceased member's photo in accordance with the Hindu culture of commemorating the dead. A knot of pain rose in her chest, and the air thickened. She blinked and tears spilled down her cheeks.

"Just think how much she endured." Megha crept behind. "All that suffering stopped, and the pain has gone."

Did anyone really care? Because life clearly continued to roll for the Dhanrajs like before. The gardeners still weeded and trimmed the hedges. The front lawn had resumed its original perfect state. Servants still mopped and cleaned the house all day. Mummyji attended all her social events and lunches at the club. Naina continued to be depressed and on constant bed rest. Rakesh clocked his hours at work and now returned at seven sharp every night.

"I was only a baby when my mother died. I know..."

Her gut roiled with regret. This was about *her* mama. Not Megha's mama who had died over twenty-five years ago. "I'm sorry but I need to be alone. I—"

"I understand." Megha resumed her position on the sofa. "Bhaiya said you might be a little curt but not to worry and no offense taken." She patted her bulging tummy and propped her feet on the coffee table again.

Sheetal turned around to face her. "What do you mean, a little curt?"

"Just that you haven't been yourself lately and you should have someone with you. That's why I'm here."

"Oh?" Sheetal crossed her arms. For ten years Rakesh had never worried about her being alone, now suddenly he appointed Megha to take charge?

"He said you might need a friend."

"Really? If he's so concerned, then why doesn't he take time off to be my friend?"

Megha dropped her gaze for a moment, then, "Have you spoken to my mother-in-law about my having the baby here?"

"I...we haven't had time to think about it yet." Rakesh would never refuse, and the time fast approached for her to make a decision. "There's too much on my mind right now."

"I'm due in three months and..."

Weeks had sailed by since Rakesh's abuse and Mama's death, but no one cared.

"Are you listening, Bhabhi? I'm talking to you."

"I was talking to you too, but I don't think you're listening. Please, leave me alone."

"Suit yourself. I'm only here because Bhaiya asked me to. I don't need to be here, you know."

"I will talk to your in-laws sometime next week."

Megha stomped out of the room.

Sheetal closed her eyes and took a deep breath. She could almost imagine the outline of Mama's features taking form in the blank canvas of her soul. *"It is easy to hold on to what you have."* Mama's voice played in her mind. *"But the difficulty is in letting go."*

She had to find a way and let go.

Sheetal walked up to the easel and mounted a new canvas. She brushed a horizontal line a third of the way down to anchor grief. Then she dipped a brush on her palette, swirled the bristles in yellow paint and dotted a ball of paint on the upper half of the canvas. She swirled some milky blue to the left and right of the yellow ball and circled the brush to give the clouds a wispy appearance. She filled blue and pastels in wide open spaces. Five hours later she dotted a U-shaped garland of flowers along the lower third of the canvas. On the upper half, she filled the empty spaces equidistant from the central sun with fragments of a broken rainbow tearing its way through the clouds. She stepped back and a wave of relief washed over her. Now all she had to do was find the painting a home.

THE NEXT DAY SHEETAL SIGNED THE RETURN DELIVERY OF SIX PAINTINGS OF the Himalayan Mountains. Heartbroken, she stacked them beside the orchids, regret welling for income lost. Only two hundred and fifty thousand rupees had been deposited in her account and her savings totaled about eight hundred thousand rupees.

That afternoon Sheetal perused the walls of the Dhanraj residence for a place to hang the broken rainbow painting. However, the lighting in a corridor was either too bright, too dull, or some artwork or a statue clustered the wall. After much searching, Sheetal found a corner close to her bedroom that felt right. She removed an old painting and mounted hers careful not to touch the wet paint.

Rakesh, who happened to be passing by, stopped. "No substance in this painting."

Sheetal dragged the painting off the wall. So typical of a Dhanraj to lose sight of the obvious.

At that moment Mummyji and Naina, who were heading for the east wing, stopped and Mummyji pumped both hands on her hips. "Stars. You need stars, I tell you. Fill the sky with hundreds and you'll have more diamonds than you can imagine! Here, let me show you what I mean." Mummyji led Sheetal and Naina to the studio, grabbed the Himalayan painting Sheetal had tried to fix in vain and positioned it on the easel. Then she grabbed a brush and dipped it in some white paint. "You don't mind, no? It is rejected work, anyway."

She wouldn't dare.

Mummyji marked several asterisks in the sky. "See, Naina! How pretty are stars? How much brighter they make this painting? So easy, even you can do."

Sheetal reached for the paintbrush, but Mummyji arched her hand away. "You're ruining my work. Look what you've done!"

"Arrey! What's to ruin when the painting is already so miserable?

You are painting in my house, and this is my property. So, what harm if I correct it, I tell you? I am only brightening it. So easy, this. And you make it look like painting is a talent. Watch, Naina. How I fix this." Mummyji dipped the brush in some yellow and proceeded to dot the left side of the mountains.

The blood rushed to Sheetal's head, and she tightened the fingers of her hands into fists. So, what if the paintings had been returned? The work had been created by her and paid for by supplies she had earned. She was about to grab the brush from Mummyji when her cell phone rang. She marched to the doorway and pulled the phone out of her sari pouch.

"Hello?"

"Sheetal?"

"Yes?" The air stilled. "Who...who is this?"

"Arvind."

Her heart skipped a beat. "Where...where are you calling from?"

"Mansali."

"How did you get my number?"

"From Yash."

Only Dr. Chaturvedi and the staff had access to that kind of information. "Is everything all right?"

"Yash is fine. I'm worried about you."

Sheetal tightened her grip on the instrument. "You shouldn't call."

"Yash told me about your mother. I'm so sorry."

Sheetal opened her mouth to say something, but the words didn't come.

"Sheetal. Are you there?"

"Yes. I...I—"

"I know. It's hard...what happened."

"The cancer. We all..." She broke off. "There was nothing more anyone could do."

"I lost my mother years ago. I understand how you feel. Are you okay?" He paused. "I mean. Really? Are *you* okay?"

Sheetal took a deep breath to raise the pitch of her voice. "I need time."

"We all do. It's what gets you through. You will, but slowly."

"Sheetal?"

"What?"

"Sheetal?"

"What?" Where was the voice coming from? She lowered the phone and stared at the receiver. The voice didn't sound like Arvind. She pressed the phone to her ear again.

"Who is it?"

Mint scented the air, and Sheetal turned. *Rakesh. How long had he been standing in the corridor?* Her mind raced. *The conversation? How much did he hear?* She pressed the phone to her ear. "I'm talking to Papa." The one-two, one-two steps of Rakesh's shoes synched with Arvind's breathing as Rakesh crept closer.

"Hello? Sheetal?" Arvind said.

"Here. Let me talk. You seem fizzed." Rakesh lifted the phone from her grip and pinned it to his ear.

"Hello? Hello? Are you there, Papa?" He raised his eyebrows.

The floor and ceiling spun. Her fingers trembled and she locked the fingers of both hands in a fist.

Rakesh beeped off the phone and handed it back. "He hung up for some reason. You don't look good. Something wrong?"

"I'm fine. I...I just need time."

"Time. It's what gets you through. Slowly."

WITH A HEART AS HEAVY AS THE FRAMED CANVAS, SHEETAL TOOK THE painting of the broken rainbow and the six orchids to the Prasad's on New Year's Eve. She timed her visit to conflict with the Singhal's New Year's Eve party because she had no interest to make small talk with friends and acquaintances, nibble on appetizers and pieces of naan or sip drinks surrounded by drunks when her heart still ached with Mama's absence.

Sheetal entered Papa's office and slanted the orchids against a wall as Papa slowly swiveled in his chair to face her.

"Ah, you're here, Beti." Papa had lost a lot of weight since Mama's death and no longer sat upright but slouched in his seat.

Cracks now ran along the length of the office wall and some of the beige paint chipped and peeled. Dust had settled in tiny nooks and corners and papers were scattered everywhere. The glory of Prasad Bhavan no longer existed. "Look, Papa." She propped the broken rainbow painting on a chair to face papa and tilted it against the headrest. A view of the topiary hedge of peacocks and elephants from the window behind Papa reeked the evening light.

Papa pushed his glasses up the bridge of his nose and a watery film filled the lower cradle of his eyes. "It's...it's Indu, isn't it?"

"You see her?" Sheetal swallowed the lump in her throat. "You see Mama?"

"I only see your Mama and nothing else." He dabbed his cheeks with the back of a shirt sleeve. "I see her everywhere."

Finally! Someone could see past the illusion of Mama wearing a floral garland, her forehead dotted with a fading yellow bindi, and rainbows spilling from her eyes. Sheetal sank into a chair with relief. "I think of her all the time. I miss her, Papa."

Papa rose to his feet and came around the desk. He pulled a chair and sat beside her. "She's gone and left us. I never realized how much she meant until now." Papa took off his glasses and put them on the table. He dabbed at the tears with a corner of his handker-chief. "She was and always will be everything to me in this lifetime." He gestured to the painting. "It's more than beautiful. It's a priceless work of art."

"Put your glasses on, Papa. You'll see better."

Papa shook his head. "What's the use when I see so much more now without them? What hurts even more, is that your mother will never know the truth. If only I'd listened more."

"What do you mean?"

The half-dipping sun glowed behind the hedge. "She always said I shared too much information with Vikram about the business and gave him more responsibility than he deserved. Can you believe Vikram's been running board meetings without me and authorizing paperwork without my approval? Legal documents."

"Since when?"

"Before Indu—I don't even know. I—"

"Can't you do something?"

"He has too much control now, and it's all my fault. Indu tried so hard to warn me, the same way she warned me against you marrying Rakeshji, but I..."

"Rakesh?" She froze.

"Indu never wanted you to marry him."

"But she always said it was what you both wanted and the right thing to do."

"It's what I wanted." His gaze fell to the floor. "She warned me, not once or twice, but several times that Rakesh would never make a good husband. She said Arvind truly loved you."

Her heart knotted. Did Papa realize he was admitting they'd chosen wrong? "Why didn't you or Mama say anything for so long?"

"And risk the stability in your life? Indu didn't want the past to haunt you again. But after we saw you that day covered in all those bandages and blood, she reminded me of my mistake." The sinking sun cast long dark shadows between them. "Is this the first time he's done this to you?"

Sheetal shook her head. "Once or twice before, but he's never gone this far."

Papa propped both elbows on his knees and cradled his head. "How did I let this happen?"

"It's not your fault. You didn't know."

"But why didn't you tell us?"

"And bring shame to the family? What would you have done? Agreed to a divorce? The last time I left him and came home you waited for a month—no, two months, and told me I had to find a way to work things out and make peace with my husband and family for Yash's sake."

"I was wrong. So wrong." His voice cracked. "People like us, not born rich. I worked so hard to bring us this far. I did not want you to live those dark days when I couldn't even afford to buy you a proper bed, a clean place to live, or your own room. I know what it means to live scarcely. To not know if you can provide food for your family for one week or the next because you can only think of today. But never did I imagine that people with so much can stoop down to so little." The last of the day's light raked in the dark green of the front lawn. Papa switched on a table lamp, and an umbrella of yellow spilled all around. "You are wise to keep your earnings in a separate account and enroll Yash at boarding school." He reached over and ran a palm gently on her shoulder. "For no fault of your own, you suffer." Then he broke down and his voice cracked. "Can you forgive me?"

An ache welled up her chest. "Let it go, Papa."

"I'll talk to Rakesh and see what I can do."

"There's nothing you can do. No matter what happens the fault is always mine."

"No one deserves to live like this and be treated this way."

"It won't happen again." She put a hand on his arm.

"How can you be sure?"

"Because I won't let it happen."

"Come and stay with me and leave him. I mean it. You don't need to go back."

She'd promised Mama that she'd take care of Papa. By running away wouldn't she burden Papa with more responsibilities? "Rakesh will demand custody of Yash and he'll fight me till the end."

"Then take Yash and leave."

Sheetal numbed.

"I'll support whatever decision you make." He patted her hand.

"Where do I go from here?"

"I'll call Ashwin in New Jersey and inform him of your situation."

Papa was overreacting. "I'll figure something out. Trust me. There's no need to go anywhere."

"For so long I trusted Rakesh when it should have been you. I'm such a fool."

"Papa—"

"Promise me. From now on you will make the decision that is right for you. Even if it hurts, you must fight to protect the ones you love. Because once they're gone, there's nothing left."

23
RUST

Rakesh slipped the receiver back into its cradle on the office table and every tight-wired chord in his body sagged with relief. He hadn't expected Tanaka to agree to the partnership so quickly. He was prepared for a barrage of questions, arguments and possible cancellation of the meeting. Instead, Tanaka surprisingly agreed to partner with Dhanraj & Son and scheduled for them to meet in New Delhi on April fifth to complete all the legal formalities and signing of documents.

Rakesh flexed the fingers of his left hand. At last! Things were falling in place. His attention fell to a photo of Sheetal and Yash, their cheeks pressed to each other, smiles revealing evenly set white teeth and a sparkle in their eyes. They looked so happy—without him.

Chopra. The word revolved in his head. What were the odds that Sheetal had found Arvind Chopra after all these years? *Impossible. Clearly a mistake somewhere.* Adrenaline surged through his veins, and he took a deep breath to keep calm. Sheetal didn't have the gall to skip one Karva Chauth let alone think of another man! Still, he had to be careful. Stay in control. The Japanese were watching his every move.

The intercom buzzed.

"Yes?"

"Dr. Chaturvedi is on the line," Reshma said.

"Who?"

"The principal of St. Paul's School. You scheduled a call with him."

Rakesh crossed his legs, lit a Robusto cigar and waited for the tip to glow. Then he picked up the receiver and pushed on a button. "Hello? Rakesh speaking." He exhaled and clouds of smoke curled up in the air.

"Ah, Mr. Dhanraj." Dr. Chaturvedi's voice oozed through the speakers. "How nice to speak with you."

"How's the weather in Mansali? Cooler than Raigun, no doubt."

"Well, of course, it's very cold up in the mountains, Sir. But another month or two until spring. Which reminds me, I hope you'll attend the annual spring concert on April fifth."

"Sheetal will be there." Rakesh perched the cigar on an ashtray. "I have a business meeting in Delhi that day." An awkward silence filled the receiver, and Rakesh waited for Dr. Chaturvedi to speak.

"So, I um...I assume you want to talk about Yash? Yes?" Dr. Chaturvedi stretched the vowels. "He's doing well in school."

"I'm sure you're aware of that unfortunate accident over the holidays."

A pause followed by the sound of heavy breathing. "Why, yes... yes. Perhaps um...he still needs a little time to adjust and settle in—"

"Do we need to come?"

"Oh no, no, no. Not at all," Dr. Chaturvedi said. "I'm sure every-thing will be fine. If um...there are any concerns, you understand, we notify the parents immediately."

"Of course." Rakesh reached for the cigar and raised it to his lips. He chewed on the end, savoring the deep tobacco flavor.

"I am, um...assuming this is not about Yash, then?"

"No. It's about a Mr. Chopra."

"Yash's House Master?"

"Yes."

"What about him?" Dr. Chaturvedi's voice tightened.

"Tell me everything about this Mr. Chopra."

"B...but that's confidential. I'm um...not at liberty to discuss—"

"We're not discussing him. I just want some information."

"I'm...I'm sorry. It's against the rules."

"Oh come, Doctor, bending the rules a little won't hurt anyone."

"It would be a breach of trust, Sir."

Dr. Chaturvedi held a reputation for being on the perpetual lookout for kind donations. Rakesh uncrossed his legs and stretched them out. "I heard you're falling behind on funds and you're having trouble keeping up with rising costs."

Dr. Chaturvedi coughed. The rattle of phlegm in his throat followed by heavy breathing oozed through the pores of the speaker. "The problem, um...Sir, is that—"

"I'll have fifty thousand wired to you by tomorrow morning." Rakesh glanced at his watch. He still had to go home, shower, dress and make it to the Singhal's party fashionably late.

"Oh...aah...well, you see..."

"Sixty-five. Better?"

"Yes, Sir!"

"Let's start with the name. His first name."

"Arvind."

Rakesh tensed. Couldn't be. Had to be someone else. "Where is he from?"

The sound of papers being ruffled filled the receiver. "New Delhi. He's a graduate of New Delhi University. But originally from Raigun."

Rakesh crushed the cigar in the ashtray.

RAKESH STAGGERED UPSTAIRS AND PAUSED AT THE LANDING. HE LET GO OF the banister and struggled to stand, however, the passageway spun and tilted. He grabbed the wall for support and planted one foot ahead of the other. *Arvind—eh? After all these years he comes back.* He focused on the third door ahead. Big mouth Naina must have told Sheetal something about him and turned her against him.

He turned the knob, swung open the door and stared into the swaying darkness. "Wake up." Barely able to cup his lips around the words, wetness drooled down the corner of his mouth. "Come on, bitch. Let's make your new year happy. Up!" He brushed a sleeve across his chin but brushed the air instead.

The room flooded with light, and Rakesh raised an arm to shield his eyes. Naina was talking...saying something, but the words blurred like the dark green of her nighty. Two? How could there be two of her? Rakesh blinked and shook his head. He leaned on the door for support, but the corridor tilted right.

"Out! Get out! ...My room," she yelled.

Her voice echoed all around and in his head. Rakesh raised both hands and rammed his palms against his ears to block out her screams, but she was getting closer. Her face, a mass of contorted brown wrinkles, swung to the left and right. He lunged, and she slipped from reach to the corridor. *Stop moving.* He opened his mouth, but the words locked with his tongue.

"I'll call..."

"What did you tell my wife? You told her about Kartik, didn't you?"

"I didn't. Promise. I—"

Rakesh reached out and pounced, but Naina moved out of reach. He reeled forward and stopped at a horizontal rod of marble at pelvis height, grabbed it and leaned over the edge as bile sizzled up his throat. A brown and white puddle below mingled in each other's ebb and flow. "D'you even know what shit I'm in? My wife hates me coz of you." He maneuvered himself to face her, but three Nainas appeared and each one raised a hand to cover the nose. "Three hundred and fifty million!" He let go of the railing. "Where's it all gonna come from? Can you count that high, bitch?"

She stood inches away from reach, all three of her faces covered in webs of stringy black hair.

"All fucked up because of you. My son, bitch! Nearly died coz of you."

"It was an accident!" she screamed. "But...you made me kill our father...The whole episode's over for you. I...I live with the guilt every day."

Rakesh struggled to make sense, but she kept shifting out of view.

"You stood...behind the curtains, watching. Making sure I gave Papa that tea. How did I know it was poisoned? I was just a girl... Only seventeen...threatened. You trapped me." She neared him. "I'm going to tell everyone what you made me do."

He cocked his head back and laughed.

"Mummy!" Naina screamed.

Rakesh lunged and clamped her mouth shut with a palm. "Shut up!" He pressed hard, desperate to mince the words against her tongue. He tilted her back, further, harder, until her eyes bulged, and her black pupils shrank to the back of her head. Her chest heaved against a palm as she struggled for breath, and adrenaline surged through his body. Squeeze. Suck every rupee out. All three hundred and fifty million. Her skull would snap any second. "Give my money back!"

Then a burn spread across his cheek. The room spun. He reeled away and lost balance. The balcony railings, pillars and doors revolved. The walls of the mansion and floor tilted. Blood rushed to his head, and he slammed against the cold marble floor.

"Leave her!"

Pushpa?

Crunch. His mouth warmed.

Everything blurred.

Everything black.

24
STATIC

Later that morning after Sheetal returned from the Prasad's, the servants whisked her into the Marquette Dining Room where Mummyji and Naina were having breakfast. "You are here at last!" Mummyji jumped to her feet, and the chair reeled back. "Rakesh almost choked my Naina early this morning before he knocked down drunk. Six servants, I tell you. Six servants dragged him from the corridor to the room and they refused to help him change into fresh clothes. What a way, I tell you, to start the new year."

Naina raised a hand to her throat and rubbed it gently. "He tried to strangle me."

What a shame he didn't. Sheetal bit her lip. Mummyji's tendency to over-dramatize anything concerning Naina made it hard to gauge the truth.

The morning buffet breakfast in sterling silver chafing dishes graced the length of a hutch. Sheetal's stomach growled, and she lifted the lids one by one. However, the spread of grilled tomato and chutney sandwiches, steaming, fluffy, white idlis, light green coconut chutney and *poha*, flattened, spiced yellow rice flakes sautéed with mixed vegetables, didn't whet her appetite. The thick scent of citrus detergent overwhelmed the air. Clearly, Mummyji must have rung in the new year with a wholesome round of cleaning.

"What am I to do?" Mummyji pumped both hands on her hips. "You leave your husband, a drunk, I tell you to..."

Sheetal nicked a corner of the triangular-sliced sandwich and popped it in her mouth but tasted nothing. She helped herself to some poha and took a seat.

Mummyji sat down again. "You don't think before going to spend the night at your parent's home. For what? To put up some painting?"

"It's not *some* painting. It was my mother's painting—"

"It's him, I tell you. This sick husband of yours who is alive and breathing who you should be taking care of. Isn't that why you fast on Karva Chauth? Your responsibility lies here with him and *this* family first. You think I am sitting around here for fun? Ashok put me in charge of the whole mansion and estate in that will, I tell you, for a reason. Can you imagine the responsibility I must carry, I tell you, because he is no longer alive? And I must live that responsibility every day."

"My mother still lives in my heart." Sheetal shoved a spoonful of poha in her mouth and chewed, but the yellow puffy rice flakes tasted bland. The spoon fell from her grip and clanked the plate.

Laal Bahadur, the chef peeked out the kitchen door. "Food is not good, Choti Memsahib?

Mummyji's expression darkened. "You ask her, Laal Bahadur. But you don't ask me if the food is to my satisfaction?"

"It's fine." Sheetal smiled. "But I think I burnt my tongue last night, so I can't taste much." She turned to Mummyji. "I've been struggling for ten years to live with Rakesh. But he's—"

"And obvious—no? How successful you are. Or your marriage wouldn't be in a mess."

How dare she! "All this time you've been treating me like I don't exist and I'm invisible. Now suddenly when things go wrong, you hold me responsible?"

"Like every married woman, you are responsible for your husband and the state of this family."

"As Rakesh's mother, even if you are his stepmother, perhaps you should claim responsibility too? After all, this is *your* family and *your* responsibility, isn't it?"

Mummyji scrunched her face.

WHEN SHEETAL ENTERED HER BEDROOM, THE THICK, HEAVY STENCH OF liquor and urine caused her to hold her breath. She raised a hand to her face as a face mask. Rakesh lay on his back in the middle of their bed, dressed in last night's tuxedo, sunlight spilling through the open curtains.

Bluish-gray bruises shadowed his face. Sallow skin clung to his temples, nose and eyes and sagged at the corners. If only the media could see the flamboyant, titanium silver knight in all his glory! Sheetal inched closer. Saliva drooled from the corners of his lips and hung off the curve of his blood-crusted chin. The jacket wrinkled in folds clearly a size too big. Had he lost more weight and his mind too? Or had the rust of the Dhanraj label finally tarnished him?

Since none of the male servants wanted to help Rakesh out of his soiled clothes, Sheetal decided it best to leave him in his filthy state and to later have their bed sheets stripped and burned.

Anything proved easier than dealing with Rakesh Dhanraj, and she had done more than her share for one lifetime.

A MONTH LATER, SHEETAL WORKED ON THE SEVENTH IN A SERIES OF TWENTY desert paintings for the Solange Art Gallery and now signed each work 'Sheetal' without the Dhanraj label.

She instructed the servants to serve her evening coffee upstairs because she didn't want to spend any more time making one-way conversations with Rakesh. At precisely five that evening, Roshni wheeled in the evening coffee and handed her an envelope from St. Paul's School.

Sheetal dropped three cubes of sugar in the cup, added some warm milk and stirred her coffee with a spoon. She took a sip, put down the cup and peeled open the envelope's flap. The invitation for the annual spring concert on April fifth requested parents to make their reservations in advance.

Six more weeks until she next saw Yash. She took comfort in the fact that at least he answered her calls with monosyllables now. He must be busy studying for his mid-terms, she figured, which is also why he ended phone conversations quickly. She went to the Japanese garden to give Rakesh the letter and found him and Megha sipping tea. "I forgot to tell you, but I received an invitation from the Solange Art Gallery. They've requested twenty paintings."

Megha and Rakesh sipped their tea without a word. "This also came in today's mail from St. Paul's." She handed the letter to Rakesh, but he didn't bother to look.

Megha looked at her watch and let out a *whoosh* of air. She rubbed her belly and leaned against the backrest.

If Megha wanted to show attitude, fine. She couldn't care less. "The concert is six weeks away and we should make reservations. I can stay on until after Yash's finals and bring him home." Sheetal had calculated that if she couldn't complete twenty paintings in the next six weeks, she still had a good three weeks after her return from Mansali.

Rakesh took the letter, raised an eyebrow, and handed it back without reading it. "I have to be in Delhi for a meeting with Tashukomo Electronics that day, so I won't be going."

Sheetal exhaled in relief. She'd get alone time with Yash again. "But you promised Yash you'd go. He's—"

"I don't have time." He waved a hand. "Anyway, you're happier on your own."

THREE DAYS LATER SHEETAL WAS WORKING ON A DESERT PAINTING WHEN THE landline phone rang. She waited for someone to take the call but after six rings she marched to the sofa and grabbed the receiver.

"Hello?"

"Hallo?" A woman said. "Hallo? Calling from Mansali, St. Paul's School for—" Static crackled the air waves.

"Yash?"

Sheetal's heart flipped. "Hello? Yash, Beta. Is that you?"

"Sheetal?"

"Hello?"

"Sheetal? Is that you?"

"Arvind"? She tightened her grip on the receiver and prayed no one else picked up the other phone downstairs. "Is Yash—?"

"That's why I'm calling. I tried calling your mobile, but you didn't pick up."

Sheetal patted her waist for the sari pouch. "I...I must have left it in the room. What's wrong? Is Yash all right?"

"He's...he's having trouble."

"What trouble?" She walked across to the window.

"He can't focus and he's falling behind in class."

Impossible. Her attention fell to the driveway below and she glanced at her watch. It was 6:45 p.m. Rakesh would be home soon. "Maybe the rehearsals and practice are too much for him."

"What rehearsals?"

"The spring concert. I received the letter about the event and there's only six weeks left, plus the children have mid-terms right now."

"He can hardly talk clearly." Arvind's voice crackled through the static. "Barely manage full sentences and—"

"What do you mean?"

"He was pulled out of the concert weeks ago."

"He must have been nervous from stage fright." Or perverts? Fear gripped her soul. Were older boys hurting him?

"The organizing committee gave him several chances, but Yash refused to—" Static interfered. "I know because I'm one of the organizers. I saw him, Sheetal. He wouldn't even open his mouth. He refuses to talk."

"Perhaps he can't take the pressure after the overdose incident."

"This has nothing to do with the pressure of the overdose, concert or schoolwork."

"I don't understand."

"It's about you."

"It's my fault. I broke my promise. I told him I'd let him stay with us in Raigun and enroll him in school here. You shouldn't call." She looked over her shoulder, relieved she was alone. "I'll be in so much trouble if anyone finds out."

"How much more trouble, Sheetal?" His voice stormed against the static. "I know what he does to you."

"Who?" The breath tightened in her throat. "Who does what to me?"

"Rakesh."

Sheetal's attention flew down to the black iron gates, still locked in position. They would swing open any second, and Rakesh would be home.

"I know what he does to you."

Static crackled. "I...I can't talk. Don't call again."

"Listen, Sheetal. I know everything."

"I don't know what you're talking about." She lowered her hand

and crimson glass bangles tinkled down her wrist like the blood that had crusted the surface several weeks ago.

"Rakesh hits you."

Sheetal raised a hand and pressed the bindi on her forehead.

"You can't live like this, Sheetal. It's wrong."

"I—"

"He's insane."

"The business. He's—there's too much pressure in the office."

"He'll kill you one day, Sheetal. That's what he'll do next."

"He's sick."

"You need to leave. Get away from him."

"You don't understand."

"Listen to me, Sheetal!" he bellowed. "Find a way. Any way and leave him."

"I can't." Her head throbbed. "I'm married."

"Can't you see what he's doing?" Arvind's voice hardened. "He will kill you next time."

"I—"

"I know everything, Sheetal. Yash told me."

She numbed.

"He was there, Sheetal. He saw Rakesh—" Static crackled.

"He was sleeping."

"...Whip...belt...blood...from your bedroom, open doorway... saw him beat you..."

The words exploded with static. Sheetal tightened her grip and closed her eyes. *What did Yash see? How much did he—it didn't make sense.* "Why didn't he say something for so long? I've been calling him every weekend—"

"Say what? To whom?" Static crackled and Arvind paused. "Sheetal? Are you there?"

"Yes... I..."

The iron gates swung apart, and Rakesh's black Lamborghini curved around the driveway.

"I... I have to go."

"He's petrified. He stammers when he does talk and fidgets all the time. He's so nervous and shaken up. If there's no improvement, you'll be called to take him home."

No.

"You have to find a way out of this mess."

A plan. She needed a plan. But first, she had to establish herself and stand on her feet to become independent. She needed to figure out a way.

"Leave Rakesh and come with me."

He was out of his mind. "I can't. I...I have to go. Rakesh will be here any second." A clicking sound, the whirr of static filled the receiver, and she beeped off the phone. Sheetal rushed out the door and peered over the balcony just as Rakesh entered.

Seated comfortably on the Bradford Browns beside the telephone, Naina glided her fingers back and forth over the hump of the receiver.

"On the phone again?" Rakesh looked up.

"I was talking to Papa." She tucked the receiver behind.

He grunted and walked off.

That evening the Dhanrajs sat down for dinner when Rakesh stormed into the Marquette Dining room and headed straight for Sheetal with a black vinyl folder.

Goosebumps puckered the length of Sheetal's arms. *An account of Arvind's phone calls? A file for divorce? Custody papers for Yash?* Megha on her right, and Naina and Mummyji across the table, stiffened in their seats.

Rakesh curved around the table's sharp edge and stood behind her. "I need these papers signed."

He was going to take custody of Yash.

Mummyji tore a piece of chapati from the stretch of circular, whole-wheat flatbread, folded it into a shovel and scooped a little vegetable gravy from one of the four varieties clumped in neat little mounds on her plate. Then she shoved it between her teeth and chewed. "What now?"

"I need half your company shares. The two of you."

The 'two of them' referred to Megha and Naina. The Dhanraj fortune didn't include her because she didn't own a share of Dhanraj & Son. She was the sole heiress to Papa's share of Induslink Corporation.

Before his death, Ashok Dhanraj had split the shares of Dhanraj & Son between Rakesh, Naina and Megha. Megha and Naina owned fifteen percent each and Rakesh owned seventy percent along with some commercial estate in Raigun. Mummyji owned the Dhanraj mansion and estate valued at seven hundred and fifty million rupees. However, the caveat that she remain a widow and manage the family, mansion and estate locked her into the role of a caretaker. If she forfeited her duties in any way, she risked losing her inheritance.

Mummyji clapped in excitement. "Are you going to certify a profit? An increase in earnings, I tell you? Hai Ishwar! Just the thing we need with so much remodeling to be done. The kitchen, dining, and sofas, so old, they are, I tell you." Her eyes widened until the eyebrows almost touched the white strands of hair crowning her forehead.

"There's something you need to know," Rakesh said. "I had mortgaged the mansion, estate and some of our other properties to finance Naina's wedding. I'm having trouble paying the interest and I'm running short of cash. I default any longer and the bank will take over."

"Ai-ee!" Mummyji gasped. "Hai Ishwar! What does that mean?"

"I forged your signature."

Mummyji's jaw dropped open and a ball of mashed food almost rolled off her tongue.

"All that's in the past. We might be out on the streets if we don't sell our shares. Look, I did what I could to tide us over and now you two need to sell."

"Sell her shares? Forge my signature!" Mummyji yelled. "What next?"

"Tashukomo Electronics is ready to buy a stake in Dhanraj & Son. It'll mean a fifty-fifty partnership. If you both sell at least half your shares and I do the same, we can meet them at the halfway mark."

"But the shares are all Naina has," Mummyji said. "You can't expect her to give them up. Hai Ishwar! Why, you already mortgaged my inheritance. I'll have nothing left."

Because Naina was Ashok and Pushpa's secret lovechild, Mummyji lived with the assumption she was entitled to Naina's fifteen percent inheritance.

"What do you think I'm struggling with? A three hundred and fifty million debt!"

"I told you so many times to pay attention to the business. But no. Always more interested in wasting time at parties and clubs. How could you let this happen? How do you expect us—" she glanced at Naina on her right "—to survive with nothing?"

"If we pool our shares, we can live as we do now and still have a comfortable life."

"Why my shares?" Naina interrupted. "Find some other way."

Mummyji narrowed her eyes at Rakesh standing behind. "Pool all the shares so you and your wife will have full control. How will we know what is going on behind our backs, I tell you? You already mortgaged my property without telling me. What else will I, my Naina, have left but our jewelry and clothes? Or will the bank take that too?"

"You make it sound like I'm throwing you on the streets," Rakesh said. "We're in this mess because of Naina and because I overspent on her wedding."

"Who told you to spend?" Mummyji crossed her arms. "I certainly didn't. I told you to forget that Black Pagoda idea because of all the bad luck it brings. Look what it did to my daughter.

Returned nine months later, divorced and homeless! Hai Ishwar! I told you, but did you listen? No."

Mummyji suggested that Rakesh choose an alternative theme that bore no element or association to bad luck. However, Rakesh dismissed her superstitions and went ahead with the construction of the Black Pagoda.

"I never asked for an expensive wedding." Naina tore a piece of chapati, scooped some gravy and dangled it above her mouth like bait.

"I don't care what you did or didn't ask for. We've got to work together," Rakesh insisted.

"Your idea. Your problem. Your shares, not mine." Naina dropped the food in her mouth.

"Of course, not." Rakesh's tone calmed. "Why should you give away your shares? How could you? If I remember correctly, you were busy reeling in your wedding dowry while I was putting together a fucking wedding for you."

"Mummy!" Naina turned to Mummyji. "Did you hear what he said? Remember how he tried to strangle me? I nearly died!" Tears rolled from the corners of her eyes. "You almost—"

"Stop crying!" Rakesh screamed. "It's all you women are good for. Turning on the waterworks when things don't go your way. It's what you spent your whole fucking life doing and got away with."

"That's no way to talk." Mummyji raised her voice. "It's not her fault you can't manage your anger issues. The expense of the wedding was your decision entirely, I tell you."

"I did it for *you*. For *her*. And what did I end up with? A huge debt. Did either of you ask for a simpler wedding or something less extravagant? You didn't even make your marriage work. Nine months, all it fucking lasted!"

"Such language!" Mummyji yelled. "Not her fault she couldn't adjust. She's been brought up as a Dhanraj and all its privileges."

"Then she should have got used to theirs. Privilege or not. She married into their family, not the other way around."

"It's all over and done with," Mummyji said. "Who cares now, anyway?"

"Life moves on. Look at Ajay. He remarried and had two children." Rakesh pointed to Megha. "Megha is expecting her first baby. She accepted the family she married into. And Naina's been rotting for ten years because she couldn't do anything with her life."

"Nothing wrong with my Naina. She's as good as any woman to have children."

"Really?" Rakesh's voice lightened with the turn of conversation. "How? By cloning herself? I don't see anyone marrying her."

"Mummy!" Naina turned from Rakesh to Mummyji and back. "Just look—"

"Brat," Rakesh grunted under his breath. "All I want are these papers signed by tomorrow." He dropped the folder on the dining table and threw a pen across. "Ditto?"

"I have nothing to do with this and my Naina doesn't either."

"Those shares will be useless if we don't pay back," Rakesh warned. "You'll be left with scraps of paper."

Megha wiped her fingers on a napkin, signed the papers and handed them back to Rakesh.

Raj's income was Megha's back up, but clearly her security lay in Rakesh's hands.

25
RUINS

Rakesh paced the office when a knock sounded at the door. Vipul Sahib peeked inside. "It's seven, Rakesh. You should go home."

"I don't know what to do, Uncle." Rakesh turned to face him. "Selling the family shares was my last choice, and Naina refuses to sign her shares." He sank into his chair. *Arvind. Not only did that bastard find Yash, he tracked Sheetal down too.* "Maybe this is how it's supposed to end. An empire crushed by the very family that built it."

"It doesn't have to be that way."

"There's no choice."

"If there's one thing I know, you're a survivor. A fighter." Vipul Sahib smiled. "You'll figure out a way."

To deal with Arvind, yes. "I hope so. But you shouldn't have stayed back so late."

"And leave you alone?"

"I'm used to it. Anyway, I've been meaning to ask, what happened to Girish's sister?"

"We loaned him the money just like you said, and it's done wonders for us too. News spread within a week. Girish speaks of nothing but your good nature, your understanding, and his loyalty shot through the roof. But we've had more employees approach us with their wish list and now I don't know who to turn away or how."

"Help the weakest first, like someone with a sick child or an ill mother. We don't have an open account, so you'll have to think it through."

"Just as I feared."

"Did our attrition rates go down?"

"Substantially. Everyone is beginning to believe in you and the company again."

Rakesh nodded. "That's a start."

"Girish wants to meet you and thank you for—"

"I don't need to get involved."

"But—"

"I need to be alone, Uncle."

Vipul Sahib nodded and sighed. "Sheetal must be waiting. Go home. Being alone never helps." Then he left and shut the door behind.

Rakesh made his way to the matching side cabinets housing a decanter of scotch, an ice bucket, several crystal glasses, and he poured a drink. The fourth in the last hour. A white noise buzzed. What did Vipul Sahib say just now about Girish and employee loyalty? Rakesh pressed a palm to the back of his head and curled his fingers tight to push the thought forward. But the buzz got louder. What did Dr. Kishore say? His fingers trembled. He reached for the drink. The coolness of the glass filled the width of his palm, and he curled his fingers around the tumbler. "You, Dad...I want to be like you!" Is that what Arvind said? No. Vipul Sahib? Couldn't be. Girish? Did Girish want to be like him? He shook his head, so the buzz stopped. Yash wanted to be like him. Yes, that's right. Or did Yash want to be like Arvind?

Rakesh placed the glass on the desk. The stuff would surely kill him one day and he couldn't afford to lose control.

On his way home that evening Rakesh stopped at a coffee shop and sobered himself with some black coffee.

He popped into Sheetal's studio and found her at work on another painting. An orchid mounted the broken window he was supposed to have fixed weeks ago. "I came to remind you of the charity dinner at seven on Thursday. Don't embarrass me again by running off to your father's."

Sheetal glanced at him and resumed her work.

"How is your father by the way?"

"He's lonely with no one to talk to and finds it difficult without Mama."

Rakesh leaned against the door's edge. "If something happened to me, would you miss me?"

Sheetal paused. "I fast every year on Karva Chauth. Nothing will happen to you."

He walked around the canvas and faced her. "We can't prevent or predict the future even if we don't want something to happen. Like how, despite knowing your mother had cancer, there was nothing you could do to stop it."

Sheetal's jaw dropped. "How can you even say something like that?"

"It's a fact. Anyway, you're going for Yash's concert?"

She gave him that stare again, like nothing he said made sense. "We've talked about this before. It's the same day you have the meeting with the Japanese in Delhi. Of course, I'm going. Are you sure you can't make it?"

"I've made your booking at the Plaza Royale this time. I didn't forget. But sounds like you don't want me to go."

"I didn't mean it that way."

"Which way did you?"

"I was just asking."

"Checking, Sheetal. You were checking."

26
FALLING

With fourteen paintings out the way and only six to go, Sheetal brimmed with confidence. All twenty paintings would be completed, framed and delivered to the Solange Art Gallery on time. Her new signature, 'Sheetal', stood out on the lower right corner of each work in liquid gold, free of the Dhanraj label.

Roshni wheeled in the evening chai and handed her an envelope. Sheetal ripped it open and read the letter when her cell phone rang. "Hello?"

"Madame Sheetal? Patel calling from Taj Resort, Calcutta. I am taking a look at your work in Raigun Cricket Club and other places. I talked to Mr. Bhattacharya at Sheraton and Mr. Kannada at Renaissance Hotel. I am also hearing you are taking part in Solange Art Gallery. And your work is very good."

"Thank you. I'm actually working on Solange's collection right now." Sheetal grabbed a pen, flipped an envelope on its back and sat on the sofa ready to jot notes.

"Then it will be even more of a privilege to have your work on display in our hotel's new wing. I was thinking perhaps you could..."

She scribbled as Mr. Patel detailed a series of seven paintings on twenty-four-by-thirty-inch canvases with the theme of earth and water with a due date of May fifteenth. Considering she was ahead of schedule, Sheetal calculated she could easily complete the requirements for Solange *and* the Taj Resort.

"We can pay seven hundred thousand rupees total." Hesitation crept into his voice. "Is this good for you?"

One hundred thousand rupees per painting? She'd never been paid that much for a single piece so far. Sheetal took a deep breath to control the excitement. Word of her good reputation had begun to spread. "It's fine. Totally fine. Thank you for the opportunity, Mr. Patel. I'm sure—"

"What's this I'm hearing, I tell you?" Mummyji called from the doorway.

Sheetal turned and covered the mouthpiece with a free hand. "I'm on a business call."

"I don't care about your business. This is important, I tell you."

Sheetal noted Mr. Patel's contact, promised to call him soon and ended the call.

"The ladies from the Royal Society Ladies Group seem to have sent you something."

Sheetal tore open the envelope from Mummyj's club, flipped open the letter and skimmed over the print.

"Invitation, no?" Mummyji peeked from the side. "I am right, no?" She thrust an arm forward and spread her Kit-Kat-thick fingers apart. "Let me have a look, I tell you."

Sheetal held the letter high out of reach.

"Did my club members invite you to the Tuesday lunch—no? Along with the other daughters-in-law?"

A chance to finally get even.

"They could have easily told me, and I would have told you. Absolutely no reason to mail you an invitation when we are in the same family and share the same last name, I tell you."

Sheetal pretended to read the letter again. "Oh, look! They're inviting me to join the group. And...and..." She feigned excitement. "Take over as president!"

Mummyji's forehead crusted with wrinkles. "Ai-ee! They...they... never told me anything. I will find out who is trying to overthrow me behind my back, I tell you. I am president of the club, and I should be making decisions." She wagged her finger in the air. "Make them answer to me, I will."

"I'm happy to do a joint presidentship," Sheetal suggested. "We can run the club together. That way you won't have to give up your position." Perhaps Mummyji would also agree to the idea of running the Dhanraj household together and then she could control expenses.

"You're thinking of joining?"

Sheetal shrugged. "I'm not sure because I don't really have time for all this since I'm a working woman and I have deadlines ahead."

"Really? I don't see you as a *working* woman." She emphasized working as if it were a contagion.

"Oh. How do you see me then?"

"Like myself, only less capable. Without the benefit of my experience or knowledge. Your painting is more like a hobby, I tell you, to help fill up your day without Yash. And next time you think of becoming president, start your own club as far away from mine as possible. I worked hard to build my life and reputation, I tell you. There were days when I had to go without food or extra clothes. The rain poured so hard, my tin roof drummed all night, and puddles— oh so many puddles around my bed." A tear drop lingered on the corner of her eye, and she drew closer. "Do you know what it's like to sleep with nothing more but a thin cotton mattress between you and the cold, hard floor?"

"I...I—"

"Do you know what it's like to manage with just three pairs of clothes? No. How could you? That's why I'm still here with all the madness. Ashok tied me down to this family's welfare, and if I fail in my duties, I lose it all and become penniless again. I have lived the homeless life before, but never again."

Sheetal knew Mummyji originated from the lower class and had struck it rich by tagging on as Ashok's mistress and wife. But she had no idea that Mummyji had grown up in the slums.

"I wasn't born rich either," Sheetal blurted. "Papa worked so hard to get us where we are today."

"Your father, no? Not you, I tell you."

"What do you mean?"

"Your father worked hard to get you where you are. But what did you do?"

"I was only nine. What more could I do? But what about your family? Where are they all?"

"My parents had nine children, seven girls and two boys. I was third in line and only fifteen when I was labeled ready for marriage, I tell you. But after my second sister married, Baba had no money for my dowry. Not like you, Ms. Working Woman, who waltzed in with an Italian car for Rakesh, designer after designer wear, and truck-loads of gold and silver."

Sheetal's heart grated with guilt. Wasn't Mummyji responsible for having set those expectations in the first place? And hadn't Mama and Papa done their best to live up to those very standards?

"They sold me."

"Who sold you?"

"My Baba sold me to an upper class family as a nanny for the children. But the husband was no good and began making eyes at me. I was young but smart and before he could get his filthy hands on me, I ran away."

"Where?"

"Ah...now you want to know where so you can poke fun and humiliate me, I tell you?"

"No. I—"

"Enough for you to know I survived cleaning people's filthy dishes, washing clothes, sweeping and mopping. And then I met

Ashok, a good, kindhearted man—but tell me, can you do even half of what I did? Can you endure a life of real hardship?"

Her heart welled in her throat. She hadn't meant to hurt Mummyji.

"You call yourself a working woman, no? Tell me, are all these paintings really work or a fraction of hard work, I tell you? Because I worked harder, much harder than you."

Sheetal opened her mouth, but bubbles of air trapped in her throat.

"Just because you are Rakesh's wife, I tell you. Doesn't make you better than me."

"I never—"

"You think I am blind? I see how the servants and Laal Bahadur wait hand and foot to do your bidding. Choti Memsahib this and Choti Memsahib that. They team up to play cricket with your little family and prefer to make your coffee over my chai.

"Rakesh is the one who—"

"Aah, blame the husband. No one can argue with him, I tell you. Rakesh tells all the servants to do your work first and you walk around like you own it all. Your head is always high in the clouds when you prance off to charities, and dinners in flashy, designer clothes. Why should my Naina sell her shares of the company to put us on the streets when you, Ms. Working Woman, are enjoying the life for free?"

Free? Sheetal grit her teeth. Yash was in boarding school because of Naina and Mummyji, and she had been paying the price for the so-called 'freedom' for ten years.

"I worked hard, too hard, to build my life and reputation and I won't give it away to anyone. Especially you."

TWO DAYS LATER AT THE DINNER TABLE, MUMMYJI ANNOUNCED THAT NO ONE was to use the landline without her permission because Ajay Malhotra was expected to call for Naina.

According to rumors, Ajay Malhotra had recently divorced his wife after she was caught in an extramarital affair. The woman's maiden family refused to take her back. The Malhotras denied the woman entry into their home and access to meet with her children. A fallen woman, Ajay's wife jumped off a ten-story building and her death made the front page of The Raigun Herald.

What didn't make the headlines traveled through the community grapevine. The next rumor to follow was that Ajay had been impotent and encouraged his wife to engage with a male friend. He ended up fathering two children, proved his manhood to the world, and all was well until the male acquaintance and his wife fell in love. Then Ajay turned the tables on his wife and labeled her a whore in public. The glorified story turned into the talk of the town. Pictures of the dead woman and her lover dominated the front page of The Raigun Herald for a week as a warning to all women who were tired of their stale marriages to stay put.

THE NEXT MORNING, SHORTLY AFTER RAKESH LEFT FOR THE OFFICE, MEGHA arrived with the explanation she was running errands and decided to drop in on the spur of the moment to check up on Sheetal. However, Megha spent all day at the Dhanraj's. Sheetal figured Megha was hanging around on purpose to remind her of the baby's delivery date fast approaching. Sheetal didn't want to take on the responsibility of Megha's childbirth, but she couldn't outright say no to any member of the in-laws. If something went wrong or any mishap was to fall on Megha or the baby, the blame was bound to fall on her shortcomings, so she played along tactfully avoiding the topic and giving Megha any confirmation until ready to make a decision. Plus, with Yash in such an unstable state, how would she manage Yash over the summer holidays and the delivery of Megha's baby?

Later that evening in the dining room, when Megha heard about Mummyji's plans for Naina to remarry Ajay, she joined the heated conversation. "You can't send Naina back."

"I don't see why not." Mummyji pumped both hands on her hips. "She'll fit in so well as a mother to two children. Besides, the Malhotras are so much better off financially now than before—no? And my Naina is still untarnished and available, I tell you."

"And she'll probably stay like that forever considering Ajay can never give her children of his own," Megha added.

"It's not always a question of giving, I tell you." Mummyji let her arms fall to rest by her sides. "It's a question of being able to provide for. Now, if you were truly happy in your family, you wouldn't be here so often, would you? Not right for a girl to visit the mother's home this frequently at such short notice, and today—*no* notice even. Uninvited?"

"Rakesh Bhaiya called last night for me to spend the day here, and I'll leave the moment he's back. It's not like I have to—"

"Didn't you say you were here because you had some work?" Sheetal intervened. "You mentioned errands in the area?"

"Yes." Megha pursed her lips. "I—"

"Work, no work, doesn't matter." Mummyji huffed. "We all know how much you miss the comforts of being a Dhanraj."

"At least, I have a husband's home to go to unlike Naina who was kicked out in nine months."

"Only because she discovered, I tell you, that Ajay was impotent and hiding the truth. Or at least that's what we will tell the world. So, it's not really Naina's fault now, because they were hiding their own dirty little secret—secrets that only come out of hiding after marriage. These arranged marriages, I tell you. People use them to hide so much! Besides," Mummyji waved a hand in the air, "for how long can Ajay continue without a wife? He needs a woman as much as Naina needs a man. It's mutual."

"She's still mentally sick," Megha said. "Anyway, what makes you think they'll agree to this?"

"What choice do they have, I tell you? He's physically inade-quate. There's no cure to his...his..."—she wrinkled her nose in apparent disgust—"incapability. It's all automatic."

"It's wrong," Sheetal intervened. "You're going to ruin both their lives again."

"What's to ruin when it's already ruined? They'll make do with each other. Find a way and compromise. Isn't that what your and Rakesh's marriage is all about?"

Sheetal stared, speechless.

"Don't look at me like that. It's life!" Mummyji sat at the table and spread a napkin over her sari. "You don't marry for love. You marry to fit in with society. To...to get on."

Clearly Mummyji's mission focused on giving Naina's hand to the best offer with no thought for long term consequences. "Two innocent lives will be ruined because of a false marriage of conve-nience. What about the children?"

"Children?" Mummyji swiped the air with her hand. "They know nothing about what's good for them. Food, shelter and clothing is all I ever needed to grow, I tell you. But Baba—" she stopped. "Anyway, every woman must be paired with a man. It's the law and the only way society will accept you."

Just then the phone rang.

Mummyji threw her napkin on the table, jumped to her feet, and reached for the phone on the hutch. "H-a-l-l-o?" she raised the pitch of her deep voice. "Malhotraji? Expecting your call, I was—Hallo?" She stopped, turned to Sheetal, and gave her the instrument. "For you."

"Who is it?" Sheetal asked.

Megha abruptly rose from her seat and left the dining room.

"How should I know?" Mummyji thrust the receiver into Sheetal's hands. "One of your business clients, I think. Working woman that you are! Get off that phone quickly and use your mobile." Then she sat down again.

"Hello?"

"Sheetal?"

Arvind. Sheetal left the dining room and hurried to the temple, tucked behind the stairs. "You have to stop calling me on the land-line. Do you know how much trouble I'll be in?"

"I called your mobile, but you didn't pick up. It's urgent."

Sheetal patted her hip. Nothing. She must have left her phone in the studio.

"Yash's having a lot of trouble." Static crackled splitting Arvind's words in pieces. "He's bed-wetting...stammering. He can barely... himself."

"I...I don't understand. Yash was never like this. I can't hear you. Hello?"

"It's Rakesh's..." Arvind's tone crackled again. "He did... responsible.

Sheetal pressed the phone to her ear and backed against a wall.

"Was probably sleeping when...some noise...woke him...went to find you and...whip...blood—"

Her heart sank grating her stomach. "I talked to Yash the morning he left, but he didn't say anything."

"Scared, dammit! The boy is petrified. You have to...take him."

"Without an official letter or call from the school? I'm not even supposed to know yet."

"How can it be official...I haven't filed... yet... Can't...go on...too long. You have to...out of here."

"There's a week and a half until the concert."

"Leave...Raigun."

Her knees gave way. She slid down the wall and landed on the floor. "Where will I go?"

"Just get...from here." The static ended. "I'll manage the rest."

Why was everything so simple to him? Like all she had to do was walk out the door and never return. She pulled her knees into her chest. She needed more time. Time to build an adequate pool of savings. Time to stand on her feet and support Yash. "It's wrong. I can't just..."

"Hello? Sheetal? You there?"

How would she face society? What would she tell people? What would The Raigun Herald publish about her? A chill shuddered up her spine. "I need time."

"You don't have time."

"I'm not ready."

"How much longer? Another ten years good enough? Then Yash can grow up without a mother. And when Rakesh beats him up one fine day, then there will be two dead instead of one."

She ran her fingers through her open hair and tightened her grip at the ends.

"You can't trust anyone."

The receiver slipped from her fingers, but Sheetal caught it in time. Two innocent lives ruined because of a false marriage. Didn't she just say that to Mummyji?

"He's your husband and look what he did to you. You have to leave him."

The air thickened. The wall. The floor. Everything spun. She flattened a palm on the floor. Then Arvind planned her escape. Static resumed. Sheetal loosened her grip on the receiver. He couldn't mean what he was saying. This wasn't real. This wasn't happening.

"He's never going to let you go. Do you hear me?"

Sheetal rose to her feet. "Hmm..." She kept her voice low.

"You have to do this alone and you can't tell anyone."

Sheetal made her way upstairs as Arvind confirmed the location where they were to meet. The words fluffed like cotton padding as she pinned the phone to her ear, bore right at the landing, another right to the east wing, another to the south and flung open the door to her studio.

"And when I—then we leave," Arvind continued.

A gust of wind whooshed and swept the hairs on her skin. The aroma of dark roast coffee. Where was it coming from?

Rakesh stood before a desert painting mounted on an easel, a mug of steaming liquid in hand. He raised the mug in a toast and approached.

"Hello? Sheetal?" Arvind asked. "Are you there?"

"Sheetal!" Rakesh tilted the mug to his lips and took a sip. He had her cell phone. "You're here."

"Hello? Are you there?"

"I...uh..." She didn't know where she was anymore.

27
CRUSHED

Sheetal reached out and the receiver almost fell from her hand while Arvind was still on the line. "I...I didn't know you were here, Rakesh. You're home early."

"Meeting fizzed. I came for you." He held out an open palm.

Sheetal slipped her right hand in Rakesh's, but he withdrew. She curled her left thumb over the receiver to feel for the button that would disconnect Arvind's call, but Rakesh snatched the phone.

"Who you talking to?"

"Yash."

"On a weekday?"

Why was Rakesh home early on a weekday? And why was he asking who she was talking to? Was she under some kind of watch? "He wants to know when we leave for Mansali. He misses us."

"Did you tell him I won't be there?"

"He'll be heartbroken. You didn't go last time."

"Never know. He's hosting the show, and I may just change my mind." He pressed the receiver to his ear. "Hello? Anyone there?" He paused. "Seems like he hung up." Then he walked off with the receiver, carefree and powerful with all the controls.

WITH TEN DAYS TO GO UNTIL THE TRIP TO MANSALI, SHEETAL OPENED A folding door in her walk-in closet packed with travel gear and accessories and rolled forward the twenty-four-inch soft-top VIP suitcase she'd taken on the previous trip. Her attention fell on a graze crusting the surface. The VIP had sufficed for the week-long trip and survived impact on hitting the train platform at the coolie's hands, but she needed something sturdy and durable going forward.

Three Louis Vuittons stacked side by side had served to escort all her personal belongings when she'd moved in after marriage. The only other time she'd used the triplets was when she left Rakesh for Mama's place to get away from the Dhanrajs for a while. The triplets were good for travel in comfort and style.

She slid open the door some more and a twenty-eight-inch hard-top black Samsonite lay tucked in a corner. She grabbed the handle, rolled the suitcase forward and laid it face down. *Should be strong enough.* She kneeled beside the suitcase, unclasped the metal latch, flipped open the lid, and pulled out a string-bag crumpled in a corner. Then she ran a hand along the inner perimeter. The Samsonite would suffice for a two-to-three-week trip. But how on earth could she pack her life in its cavity? Her chest tightened. Could she really leave?

She closed the suitcase and up-righted the four-wheel spinner. Maybe she could move in with Papa? No. Rakesh would perpetually be at her throat and demand custody of Yash. Maybe she and Yash could go into hiding with Kavita and Gaurav? She pressed her palm against the outer fold of the wooden door and rolled slid it toward the closet's wall. Kavita had more room now in her new two-bedroom flat with running water, electricity, and proper amenities. Surely Kavita could accommodate her and Yash for a while. Besides, Rakesh would never care to look for them in northern Raigun, the middle class and poor man's abode. The magnet clicked on meeting the wall's edge and she stopped. When Megha had gone missing eight years ago, Rakesh cruised every street corner and alley around Raigun University's campus for days. He stepped into seedy bars and almost got run over by a lorry in the middle of the road. Not just that. He'd spied on her and Arvind at The Broken Fort. Of course, he would hunt her down.

She packed in the privacy of her closet so that should Rakesh happen to enter the bedroom, he wouldn't see what she was taking. Still, with all the noise she made, he'd guess she was up to something.

Half an hour later, Sheetal's clothes stacked five inches above the suitcase's rim, but she didn't care because unlike Megha there would be no attempt to return to lost luxuries. She piled more saris, shawls and footwear and pulled down the lid, but it wouldn't close.

"Sheetal?" Rakesh called to her from his closet. "Ready in twenty-five minutes. We need to be at the charity dinner by seven. Don't be late."

Dinner! She raised a hand to her forehead. How could she forget? The contents of her suitcase slipped down the sides and pooled in a heap on the carpet.

She dumped the extra clothes on a shelf, shut the Samsonite and wheeled it behind the folding closet doors. She pulled an ironed sari off a hanger and changed. She pleated the silk fabric running from the front of her hips to her toes and tucked it at the waist.

"Are you ready?"

Her fingers trembled and the pleats pooled on the carpet. He shouldn't notice her hesitation. She curled her fingers into a fist, took slow, steady breaths, re-pleated the sari and tucked the folds in her petticoat. How could running away make any sense? Arvind had asked her to run away on the day of her wedding and now he was asking her to do so again. People like him, maybe...maybe that's all they knew? To run away and leave troubles behind. But people who had a family, a child, and a social life to keep intact couldn't just leave it all. There had to be another way.

She sat down at her dresser to apply makeup just as Rakesh entered her walk-in closet.

"What's this?" He tapped the jewelry box on the dressing table, his eight-carat diamond engagement ring a contrast to the colored glass.

"Something I picked up from a stall in Mansali. I just love all the colors."

"Too gaudy, bright and cheap. Best left here so I don't have to look at it every night before I sleep." Then he spun on his heels and left, slamming the bedroom door behind.

SHEETAL WAS HALFWAY DOWN WHEN RAKESH WENT BACK UP, TAKING THE stairs two at a time. "Forgot something important. Wait for me downstairs."

Sheetal reached the landing, surprised to find Mummyji seated on the Bradford Browns.

"Such a shame, I tell you. Naina's not well or she could have joined you at the charity dinner."

"It's a public event." Sheetal emphasized public.

"And what's the saying, I tell you? Charity begins at home. Hai Ishwar, if you wanted, you could have—"

"Where's Naina?" Rakesh hurried past clutching a brown packet.

"What do you want?" Mummyji crossed her arms.

"Same thing you do. I want her settled in her own family."

"You suddenly care for her? What's wrong with you? What are you up to now, I tell you?"

"Why would I have spent all that money on her wedding in the first place if I didn't care? There's nothing more I want at this point than to see Naina where she belongs. With a family of her own. I'll do what it takes to make sure that happens."

"Like?"

He handed her the packet. "Ayurvedic tea. If nothing else, maybe this will work."

"Never heard of such a thing, I tell you. Who ever heard of cure with tea?"

"It's from a reputed pharmacy. Alternative medicines take longer but they're effective and worth the effort if Naina's cured for good."

"Hmm..." Mummyji held the packet between the tips of her fingers and swiveled it this way and that. "*Bharat Chaiwallah.* Never heard of them, I tell you." She handed it back to Rakesh.

"They are reliable people and reputed in Ayurveda, medicinal and herbal teas."

Mummyji snickered. "I don't understand your sudden bout of affection for Naina, I tell you. After all these years."

"If I was up to something, I wouldn't have thrown her a nine-hundred-million wedding. It's always been the best for Naina, the most expensive for Naina, the most elaborate for Naina. Now, all we need is for her to get on her with life so we can get on with ours. But you're always suspicious."

"Hai Ishwar!" Mummyji scrunched her nose. "What else did you expect, I tell you, after the way you behaved last time? You nearly killed and choked her to death."

"I was drunk. I...I didn't know what I was doing. I said I was sorry."

"I don't remember you saying so."

"All right, I'm sorry. There. Said it."

Did he mean it?

"I don't think she'll touch any of this tea business if I tell her you—"

"Tell her a friend from your club ordered it. Make up something. As long as she gets better, there's a hope of her getting back with Ajay—or anyone else—and we can live in peace."

"I don't see how—"

"You want the world thinking she's cured and normal. But you don't want treatment. You don't want gossip. You don't want to spend the rest of your life taking care of her either. Do you?"

Mummyji straightened. "How dare you assume I want nothing to do with her, I tell you. She's my daughter."

"Look at your life." He softened his tone. "You can't go anywhere you want *when* you want. You're tied down and stuck between these four walls because of her. I know how tired and frustrated you must feel. Look at how exhausted you are and how desperately you want it all to end."

Mummyji sank against the backrest, and the flab around her midriff compressed and protruded like two tires as Rakesh droned on.

"You deserve much better. I know I've been unfair and wrong for many years and it's time to set aside our differences so we can all finally be free." He coaxed the brown packet back into Mummyji's hands.

"Do you really think she will be...normal again?" Mummyji's voice cracked.

"We have to try." Then he grabbed Sheetal by the wrist and marched her to the front door. "We're running late."

Sheetal lengthened her strides to keep up, hope growing in her heart. Was he really going to set things right for all of them? Did he also feel he had wronged her? Was he also willing to make amends between them?

The Lamborghini's door arched up, but Sheetal paused. "You said just now it's time to set things right for all of us, so we are free."

He strode around to the driver's side.

Sheetal looked across the Lamborghini's hood. "What did you really mean?"

"How does it matter what I meant? You don't care, anyway."

. . .

ATTENDEES DRESSED IN COLORFUL SARIS, SALWAR KAMEEZES, SWANKY TIES, and dark suits graced the dance floor while many milled around the buffet table and lounge areas. Waiters dressed in black suits and white shirts served trays of champagne and hors d'oeuvres to the guests, the air thick with the fragrance of perfumes.

Sheetal walked beside Rakesh for an hour, her hand perched in the crook of his elbow. She greeted the glitterati of Raigun with a forced smile. Finally, Sheetal wiggled her fingers to loosen her grip, but Rakesh tightened his hold. *Calm.* Sheetal forced herself to relax. She mustn't trigger suspicion.

"Something wrong?" he asked.

"No. Why?" A high-pitched laughter escaped her lips. "Just look at everyone. The food and décor are so well organized. Aren't you having a good time?"

"I can't speak for anyone else, but you're having more than a good time."

"Really? What makes you say so?"

"Because..." He flipped open his mobile. "You're not yourself."

THE NEXT MORNING SHEETAL CHECKED HER SUITCASE FOR THE TWENTIETH time, and added another salwar suit, a new sari and bottle of hairspray. She assessed her luggage and threw in some extra safety pins, a bottle of moisturizer and another pair of sandals for good measure. She skimmed hundreds of saris dripping off hangers and ran her fingers along the gold and silver tassels, sequined trimmings and network dangling from the pallus. The time had come to let go.

WITH TWENTY-FOUR HOURS UNTIL THE TRAIN'S DEPARTURE, SHEETAL decided to clean up and organize her studio one last time. She grabbed several brushes she'd left on a dirty towel to dry, tubes of paint and rags then stopped. If she cleaned up, Rakesh would grow suspicious. She left two brushes on the towel and ran her fingers over the edge of the nineteenth painting for the Solange exhibition. To think she could have been in the company of Tagore and Husain and possibly embarked on a journey to international fame. Her heart fisted in her throat. For so long she had accused Mama of giving away everything she had worked so hard for and now here she was doing precisely the same.

She grabbed the painting of the Himalayan Mountain propped against the windowsill and was about to put it away when Kannada's comment made her stop. Didn't he say the paintings were too dark and depressing? Kannada had probably examined her work in the wrong lighting or from the wrong angle. Or maybe he'd had a bad day and that affected his opinion?

She grabbed two more mountain paintings and slanted them against the wall in a spot of sunlight. She stepped back ten feet but the sky, background and mountains really were a dull gray and almost black in some parts. She moved the paintings to another spot of sunlight and brought three more rejected mountain paintings to view. Her heart sank. Kannada was right. Flaws marked her work.

The sound of feet shuffling outside her studio and the odor of stale chutney reeked from behind and she turned.

"Eh-na?" Naina asked. "You leaving again?"

"Tomorrow, but I'll be back."

"I'll be going too." Naina stood in the doorway. "You'll see."

"Where?" *A mental asylum?*

"They called this morning." She sneered. "Ajay is ready to marry me again."

"What about the children?"

"Mummy promised to send fifteen servants this time and a nanny for those children along with a better dowry."

Fifteen servants and another dowry? Where was Mummyji going

to get that kind of money from? "They need a mother. Not a nanny or a dowry."

Naina crossed her arms. "I know."

"You can barely handle yourself. You're putting two innocent lives at risk."

Naina brushed her fingers in the air.

"How can you be so selfish?"

"Me?" Naina's eyes widened. "You send your own son to boarding school. Your career is all you care about. That's why you got rid of him, na, for yourself. And you call me selfish? Look, na, who is talking?"

Bile crept up Sheetal's throat. "How can I keep Yash here when he's not safe? He almost died."

"Didn't, though."

"You left your pills around. How will you keep two children alive when you almost—"

"I didn't. I didn't kill anyone! He told me to." She barged into the studio and slammed the door behind her. "He watched from behind the curtains the whole time. And I—" she broke into sobs "—had to give Papa the cup or Rakesh threatened to take away my shares of the company. Papa died because of me." Thick tears trickled down her grimy cheeks. "But it wasn't my fault. He *made* me do it."

"I don't understand."

"I didn't either, but Rakesh wanted the company and said it was the only way."

"Only way to what?"

"Get rid of him."

"Who?"

"Papa." She grabbed Sheetal by the shoulders.

"Rakesh wanted to get rid of your father?"

Naina nodded. "He made sure I gave Papa the cup while he watched from behind the curtains." Tears streamed down her cheeks. "And he watched Papa die at my hands. The doctors said it was a heart attack, but I know there was something in that tea that caused the attack."

"Why would he do such a thing?"

"He wanted control of the company." She drilled her fingers.

Rakesh had a temper and an insatiable greed for power. But murder? There had to be a mistake. "This cup you gave—"

"He made me give it and said Papa had better drink it or he would take everything I owned, and I'd be poor and homeless for life."

"Does Mummyji know?"

Naina shook her head and let Sheetal go.

"Does anyone know?"

"No."

"Why didn't you tell her or anyone—someone, about this for so long?"

"Rakesh threatened to hurt even kill me if I did. Don't you see? Don't you think I want to get better and be normal like you? But I can't risk therapy because what if I speak the truth by accident? I'll be convicted of murder."

Sheetal numbed. Poor Naina. Her depression had nothing to do with being Ashok's favorite as Mummyji had everyone believe. Naina was wasted because of a murder she had been forced to commit. Sheetal took a deep breath and slowly exhaled. "An autopsy must have revealed the—"

"Rakesh ordered an immediate cremation and lit the pyre himself. He said autopsies went against the family's religion."

Since when did Rakesh care for religion?

"And the doctors agreed Papa suffered a heart attack." Naina swiped a few strands of hair away from her face.

"Why are you telling me this now after so many years?"

"I tried so hard to spend some time with you alone. But you want nothing to do with me and you're always trying to run away."

"That's not true." Sheetal bit her lower lip.

"Whenever I try to talk to you, na, you always have to go some-where or be someplace else."

Sheetal gulped. "Why are you speaking up now?"

"Because Rakesh tried to strangle me the other night."

To think she'd secretly wished Naina had died. Guilt wedged in her heart with regret.

"When you married in this family, na. I tried to warn you so many times that he was having an affair, but Rakesh wouldn't let me come near you. So, when you went to your mother's house for two weeks, I destroyed all your artwork on purpose. I ruined your studio in the hope you'd see the damage and be horrified enough to leave and never return. But you're so foolish you came back and stayed. And you believed Rakesh over me."

Her heart fisted in her throat. For so long she had thought ill of Naina and cursed Naina, when all Naina had wanted was to save her from a life of self-destruction.

"Even now. He's having an affair with—" She stopped.

"With whom?"

"I...I can't say."

"Why?" Sheetal's knees buckled and she sat on the table's edge. "Speak up."

"He'll hurt me like before or worse. You have to believe me. I wasn't trying to harm Yash. I never would. It was a mistake. But Papa's death wasn't an accident, and now he's after you."

The room spun.

"Can't you see, na? My suffering has always been because of Rakesh. I don't want to marry Ajay again after all I've been through. But it's my only way out. Once Rakesh gets you, it's over."

Chills shuddered up her spine.

"I...I know what you're planning," she whispered. "I heard you on the phone. You have to leave, Bhabhi." Naina's breathing grew heavy and her face inched closer. "Get away from here before it's too late."

Sheetal closed her eyes to still the confusion. *So, Naina had eaves-dropped on the conversations with Arvind. How many times? What more did she know?* She couldn't trust anyone. "I don't know what you're talking about."

"Don't lie, Bhabhi."

"I—"

"I've watched you struggle for too long. If you stay, you'll end up worse than you can imagine. But think of Yash's future."

"You've hated me all these years. Why are you suddenly trying to help?"

"How can I hate you when I look up to you? You're the one who hates me. You have everything. You are everything I can never be." Her breathing thickened. "You are independent, strong, you even run your own business. But none of this will last. He will take away everything you've built. I know Yash almost died because of me." Naina touched her gently on the arm. "But you, his mother, are the only one who never blamed me for what happened."

Sheetal cringed. She'd never hated herself more.

LATER THAT DAY SHEETAL WAS ABOUT TO LEAVE HER BEDROOM WHEN ROSHNI handed her a yellow Manila envelope. Sheetal flipped the envelope but there was no return address. She shut the bedroom door and peeled open the flap. *Could this be the escape plans or tickets from Arvind?* Her heart raced and she tipped the contents into an open palm. A CD slid out. Sheetal peered inside but there was no letter, no card or indication of the sender. She popped the CD in the deck and hit 'play.'

Nothing.

Sheetal swiveled the volume knob, sat on her bed, and pulled her knees in to her chest. A loud thump like an amplified heartbeat echoed between the walls.

Muffles. Static. Clicks. Thuds followed. As if someone was trying to position an instrument for recording.

Silence. Groans. The groans faded. Then a deep, heavy panting filled the room. Long drawn exhales followed by quick, short rasps and two male voices, one slightly higher in pitch than the other, levitated in a rising crescendo. The sound of kisses, at first light and feathery, then harder and more pronounced filled every corner of the room. Deep moans of pleasure. Heavier breathing and panting now folded, one into another, until Sheetal could no longer tell apart the voices. Foul language cursed the air, and a gruff, male voice commanded the other to hold and squeeze him in all the private places.

"Ditto."

The hairs on her skin stood on ends. *Rakesh with another man?* Her mind was playing games. The moans and groans of two men making love continued to fill the room. Sheetal jumped off the bed, disgust crawling through every nerve.

"Ditto. I'm fizzed." Rakesh's voice boomed. "What a fuck!"

Sheetal sank in a heap on the floor. She was going to be sick.

NEXT MORNING SHEETAL PACKED ALL HER SIGNIFICANT PAPERS AND documents in the Samsonite: a bank book, two passports and Yash's birth certificate. Then she went to the bank and withdrew all her jewelry. As she stashed the jewels in a handbag, she couldn't believe four months ago she'd been willing to sell these very assets to help Rakesh. What a fool she'd been. She pushed the metal drawer back into its hollow cavity, handed the clerk the key outside the vault, signed the log and asked for assistance to close her account.

Puneet Gupta, the bank manager, came rushing out of his office.

"Madame, are you not happy with the bank's services? A member of my staff just told me you are closing your account with us."

"Oh, it's temporary," Sheetal assured him. "I'm withdrawing for personal reasons. But I'll open another account very soon." Then she left with enough travelers' checks, bank drafts and foreign currency to tide her over for several months.

28
SNAKES & LADDERS

S heetal made her way down the Dhanraj stairs for the last time as the sun cut across the tessellation of black and white tiles.

The servant had aligned Sheetal's suitcase with Rakesh's as if both were heading for one destination. However, Sheetal was to leave for Mansali in half an hour, and Rakesh, who was at the office, had the late afternoon flight to New Delhi.

Mummyji rushed in from the dining area. "All ready to leave, I tell you? Rakesh said for you to leave his suitcase here and not to drop it off at the office."

"I wasn't planning to."

"And as for making up all that nonsense about being invited to my club and suggesting a joint presidentship and then going so far as to replace me! Well, asked everyone, I did, I tell you, and found out the letter was an invitation to a lunch like the ones sent to all the other daughters-in-law. But you really are trying to take my place, aren't you?"

"It was a joke." Sheetal shrugged. "No harm done."

"A joke? I'm not stupid, I tell you. I know what you are up to. Meaning something else altogether."

"I just wanted to know how you'd feel about us being equals."

"What does that mean?"

"The same. Equivalent. Share. Half-half."

"I know what equal means. But how could you even think it possible, I tell you? You will need decades of grooming to achieve half of my accomplishments and reach my status. Why, everybody knows what a good mother and wife—"

"What kind of wife were you, having an illegitimate child before your wedding?" Sheetal hitched the strap of her travel bag, packed with assets, along her shoulder. "What kind of mother are you when you can't even raise one child right? You hide Naina's illness and pretend it doesn't exist. But she has problems and needs help."

"Ai-ee!" Mummyji squeaked as a servant wheeled the Samsonite toward the car parked outside. "I *am* getting her help. Ajay's family called, I tell you—"

"I'm talking about medical, professional help. Real help."

"No more doctors and therapy. No more of this Elavil nonsense. I have a cure from a specialty pharmacy. Each gram is so costly!" Trapped in a false sense of security, Mummyji refused to look outside the make-believe world Naina's illness had roped her into as her caretaker. "Now, of course for Naina's wedding, I'm going to put together—"

"Oh! You stupid woman! How can you think of a second wedding when we are already in so much debt?"

"Ai-ee! I will tell your father about your unacceptable, intolerable behavior. Such language is all Rakesh's bad influence."

Sheetal marched up to the pair of elephants saluting each other near the Fulton whites and stood face-to-face before Mummyji. "You know why I put Yash in boarding school? So he's away from your bad influence and doesn't turn out like you."

"How dare you—"

"I'm leaving now."

"Of course, you should leave." Mummyji's expression melted into a grin. "The good news, you have heard, no?"

"Naina's going to marry Ajay, right?" Sheetal pumped a hand on her hip. "I know. The *whole world* knows that you will dangle them like puppets on your string."

"Think what you want. But Rakesh is planning for Yash to stay here in Raigun." Mummyji clasped her hands behind her back and circled Sheetal.

"Rakesh and I were discussing that for some time until Yash ended up in the hospital. And then we changed our mind."

Mummyji waved her fingers in the air. "Obviously, Rakesh hasn't told you, I tell you, or perhaps he's chosen *not* to tell you." She paused and reversed direction. "Only last night we confirmed about Yash living here permanently. And the matter is settled because this will be your last trip to Mansali. All this running to and from Mansali without a husband or family will be over for you now and you will be more at home Mrs. Independent Working Woman."

Sheetal spun on her heels and left.

Two hours later Sheetal followed a coolie carrying her luggage and was about to board the Delhi Mail train when her mobile rang. She took the call but the hustle and bustle of passengers, the *clack-thack* of feet on the concrete platform and calls from vendors clouded her hearing. "Hello?"

"Beti?"

"Papa?" A group of people brushed past and knocked against her in a rush to catch a train on the adjacent platform. "Papa, I can't hear you." The coolie hopped aboard the train with her suitcase, and she pressed the phone to her ear. "You have to speak up."

"I spoke to Ashwin and...him...everything."

The train whistled, and she cupped her left ear with a free hand. "I can't hear you."

"He said...arrange...visas..." His voice faded under the hollers of food hawkers' yells as they pushed carts along the platform. "Passports? You...carrying...right?"

"Yes." She grabbed the metal handrail and raised a foot on the first step when several people exited, forcing her back on the platform.

"Cash..."

She swung back on the step and struggled to upright herself. "Yes, Papa. I have cash."

"Good. I was...to send...but it's gone. All tied up. Vikram blocked all my money. Can't believe he did...to me."

People bid farewell to passengers aboard. "How could he?"

"After all I did for him and his family. He deceived me."

"What did he do?" The coolie emerged from the carriage and signaled that he'd stowed her luggage. Sheetal climbed aboard and fished her wallet out of the travel bag as the coolie hopped off. "What did he do?"

"...papers. I don't remember...and how...when I didn't sign them? But...my signature..."

The train lurched forward, and Sheetal thrust five hundred rupees into the coolie's open palm. Then she hurried in the compartment, turned left and rushed down the narrow corridor "I didn't hear what you said, Papa."

"I said not to worry. I called Ashwin and he's flying down tomorrow. My lawyers will look into this and make sure I get every paisa back. I will call Hemu, let her know what her son has done, and threaten to shame them if she doesn't make Vikram—this noise. What is all that noise? Where are you?"

"On the train to Mansali."

"Good, Beti. And don't come back. Take Yash and go with Arvind."

The air stilled. *How did Papa know?*

The train hollered a whistle and lurched, throwing Sheetal forward. She grabbed the corner of a berth and steadied herself.

"Don't worry about me, I will fight. If there's one thing I've learned from you, it's how to fight back. Stay with Arvind. You hear? Trust him, Beti."

"I—Yes, I—" The line went dead.

The engine tore through the dark terrain scattering birds in the sky. Sheetal called Papa several times but couldn't connect.

LATER THAT EVENING, WHEN SHEETAL WAS TWO HOURS AWAY FROM Dholakpur, her phone chimed, and she flipped it open. "Hello?"

"Hai Ishwar! Gone. All gone." Mummyji burst into tears.

"What happened?"

"Naina." Her voice crackled. "I called Rakesh, and he's not picking up the phone. He must be on the Delhi flight. There's no one, and I'm all alone in this big house."

"Where are all the servants? Janvi? Roshni? Where's Naina?"

"I can't wake her up." Mummyji took a deep watery breath, congestion clogging the words. "I've been trying for half an hour, but she won't move. And—Hai Ishwar! There's foam all over her mouth, I tell you!" Her cries vibrated with the *thaka-thaka-thunk* of the train.

"Call a doctor."

"He's on his way and should be here soon. Hai Ishwar! What did I do to deserve this?"

The Delhi Mail hollered a warning for something to move out of the way, and Sheetal jostled from side to side with the rattle of Mummyji's sobs. "Is she breathing?"

"I...I don't know."

"Check. Put your finger under her nose. Check her pulse."

The train's *thaka-thaka-thunk* filled the silence.

"Can you feel anything? Is she breathing out air?"

"Nothing." Mummyji's sobs thickened.

"Did she eat or drink anything before—"

"I...I don't know."

A shiver ran up Sheetal's spine. Did Naina overdose on Elavil and commit suicide?

"Hire a car the moment you reach Dholakpur, I tell you." Mummyji's voice tightened. "Have someone drive you home imme-diately!"

Sheetal tightened her grip on the phone. "I'm on the train and I can't. Yash—"

"Forget Yash!" Mummyji's voice grew hysterical. "All you think of is your son, your family, your everything when everything of mine is falling apart."

"You refused treatment. You chose not to—"

"She's weak, and not strong like you. Get off at Dholakpur and come home."

Sheetal flipped the Nokia closed, tossed it in her bag and zipped it shut.

29
PROMISES AND BITES

Sheetal checked-in at the Plaza Royale, a holiday resort comprising of fifty-two villas and cottages scattered over acres of hilly landscape. A narrow concrete road wove from the resort's security checkpoint to the reception and threaded the outlying residential properties in one grapevine.

The receptionist looked past Sheetal's shoulder as if in anticipation for someone else to join her.

"I'm staying alone for the next two weeks," Sheetal clarified.

"Your reservation is for one of the outlying cottages. Number forty-two." The receptionist swiped Sheetal's credit card.

Why did Rakesh make reservations in a remote location tucked away in a corner of Upper Mansali? Families or couples who wanted privacy and time together were more suited to this resort-style setup, certainly not a person traveling alone.

The bellboy drove Sheetal in a golf cart around the hilly landscape from the reception to an outlying villa. The five-minute ride trailed up gentle slopes as the bellboy went over important details like how the reception desk needed at least a fifteen-minute warning if guests wanted to reserve a golf cart to get from their villa to the reception or main gate, and how this road presented the only mode of transportation at the resort. The only restaurant at the reception was open from twelve to three for lunch and six to nine for dinner. The villas were designed to accommodate two or three families and smaller cottages, a family of four. The bellboy parked the golf cart outside 'Cottage forty-two', grabbed the Samsonite, unlocked the front door with a key, and Sheetal followed. *"Yahaan rakhoon, Memsahib?"* He asked if he should place her luggage to the left beside the four-seater dining table and kitchenette.

"No, in the bedroom please."

The bellboy took her luggage down a narrow corridor ahead and turned right into an open doorway.

A cozy living room took up the right of the hall. An entertainment unit backed against a wall on the right and looked out at a maroon sectional sofa, a matching single seater and a wooden coffee table. Sunlight streamed in from a glass patio door to the far right over-looking a wooden deck and bathed the two-seater in a pool of light. Small, but cozy. In any case, she would only need the cottage for a few hours.

The bellboy emerged, walked down to the kitchenette, and almost knocked over a standing lamp in a corner. However, he caught the lamp in time, settled it back on its base, and in fifteen steps reached her. The living room equated to half the size of her bedroom in the Dhanraj mansion. Sheetal dropped her handbag on the single-seater, took the bunched keys from the bellboy and placed them on the dining table.

"I've placed your luggage in the larger bedroom," he said.

Larger? "How many bedrooms here?"

"Two. Is there a mistake?"

"No. It's fine." She tipped him and shut the door.

She walked over to the kitchenette and ran her palm along the smooth counter equipped with a toaster, an electric kettle and a mini fridge tucked below. The slab of granite turned a sharp right to a two-ring gas stove and four knives wedged deep in a wooden block at a diagonal.

Sheetal walked across to the patio, content at the proximity of the living and dining spaces. Two arm-lengths and she could have touched the ceiling, unlike the Dhanraj mansion where she had to swim up against tides of marble. She cut through a gap between the sofas, twisted the already-pegged key in the lock and slid the glass door open.

The fragrance of wet earth and grass perfumed the air. Sheetal stepped on the deck and planks of wood creaked. Two chairs had been overturned on a patio table, and Sheetal up-righted both. The closest lodging in the distance approximated the size of half a thumb. How lush and green the surrounding hills rolled. So wild and so free! Specks of gray road peeked intermittently from between the earth's rounded folds as if playing hide and seek. She leaned over the deck's railing and peered right. A ribbon of concrete trailing from the cottage's doorstep disappeared and peeked up again with the rising landscape to join the main road. She took a deep breath and moistened her lips savoring freedom. If only she could have given Papa some relief from all the mayhem he was probably dealing with in Raigun.

She went back in, fished her cell phone from the handbag and punched Papa's number. The ringing reverberated. What happened to Naina? Who would manage the delivery of Megha's baby? The ringing stopped and she put away the phone. Those were not her problems anymore.

THAT EVENING SHEETAL WAITED OUTSIDE DR. CHATURVEDI'S BUILDING FOR Yash. Grass carpeted the landscape, birds chirped in trees lush with green leaves and the horizon had been painted a cloudless dark blue.

Sheetal tapped her fingers against her thigh in anticipation. Yash would be fine. Everything was going to be fine.

A lone figure in a half-sleeve white shirt and pair of navy blue trousers emerged from the auditorium. Sheetal squinted for a clear view. *Yash?* She waved. However, the figure didn't look up. Must be someone else, like the other boy she had mistaken for Yash last time. Still, she walked toward him just in case it was Yash. The boy dragged himself, his head lowered, and hands tucked inside the trouser pockets. Yash would have waved to her by now and run at full speed. Must be someone else. Someone who lacked spirit and zeal. Fifteen feet away she couldn't deny the truth any longer. The boy was Yash.

Sheetal fell to her knees and cupped Yash's face in her palms, but he kept his eyes lowered. She crooked a finger under his chin and raised his head, but he refused to look up. "What's wrong, Yash? Look at me." She ran her fingers through his hair, down his cheeks and winced at the sharp slants and angles that defined his face. She touched his nape and ran her hands across the shoulders of his half-sleeve shirt. Bones piqued the pads of her fingers and her heart ached at how thin and wiry he'd become. "I'm here, Yash. I came for you."

He raised the umbrella of his eyelids, his expression blank.

"Talk to me, Yash. Say something."

Nothing.

Her heart grated the pit of her stomach. Sheetal pulled Yash to her chest and hugged him tight, but he didn't fill the width of her arms. Instead, he squeezed in just a half of her embrace. "Say something," Sheetal whispered in his ear. "Look at you. So thin, so weak. What happened?" She ran her thumb over his forehead, brushing aside a lock of hair. "Did someone say something? Do something to you?" She circled a shoulder with the pad of her thumb, then fanned her fingers across his back and slid the other hand down his arm. "What is it, Yash? Tell me. Speak, Beta, who's done this to you?"

He jerked ever so slightly, a minor motion of the head.

No? Was that a no? "You can tell me anything, Yash. I'm your mother. No one can harm you now."

"C-can't," he whispered.

"Why?"

"He t-t-told me n-n-not t-to."

Stammering? Her heart welled in her throat. Yash had never stammered in his life. "Who?"

No answer.

"What did he say?" She held both hands and tightened her grip on his fingers. "Do you love me?"

He nodded.

"Do you trust me?"

Another nod, this time pronounced.

"Then tell me."

Yash inched away. "D-d-do you l-l-ove m-me, M-um?"

Her heart fisted in a knot. "Of course, Yash. I love you more than anything in the world."

"Then t-tell the t-t-ruth. W-w-what D-daddy did t-to you that n-night. W-was it a m-mistake? You s-said it was a m-mistake."

The breath tightened in her throat. Yash wanted the truth, the very truth she'd spent years running away from. "He was hurting inside. He wanted me to feel his pain." She stopped. Why was she justifying Rakesh's actions again? Who was she saving Rakesh from and why? He had hurt, beaten and accused her of being with another man when he had been cheating on her with another man all along! "He was wrong. He had no right to, but he wanted to hurt me."

"On p-purpose?"

Sheetal nodded.

Yash wrapped his fingers around her wrists where the bandages had been and pressed lightly. "D-does it s-s-still hurt?"

"Not anymore. And he's never going to hurt me again, I promise." Another figure in the distance dressed in a half-sleeve white shirt and khaki pants was heading toward them. Sheetal rose to her feet, bending down at the waist to Yash's height. "What did he tell you not to tell me?" She held him by the shoulders and the bangles collided with one another. "Who told you not to tell me?"

"I c-can't s-say."

Sheetal tightened her grip.

Tears rolled down his cheeks. "I-if I t-tell, he'll d-do the s-same t-to m-me."

Sheetal looked up. Arvind was getting closer. And quickening his gait like he anticipated Yash would reveal something. "Who?" She drilled her fingers into him. "*Who* will do *what* to you?" Had Arvind threatened Yash into revealing details about her and Rakesh so he could divert her from Rakesh? So he too could know their inner secrets like Mummyji? Were the boys in the hostel perverts? Was Arvind a pervert? A chill ran through her veins. "Who, Beta? You have to tell me who. Help me to help you."

"You're hurting m...me, M-Mum."

Sheetal loosened her hold. "Who?"

"B-but then he'll hit m-me. And hurt m-me."

"No one will ever hit you." Sheetal looked him in the eye. "I promise. But you *have* to tell me who's doing this." Yash tried to wriggle out of her grip, and Sheetal firmed her hold. "Listen to me. I've been working very hard so we can leave this place and never come back. I am doing this for you, only you. But you have to tell me the truth or you and I will come back to all this. Understand?"

Arvind was meters away now and not too far from hearing range. He had loved her. He still loved her. He would do anything for her. Is that why Arvind had discussed Yash's condition off school records and via private phone calls? Bile rose up her throat. "Quick, Yash. Tell me quickly. Who's threatening you?" She could change plans. Contact Papa. File for a divorce. Take custody of Yash. *How?* Somehow. But if Papa had signed everything over to Vikram, then Papa'd be left with nothing. She'd be left with nothing. And she would inevitably lose Yash to Rakesh. The sky inked purple. She'd call Uncle Ashwin tonight. He'd know what to do. "Quick. We don't have time."

Arvind was marching at full speed.

A gush of air escaped from the corner of Yash's mouth, and his lips wrinkled unevenly.

"Yes," she encouraged him. "Go on."

"D... D..." His lips inched apart, the joint between his trousers darkened and the stench of urine overwhelmed.

"Yes, Yash. I'm here. Tell me." Arvind was four feet away. "Tell me!" she begged. "Please."

Yash opened his mouth and the word spilled like liquid down the empty karva of her soul.

"D...Dad."

SHEETAL WALKED WITH ARVIND TOWARD THE SPORTS FIELD, AND HER attention meandered to the conifers turning gray in the evening light. She had sent Yash to change into a fresh pair of clothes so she could talk with Arvind in private. She sat on a bench.

"What's wrong?" Arvind sat beside her.

"Nothing."

Arvind pulled something from his pocket and handed it to her. "Tomorrow evening. Platform number six."

Sheetal took the ticket and held it between her thumb and index finger. The ticket read: *Red Fort Express, Bogie number 50042.* "I can't believe I'm giving up thirty-two years of my life. It's just—there's so much—a lot of—"

"Shit, yaar, Sheetal! I'm giving you a chance to start over and live."

Her forehead pulsed. "You make it sound as if I've been dead."

"What kind of a life have you been living? First, your husband beats you, then he threatens Yash. Isn't it obvious that there was never a need to go through with any of this?"

"You're saying eloping with you would have led to happily-ever-after?"

"I'm not saying anything."

"You expect me to predict the future?"

"You don't have to be a psychiatrist to figure out Rakesh Dhan-raj." Arvind leaned forward and propped both elbows on his knees. "The man speaks for himself."

"Just say it."

"I don't think you trust me."

"You think I can trust anyone after all I've been through? How will we manage with different last names? People will become suspicious, and I can't tell anyone I'm a Dhanraj. But as Sheetal Chopra, as husband and wife and with Yash as our son, no one will suspect."

"True." He steepled the fingers of both hands. "I have a better idea. No use pretending."

"Why would we pretend?"

He turned. "What do you mean?"

"I thought you said you didn't marry all these years because you still loved me."

"I do."

"So aren't you going to..." She gulped but the question lodged in her throat. She couldn't bring herself to say the unthinkable when she'd been a big enough burden.

"I have friends and family who will take care of you and Yash."

"And you?"

"I won't be able to return to St. Paul's. That's obvious. I'll figure out my life later."

"You're going to leave us?"

"I'll take you as far as I can and leave you in good hands. Promise."

"Where? With whom?"

Silence.

Her heart. Her throat. Everything ached and tears crept at the corner of her eye. "You're not telling me anything. Why? Why can't you marry me?"

"You want me to marry you?"

"Don't you love me?"

"I will always love you. But I can't marry you."

"Why?"

"Because, I...I just can't. I have to let you go."

"What do you mean?"

"There's no telling what Rakesh will do."

"Rakesh is gone. What more does he have to do with us? With me? I left him for you."

"No, Sheetal. If you left him for me, then it's wrong. You're leaving him for you."

"But I love you." The ache in her heart welled up her throat and everything blurred. "Since we met, I can't stop thinking about you. And us, together. You're all I have, Arvind."

"I love you too, and I spent the last ten years of my life wondering why you never came with me. I don't want to spend the next ten years wondering why you did."

"I don't understand. What more can he do to me? To us? He won't know where we are. Rakesh won't—"

"It's not that easy."

"Ten years ago, you jumped over my balcony and told me to walk away from it all. You told me to marry you. You said it was easy and all I had to do was leave and forget about what everyone would say." She took a deep breath. "Well, I did. And...now you want nothing to do with me? Why? Because I have a son? Because I'm married once—"

"Because you need to do this for you and for Yash. If I marry you, Rakesh becomes right. You and I become wrong."

Like Ajay Malhotra's wife? Wronged, to begin with. Then proven wrong again because she had fallen in love with another man? "Why did you help me then, Arvind? Why the phone calls? Why the worry? You should have left me where I was. Why the promises? Why the lies?"

"I promised to help." His voice held firm. "That's all. Anything more is stepping over the line."

"What line? I crossed all boundaries for you."

"For Yash. You're doing this for Yash and for you. Not for me. You just said so yourself. If it were for me, you would have left Rakesh ten years ago." He closed his eyes and docked his forehead on his knuckles.

"Are you and Rakesh in this? Together?"

"What?"

"Have you teamed up with Rakesh against me?"

"Are you out of your mind?"

"What am I supposed to believe when you don't—"

"You are my responsibility, and I don't want to take advantage of you. Do you honestly think Yash will ever accept me as his father? Do you think we can ever live like a family? A real family? What will everyone say?"

The blood rushed to her head. First Kavita assumed she had the right to decide her life and now Arvind. What responsibility called someone to put their life at risk for another without a fee or expectation in return?

The darkening grass, the purple-gray sky, the air suspended in motion.

"I have a room booked at Jatinder Bhai's guest house if you don't want to stay at the hotel. You can move—"

"No. I'll stay put just in case Rakesh calls and checks with reception. We stay with the plan. You're right. There's no telling what he will do."

"Tomorrow evening, I will stay in the auditorium until the show begins so everyone sees me around and I have things set in place. When the concert begins, Yash and I will meet you outside, near the stairs somewhere. Then we leave. I've told Yash everything."

"What did he say?"

"He looked relieved but scared. And confused. Should this fail—"

"You're expecting something to go wrong?"

"No. But we've got to be careful in case Plan A falls apart. Plan B, I send a car to the hotel lobby. Where are you staying?"

"Plaza Royale."

"The driver will meet you in the lobby at eleven o'clock. The Red Fort Express leaves at three in the morning. It's our only hope because travel by car through Dholakpur isn't safe, and anyway, the next train isn't till later that afternoon at four. We can't afford to miss the morning one, you understand?"

Sheetal nodded.

SHEETAL HARDLY SLEPT THAT NIGHT AND SPENT THE NEXT MORNING rehearsing Arvind's plan. When she couldn't take the stress anymore, she stepped out on the deck for a breath of fresh air and focused on the wide rolling landscape. Then she ordered room service.

Forty-five minutes later a bellboy set the patio table for two with an embroidered tablecloth, crockery, silverware, a small vase of flowers and set pots of spicy dals, vegetable curries and naan.

Sheetal had told him to lay the table for two so the loneliness wouldn't pinch. For ten long years, succulent meals had graced the Dhanraj's dining table, but everything tasted bland. Now she could smell aromas like hot cayenne peppers, garlic, fried onions and cumin seeds that crackled and exploded in anticipation of freedom in every bite. She chewed hastily, swallowing each morsel and savoring the flavors.

At three that afternoon, Sheetal packed her essentials in a khaki string bag: one ordinary salwar suit to change into from the sari she would wear at the concert, a pair of Nike shoes because she couldn't walk around the train station in dressy stilettos, passports, papers, her train ticket, a torch—just in case the lights went out, cash, travelers' checks and jewelry. She shoved the bag in a gap between the cupboard and the wall so she didn't accidentally misplace it.

Then she debated whether to bother dressing up in a fancy sari because she wouldn't really attend the concert anyway. Perhaps something not too dressy would suffice. On second thought, casual clothing would draw even more unwanted attention.

Sheetal was folding the front pleats of her sari and calculating the hours they would have from the time they reached Lower Mansali to the train's departure at three tomorrow morning. There would be plenty of time. No rush. Her breathing calmed. Maybe everything would go smoothly after all.

A knock sounded at the door.

"*Kaun hai?*" she asked from the bedroom.

Silence.

Sheetal continued to tuck all seven pleats at the petticoat's waist when another knock followed. "Who is it?"

"Room service."

"I ordered room service hours ago and lunch was delivered." She twisted a lipstick cap off. Someone had probably mistaken this cottage for another or come to clean up. She was about to apply the frosted pink color when a third knock rapped. She leaned out of the bedroom's doorway to make herself clearly heard. "I told you, I didn't order room service and I don't need anything cleaned. Now, please go away."

The knocking continued.

Sheetal thumped her lipstick on the dressing table, marched to the front door, swiveled two bolts to the left and twisted the key in the lock. "I told you I—" The door swung open, and Sheetal stepped back. Her right heel caught in the skirt of her sari, tugged at the folds, and she staggered and grabbed a chair for support.

He marched in. Two strides.

The words bubbled, trapped in her throat. "I—"

"Promise. I won't bite."

30
FEAR

Sheetal stepped back, fumbling for the right words as the sari pleats came undone. "I...I wasn't expecting you."

"I wasn't expecting you to." Rakesh blocked the view of the setting sun, and his broad frame swallowed the light. He entered, dragging the scent of mint, a suitcase in one hand and a hand-carry with the other. He kicked the door closed with the back of his heel, and a thud shook the wall. Then he paused, surveyed the interiors, marched ahead to the corridor and put down the hand-carry.

Rakesh's head fell three feet short of the ceiling. Two strides and he reached the corridor's middle leading to a bathroom and both bedrooms. He swung open a door on the right and peeped in Sheetal's room. "Sweet." Then he marched ahead, swung open a door on the left, wheeled in the suitcase and emerged seconds later. "Comfortable?"

Her heart pounded. Thank goodness she took the initiative to dress up. Was he going to share her room? Sleep on the same bed? Use the other for storage? Storage of what?

"Too comfortable?"

"I... I thought you'd be in Delhi." She raised the pitch of her voice to sound casual. "On business."

"I am on business."

"But the Japanese. Tashukomo Electronics. Didn't you say—"

"That can wait." He yawned stretching his arms wide and appearing to touch the sides of the villa as the ring sparkled in the yellow light. His arms drew down and the ceiling appeared to succumb to his pull. "Too small." He shook his head.

He sat on the three-seater and spread his arms along the backrest taking up the space.

"I'm guessing you're here for Yash's sake?" With no official news from the school that Yash had been replaced, Rakesh would be expecting to see Yash take center stage. "I was just getting ready for the performance. Yash will be so—"

"I came for you."

"Oh. You—you must be tired after the long trip."

He rose, grabbed the hand-carry and unzipped the mouth. Then he pulled out three bottles of Blue Label and stacked them like trophies in an open cabinet above the toaster.

Was he planning to drink them all tonight?

"Aren't you going to ask me for chai?" He returned to the sofa area but didn't sit.

She prayed her sari sealed the heaves of her chest. "I'm still getting dressed."

"So?"

"We need a car. How—how about you call the front desk?"

"I will." He walked to the patio door. "You've been busy entertaining, I see. Table for two without me?"

She froze at the implication. "I was alone and ordered room service, but the bellboy assumed I was ordering for two. The other place setting is untouched."

"You must have quite an appetite. Room serviced?" He closed his eyes, tilted his head back and laughed.

Sheetal grabbed the edge of the dining table for support. "I have to finish getting ready. We'll be late."

"You never even invited me."

"In Raigun. You said no, remember?"

"Didn't try hard enough. Doesn't matter, anyway. After this, it's over. You're going home."

Her mobile chimed.

"Take the call," he ordered.

She went to her room and fished the Nokia mobile out of her travel bag. The caller ID showed Mr. Patel from the Taj Resort. *Good.* The phone call would prove business as usual. She pressed the phone to her ear. "Hello, Patelji?"

The phone was snatched, flung across the room, and splintered on impact with the wall. She spun around, her breath trapped as he grinned.

"Now that future interruptions are out the way, a few updates. I filled out all the transfer certificates at Dr. Chaturvedi's office on my way down. Yash will study in Raigun going forward. We leave tomorrow afternoon on the four o'clock train—"

"Yash," she interrupted. "Did you meet him?"

"No. Why?"

"Does he know you're here?"

"No. But you sure as fucking hell don't look happy. Anyway, he'll find out soon enough."

The welcome reception outside the auditorium's main entrance swarmed with people as a photographer asked groups of attendees to pose. Men and women dressed in shimmering attire stopped to chat and mingle with Sheetal and Rakesh, no doubt keen to be seen and photographed with the Dhanrajs.

Her wrist in Rakesh's grip, Sheetal looked out at the steps leading to the grassy area below where she'd met Yash just yesterday evening. She was supposed to meet Arvind and Yash on this very spot in about half an hour's time. She drifted outside Rakesh's permissible radius, but he pulled her back. She smiled at the crowd and kept calm like a repeat of the charity dinner's performance before they'd left Raigun. *Just play along and he might not know the difference.*

Sheetal sat next to Rakesh in the middle of the VIP row in the brightly lit auditorium. She looked behind at rows slanting upward, giving spectators a clear view of the dais. Her attention flew to exit signs in neon red stamped in regular intervals along the auditorium's walls. She leaned past Rakesh and caught sight of an exit on the right.

The stage curtains parted, the bright lights dimmed and music played. Yash and Arvind were probably waiting for her outside. She had to get out. But how? Did they know Rakesh was here and that she was stuck with him? No khaki bag, no cash and no documents. Even if she did manage to escape, she couldn't leave. Her heart raced. "I need to go," she whispered as the hall plunged into darkness.

"Where?"

"Ladies' room."

"Hold it." A drum roll sounded, and he clamped her wrist.

Her heart, her head, everything thumped loud and wild.

This year's concert was a tribute to the legendary actor, producer and director of Indian cinema, Raj Kapoor. Renowned as India's Charlie Chaplin, Raj Kapoor frequently performed roles where he portrayed a tramp or a tragic lover with a female lead actor. Because St. Paul's was an all-boys school, some of the boys had to dress up in saris, salwar suits, and play the role of leading women in the musical sequences of various Bollywood hits.

About thirty of Raj Kapoor's famous songs, acts and dance sequences were woven into vignettes. Each clip belted out a new song and new actors. Scene after scene rolled on and off the stage like the episodes in Sheetal's life. The long, languid calls of the violin reminded her of the endless search for a husband's love. The tinkle of piano keys, her love for Yash, Mama, Papa, and the struggle to keep life bound and intact. Drum rolls called to mind Rakesh. The CD. The threats to Yash's life.

An hour into the performance, Rakesh leaned toward her. "Where's Yash?"

She had spent all evening rehearsing the words, so she sounded natural. "He's not hosting the event."

"You knew Yash wasn't hosting?" Rakesh hissed.

"He told me yesterday when I met him."

From the spotlights on stage, Sheetal could just make out Rakesh's twisted expression.

"Who the fuck"—spectators seated in the row ahead turned behind—"kicked him out?"

"No one." Sheetal kept her voice low. "He couldn't present."

"*Couldn't?* Couldn't go on stage like that boy up there?" He gestured to a boy who announced the next series of musical clips. "You turned Yash into a fucking coward, like yourself."

More heads turned in their direction.

She lowered her head. "He's not feeling well."

"And you knew about this?"

"I—"

"Why didn't you tell me?"

"I didn't expect you to be here. You said you were going to New Delhi."

"Then why are you here?"

"I told you...I found out yesterday."

"Bullshit."

Applause filled the arena and the curtains clapped to a close for an interval.

"You're not really here for the concert, are you?" Rakesh firmed his grip on her wrist. "There's something else. I can tell."

Her hand numbed and she could barely feel the bangles on her wrists. "You're hurting me." Lights bathed the auditorium in yellow, and people who stayed back swiveled their legs to let others pass through. However, no one dared trespass Rakesh and Sheetal. They exited via the aisle's left.

"I'm only here because of Yash," Sheetal said. "You know that."

"Then why come for the performance if he has no part? You could have stayed back at the villa."

"And do what? Do you remember Megha?" Sheetal firmed her voice. "Remember what she was like before? How she used to talk, dress and keep to herself?"

"What does Megha have to do with Yash?"

"She was so unstable...so broken inside."

"Sweet! Women talk. Just what I need."

"It's precisely what's happening to your son. He stammers. He's lost all confidence. He's broken inside. I wonder why?" She snatched her hand away. "What did you do to him?"

Rakesh's features tightened and his face turned a shade of dark yellow. "Oh, you think it's my fault when you're the overprotective one?"

At that moment, Dr. Chaturvedi made his way through the narrow aisle of seats, cane in hand. "Aah. Good evening, Mr. and Mrs. Dhanraj."

Rakesh and Sheetal rose, and Rakesh shook his hand. "Good evening. Quite spectacular. A lot of practice and hard work has gone into this performance." Then he leaned toward Dr. Chaturvedi and whispered something.

Sheetal inched closer to hear what he was saying.

"Why was I not informed about my son?"

"Informed about what?" Dr. Chaturvedi asked.

"It is my understanding that he's not hosting the concert as he should be. He auditioned and got through. Then why wasn't I told he... There's a problem?"

"Problem? Um...what problem?"

"Isn't there a school policy about informing parents when something is wrong?"

"I...ah...yes. Maybe we can discuss this later?"

"Now. And why didn't you say something when I called you a few weeks ago?"

Rakesh called Dr. Chaturvedi? For what?

"I, um...don't seem to understand what's going on." Dr. Chaturvedi turned left and right. "My apologies but perhaps I—"

"My wife just informed me."

Dr. Chaturvedi winced as more people turned to look their way.

"Something about no confidence." He waved a hand in the air. "Can't talk right. Why didn't someone say something?"

People nearby spoke in hushed whispers.

"Ah...I...um...didn't know myself." Dr. Chaturvedi nodded and gestured to the crowd that everything was all right. "I have no idea. Had his House Master informed me, I most certainly would have—"

"This House Master. I want to see him now."

"Perhaps a little later as scheduled?" Dr. Chaturvedi lowered his voice and gripped the backrest of the nearest seat.

What schedule? Rakesh wasn't even supposed to be here.

"Now!" Rakesh demanded. "I want all this sorted out, now."

"It's the middle of the concert. Perhaps, um...if we waited for—"

"I don't wait, especially after I've paid for it." Rakesh grabbed Sheetal by the wrist.

Did Rakesh bribe Dr. Chaturvedi? If she'd donated one of the orchids, perhaps she could have bought the man's loyalty first.

Just then, Dr. Chaturvedi's eyes widened behind the frames of his thick, black glasses and he whispered something in Rakesh's ear. He pointed to the dais in front and then summoned a teenage usher. He whispered something in the boy's ear and sent him off.

"What was that all about?" Sheetal tried to worm her hand out of Rakesh's grip, but he tightened the hold.

"You'll see."

A figure in the distance cut through a throng of people and headed toward them. *Arvind.*

Dr. Chaturvedi coughed and broke the silence as Arvind neared. "Let me introduce you both."

Arvind smiled and then turned to Dr. Chaturvedi.

"Meet, um...Mr. Chopra. Arvind Chopra." Dr. Chaturvedi turned to Rakesh. "Mr. Rakesh Dhanraj. I'll leave you, gentlemen. I, um...think you two have some catching up to do." Dr. Chaturvedi left.

He knew everything. There was no escape now.

Arvind reached to shake Rakesh's hand. "Hello, I'm Arvind."

Rakesh's jaw tightened. "Arvind!" He let Sheetal go and shook Arvind's hand, towering several inches above. His knuckles tightened and paled around Arvind's hand. His fist and face turned a darker shade of yellow while Arvind's swelled to a richer shade of brown. It was like watching scotch and coffee fill a single cup, each vying to outdo the other's color. "So, we finally meet. Heard much about you and how you're taking care of my son." He let go of Arvind's hand.

"An honor to meet you at last," Arvind replied.

"The honor is all mine."

"Yash talks a lot about you."

"As my wife—you. Not that she tells me anything, of course. But I know. And oh"—Rakesh turned around to face Sheetal— "I forgot to introduce you to my beautiful wife, Sheetal. But then, you two already know each other, I hear. And you already know my son. In fact, you know everyone and everything there is to know about me. Except me."

Sheetal pressed her palms together in the customary Indian greeting.

"Oh, come now." Rakesh pulled her forward and squeezed her between him and the backs of seats until she was standing right beside Arvind. Rakesh nudged her closer to Arvind. Uncomfortably close. "You're behaving like strangers. All this pretending, save it for the kids on stage. You guys are old friends. Good friends. *Very good friends.* Ditto?"

"Rakesh, he's just Yash's House Master, nothing more."

"Of course." He grinned. "Or how else would you have found him again after all these years?"

"We just happened to meet. I told you—"

"Things don't *just* happen. They're either meant to. Or not. And I'm here to make sure. Not." Then he grabbed her by the shoulders and firmed his grip. From the pressure of his hold and the way his fingers were digging into her shoulder blades, he was using her as a cane to steady himself. "I hear my son is unwell."

"He's up there with all the other students," Arvind said. "If you would like—"

"Was it not your duty to report this to Dr. Chaturvedi?"

"Report what?"

"This problem Yash is having. My wife just told me."

"I didn't think it was that serious."

"Mr. Chopra, I'm his father. I'll decide what is serious and what isn't. And when it comes to my family, I make the decisions around here. Understand?"

Arvind looked him in the eye. "Perhaps *you* need to understand that Yash is in this state because of you. Just because you run the country's biggest business empire, doesn't mean you can run a child's life."

The pressure of Rakesh's grip tightened, and the floor felt as if it would give way.

"Do you have a doctor's degree, Mr. Chopra?" His voice was calm. Deathly calm.

"No."

"Then I suggest you stop giving recommendations on my son's treatment."

Arvind slid his hands into his trouser pockets as people filled their seats again and a small crowd gathered around. "It's not just your son. Anyway, I should be heading back. We still have the rest of the show. It was good to meet you. Finally." He nodded to Rakesh and then Sheetal, avoiding eye contact before turning to leave.

"Ditto." Rakesh raised his arm in the air. "The show must go on." He swayed an arm. "May the best man win."

The lights faded. Arvind disappeared and the auditorium was blanketed in darkness once again.

"I...I think we should leave," Sheetal whispered.

"Why not? Somewhere far away, perhaps?"

THE REMAINDER OF THE SHOW WENT ON AS SHEETAL REHEARSED PLAN B. A car would be waiting for her outside the hotel lobby at eleven o'clock. Obviously, Arvind now understood why she failed to meet him and Yash shortly after the performance began. Her only chance was to make it to the waiting car. But how? She wasn't in the hotel's main building, but in a villa in a resort kilometers away from the reception, out in the middle of nowhere. How could she have forgotten to inform Arvind yesterday? If he sent a car to the reception, she'd never make it there on foot. The car had to meet her outside the villa. She had to tell Arvind. But how? Rakesh was not going to let her out of sight for a second.

The curtains drew to a close, and the audience applauded and cheered.

"Come." Rakesh grabbed Sheetal by the hand, rose to his feet and cut his way through the aisle, knocking down people in their path like dominoes. When they reached the auditorium's entrance, he ordered a security guard to go find his son among clusters of students sitting near the stage.

Minutes later, Yash arrived, dressed in school uniform. He slid his hands into the side pockets of his trousers. "H-h-hello, D-dad."

Rakesh bent at the waist, towering a full two feet above Yash. "What's this I'm hearing, Yash? You were replaced as host for the performance? I would have been so proud of you. You let us down, Yash. All of us."

"I'm s-s-sorry." The pockets of his trousers swelled as his hands fisted.

Rakesh shook his head. "You don't look sorry at all. Look what your mother turned you into."

Sheetal lunged and reached out to hold and protect her son, but Rakesh yanked her back and pulled her to his side.

"Now here's the plan. We're taking tomorrow's train back to Raigun. All three of us. You've always wanted to live at home like other boys. Right? You'll be in a new school, and you'll have new friends."

Yash nodded. "B-b-ut my exams?" He paled, turning to Sheetal in apparent desperation. "I have t-to g-give m-my f-final p-papers."

Rakesh rose to his full stature. "We'll see."

"I d-don't want t-to g-g-go." Yash's trousers darkened at the crotch, and the air reeked of urine.

Rakesh wrinkled his nose and turned on Sheetal. "Look what you've turned him into! Look." He reverted to Yash. "You go where I take you. Understand?"

Yash stood rooted to the ground.

"Have your bags packed and be ready first thing tomorrow morning."

People were spilling out of the auditorium.

"I will come pick you up. For me, Yash. Do it for me." Then he turned to leave, dragging Sheetal who struggled to keep up.

She craned her neck to see Yash as the distance between them increased. "Cottage number forty-two." Sheetal mouthed to Yash as the ground swept beneath her feet. "Cottage forty-two."

Yash nodded.

"Understand?" she asked, voiceless.

Yash continued to nod, his expression blank.

31
DRINK AND KILL

Rakesh slammed the cottage door closed and hurled Sheetal across the carpet.

She tripped over the pleats of her sari and hit the sofa's edge. A sharp pain seared up the left of her nape and ear. Rakesh was about to strike when Sheetal raised a hand and turned away. The hand bearing his ring came down. Sheetal numbed and gasped for air. She cowered at the threat of another blow when something warm, wet and sticky oozed down her cheek. Her eyes stung. She blinked, squeezing them hard so she wouldn't cry. Rakesh hated tears.

"Fucking bitch!" Spittle sprayed with the words. His bloodshot eyes loomed like two yellow moons out of focus as he struggled to balance and the hip flask, pegged to his belt, swayed with his tilting momentum. "It wasn't about Yash, was it? But all about you. Am I not man enough?"

Sheetal took small shallow breaths as he paced the room. Not too long before he would kill and drink or drink and kill. Either way, she was going to die. *Must keep him drinking and talking.*

He pulled out the flask, unscrewed the cap, raised it to his lips and gulped the liquid. Then he brushed the sleeve of the blazer across his face, staggered to the dining table and thumped the bottle on the surface. "What is it you like, eh? That dark skin? That beard? Is that it?"

She turned away, keeping watch from the corner of her eye should he strike.

"What?" he screamed.

Ripples shuddered throughout. She had to answer. Say something quick. And keep her eyes down. "Nothing," she whispered.

He torpedoed across the room, grabbed her by the shoulders and forced her onto the double-seater, pinning her against the fabric. Then he pressed his lips down on hers and sucked hard drawing the breath from her lungs.

Scotch and vomit sizzled across her tongue. Nausea crept up her throat and she suppressed the urge to retch. She couldn't breathe. She receded back against the fabric and turned away.

"Something wrong?" His fingers inched down the cleavage of her blouse and his sharp nails grated. "Don't want me anymore, do you, bitch? You want that son of a bitch!" His breath burned. "Yash likes him. You like him. Try him out, did you? What-was-he-like, Sheetal? Was-he-all-you-wanted-in-a-man?"

The haunting melody-tone. The nightmare was happening all over again. She was going to lose control and her bladder would spill any second.

"What the fuck do you see in him? Nothing. Hear me! He has nothing. Not even a fraction of what I do. Shares a cottage with fucking students. Doesn't even own a home, and you were ready to leave me for him and take my son with you? How dare you? Yash is mine! He belongs to me! He's my blood." He touched her on the right cheek. "Now how did that happen?" He licked his finger. "Sweet." He pressed his lips against the wound and sucked hard.

Pain sizzled. She gasped for air. *Calm. Keep calm. Let him have his way.*

He withdrew and streaks of red contoured his lips. "I gave you everything. A studio for those damned paintings. A career. A business, Sheetal, that was fucking doing better than mine! But nothing I ever do is good enough. Why?" He made his way to the kitchenette and grabbed one of the bottles he stacked that afternoon. He unscrewed the top, put the bottle to his lips, took a drink and lowered it. "We'll see how successful you are when I smash your studio this time. No more Naina. That tea will get rid of Naina for good."

Fear paralyzed. The ayurvedic tea from Bharat Chai Wallah.

"This time *I'm* going to burn those paintings and put an end to all your nonsense. Watch your fucking career go up in flames." The bottle swung in his hand, and scotch spilled on the carpet. "Tell me, Sheetal." He fell in the single-seater recliner and lengthened his feet on the coffee table. "What do you like about him?"

Twice. He had asked her the same question twice. "Nothing."

"You were going to run away with him, right, and take Yash?" He drank some more.

If he knocked out, there was enough space to crawl and squeeze between the sofa's edge, to the dining, and make it to the front door and escape. But where would she go in the dark in the middle of nowhere? The hotel lobby was an easy two to three kilometers out. Even in this half-delirious state, Rakesh would get her. Her drawstring bag. She couldn't leave without it. She had to keep him talking and drinking until he was out.

He swung the bottle in an arc up to his mouth, took another sip and lowered it. "Running-away-from-me, right?"

"I...I didn't know what to do." She inched to the sofa's edge and slid down on the floor. *Power. He craved dominance, control and power.* "I didn't think you loved me anymore."

"Fucking bitch!" His speech slurred. "Liar."

"You love someone else, Rakesh. I heard you and him on the tape. It sounded like you were...like you both were..." *Pretend. Pretend to be helpless. Weak. Lost.* "You were making love to him on the tape, and—"

"Why, that son of a bitch! Double-crossing—" He thumped the bottle on the table and scotch erupted, splashing tiny puddles on the wooden surface.

"I...I didn't know what to do. I wanted to ask, but I was scared. What if you said you didn't love me and loved him more? Then, where do I go? How do I live without you?"

The creases around his eyes smoothed. "You...you...withdrew money and closed your account."

"I had to, Rakesh. They were lying." Rakesh hated dishonesty.

"Gupta Sahib said you closed the account for personal reasons?"

"They were giving me a lower interest rate. Did Gupta Sahib tell you I was planning to open a new account? A joint account in both our names? They can't mislead me again."

"Hmph." He grunted.

"Oh." She eased her tone to make light of the matter as pain burned across her face. "He must have forgotten."

He reached for the bottle and drank some more. "You were on the phone with him. Why?"

"Who?"

"You know fucking who! Arvind. That's who. Megha told me of your plans to run away."

Megha? She didn't even live with them?

"You talked with him three times." He rose, turned around and paced the room, struggling to balance.

The static on the phone hadn't just been Naina's interruptions. Megha was spying for Rakesh. That explained her frequent visits on short notice. No notice, and always to tide-over Rakesh's absence. The brother-sister partnership wasn't simply a heightened security measure. The two worked as a team and were the real Dhanrajs. The turf had always been theirs to secretly rule, control and protect. For so long she had believed herself to be the sole outsider, but Mummyji and Naina were the true exiles struggling to hold their ground. With Naina gone, Rakesh would continue to play Mummyji and her against one another so they could never unite.

"Why-the-calls, Sheetal?"

"He...he wouldn't stop calling. He wanted me to run away with him, still thinks I love him, and that he has a right over me." She lowered her tone. "I...I didn't want to trouble you with such trivial things. It's you I love, not him. And you've got so many worries... pressures of the business and the debt. I played along, Rakesh. I let him believe what he wanted, thinking he'd eventually go away. I came for Yash just like you said. I think Arvind's hurting our son and doing things to him. Things you said happen to boys in a hostel."

He nodded as if in agreement and grunted. "Why, that fucking—"

"It's you I love, Rakesh." She dabbed her wounded cheek with the pallu and cringed as sharp zari embroidery pricked her raw skin. Rakesh sat down again, and she inched toward him, maneuvered to the right of the armrest so she could duck and shield herself from a blow should he strike. "I...I love you." She glanced up at a digital clock near the gas stove. Nine-thirty. *Ninety more minutes.*

He grabbed her by the hair and the skin strained against her scalp. Sheetal tried to pry his fingers off, but he tightened the pull and pain seared.

"Fucking bitch, liar! It's him. It's always been Arvind."

"No." Hot wet tears streamed down her face. "You. It's only been you."

He twisted harder.

"I'll prove it." He let go, and she dragged herself to her knees, shuffled forward until she was in front of him and positioned herself between his thighs. Then she leaned into his face, took a shallow breath and closed her eyes. Bile raced up her throat and she gulped. She pressed her lips to his and exhaled, her lungs on fire. She was going to be sick.

He pulled away. "Games, eh, to play with me? I bet you did much more for Arvind. I'm done with you. Fuck off!" He pushed her away.

Sheetal staggered to her feet and slowly made her way down the corridor. She skimmed the kitchen counter, the toaster, the sink and finally the wooden block of three knives. She paused. *Four. There were supposed to be four.* She walked to her room and closed the door leaving a crack open. Then she peeled off the sari, slipped on a salwar suit and donned a thick nightgown in a beam of moonlight cutting past a silhouette of trees and window rails to stream through the glass.

Glass clinked on wood. Feet shuffled on carpet. Silence. She dabbed her cheek with the petticoat she'd been wearing, and the fabric grew moist and dampened against her fingers. She tossed the petticoat on a suitcase lying open near the foot of the bed. Then she slipped between the sheets, pulled the covers up to her chin and leaned over the bed's edge to peer through a crack in the open door. No sign of Rakesh. She didn't want to risk being seen by him, so she eased her head back onto the pillow and pulled her wrist out from beneath the covers to check the time on her watch. Ten-fifteen. *Forty-five minutes to go.* A car. She prayed. Let there be a car waiting outside.

Slowly Sheetal pulled the covers aside and eased her legs until soft carpeting padded her feet. She rose and neared her bedroom door. Nothing. She stepped out in the corridor, tiptoed to the end, and could make out through the light of the moon the coffee table's outline, a half-empty bottle and puddles of liquor reflecting the moon's light. A few objects littered the floor. Sheetal inched closer. Rakesh's shoes and socks. A shadow, like that of a person, doubled over the recliner's back, caught her attention. Had Rakesh collapsed? Sheetal slid one foot ahead of the other. "Rakesh?" she whispered.

Silence.

"Rakesh?" She flattened her palm on the form and her fingers sank into the fabric. The blazer. She blinked and scanned the living room. Then she walked back up the corridor, past her room and bathroom and paused outside the other room. The door was ajar about two inches wide, and she pushed it open a crack more. Rakesh lay flat on his chest, fully dressed and knocked out.

She looked at the time on her watch. *Thirty-five minutes left.*

Sheetal crept back to her room, peeled off the nightgown and rolled it into a ball along with several saris, salwars and pillows. She arranged them lengthwise where she had just been sleeping and then rolled the covers back over and patted a sleeping figure into shape. She went to the cupboard, pulled out the khaki string bag, tucked it under her left arm, wrapped the matching dupatta around her neck and slipped on her Nike shoes. Then she tiptoed to the front door and turned the double bolts and knob. The door was locked. Sheetal rattled the knob and stopped. *He was bound to wake up with all this noise.* She scanned the dining table for the bunched keys. Gone.

Sheetal tiptoed to the patio door, pressed her hand against the sheet of glass and slid it to the right. The door wouldn't move.

She groped in the stream of slanting moonlight for the key pegged in the lock yesterday afternoon. A cold, metallic knob jutting out the patio door filled her palm. No key. *Fallen. The key must have fallen somewhere.* She sank down on all fours and groped the area between the sofa's back and the patio door. Nylon fibers filled her palms as the moon continued to spill white light on the wooden porch and grass outside. There were two ways in and out of the villa and Rakesh had the keys to both. He had planned this all along. The isolation. Privacy. Up in the mountains in the middle of nowhere. Hold her hostage.

She stole her way to the corridor, pressed her back against the wall and peeped around the edge of Rakesh's door. *Still fast asleep.* Sheetal entered the bathroom and sat on the bathtub's edge. Every door, locked. Every window, barred behind a sheet of glass. Every sheet of glass, railed by metal bars on the outside. And the patio glass door, locked. *"Let's say I know what's going to happen."* Rakesh's words swirled in her mind. *"Do I do something about it, or just let it happen?"* She glanced at her watch. *Twenty minutes.*

She had to get out.

Sheetal cocked her head back and noticed a square portion of the wall, two-by-two feet in dimension, and ten feet off the floor, knocked out and covered with a lattice mesh. The mesh appeared to serve as a temporary covering for an incomplete window that needed repairs. Only four nails, one in each corner, appeared to hold the wire mesh in place.

Sheetal eased open the bathroom door carrying the string bag and tried to minimize light-spill from the bathroom into the hallway. She tiptoed to the kitchenette, pulled a knife out of the block of wood and pinned the blade against her index finger. The narrow-pointed blade would do the job. She returned to the bathroom, closed the door and punched the lock in place.

RAKESH STIRRED. A NOISE CAME FROM SOMEWHERE. WHITE NOISE. HE TRIED to open his eyes. But his head pounded. Cold. He was so cold.

SHEETAL PULLED DOWN THE TOILET LID, NESTLED HER STRING BAG IN THE bathtub's corner closest to her and climbed on the commode. She ran her fingertips along the vinyl frame feeling for nails and extra screws. *Nothing.* She stepped down, pulled the knife out of her bag and rolled the bag into the bathtub's corner again. However, the mouth of the bag opened, and the torch rolled out and clanked in the porcelain tub below. *Did he hear?* Sheetal stuffed the torch back in, climbed up with the knife in hand, pushed the pointed tip into a screw and rotated it counterclockwise. The screw budged, and bangles tinkled down her wrists. *Too much noise.* Sheetal pulled the bangles off one by one and clumped them in a heap on the bathtub's corner before progressing to the second screw, the third, and then the fourth, spinning each in the same direction. The screws twirled like merry-go-rounds spinning her closer to freedom. The vinyl case loosened from the wall's edge. Sheetal spread her hands to catch the mesh, but the frame hit the commode, clanged, twanged and banged against the bathtub's corner and knocked the spiral of bangles down.

RAKESH ROLLED ONTO HIS SIDE AND OPENED HIS EYES. THE WALL BLURRED. *That noise. That damn noise. Where was it coming from? And why was it so hot?*

SHEETAL GRABBED THE STRING BAG, TIGHTENED THE MOUTH, SWUNG IT behind and slid her arms in both hoops. She raised her arms, grabbed the ledge and curled her fingers around the windowsill as light from stars and gibbous moon poured from the night sky. She had to get herself up. But how? She had nothing to help gain height. She flattened both palms on the five-inch broad sill, pushed off the commode and pulled herself up, flattening and locking both elbows at ninety degrees. She lugged her body up the wall and through the window. The upper half of her torso hung outside and the lower half in. Cold mountain air brushed past. Sheetal pedaled her toes against the wall and pushed. Her body swung up and she plummeted. Falling. She was falling. She hit the ground and damp grass smacked her in the face. She got up on all fours and spat dirt. Then she wiped her face with her sleeve, clambered to her feet and ran.

RAKESH MARCHED INTO SHEETAL'S ROOM AND POUNCED ON HER SLEEPING frame, but his hands sunk into cushions of fabric. He threw back the duvet, and balls of Sheetal's clothing unraveled. Rakesh straightened to his full height and roared.

A LION? A BEAR? SHEETAL STOPPED IN HER TRACKS. THE BLOOD-CURDLING call sounded like a beast. She looked at the time on her watch. Eleven. She ran, her heart pummeling to keep up with her legs. She crunched grass, stumbled over uneven terrain. *The car? Where was the car?* She stopped on the crest of an upward slope to catch her breath. The road lit silver by the moon was broken by the outline of a silver bonnet. *The car!*

A figure near the car waved for her to hurry. *Jatinder Singh!*

Light flooded the grass from behind. She looked over her shoulder and from the corner of her eye, the villa was bathed in yellow. She turned and pounded one foot ahead of the other as wind rushed through her hair. She was getting closer. Closer. She skidded to a stop and lunged against the vehicle.

"Hurry, Madame." Jatinder opened the back passenger door. "Getting late, we are. No time. Rushing must."

Sheetal scooted in the passenger seat, Jatinder slammed the door shut, revved the engine and sped into the night.

32
RED FORT EXPRESS

"*Jaldi karo.*" Adrenaline zipped through Sheetal's veins as the car revved along the concrete road.

"Hurrying, Madame." Something darted in front of the windshield, and Jatinder slammed on the brake thrusting Sheetal forward. "Very sorry, Madame." He turned around in apology. "I no good in emergency. But I trying my best." Then he roared ahead at full speed.

Sheetal clutched the bag to her chest and savored the ripped fabric grating her palms. The car swerved to the left and right, and Sheetal grabbed the seat in front for support.

"No worrying, Madame." Jatinder looked at her in the rearview mirror, his cherry-button eyes sparkling. "No one hurting you now. I am promising Arvind Bhai I make sure you reach station on time. Train leaving three o'clock. Red Fort Express, Madame. Always punctual, like myself. I check and confirming before I am leaving to…"

Sheetal relaxed in the warmth of the beaten leather seat and snuggled in the contours of foam jutting through the seat's cracks and scratched surface. The gibbous moon lit their path and the dark landscape glided outside her window. Today was *Chauth*, the fourth day after the full moon, but fear would not hold her back.

Then the vehicle eased to a stop before a yellow-and-black striped horizontal bar.

"What is it?" She sat up.

"No you worrying, Madame. Gate-pass to outside hotel. You covering your head and face with dupatta and guard not seeing you. Less difficult. You are having blood on face. If guard is seeing, we are having problem."

A security guard emerged from a booth and approached them.

Sheetal glimpsed herself in the rear-view mirror. A gash cut across her cheek and her face was puffed and dotted with bruises. She could easily pass for a battered villager or Jatinder's servant, and no one would know the difference. Sheetal covered her forehead with the dupatta and lowered the veil so it covered half her face.

"Eh." The security guard gestured for Jatinder to lower his window. "Where you go?"

"My wife is with me on food delivery," Jatinder explained in Hindi. "Cottage forty-two ordering food from my dhaba and I delivering. Now I take my wife to her mother's. Her name is Janki."

The guard peered in from Jatinder's window, and Sheetal lowered the veil down to her chin.

"Afraid to stay alone in dhaba. Just married."

The guard nodded, returned to his cubicle and pushed on a button. The horizontal bar lifted, and Jatinder rolled the car forward with ease.

"Hurry, Jatinder."

He glanced at her in the rearview mirror. "Slowly, Madame. So, no one is becoming suspicious." The car rounded a bend away from the guard's view, and Jatinder revved the engine at full speed as he took a left down toward Mall Road. He honked at cars, auto rickshaws, bicycles and *tongas* to get out of the way. He screamed at pedestrians to move aside and forced them to dive for cover along dirt-lined pavements. The headlights cracked the darkness as he tore down the road lurching the Ambassador left and right. "You eating food, Madame?" he yelled amidst the commotion.

Her stomach growled as she swayed side to side. She hadn't eaten since lunch.

"You looking, Madame, on your left. Below seat. Bag with *tiffin* box. My wife packing something for you. Maybe also some towel for you to wiping your face."

Sheetal ran a hand below the seat, grabbed a plastic bag and unraveled a knotted cloth inside. She pulled apart thick steel clips banding four steel-towered containers, un-stacked the *tiffin* boxes and pulled the lids off each. Three vegetable curries and a small bundle of chapatis!

"Simple food, Madame." Jatinder's voice took on an apologetic turn. "My wife is not knowing fancy items. Also, she is not knowing good manners of high class people. Like cleaning your hands with wet napkin before eating. Sorry, Madame. Simple girl from simple village. But I asking her put towel for you."

Shame veiled from head to toe. To think she had openly taken offense at Jatinder's English, hospitality and humble manners. She had judged the man from his clothing, the state of his battered vehicle, his dingy restaurant and the food he served. Now here, Jatinder and his wife shared their dal and roti without any expectation in return. Guilt clawed at her heart, and she hated herself. How could she ever repay him? "Thank you. You must thank your wife for me as well. And I am so sorry if I said anything to hurt or offend you or your wife."

"Not me, Madame. Arvind Bhai is remembering you must not be eating. But you no worrying, Madame. No need for saying sorry when you doing no wrong. Eat. Hot food. You having long journey ahead because no taxis driving now. No man risking journey at night so your husband no follow. Arvind Bhai and Chotta Baba already going and must be halfway down." Then he patted the steering wheel with a firm nod of the head and revved the vehicle onward with a loud, "Chal Chamkeeli!"

"I UNDERSTAND, SIR." THE HOTEL MANAGER IN A NAVY SUIT AND TIE nodded.

"You don't. That's my wife." Rakesh yelled. "Some guy kidnapped her."

"But no driver will take you down at this hour. It's too dangerous and it's against the Mansali Tourist Board Association's rules and regulations."

"Fuck the tourist board." Rakesh swaggered and leaned on a sofa for support. The Plaza staff swayed around, and he tightened his grip on the sofa's edge. "Fuck all your rules and regulations. I saw him leave in a silver Ambassador parked outside our villa. His name is Arvind Chopra and he works as a teacher at St. Paul's."

"I understand, Sir. We'll call the police and file a report immediately. They can block—"

"I want my wife. Now."

"But sir, it isn't safe to drive at this hour. We should file a report first."

His head throbbed. "Now. Call a taxi now!"

"There isn't a single car that will take you down. No one will." Sweat beaded the manager's forehead.

Rakesh sucked in his chest. "You have a car?"

"Yes."

"You drive?"

"Yes."

"You know the roads?"

"But, Sir—"

"You know who I am?"

"Rakesh Dhanraj, Sir."

"Good." He nodded. "Get moving!"

RUGGED MOUNTAIN SHRUBS SCRAPED THE AMBASSADOR'S LEFT WHILE THE empty road on the right careened by. "I think Arvind Bhai and Chotta Baba reach Lower Mansali by now," Jatinder said.

"How much longer?" Sheetal glanced at her watch. It was twelve. She had three hours until the train's departure. "We'll never make it at this rate."

"Another hour and half remaining. But you no worrying, Madame. We having plenty of time."

"I know." Sheetal instantly regretted the authoritative Dhanraj tone. "What I mean is, I know, but what if something goes wrong?" The possibilities of doom were endless considering the sharp curves of the roads and hairpin turns. Shadows of boulders hanging off cliff tops threatened to avalanche any second. Black painted the surroundings except for the narrow strip of concrete illuminated by the car's headlights. Sheetal glanced out the window. The car screeched as the rudder grappled for the cliff's surface. The vehicle gained momentum and plunged downhill. Treetops and mountain caps glowed under the torch of the moon's beam.

'May my death precede that of my husband so that I can enter the chitaa as a bride.' The words circled her mind, but a determination set in. She was *not* going to die before Rakesh. The vehicle eased along a winding path, slowed and halted. "What happened?"

"Chamkeeli, Madame," Jatinder said. "Is having mood problem."

"Mood problem?"

"She no like driving at night. Once before I try, Madame. She stop. She old and rusting, Madame. But reliable. You no worrying. I take you, somehow."

Leaves rustled in the night breeze. Everything stilled, and Sheetal tensed.

"I knowing, Madame, what do." He stepped out, walked around

to the back of the vehicle and hoisted both the boot and engine's hoods up. "Chamkeeli no liking high speed we are driving. Cannot blame—no? Like wheezing for car, Madame."

A shudder ran up her spine. "But he'll catch up. He saw us leave and is right behind. How long will it take for your Chamkeeli to stop wheezing?" She tightened her fingers around the string bag and pressed it to her chest.

"You no worrying, Madame. We having plenty time."

"We've got two hours left." Her voice cracked with the snap of branches in the darkness. "We have to get down there. Do something! You don't know my husband. He'll kill me!"

"Trust me, Madame." Jatinder's cherry eyes sparkled in the night. "Everyone knowing him."

"Drive! You fucking fool, drive!" Rakesh clutched the sides of the Maruti's front passenger seat. "Look out!" The Maruti Zen, a mere toy on Mansali's mountain roads, screeched as they careened around the mountain's path and the back tires spun in search of flat ground. A split-second later they swerved almost running over a cliff. "Fucking kill me, why don't you?"

"I'm sorry." The manager shivered. "I've never driven on these roads at this time of night."

"You live here, dammit!" Rakesh swerved to the right and rammed into the manager's arm. He glanced ahead at a thin stretch of concrete road that crumbled to a broken railing further down and held his breath. "Watch out!" Rudder grappled for road in a spinning frenzy. "Fucking hell! How much longer?"

"It's three hours down. Sometimes more, Sir."

Rakesh ran his tongue across his lips, savoring the taste of Sheetal's blood. "Sweet."

"Provided we get there in one piece."

"What do you mean?"

"This is a tiny car, Sir." Shadows rushed in the headlights' periphery. "The Maruti is too light a vehicle for these mountains. It's not meant for such difficult drives. A sturdier car with an experienced driver is what you need."

Overhanging branches scratched the bonnet of the vehicle while rocks and bits of broken mountain road rushed on both sides. "Why didn't you say so before?"

"I tried to tell you, Sir. I'm new but—"

"Fuck!" The car careened around the stump of a fallen tree, and Rakesh swerved and hit the manager's arm again. "An inexperienced manager! All I fucking need today."

"Oh no, Sir." He glanced at Rakesh with a nod of the head. "I've been managing this hotel for the last five years."

"What are you new at?"

"Driving, Sir. I got my license last week."

Sheetal glanced at her watch for the umpteenth time sitting in the stationary car with Jatinder Singh behind the wheel. "Is she ready now? Your Chamkeeli?"

He turned the key in the ignition, and the engine wheezed. "Chamkeeli no starting, but better than before." Jatinder rummaged through the glove-box compartment. He tried the ignition again, but the engine choked and spluttered. "Day time easy to fix, Madame. Night becoming difficult." He glanced up in the rearview mirror and smiled in relief. "I see light. Another car coming, maybe can help."

"Where?" Sheetal turned around and saw a pair of headlights chase shadows through the wiry arms of trees.

"Up there, Madame. Coming down. I see some light, then going away. Help maybe coming."

Rakesh.

"What, Madame? You are crying."

A diya-like light flickered in the rearview mirror. "He's coming to kill me."

"No, Madame. I am thinking some way out." Jatinder swung open the driver's door, jumped out and made his way to the front. He ducked under the hood. "Maybe if I am joining these two wires and trying... But cannot see, Madame. It is too dark—no? Chamkeeli—"

"Here!" Sheetal hopped out of her seat and handed him a torch. "This will help."

"Good, Madame. Very good! Why you no saying before?"

Sheetal turned to the moon and prayed for her own life.

RAKESH SWERVED DOWN-HILL. A HALF HOUR UNTIL THE RED FORT EXPRESS' departure. "What's my alternative if we miss the train?"

"Car, Sir."

The manager could drive the car to the next station and then he'd board the train.

"But it's not safe, Sir."

"Why?"

"Heavy riots in Dholakpur. People have blocked all incoming traffic and there is a curfew in the city. No car has passed in the last half-hour without a vehicle getting burned or stoned."

"I need to get through." Rakesh grit his teeth.

"They will smash and beat you down. These Hindu-Muslim riots are getting out of control."

Pebbles and chips of earth stormed the Maruti's belly. Branches drummed the bonnet as the car tilted dangerously to the left, heading for a pointed cliff. "Is there another way?"

"The Delhi Mail Express leaves at four in the afternoon."

The stench of burning rubber and bile fizzed up Rakesh's throat. "I know that! I already have tickets, but we either make it there on time or you drive me to Dholakpur."

"But—"

"No buts. Rev up and keep your fucking eyes on the road!"

AFTER SEVERAL MINUTES OF TINKERING AND WALKING FROM ONE END OF THE vehicle to the other, Jatinder tried the ignition again. The Ambassador revved a full-throated, muscular holler.

"Chal Chamkeeli!" Jatinder bellowed, slammed on the accelerator and sped off into the night.

"HURRY!" RAKESH COMMANDED. "GO FASTER."

"I'm trying my best, Sir." The car jiggled and bumped over chips of rock as the manager swerved on the mountain road.

Then, from out of nowhere, an overhanging branch loomed into view. Rakesh raised an arm to shield his eyes and screamed.

THE AMBASSADOR BRAKED OUTSIDE THE CROWDED STATION, AND SHEETAL jumped out. "Thank you, Jatinder Singh." She clutched the bag and passed a five-hundred-rupee note through the open window.

"No time for you thanking, Madame." Jatinder hollered midst honking traffic and an angry stream of headlights from waiting cars behind. "You keep money and go. Hurry up. Ten minutes. Arvind Bhai meeting you on train. Now, run!"

Sheetal stuffed the note in the bag and pushed her way through the crowd. She shoved people aside with her hand and rushed past coolies and mothers clutching wailing infants on hips. She broke hand-chains linking children to parents as calls of 'garam chai' and 'garam nescoffee' thrummed the air. "I'm sorry," she apologized to an irate mother she momentarily separated from her son. She strode through a sea of moving bodies reeking of garlic-and-onion sweat, ran up the ramp and across the footbridge in the light of yellow bulbs. A shifting ocean of people thronged the platforms below. She elbowed people aside clutching the bag to her chest in search of the right platform as smoke billowed.

One...two...three...six! She took a right down the stairs, but her knees suddenly buckled, and she was thrust forward by a mob from behind. She grabbed the banister for support and landed with a thud several steps below. Layers of crinkled salwar caught between her Nike shoes and the ground. Sheetal grabbed the seams, tucked each in the shoes' back ridge and rose against the moving tide of people. She slid her arms through the hoops of the string bag, picked up the dupatta pooled near her feet and tossed it around her shoulders leaving the ends free to hang down her back. Then she rose, took the steps down two at a time and ran across the platform.

She dodged past a crowd of laborers. A tangle of arms shoved her out of the way. Coolies carrying rusted metal trunks on their heads elbowed her aside. Trails of cheap polyester pallus dangling down the shoulders of women almost noosed her. She read the numbers printed on each carriage. 39001... 39002... She ran alongside a train parked on her left, past the first-class coupes to the second, but all the doors were closed.

"Sheetal!"

The crowd rushed forward and swept her in its tide. Sheetal strained against the crests of heads and bodies drifting north. Who was calling her? Passengers climbed through open carriage doors on an adjacent train.

"Sheetal!"

Arvind?

She looked up and struggled forward amidst the thrust of moving bodies. Then the dupatta around her neck tightened and she tugged it loose to breathe.

"Sheetal!"

The sea of strangers thickened. Scotch. The air reeked of scotch. She looked over her shoulder to the ramp she had just descended and glimpsed a sickly-yellow body weave through the rush of sturdy browns. *Rakesh!*

"Here! Sheetal! The train. Up ahead."

The guard's whistle screeched.

A train was about to leave. Which train? Passengers were filling both trains on each side of the platform. Someone in the distance called again. She drifted with the stream of people and then saw him. *Arvind!* He stood three coach-lengths ahead at the edge of a carriage doorway and waved to hurry.

"Sheetal!"

Thick, black smoke clouded her lungs. She ran pumping her legs, closing the distance between her and Arvind down to two coaches.

"Sheetal!"

A sea of bodies swept her in its tide. She lunged forward but was pulled back and anchored while everyone else charged ahead in the swelling current. She looked over her shoulder. Rakesh was just a few feet away. His fingers snaked out from between rows of shifting bodies.

Sheetal turned in the direction of the train, and the platform vibrated beneath her feet. An engine sighed followed by a chug. Sheetal struggled to place one foot ahead of the other, but her throat tightened.

"Sheetal! Fucking bitch! Get back here!"

The ground shook. Her knees buckled. She was dragged back against her will. She gasped for air. She was choking. Crumbling. Falling into a black hole. She clawed at the dupatta, yanked the noose off her head and tossed it behind in a pool of shoulders, elbows and arms.

A knife from behind glinted in a hand and the other looped around her dupatta and yanked the snake of fabric away between the dominoes of moving bodies.

People screamed.

"Run! Sheetal, run!" Arvind bellowed.

Sheetal crouched in a panic amidst the ocean of people. She disappeared, and when she glanced back a sea of people, the very people she feared, avalanched on Rakesh and buried him in a chain of human limbs.

The train to her left chugged forward. The whistle shrieked, drowning the crowd's hollers. The blood rushed to her head. The train on her left, the one she was supposed to get on, was leaving!

Sheetal ran, her shoes slapping concrete and her lungs panting to the train's rhythmic motion. She lengthened her strides forcing people out of the way and gaining momentum with the moving vehicle. One more carriage...one more carriage to go.

With one hand pegged on the train's vertical handrail, Arvind leaned away from the train's chassis and held out his free hand for her to grab. "Run!" he screamed. "He's behind you!"

Jump! She had to jump aboard. Now!

"Get back here, bitch!" Rakesh bellowed as the train picked up speed.

Sheetal stretched out her left hand for Arvind to grab.

The toes of Arvind's shoes were two feet ahead. His hand. There. Waiting. To link with hers. One...two...three. She grabbed a metal handrail on the left, Arvind's arm with the right, and swung herself up as the wind rushed beneath her feet.

She hung suspended in mid-air between two worlds.

Arvind hauled her up against the deafening grate of metal against track and pulled her away from the spinning ground below. He pressed her to his chest, and the train's rickety floor padded her feet. Sheetal melted in his arms, soaked in warmth, her breath heaving with the *thaka-thaka-thunk*. She swayed and panted to the rhythm of Arvind's beating heart.

"You made it." Arvind slammed the train door behind him.

She struggled to breathe. "He almost strangled me."

"I know." Arvind ran his fingers through her hair, cupped the left side of her face with a palm and ran a thumb over the wound on her cheek. Wrinkles crusted his forehead.

Sheetal slid her arms round Arvind's waist, and all the ghosts of the past disappeared in that one moment.

"M-M-Mum?"

Yash! Sheetal withdrew from Arvind's embrace realizing the awkwardness of being in another man's arms in front of Yash. She reached out to hug him.

"Are you ok-k-kay?"

She hugged Yash tightly. "I'm okay. More than okay." She was more so than she had been in a long time.

AN HOUR LATER, SEATED BETWEEN ARVIND AND YASH ON A LOWER BERTH, Sheetal swayed to the train's rickety motion as the Red Fort Express plunged across lakes and rivers, tearing across fields, ravines and wide mountain terrain.

Yash slept on the berth, his head on her lap, lolling to the swaying motion. Sheetal shuddered to think what could have become of Yash had they been forced to return to Raigun. She would get Yash help, find a doctor and start treatment right away. No. She reminded herself. First, they had to find safety. Sheetal curled her fingers around Arvind's hand. "Thank you."

"For what?"

"You know."

"No." He shrugged. "Tell me."

"Yash. Me. I...you. What will you do now? You have no job at St. Paul's. You're a teacher—"

"*Was* a teacher."

"And you can't go back." Her gaze fell to the floor. "You gave up everything for me. For us."

"For you, yaar, again and again. A thousand times over if I had to."

"I ruined all you had."

"I was ruined without you." He smiled and sunlight burst through the window behind him, its glory bathing fields and paddies with renewed hope.

He had waited ten years, ten long years for her, and Sheetal would wait another ten if she had to, for him. But if Arvind refused to change his mind that would be fine because life wasn't just about marriage and having children or being a good wife, daughter and mother.

Life was about living free.

The train curved around a bend chugging on and on toward the distant horizon as clouds spread a blanket of comfort in the blue sky. Sheetal closed her eyes. Everything she needed was right here. She sighed, content, and fell asleep.

A sleep she hadn't slept in years.

SHEETAL STARTLED AWAKE, A SCREAM RINGING IN HER EARS. BLACK FUMES blanketed her vision. Muffled cries for help thickened with the smoke. She inhaled but couldn't breathe. She coughed. Still, couldn't breathe. She parted her lips and gasped for air. Chauth. *Karva Chauth? Was the pallu on fire? The paintings? Were they burning?* She reached on the right for Yash, but her palm pressed against something hard. Heat sliced through her wrist, sizzled up her veins and she yanked back her hand. *Rakesh? The belt?*

"*Kholo! Darwaaza kholo!*" Knocking pounded on the surrounding walls, demanding she open the doors.

Dholakpur? Did the train stop at Dholakpur? She stood, was knocked aside and lost footing. *Hooligans trying to get on board.* She reached up and grabbed something to steady herself that felt like a branch dangling from the upper berth, but her fingers slid down the barrel and tangled with a mesh of twigs. She was knocked to the floor and the branch came down, dragging a weight and pinning her to the ground. She struggled to breathe, shoved the weight off and dragged to her feet, flattening her palm against the dead weight. *A body? Arvind?* Fear gripped. *No. Can't be.* He was with her on the lower berth. Sheetal fanned her hands and groped through the thicket of smoke. "Yash!" She struggled to yell. "Arvind?" The door. She had to find the door and get out.

"*Band. Darwaaza band hai!*" Someone screamed that all the doors were locked.

"Yash! Arvind!" Smoke plunged down her lungs and she coughed.

"*Bachao!*" Someone screamed for help. "Mum! *Bachao!*"

Yash? "Where are you, Yash?"

"*Aag! Aag!*" People yelled out fire.

The pounding of feet. Of fists on walls. Screams. Gut-wrenching shrieks drummed the air. She struggled to keep standing and hold her ground.

"Yash! Arvind!" She had to get back to the berth. Yash had been sleeping on the lower berth beside her. Was he still there? She walked further into a funnel of smoke. Hit a wall. Ran her hand across a hot surface and struck a coal-hot lever. *A door. Was this a door? A way out?* She pulled her hand back. Burning hot. "Yash!"

"M-Mum! Here!"

She fanned her hand in a blanket of black.

Something firmed its grip around her ankle, tightened, and began clawing up her shin and then her knees. Sheetal lowered her hand and flattened it on a mass of hair. The figure hugged her tight around the waist, crying and screaming all at once. "M-Mum?" He coughed. "Is it you, M-Mum?"

"It's me, Yash." Thick, black smoke billowed all around. She was not going to be trapped again. She was not going to die. She grabbed the skirt of her kurta, rolled it around her hand and pushed hard against the door, but it was stuck. The sound of twisting metal and creaking iron reverberated.

"Sheetal? Yash?"

Arvind! He was alive. "We're here." She planted her hand where Yash's head had just been. He was gone. "Yash?" She fanned her hands in the air. Smoke engulfed her lungs and she coughed. "He was here, Arvind! Just now. I don't know where—"

"Find a door!"

"I'm near one. It won't open!"

"Push hard!"

Sheetal tried again but the heat! Her eyes burned. "I can't. It's—"

"Use a cloth. Something. And jump out."

"Yash? What about Yash?"

"I'll find him." His voice billowed over clouds of smoke as people knocked into her, thumping the walls and screaming for someone to open the doors.

"He's with me! I've got him," Arvind yelled. "Now push and get as far away from here as possible. The train's going to explode."

Sheetal pushed the door's handle with all her life. The door swung open to streaks of blue sky clouded by smoke. She jumped and hit ground on impact. She staggered to her feet and ran as fast as she could, past smoke and a crowd of people trying to help passengers still aboard. The desert view cleared in the distance. She stopped and turned around. There was enough distance between her and the train. She was out of harm's way.

People spilled out the train's doors to the screech of sirens and wails of ambulances.

Yash? Arvind? Where were they? More people trickled out. There he was! *Yash!*

Arvind eased him to the ground from the carriage door. Yash landed and ran toward her. Relief flooded her veins and Sheetal staggered toward him. Arvind was about to jump off, but a mob pushed him out of the doorway and hurled him back inside the coach gutted with fire. The crowd rounded to aid victims spilling from the doors, and she lost sight of Arvind.

"M-Mum!" Yash filled her embrace and held on tight.

Sheetal pressed him to her chest and rocked him in her arms, her attention on the door. *Arvind. Come on, Arvind.*

A command to move away from the train boomed in the distance. Screams echoed. People scattered. Emergency vehicles reversed. And then she saw Arvind standing in the doorway. He was about to jump off when a ball of fire rose with a deafening explosion.

EPILOGUE

APRIL 6TH
THE RAIGUN HERALD
NEW DELHI, INDIA.

Fifty-seven people, mostly women and children were burned alive yesterday when a trainload of passengers was torched by a mob in Northern India, authorities said. Police across India braced for outbreaks of retaliatory violence.

Shortly after the train attack, two men were stabbed to death, and shops, buses and cars were set ablaze by angry mobs.

Twenty-five women and fifteen children were among the dead when mobs armed with stones and kerosene descended on the Red Fort Express at Dholakpur, carrying hundreds of tourists homebound from the northern town of Mansali.

About sixty-five other passengers were injured, thirty-eight critically, in the inferno that gutted four coaches and charred some victims beyond recognition.

When the train's emergency brake was engaged, as it started to pull *away from Dholakpur, attackers described by a state official as religious activists, swarmed the passenger cars. They bolted the doors from the outside before setting fire to the coaches...*

Rakesh paced up and down the boardroom. He twirled a pencil in his left hand, his heart pounding at a hundred beats per minute. At first, the Japanese were furious when he requested the meeting be postponed to this afternoon instead of yesterday. But after news spread of the morning's accident and the possibility that Rakesh might have lost his family, the Japanese agreed.

Board members from Dhanraj & Son occupying the left half of the thirty-seater rectangular meeting table waited in silence.

Sweat dripped down his neck. Rakesh raised his hand and traced the line of dampness with his index finger, but the drop had run behind the shirt collar and disappeared without a trace.

Like Sheetal. He tightened his grip on the pencil. She had betrayed him. Taken their son.

Rot.

"Rakesh?"

In.

"Rakesh?"

Hell. A weight pressed on his left shoulder. He tightened, took a deep breath and turned round. Vipul Sahib. The board members of Dhanraj & Son seated along the table's left, prim and pristine in formal business attire, looked at him as if anticipating a cue. Crystal jugs of water, surrounded by a moat of glasses placed in regular intervals along the length of the sparkling wooden slab divided the two countries.

"You don't look well. I think you should go home," Vipul Sahib said.

Home? Rakesh closed his eyes and snapped the pencil in two.

"You don't have to run this meeting. We can handle it. The whole team is here..." Vipul Sahib's grip tightened enough to make Rakesh straighten. "I'm so sorry." He stepped back. "I—all of us understand. You just lost your family."

Rakesh had told everyone that his family had been kidnapped, taken on board a train and they'd been missing since. He remembered the downhill ride to Lower Mansali, the crowd at the station, catching a glimpse of Sheetal, and then waking up on a pile of brown jute sacks in the middle of the platform with Sheetal's dupatta in hand.

"I can't even imagine what you must be going through."

He tightened his grip, but the pencil was gone. Like Yash.

"It's all over the news. Go home, son. We'll explain the situation. They'll understand. There's a flight to Raigun in four hours. You can still—"

"I'm here to stay and wrap this up." The Raigun Herald would have a field day now that Sheetal and Yash were missing and Naina had been certified dead on arrival at the hospital. More humiliation to put up with.

"I don't think you're in any condition to—"

"It's my decision, Uncle." He turned to face the board members and cleared his throat. "This deal is crucial. The entire company is at stake. We have to close this, swift. Sweet. No mistakes. No excuse."

Megha's delivery. What excuse would he give the Saxenas? Megha had been waiting for an answer and she was going to hate him after tomorrow's call when he'd have to say no. Pushpa couldn't handle the delivery. Hell, she couldn't handle anything since Naina died. She'd become a nervous wreck from what Janvi had described on the phone. Now he'd have to handle her too. How? Show Pushpa to Dr. Kishore? Put her on anti-depressants? Or something else? His head pounded. As if that wasn't enough to deal with. And if the Japanese found out they might just bail out. Then he'd lose everything!

Vipul Sahib took a seat beside Rakesh's empty chair. The door opened, and a string of Japanese men filed into the room and took their places on the table's empty half.

Daichi Tanaka shook hands with Rakesh. "Good to meet you, Mr. Dhanraj." He bowed. "I am so sorry to hear what happened. Is there any news of your family?"

Naina dead. Pushpa gone mad. Sheetal and Yash runaways—no, dead. Probably dead. "Nothing so far. But thank you for your concern. I appreciate you agreeing to the change of plans."

"Not at all. This is most unfortunate. I do not have the words to say how sorry I am. How we all are. But we all, at Tashukomo Electronics, hope to hear good news soon."

Rakesh nodded and gestured for him to have a seat.

"Before we begin," Tanaka stood rooted to the floor, "I want you to understand we at Tashukomo Electronics are in agreement over the proposal. But we have some conditions of our own."

Rakesh stiffened. "And they are?"

"We understand we must go through an Indian company to sell to your people. But we want our people to speak on our behalf before the media. Also, we want a stake in marketing."

Rakesh moved to the table's edge, closer to Mr. Tanaka. "That's *our* job."

"You need us. Our sales total eight hundred million. Worldwide."

"You need us more. Our population totals one billion. Domestic."

"You don't know our products the way we do."

"You don't know our people the way we do."

"Yes, you are right. We don't. Which is why we hired a consultant from *your* country to lead our marketing team and work with you. Unite. One. Hai." He nodded. "In the right direction, of course."

Rakesh tensed. A pain swelled up his chest. He leaned against the table's edge for support. "Of course. And this someone is—"

"Not to worry." Tanaka smiled. "First, we should sign the papers and get all the official matters out the way. Then move on to more trivial things. Don't you agree?"

Rakesh gestured for Tanaka to have a seat but stood rooted to the ground.

"I understand how worried you must be." Tanaka pulled a chair for himself. "With all you and your family are going through, everyone understands. We can reschedule—"

"No." Rakesh turned to a small stack of papers Vipul Sahib had just placed on the table. "Let's go ahead."

Rakesh and Tanaka signed papers for the next ten minutes. After all the formalities were complete, they shook hands as attendees filled the room with applause. The pain in his chest lessened.

"We look forward to working with you and making waves in the Indian market," Tanaka said. "An exciting moment for all of us."

Rakesh took a deep breath. "Yes. I—my team. All of us at Dhanraj & Son feel the same way."

"You are looking very unsure." Tanaka frowned. "Perhaps, it is the surprise? The stake in marketing? You and your people will be comfortable working with our new hire. He mentioned that you two go way back." Tanaka leaned closer and whispered. "He is...uh...what you call in Hindi, *jordaar?*" He meant one-of-a-kind. "You won't be sorry." Then he turned around to address all the board members. "I present to you the marketing team of Tashukomo Electronics."

A crew of Japanese men and women dressed in formal business attire filed in and stood in a line before the audience. A man in the center curled the fingers of his right hand into a fist, rammed it into his open left palm, and four fingers curved around the closed knuckle's edge. Then he bowed.

The button-pusher. Rakesh's knees weakened. He scanned the faces and clamped his jaw, feeling the pressure of molar against molar.

"We seem to be missing someone. Our Indian consultant." Tanaka shook his head. "Perhaps he is delayed." He walked to the door and was about to close it when the front curve of a black leather shoe plugged the closing door.

"I'm sorry." The sound of crisp r's thickened the stranger's accent. The scent of lemony aftershave filled the room.

Rakesh froze.

"Hello, everyone! Namaste!" He strutted in, dressed in a soft gray

Zara suit. Blond and brown highlights tinted the wavy black hair that glowed in the harsh yellow lighting. Kartik walked over to Rakesh, shook hands and leaned to whisper. "It was good while it lasted. No strings attached. And I always thought you more of a man." He tightened his grip. "But we need to move on for old times' sake."

QUESTIONS FOR BOOK CLUBS

1. Given the Dhanraj's elite class in society, what are some of the common societal pressures Rakesh and Sheetal face in the story?
2. What perspective of society does Megha's role support?
3. What perspective does Naina's role bring to the story?
4. Pushpa owns the Dhanraj estate and mansion, and she has the freedom to live her life. But is Pushpa truly free? Why? Do you know anyone in this position?
5. At the halfway mark in the story, Rakesh almost turns over a new leaf. But fails. What are Rakesh's virtues? What are his vices? Why do you think his vices overpower his virtues?
6. How do the corporate environment and Vipul Sahib influence Rakesh's world? Do you know anyone who excels in one environment and suffers in another?
7. What is the most difficult hurdle Sheetal overcomes in the story? Where does she find the strength to take on that battle?

8. What effect does Indu's death have on Sheetal? How does this serve as a turning point in Sheetal's life?

9. How does Kavita's situation contrast with Sheetal's? How does the author use such a contrast to depict socioeconomic imbalances?

10. What aspect of society do the coolie, Jatinder Singh, and the Choudharys bring to the story? Despite the socioeconomic disadvantages compared to the elite, what advantages do they have over the Prasads and Dhanrajs?

11. What are Rana Prasad's flaws? What turning points in the story propel Rana to overcome his flaws? Does he succeed?

12. How does the culture and lifestyle of the people in India affect the locals' behavior and thinking patterns?

13. Who is your favorite character and why?

14. What does being a good parent mean? Has Sheetal protected Yash by staying on in this broken marriage for her son? Do you know anyone who has dealt with a similar situation?

15. Given the level of wealth in the Prasad and Dhanraj's worlds, do you think an overabundance of wealth has limitations? If so, what are they?

16. What are some of the themes in the story? How do the secondary characters amplify them?

17. What cultural aspects of the story did you find intriguing and why?

18. How many different hierarchies in society were you able to distinguish in the story? How does a person's status affect his/her freedom or limitations?

19. The practice of Karva Chauth is still widely prevalent today, and the majority of Hindu women (worldwide) fast and pray on this day for their husband's longevity.

Why is Sheetal so rooted in her tradition? What do you think the practice means to her?

20. Do you know anyone from a different race who shares a similar cultural practice?

21. Do you think Yash might have benefited by living with the Dhanrajs instead of at boarding school? What alternative ending could Sheetal have to save herself and her son?

22. If you could come up with a different ending, how would your ending differ from the author's?

23. In what way do you think Kavita and Megha (from the lower echelons of society) impact Sheetal's decisions?

24. What are the root factors that have been holding Sheetal back from her claim to real independence?

25. Which character(s) do you love to hate in the series and why?

GLOSSARY

Aa gaye – We've arrived

Aag - Fire

Aage kahan? – Where do we go next?

Aap akele? – Are you alone?

Acchha (hai) - Okay

Acche lag rahe ho – You're looking good

Aloo matar - An Indian curry made with potatoes and peas

Ambassadors – An automobile manufactured by Hindustan Motors of India from 1957 to 2014. Despite its British origins, the Ambassador was considered as a definitive Indian car and was fondly called the 'King of Indian roads

Arrey, Behnji, jaldi karo. - Hey, Sister, hurry up.

Arrey, Bhai. - Hey, brother! (reference to close male friend)

Arrey dekho! – Hey, look!

Arrey! Garam garam dosa - Hey! Hot hot dosa.

Arrey, gori gori Memsahib! – Hey, fair-skinned Madam!

Arrey, jaldi karo, Bhaiya! Saman ootaro! – Hey, hurry up, Brother. Unload the luggage!

Arrey, koi hai? Sunno. – Is anyone there? Listen.

Arrey, Memsahib. – Hey, Madam

Arrey, Sahib – hey, Sir

Arrey, yaar – Hey, friend

Aur dost – And, what else is up, friend?

Aur Jattu Bhai? – And, what more, Jattu Bhai?

Babu – Little boy (affectionate term)

Band. Darwaaza band hai! – Closed. The door is closed!

Bachao! – Help!

Bai – Colloquial term referring to a servant or nanny

Baya - Karva Chauth gifts for the mother-in-law usually consisting of a sari, dry fruits, or money and is believed to bring good luck to the married woman's (daughter-in-law's) life

Beta – Term of affection parents use when addressing sons

Beti - Term of affection parents use when addressing daughters

Behnji - Sister (with respect)

Bhai - Brother

Bhabhi - Term of respect reserved for an older brother's wife

Bhagya - Destiny or fate

Bhavan - A large house or structure built for a specific purpose, e.g. to hold meetings or conferences

Bindi - Ornament used by women to decorate the forehead. Tiny, colorful accessories available in different colors and designs and placed between the eyebrows. Bindis were originally worn by married women to show their marital status but are now used as a form of decoration.

Chal Chamkeeli! – Let's go, Chamkeeli!

Chauth – The fourth day after the full moon

Chicken tikka - An Indian appetizer comprised of small pieces of marinated chicken cooked in a tandoor (clay oven) and served with chutney, onion rings, and coriander leaves.

Chitta – Funeral pyre

Chapati - Whole wheat, circular flatbread cooked on a griddle

Chole garam - Hot chickpea curry

Choti Memsahib – Little Madame

Chotta Baba – Little Boy

Chowki – A low wooden seat or stool

Chowkidar - Watchman/caretaker/security guard

Crore - A unit of currency measurement. One crore equals ten million or 100 lakhs

Dada – Term of respect to refer to paternal grandfather

Dadi – Term of respect to refer to paternal grandmother

Dal - Protein-rich lentil soup, a staple diet for many Indians

Dal and roti – colloquial for bread-winning/winner

Dhaba - Roadside restaurants commonly found in northern India that serve Punjabi food

Dhaniyavad – Thank you

Dhurry - A thick cotton rug

Diwali - Hindu festival of Lights occurring anywhere from mid-October to mid-November. It involves the lighting of small clay lamps filled with oil to signify the Hindu God, Lord Ram's return after fourteen years in exile and his triumph of good over evil

Diya - A cup-shaped clay lamp with a cotton wick, lit to dispel darkness on religious Indian festivals

Dosa - A rice pancake made from fermented rice and lentil batter. The dish from south India is cooked on a griddle and served with coconut chutney and a lentil soup known as sambhar

Dost - Friend

Drama—baazi - Melodrama

(Lord) Ganesh - Hindu god with an elephant's head, widely worshipped by most Hindus. Lord Ganesh is known as the Remover of Obstacles and Lord of Beginnings and is honored at the beginning of rituals and ceremonies

Fiat - The ninth largest Indian car manufacturer by sales in India.

Firangi - Foreign

Garam chai – Hot tea

Garam nescoffee – Hot coffee (Nescafe)

Ghunghroos - Anklet bells or tiny bells used to decorate the perimeter of a thali

Gujarati – A native or inhabitant of Gujarat in western India

Hai Ishwar – Oh Lord!

Hanh - Yes

Havaa! Tez havaa – Wind! Strong winds!

Hindustani - Refers to India and its people

Hira Moti – Diamond and Pearl

Idli - A savory steamed rice cake made from fermented rice and lentils, usually served with coconut chutney and a lentil soup known as sambhar. A favorite breakfast item in south India

-ji – A suffix added after someone's name as a sign of respect

Jaldi Karo! – Hurry up!

Jordaar – One of a kind

Kahaan jaana hai, Madame? Mein aapko chodh deta hoon. – Where would you like to go, Madame? I can drop you there.

Kaise ho? – How are you?

Kaka – Term of respect referring to an elderly (grandfather) male

Kaun hai? Who is it?

Karva - A small pot or vessel of water used in the religious prayer for Karva Chauth

Karva Chauth - A festival celebration that usually falls in the month of October, 4 days after the full moon. Commonly celebrated by married women from the northern part of India

Khana garam – Hot food

Khareed lo, Memsahib – Please buy this, Madame

Kholiye – Open (the door or window) with respect

Kholo bhai kholo! – Open, Brother. Open (the door or window)!

Kholo! Darwaaza kholo! – Open the door!

Koyal - Cuckoo / Blackbird

Kum kum - Red powder used by Indian women to decorate the forehead for social or religious events

Kundan - A traditional form of Indian gemstone jewelry that originates from Rajasthan and Gujrat whereby gems are mounted in gold foil instead of prongs, a technique used most often in the construction of elaborate necklaces

Kurta - A loose shirt falling either just above or somewhere below the knees of a male. Usually worn by men

Kurti - A loose shirt falling either just above or somewhere below the knees of a woman. Usually worn by women

Lakh - Used with Indian currency and a unit of measurement according to the Indian numbering system. 1 lakh is equivalent to 100,000

Lakshmi puja - A prayer performed in honor of the Goddess of Wealth on Diwali for peace, wealth, and prosperity for the year ahead

Maang – Middle parting of a woman's hair

Maharani - Queen

Maidan - An open space or area of barren ground used for sports matches. A grassy lawn area

Maji – Term of respect for 'mother' that Indu uses to refer to Asha, her late mother-in-law

Mali - Gardener

Mangalsutra - An auspicious necklace worn by married women. The new husband ties the necklace around the woman on the wedding day, which symbolizes the unity of two souls

Maruti Zen – A five-door hatchback produced and sold in India by Suzuki's Indian subsidiary Maruti Suzuki from 1993 until 2006

Masala dosa - white rice-and-lentil crepe with a spicy filling of potatoes and onions

Mera saman -luggage

Memsahib – Madame (Reference term for a woman at a higher hierarchy)

Memsahib, gori, gori Memsahib – Madame! Fair and lovely, Madame!

Moli - Religious red and yellow thread used in Hindu prayer and ceremonies believed to deliver blessings from god and ward off evil spirits

Moksha - A Hindu belief of liberation or release of the soul from the body after death

Naan - White flour flatbread leavened with yeast and cooked in a tandoor (clay oven) or oven

Namaste - Indian greeting performed with hands pressed together, palms touching, fingers pointed upward, thumbs close to the chest, accompanied by a slight bow of the head. The equivalent of 'hello' with an element of respect

Paanch-so – Five hundred

Pakoras - Deep-fried vegetable or meat fritters

Pallu - The loose end of a sari

Paneer do pyaza - - A curry of Indian cottage cheese in a rich onion gravy

Parvati(ji) - Goddess Parvati is the wife of Lord Shiva, mother to Lord Ganesha and daughter of the mountain king, Himavan and Queen Mena. She is the goddess of fertility, love, marriage, and children, worshipped for her divine strength and power

Phatafhat - Quickly

Phera - Wedding vows that constitute seven circumambulations around a sacred fire. The vows are considered unbreakable with the God of Fire held as witness to bless the couple's union

Poha - Parboiled rice that is flattened by rolling or beating dried flattened rice into flakes. The flakes are commonly used to create an Indian breakfast which is spiced and cooked with onions, potatoes, coriander leaves, and spices, and served as a breakfast dish

Puja - The act of worship

Rajma rasiya - Gravy-based kidney beans

Raj Kapoor - A renowned, award-winning Indian actor, producer, and director of Indian films until the late 1980s

Raw kidney beans which are soaked and cooked with onions, garlic, cloves, tomatoes and a blend of spices

Rangoli - Traditional art form that uses colored sand, rice grains, or powders to decorate flat surfaces of a courtyard or the entrance to homes during religious festivals. The art is usually practiced by women and girls

Roti - Whole-wheat flatbread cooked on a griddle. A staple diet for many Indians from the north of India. Like chapatis but thicker

Rupee - The common name for the currency of India. From 1995–1998, the U.S. Dollar to Rupee exchange rate fluctuated from about U.S. $1 = Rs.35 to about U.S. $1 = Rs.42. In 2022, the rupee fluctuated further, Rs.84 = U.S.$1

Sahib - Master or Sir

Salwar kameez - Popularly known as the Punjabi suit. The traditional dress of women in the Punjab region of northwestern India and eastern Pakistan. The outfit comprises a pair of trousers (salwar) and a tunic (kameez) that is usually paired with a scarf (dupatta)

Shivaji - The Destroyer of the universe, he is one of the three gods in the triumvirate worshipped for his powers to create, protect, and transform the universe. The other two gods in the triumvirate are Vishnu and Brahma.

Sindoor - A red powder (vermilion) used by Indian women to streak the part in their hair to indicate their married status

Nariyal Ka Rasta – Coconut Lane

Tava - A flat, circular griddle or frying pan made from cast iron or a non-stick pan used to cook chapatis and other Indian breads

Thalis - A large metal platter with a raised edge used for dining (as plates) and also in rituals and prayers to hold the prayer items

Theek hai? – Okay? (Or) Are you okay?

Theek ho, Behnji? - - Are you all right, Sister?

Tiffin – Tiered metal lunch box with compartments that fit on top of the other and are bound together by metal clasps

Tongas - Horse driven carriage

Tomato shorba – Spiced soup made from tangy tomatoes, spices, herbs and coriander leaves

Tum bhi – You as well

Uttapam - A crispy, thick rice pancake made from fermented white rice and lentils and topped with mixed vegetables. The dish originates from south India and is served with coconut chutney and a lentil soup known as sambhar

Wallah – Guy

Waah, waah – Yes! (cheer)

Yaar - Friend/dude/mate

Yahaan rakhoon, Memsahib – Should I keep it here?

Yeh table theek hai, Madame? – Will this table do, Madame?

Zari - Fine gold or silver threads woven in fabrics to create brocade and border designs. Commonly found in traditional Indian, Persian, and Pakistani garments

ACKNOWLEDGMENTS

Some Truths
Behind Every Series Hides A Story

The Winds of Fire Series has been a twenty-plus-year journey from conception in Singapore (2000) to publication in the US (2022), and similar to my travels, the series crosses continents. Like Dynasties (Book 1), so too Once and For All endured countless rewrites, revisions, hurdles, and rejections. Talented professionals and mammoth research have given this story the wings to fly, and any mistakes are my own.

To Lindsay Preston: seven years ago, you got the ball rolling at "Hello" and you continue to be my biggest cheerleader. Where would I be without your unrelenting enthusiasm? You are a true blessing in my life.

Deepest thanks to India's leading fashion designers, Ms. Anita Dongre, House of Anita Dongre, and Mr. Arjun Khanna, House of Classic Couture, for designing Rakesh and Sheetal's ensembles and guiding me through the lives of the rich and famous.

Sangeeta Mehta, Mehta Book Editing, New York, I am eternally grateful for your infectious enthusiasm with the characters, the Winds of Fire series and for believing in me when I doubted myself. To master instructor, David Corbett, I would not have come this far without your writing bibles, 'The Art of Character' and 'The Compass of Character'. Thank you for sharing your wisdom.

To Dr. Shruti Daga, aka little sis'—hugs for being one of my first true readers, taking on the role of medical advisor for the series, and for screaming when I made you kill characters because your profession as a cardiologist demands you save lives. What can I say? Fiction is a beast. We have many more books to write, many more characters to kill, and I promise you more homework—Today, Aways and Forever. What are big sisters for?

To USA Today Bestsellers Jade Lee (soul sister), Lauren Smith, New York Times Bestsellers Haywood Smith (Guruji) and Beverly Jenkins, thank you from the bottom of my heart for helping me navigate two decades of hurdles, rejections and endure the path to publishing. You talented ladies are my rock. Kathy L Murphy, The International Pulpwood Queen, endless thanks for heralding Dynasties and Once And For All as January 2023 and 2024 International Book Of the Month picks. Your continued enthusiasm and advocacy to speak up against domestic violence, abuse and raise awareness for mental health and self-empowerment keeps the ink flowing.

I am deeply grateful to Anshu Chopra for everlasting friendship and extra insights on Karva Chauth. I fall short of words to express gratitude to sister, Renuka Maheshwari, Praveena Baid, Samantha Thomas, Paige Santmyer, Shukti Basu, Chitra Thomas, Aarti Khater and Jayanthi Kanderi—what more can a girl ask for than sisters and friends like you?

Mom (Lalita Daga) and my late father (Ghanshyam Das Daga)... I made it through 'Dynasties'. With your love, courage, and conviction I plunged into 'Once and For All', weathered more torrential mayhem in the crazy world of publishing, and now persevere with Book three. I could not have come this far without your support. What a blessing to have parents who cheer me every step of the way. Parents who held my hand when I first held the pen and then cradled me again when my world fell apart and restored my belief in myself and a new world.

Vikhyat and Vishesh, my Golden Boys. Vik, you coined the term

'Winds of Fire' and helped navigate the entire series. Vishesh, you nailed Yash's character and debated characters, turning points and story. You both are the light of my life and I know you will always shine bright.

Your belief keeps me going…

NEVER AGAIN

BOOK 3

PROLOGUE

Why did some nightmares never end?

Why did fire and smoke fill every ounce of breath so that she suffocated? Had she died only to be reborn in another hell?

"Sheetal?" A muffled voice seeped through layers of heat.

She ran her hands over her body, fingers trapped between cotton fabric and the cocoon of a blanket.

"Sheetal?" Someone called out in the darkness.

A halo of white light floated above. Sheetal reached out and touched the whiteness. A kaleidoscope of colors shattered the horizon and disappeared. Sheetal exhaled. She was alive. Very much alive.

ABOUT THE AUTHOR

Fiction author, international freelance journalist, blogger and former newspaper reporter, Anju was born in India but grew up in Hong Kong. She has also lived and been published in Singapore, India, Australia, and currently lives in the United States with her family. Anju hopes her books will Bridge Cultures and Break Barriers.

Connect with Anju:
Connect with Anju: www.anjugattani.com

Please leave a review at your favorite online bookstore if you enjoyed this book!

facebook.com/Anju.Gattani.Author
x.com/Anju_Gattani
instagram.com/anju_gattani27
amazon.com/stores/Anju-Gattani/author/B0067M0MDU?ref=ap_r-
dr&store_ref=ap_rdr&isDramIntegrated=true&shoppingPortalEnabled=true
bookbub.com/profile/anju-gattani

Printed in the USA
CPSIA information can be obtained
at www.ICGtesting.com
JSHW082136010224
56030JS00002B/3/J

9 798986 652436